WHISKEY ROSE

BOOK 2

Jocelynne Jones

2nd Edition
ISBN 978-0-473-35043-7 (paperback)
ISBN 978-0-473-35044-4 (kindle)

Published by Little Red Hen Community Press,
Tauranga, New Zealand.
Printing: Createspace.com
Retail: Amazon.com
Cover picture: Public domain

ABOUT THE AUTHOR

Jocelynne Jones is the pen-name of a writer living in New Zealand. Retired, with two grownup offspring and a granddaughter, she is a quiet-living family person whose writing has, up until the age of eBooks, been little more than a hobby. With the establishment of 'indie publishers' Jocelynne has found an outlet for a passion that was hitherto stifled by previous publishing systems.

Other titles by the same author are:

'Whiskey Rose: Book 1' – The first part of a story about an average family faced with the constraints of caring for their elderly relative.
'Lucifer's Story' – a fantasy tale of good-over-evil, which envisions the end of evil forever. It is set in a parallel universe called Eternity. Presented in two volumes.
'Freedom: Ours for the asking' – A work of non-fiction under the genre of 'mind, body, spirit,' which explains how people have become separated from their intrinsic identity, and what to do about it.
'Guarding My Angel' – A drama based on the author's autobiography.

To Jenny.

With grateful thanks, as always!

WHISKEY ROSE

BOOK 2

STORY SO FAR...

In her seventies and widowed twice, Emily Thompson's saving grace lies in the ghostly presence of her soul-mate and father of her twins, Arthur, and the roses he tended when he was alive; especially his striking whiskey rose.

When he passed away Emily thought her life had ended, until she read a condolences card which suggested Arthur was always with her in spirit. This she discovered to be true, and for a while he not only kept company with her but also restored her vitality. ...But then she met James.

Swept off her feet by him, they soon married and lived happily until a tragic accident took him from her; which though traumatic, allowed Emily to reconnect with Arthur.

Throughout all of this her family members, each with their own dramas in life, observe in Emily a grieving widow, a contented bride and again the effect of loss. Her serenity, uncharacteristic for one so recently widowed – not once, but twice – raises a collective family eyebrow. Twins Fiona and Ruth, and granddaughter Kristine, have reservations as to the cause of her contentment; Fiona citing the onset of dementia, Kristine slowly coming to realise that there's more to her Nana's passive demeanour than that.

Yet, Emily is still part of the human world, not the ethereal realm of Arthur, even though his ghostly domain is fast becoming a reality to her. In Book Two of *Whiskey Rose* her family are faced with some difficult decisions, which will affect their own lives and more especially the future of their much-loved but ageing matriarch.

PART ONE

CHAPTER ONE

Royston excitedly looked up Alicia's number in the phone book. Something about this woman appealed to him enormously. She was every bit the opposite of Fiona, and yet in some ways quite similar.

There were two issues Royston wanted to discuss with her.

One was his concern about Emily; the other, his need to honour an obligation. The debt of gratitude he still felt towards Alicia he hoped would be suitably addressed by her acceptance of a dinner invitation. With the other – the more important of the two issues – he was sure she could be of help. At very least, the knowledge gained through Alicia's profession would be invaluable in helping Emily to recover, and in deciding where they should go from there.

Later in the day, Royston made his call.

His heart skipped a beat when she answered it.

"Oh, hello. I thought it might be you." she said cheerily, and then added with a half laugh, "After my enlightening session with Emily this afternoon I think I know what you want to talk to me about!"

"Alicia, you are right. I would like to discuss Emily with you. In fact, I'm beginning to develop a certain amount of urgency in seeking advice from some kind of professional. Kristine and I are presently at a loss to know what to do with her. Do you think I could meet you somewhere – for a meal, perhaps? ...I did suggest we should go out for dinner, if you remember."

1

Alicia liked Royston. She had felt an affinity with him even on the day they met at the golf course.

Maybe the tragic circumstances of that day drew them instantly into a close association; or maybe, Alicia reflected while she listened to Royston's concerns about Emily, he was just a really nice guy. She was ready to meet someone nice after her messy divorce the previous year.

"Yes, I do remember you saying that," she responded. "...And thank you so much for the invitation. Dinner would be lovely. Where and when would you like to meet?"

Royston was thrilled; at last he would be able to cast his worries upon a sympathetic ear. Alicia was a good-looking lady, too. Taking her out would be a privilege.

"How about tomorrow night?" he asked quickly in case the mood of the moment changed. "There's a new French restaurant in town. Would you like to try it?"

"Oh, I know the one! It's been advertised, and sounds delightful. Shall I meet you there at, say, seven o'clock?"

"That would be perfect," was Royston's eager response.

Had Alicia been able to see him she would have noticed a look of intense pleasure on Royston's face.

"By the way," she said before hanging up. "Kristine's very worried about arrangements to look after Emily when she goes back to school. I told her earlier that I might be able to help, although I don't know how. It's nothing to do with me, but she seemed very distressed about it."

"Thank you for telling me. I'll deal with it."

Immediately afterwards, Royston drove round to Emily's

Although he shared the family's general consensus that his daughter was managing with Emily exceptionally well, he also thought they should not expect her to cope alone. Kristine was, after all, still a school student. And that, to Royston's way of thinking, came first.

2

At Emily's, he let himself in through the back door using the spare key located in a new, burglar-proof hiding place.

He found the two women in the lounge, watching television; although, only Emily was actually watching it. Kristine had long since stretched out on the settee and appeared to be sleeping.

While Emily happily welcomed him and made a mandatory cup of tea, Royston realised how best he could deal with the perplexing situation, and solve a few domestic problems of his own as well.

Assuming it was alright with the rest of the family, he would give notice at his flat and move permanently into Emily's house. With the flat to finance as well as the house that Fiona still occupied; not yet mortgage free, having one less expense would be a blessing.

The sooner Kristine was allowed to return home to pick up the threads of her own life, the better.

Kristine roused from her nap when she heard Royston and Emily chatting in the kitchen.

She looked at her watch. It gave the time as eight-thirty. Had she been less surprised by her father's arrival, she might have bemoaned the fact that she was stuck at home at that hour on a Friday night. But the week past had been so out of the ordinary that no such thought entered her head. Instead, she blinked her sleepiness away and said, "Dad, what are you doing here?"

"I had a message from Alicia," Royston replied. "She said you were worried about who would look after Nana when school starts up again."

"Yes, that's right. We go back next Monday. But why would Alicia ring you about it?"

"She didn't. I rang her. It was while we were talking that she mentioned it. You don't mind, do you?"

"No, of course not. ...And I must thank her for following through on her promise. She said she would look into it."

"I can thank her for you, if you like. We're having dinner together tomorrow night."

"That's nice for you, dear. Alicia seems to be a lovely lady," remarked Emily.

She had been sitting, quietly listening to the discussion between Kristine and her father, at the same time forming her own opinion; an opinion which she now saw the need to express.

"But Kristine," she went on. "I don't want you to worry about me anymore. We'll be just fine on our own. I can manage quite well without help now. My back is much better, and I've been free of pain for weeks. So you don't need to make arrangements to look after me. ...In fact, I wish you hadn't. Quite frankly, I'm disappointed you two talked about me behind my back; especially with someone who is still a stranger to the family..."

Emily's comment took both Kristine and Royston by surprise. They looked at her; then shot enquiring glances at each other as if to say, what do we do now?

Royston immediately saw the need to take control.

It was Emily's intimation that 'we' could manage which alerted him. Despite the casual way in which she said it, Royston could see she was far from alright.

Emily, so it seemed, was still hallucinating.

Royston had intended to come right out and tell both Emily and Kristine about his decision to move in. He felt sure they would approve of the idea...he still thought Kristine would. But now he wasn't quite so sure about Emily. In light of what she just told them, would she regard his decision as an invasion of her privacy?

His previous stay with her had been for a very specific purpose – to help her get through the awful first few days

4

after her husband's death, and to prepare for the funeral. Would she welcome him now as a permanent fixture in the house, or feel intimidated by his presence?

He must be careful how he broached the subject, if he was to avoid an outright rejection of his idea...

"I'm sorry, Emily," he said with contrition. "We meant no offence but we are concerned about you; after all, it's a long time since you lived alone. Since then you've suffered both injury and loss. If you were to have another fall while on your own, there would be nobody around to help you."

Emily beamed her gracious smile at him.

On tenterhooks for a moment, Kristine felt herself relax; for she had been in a difficult position.

She understood the situation from both points of view; and looking at it from both perspectives she could see that to a certain extent each was right in their way of thinking. ...And her grandmother, though needing supervision, was very much in control of her faculties.

"Nana," she said; squatting down beside her. "I don't want to take sides, but I think Dad has a point here. It would be awful if you fell again. I realise you're feeling more like your old self now and probably are able to cope, but Dad and I will still worry. Won't you let one of the family stay with you for another couple of weeks, just to be on the safe side?"

Royston pricked up his ears. Kristine's suggestion was better than he could have hoped for.

"Yes," he said enthusiastically. "I'm sure you don't want Kristine to have your wellbeing in mind while she needs to focus on her schoolwork. ...And I would be only too happy to move back here!"

"Move?" said Kristine in surprise, "Why did you use the word 'move'?"

"I meant, stay... Well... Actually, no, I didn't mean stay."

"Dad, you're not making sense."

Suddenly Royston realised that two pairs of eyes were looking at him curiously. Perhaps it was time he explained his situation to them.

"I apologise for being so ambiguous," he began; "but I have been thinking along the lines Kristine just mentioned. You see, after Sylvia left me, I've felt the need to change my own living arrangements. Then, when Alicia told me about Kristine's dilemma, something came to mind which sounds like a good idea and will solve two problems at the same time..."

"...Meaning what?" asked Kristine as Emily looked on blankly, not really grasping what he was talking about.

Royston turned to Emily, startling her when she realised he was about to address her.

"Emily, how would you feel," he said warily; "if I were to move in here with you?"

"Do you mean, forever?" asked Kristine.

"Yes... Well, indefinitely, anyway," he replied. "What do you think, Emily?"

"Oh, I don't know," she said guardedly. "I would have to consult with Arthur. He might not like having another man living in the house with us."

Kristine shot her father a glance. She could tell from the look on his face that Emily's reaction had dismayed him.

If Emily was to be persuaded on the matter, they would both need to relate to her grandmother's perspective for a minute, if necessary sacrificing a rational response.

"Nana, I'm sure Grandpa would be very happy to have another man in the house," she said quickly.

She glared at Royston, her expression begging him not to make anything of her comment.

He picked up on it at once.

"I need to ask Arthur first," said Emily. "We do like our privacy, you know."

"Naturally," said Kristine. "Will you ask him soon?"

"Yes dear, if it makes you happy," replied Emily, patting Kristine on the arm.

"...In the meantime," continued Kristine; "would it be alright if Dad stays here with you while I go back home? I really have to get ready for school. You wouldn't mind that, would you Nana?"

"I suppose it would be alright," Emily conceded; "but I'll still need to consult Arthur."

"Of course," came their joint response.

"Well intervened," said Royston as Kristine walked him out to the car.

"Did you really think about moving in here rather than just staying for a while?"

"Oh yes. When Alicia told me you were worried about the new school term, it started me thinking."

"Thanks, Dad. I'm glad you did. It has taken a load off my mind, I can tell you!"

The Bistro restaurant stood a little way back from the road so tables and chairs could be arranged for al fresco dining.

With tiny white lights decorating trees in the kerbside area the effect, to Alicia and Royston when they walked up to it, was magical; especially as typically French sounds and aromas wafted out through the open doors.

The two new patrons warmed to the place at once.

As it was a balmy evening they decided to eat outside; not just for the atmosphere and fresh air, but because it was quieter than inside the restaurant, and they wanted a chance to talk. At least, Royston hoped to talk at length with Alicia...and not just about Emily. This woman was someone he wanted to get to know on a more personal level than just that of a visiting district nurse.

During the evening, Royston learnt some insightful facts about his dinner companion: She had recently been through a painful divorce – the outcome of her husband's infidelity with her closest friend. There were no children from their union, she told him, and she had relocated to get away from bad memories.

"I needed to make a fresh start," she concluded.

Royston, for his part, told her about Fiona...

"...So you are actually still married?" Alicia asked, a little put out.

It had not yet occurred to her that Royston might have a wife tucked away. Everything about him had suggested to her that he, too, was divorced.

Anticipating such a reaction, Royston quickly sprung to his own defence.

"But it's a marriage in name only and has been for some time;" hoping against hope that his present marital status would not inhibit a possible friendship with Alicia.

"I see," she said at length. "I'm sure you can understand though, that having been on the receiving end of infidelity, I would not like to one day find myself as the other woman in someone else's divorce case!"

Royston listened to her comments in near panic. Was he going to lose this lovely, refined new friend before their friendship had even begun?

"...However," she went on when she saw the look of concern on his face. "I have nothing against an ordinary friendship. We will, after all, be crossing paths from time to time where Emily is concerned. It's only natural that we might become friends, too."

Strangely enough, by the time Royston got home that night he realised that his intended purpose for the evening had not materialised. His plan was to seek help with Emily, but the subject did not even arise. In a way he was glad: it was nice to meet with Alicia on a purely social level. They had such an enjoyable time that he realised, in retrospect, that bringing up a worrying and depressing topic would have spoilt the whole occasion; possibly for them both.

Maybe the next time we meet, he declared privately, there will be time to get into that particular topic with her. Tomorrow should herald the beginning of a new era which will definitely include Alicia, if only on a professional basis; for with or without Arthur's permission, tomorrow all my belongings will be transferred to the home of confused, and still slightly infirm Emily.

The prospect of it was both daunting and irresistible.

"I was beginning to think you weren't coming back," Fiona caustically remarked on Kristine's late return. "You haven't forgotten about school tomorrow, have you?"

"Of course not!" replied Kristine, irritated. "Why do you think I came home now?"

"Well, you certainly led me to believe you'd taken up residence with your loopy grandmother; it's been so long."

"It hasn't been all that long... And don't call her 'loopy'! She's just in the throes of grieving, that's all. If you paid her any attention yourself, you would realise it!"

"Alright, alright; I'm sorry... Anyway, Kristine," she said, softening a little, "I'm glad you're home; I sometimes get a bit lonely without you."

"I'm glad to be home again, too," said Kristine; and for some strange reason she meant it.

In fact, home seemed almost like a refuge now; possibly for the first time since her father left. What's more, her mother's arms, as they briefly hugged, seemed welcoming; and this surprised Kristine. She and Fiona had been very much at odds in recent times. Hugging was a practice they did not usually engage in. Perhaps it had something to do with the trying environment she had been in over the last few days...

"So how is that mother of mine?" Fiona asked Kristine after she had unpacked her bag.

"As well as can be expected," said Kristine answered, not knowing what else to say; for giving a more accurate assessment would be morally wrong just now.

Knowing her mother would take pleasure in any excuse to criticise Emily, she could hardly confirm what Fiona had already suspected: that Nana was bordering on senility.

...Best say nothing about it, she thought.

Kristine did, however, inform Fiona about Royston's decision to move back to Emily's. It would be better, she reckoned, for Fiona to be given the news right from the start, rather than find out about it later on.

"He's gone back to stay with my mother? Has he lost his mind?" was Fiona's incredulous response. "Why on earth would Royston do that? It's not like he and Emily are close. I bet he's just doing it to make me look bad!"

"It's not all about you!" said Kristine, exasperated.

Just for a moment she had forgotten how unreasonable her mother could be.

"Dad was with James when he died, and then needed to break the news to Nana. It's only natural that he feels a sense of duty towards her. And besides..."

"...What now?"

Kristine paused, thinking quickly. She wanted to explain that her grandmother needed constant supervision at the moment, and that her father had taken over because of her new school term. But she could not bring herself to divulge what the situation with Emily was really like; it would have been too much like a betrayal of trust.

"...Besides," Kristine went on. "Nana should have a man around the place. She can't manage the house and garden all by herself."

"I suppose I should check in with the old dear myself," murmured Fiona.

Kristine could hardly believe her ears.

Was Fiona actually thinking of connecting with her mother again? That would really be something!

"I think that would be nice," she said. "Nana still needs a lot of support. You could spend some time with her, so Dad can get into work occasionally..."

"...Oh, I don't mean your grandmother," Fiona quickly cut in. "I mean Dad. We are still legally married, after all. It wouldn't hurt for me to talk to him now and again. I actually felt sorry for him when the husband was killed. It must have been an awful thing to go through."

"Yes, and if it wasn't for Alicia he probably would not have been able to cope with it..."

"...Who is Alicia?"

She's the district nurse. She gives Nana her check-up; and also happened to be playing on the golf course at the time of James's accident."

"...So you and your father know her well enough to call her by her first name...how is that, Kristine?" Fiona asked with a hint of sarcasm in her voice.

"I met her when she came to visit Nana... Mum, why are you adopting this attitude?"

In disbelief, Kristine homed in on the change in Fiona's tone of voice.

"It's like you're accusing her of being Dad's girlfriend or something. She's only the district nurse – there's nothing personal in it. And she seems to care about Nana: that's the main thing. You should be pleased. It means you don't have to be bothered with her yourself!"

11

Her anger rising, Kristine stormed out. So much for the pleasant homecoming, she thought angrily. She may have returned on account of school, but right now she would not remain under her mother's roof a minute longer.

Grabbing her bike, she headed for the local park.

Kristine had a favourite haunt in the park, and frequently biked there in order to clear her head when something was troubling her.

A rocky outcrop overlooked the lake and the path that meandered around it. She made her way up there now, and propped her bike against the crash barrier around the edge. Then she perched on it facing outwards, her feet dangling over the bank; as though turning her back on the world she wanted to escape.

It was enlivening for her to sit there, with the prevailing wind providing enough breeze to blow away the cobwebs from her mind and freshen up her face.

Eagerly, she faced into the wind, allowing it to flow over features wearied from too much care and responsibility at a time when she should be refreshed and revitalised ready for school.

She thought about the girlfriends she did not have a chance to socialise with during the holidays because of family commitments.

She envied the fact that they would have enjoyed their holiday; a break that should have been like a springboard for the final leap towards the end of her secondary school days: a special occasion in anyone's life.

To her knowledge she was the only one from her social circle who had aspirations to further their education...but that shouldn't prevent them from remaining her friends, if she could still call them friends after fobbing them off over the last week or so.

"Oh, Nana!" she cried into the wind.

In desperation, she groaned as the reasons behind her dilemma came to mind again.

If only James had not died, Kristine moaned. If, instead, he had recovered from his accident, Nana would once more be bright and independent...and she would still be living the life of a normal teenager rather than acting as the caregiver of an old lady; albeit her grandmother!

Kristine brushed the thoughts and their accompanying feelings aside; for there was no point in dwelling on them. Thinking wasn't going to change anything. She just had to accept that from now on her life would be different.

While she picked up her bike to go back home an image flashed through her mind of womanhood lost. ...Of all the years ahead that should be spent pursuing a career, a happy social life and ultimately marriage, instead of being governed by the responsibility of care to somebody who, as far as the world was concerned, had already begun the downward spiral towards senility.

A sickening lump formed in Kristine's throat with the thought of it.

"I must stop all of these depressing thoughts," she told herself as she cycled home, aggressively forcing her bike through the strong head wind. "She is my Nana and always will be. How can I in good conscience put my own selfish needs ahead of hers?"

But the last remark was made with enough reluctance to trigger an avalanche of tears, the saltiness of which stung her face in the wind and dried to a crusty film during the ride home.

When she got back Fiona was quick to notice redness in her eyes.

"Have you been crying?" she asked; her in an accusing rather than sympathetic manner.

"It was just the cold wind," replied Kristine with partial honesty. "I went for a ride to the park."

"...The park?"

"Yes. I go there when I need to get away."

"Hmm... That's somewhere I haven't been to for years. Dad and I used to enjoy walking along the footpath by the lake. It was nice..."

For a moment Fiona's thoughts drifted back to happier times; giving Kristine the chance to slip away from her.

She cleansed her sore eyes with cold water from the bathroom tap; then glanced up at her face in the mirror.

"Gee, I look a mess," she said, and tidied her hair.

Then she went back out to her mother, only to discover that she was on the phone.

"Who are you ringing?" Kristine asked as Fiona waited for the call to be answered.

"I thought it was time I gave your father a ring," she said with intent; "What with everything that has happened in recent weeks."

"Wow, that's a switch!" said Kristine in surprise.

A few seconds later, Fiona put the phone down; a look of disappointment on her face.

"He's not at the flat," she called through to Kristine who was pouring herself a glass of lemonade. Then, walking through to join her, she said, "What a pity. I really felt like talking to him. I guess he must have gone out somewhere with that Sylvia woman. I'd almost forgotten about her."

Immediately Kristine swung round.

"...So you haven't caught up with the latest gossip over that, then?"

"What gossip?"

"...Dad and Sylvia. They've split up!"

Fiona sniggered scornfully. "I can't say I'm surprised," she said. "I knew it would never last. From what I've heard

14

Sylvia was much too common for him. Dad and I may have had our differences, but I'll say one thing for him: he had good taste. I'm glad he sent her packing."

"It wasn't like that at all," said Kristine mockingly. "In fact, Sylvia walked out on…"

"…Well then…it serves him right," sneered Fiona.

"It was only because he helped Nana after the accident. In fact, he's there now, if you still want to talk to him."

"Your father's a glutton for punishment alright. She's not even his own mother!"

"No, but he obviously cares for her; which is more than can be said for you!"

"Alright! That's enough! I've already decided it's time I contacted him again; both of them, in fact."

Kristine softened.

"Do you really mean that?" she asked hopefully.

"I just said so, didn't I?"

Kristine paused to draw breath for a moment while Fiona's surprise decision sunk in.

A part of her was thrilled that at long last her mother was climbing down off her high horse and thinking of re-joining the family unit.

…But another part of her was not so sure.

Should she encourage reconciliation between the two of them when Emily's behaviour was so unusual?

She knew her mother well enough to foresee a negative reception to Emily's flights of fancy. And as for her father… Kristine was sure Royston harboured no ill feelings against Fiona, but would he want to reconnect with her under such trying circumstances?

Somehow she didn't think so.

And then something else occurred to Kristine: If Fiona was determined to contact her ex-husband, then maybe it would be best if she came clean and told her mother the true extent of Royston's plans...

"By the way, Mum," she said apprehensively. "I think I should explain something to you: something I didn't tell you earlier because I wasn't sure how you'd react. But if you're intent on being in touch with Dad and Nana again, then it's something you should know."

Fiona looked at her curiously. "You're babbling, Kristine. What are you talking about?"

"Dad is about to move over to Nana's..."

"...You've told me that already."

"I know I did. But what I didn't tell you is that he's going to be living there permanently."

"Why, for goodness sake? She's not an invalid anymore. What's he playing at? I tell you, he's just trying to make me feel guilty for ignoring her..."

"...Mum, of course not! He's going to live there because he's given notice to vacate his little flat, and because Nana needs constant..."

All of a sudden Kristine realised she was revealing too much information. The last thing she wanted was for her mother to learn of Emily's hallucinating – she would very quickly have her committed to a mental facility.

"...Constant what? Constant supervision; isn't that what you wanted to say?"

Kristine was beginning to feel trapped.

"No...now you're putting words into my mouth!"

And that was indeed the truth: Kristine had deliberately refrained from saying any more. She had no intention of even implying Emily needed supervision, for in her heart she knew it was not really the case. As far as Kristine could so far make out, her grandmother was still capable of looking after herself.

...Me and my big mouth, she thought helplessly.

"Well then...what were you going to say?" asked Fiona impatiently. "You definitely suggested she needs constant something or other."

"Yes, of course she does. She needs company and a sense of security. Like I said before; she needs a man there to help her. She's a lonely old widow who has lost two husbands, and is still incapacitated after that fall. And she needs to have her own flesh and blood take an interest in her instead of being critical!"

Kristine's temper was rising again; she didn't like being backed into a corner; yet Fiona was unrelenting.

"She's got Ruth, for goodness sake! Where has my lazy sister been all this time?"

"Auntie Ruth has Uncle Wilbur to take care of. For all I know, his health is still an issue for her. She got a heck of a scare when he had that turn at his party. And although she would like to be more involved with Nana, she can't. You, on the other hand have nothing to do all day but laze around at home and complain about anything that comes to mind. You don't care for her – or anybody else in our family for that matter!"

"That's not true! ...And I don't sit around all day – I have my little job. As for Nana; I have always cared for her in my own way..."

"...Oh, come off it, Mum! You haven't been near her for ages. If you did go to see her you would just start finding fault again. To be honest, she can do without you in her life. Just leave it to Dad and me. We care about her, and she accepts what we do for her. That's what matters. Now, if you don't mind, I need to prepare for school tomorrow!"

Kristine made for her room. With a headache that started to pound within her skull, she pulled her school bag out of the closet and dumped it on the bed.

17

Then she walked over to her bookcase, the shelves of which were filled with textbooks accumulated throughout her senior years at school.

She squatted in front of them, her eyes skimming over the titles, ready to pull out the ones she would need for the morning. But she could not see them properly. Her mind had gone blank and her eyes seemed to be glazed over from the migraine that was threatening to take hold. So instead she threw open her window for some fresh air and sat for a while, breathing it in.

"I must pull myself together..." she told herself sternly; "...or I'm just going to lose it before school even starts!"

Kristine placed her hands over her face and, as though something had snapped inside her, she burst into tears. At the end of her tether, Kristine gave full rein to her tears, fearing neither witness to them nor intrusion upon them; for she knew Fiona would not bother to come and talk to her...she never did.

Throughout the night, in which she slept surprisingly soundly, Kristine's exhausted mind endeavoured to work on a solution to her dilemma. If she was to successfully conclude her final year of schooling, she needed release from the constant oppression. Her time looking after Emily was one thing – that could not be avoided. Demanding though it had turned out to be, it was still a pleasure to do it; but her mother's nagging was something else. It was getting her down more and more these days...

By the time she finally awoke, part of the solution to her problems had revealed itself to her. If she did nothing else to better her situation during the course of the year, she should at least do this one, vital thing. She needed to get out from under the depressing affect her mother was having on her.

Emily liked the thought of having Royston with her again; she had missed him.

His presence there during her initial grieving period had been more as a substitute for her husband, and she had in some ways regarded him as though he was indeed James; to the extent that when he left to go back to his flat it was the persona of a husband she found herself missing, rather than Royston himself.

Yet, this time there was no mistaking in her mind just who had come back into her house, or rather, who had not come back to it; for she knew in her heart, now, that James had withdrawn, and returned her to Arthur.

"Here, let me help you with those heavy things," Emily said as Royston began to carry in his belongings.

Having moved out of Fiona's with only a few items, he still possessed comparatively little to bring into Emily's, but just at the moment there seemed to be an awful lot of mainly clutter.

From behind the bulky cardboard box he was carrying, Royston said, "Thank you, Emily, but I can manage. I don't want you to hurt yourself, lifting heavy boxes."

So Emily could do nothing except stand back and watch as the boxes, bundles of bedding and numerous smaller items gradually covered the floor in her lounge.

"Don't worry; this will all be gone in a jiffy," he assured her when he saw the look of consternation on her face.

"I'm not worried about the amount," she said. "But I am wondering where you are going to put everything once you've finished unpacking!"

Royston laughed. He closed the front door with his foot after the last of his boxes had been brought in.

With a smirk on his face, he said, "Very soon you won't even notice my stuff. Everything will just disappear into the woodwork."

"I hope you're right. Arthur has never liked the house to be in a mess."

Royston sighed, as one who has just remembered the burden he must bear.

"Ah, yes: dear Arthur," he muttered as he took the first of many boxes into his reclaimed bedroom. "Where would we be without Arthur?"

During the afternoon, Emily answered a frantic phone call from Kristine.

"Hello, dear," she said cheerfully. "How are you? ...And how was your first day back at school? Will you be able to come round to see me like you used to...?"

"Nana!" Kristine said tersely, cutting across the onrush of questions. "Sorry to interrupt...I'd really like to chat with you, but I actually rang to speak to Dad."

Though taken aback that Kristine wanted to sidestep their usual small talk, Emily nevertheless heeded the note of urgency in her voice.

"Yes, of course you can. He's just putting some more of his things away." Then she added, as if compelled to do so after decades of ingrained thoughtfulness, "Is everything alright, dear?"

"Yes, Nana! Just get Dad...please! I really need to talk to him – right now!"

"What's wrong, Kristine?" asked a concerned Royston when he came to the phone. "Emily said you seemed to be worried about something."

"No! Nothing's worrying me; that was just Nana's..."

"Why did you insist on speaking to me?" Then, before Kristine could answer, he asked, "By the way, how are you getting on back at school?"

"Oh, Dad! You're as bad as Nana for asking too many questions at once!"

"Sorry, it was purely unintentional. What do you want to talk to me about?"

"…Not on the phone. Can I meet you somewhere for a few minutes? There's something I need to discuss with you urgently – and in private."

"Well, ordinarily I would say, yes – Emily should be fine on her own for a short period of time. But I'm still in the process of moving in here. You should just see the lounge floor. It's cluttered up with my stuff. I wouldn't want her to trip over anything…"

"…So you're saying you won't meet me."

"I don't know, Kristine. You've caught me a bit on the hop. I suppose I could excuse myself briefly and ask Emily to keep out of the lounge until I get back. That shouldn't cause too many problems for her. Give me a minute. I'll go and speak with her now."

Royston put down the phone. A moment later he came back to Kristine.

"Yes, that will be alright. Where do you want to meet?"

"At the park. Mum says you're familiar with it. Do you know where the lookout is?"

"Round by the lake? Oh yes, your mother and I used to go for walks there…"

"…I know. I'll see you there in a few minutes. Give me a bit of a head start because I'll be on my bike."

By the time Kristine arrived, Royston had already parked and was waiting by his car. He waved as she approached.

Kristine stopped right next to him, the tyres skidding to a halt on loose gravel.

She removed her bicycle helmet, and straight away he could see the strain in her face which prompted her to contact him. Royston commented on this while she caught her breath.

"Come and sit in the car with me; then we can talk," he said as he took the bike from her and propped it against the crash barrier.

Kristine gratefully accepted his offer to sit in comfort for their chat. Although she was hot from her ride, it was windy at the exposed lookout and she did not want to catch a chill on top of everything else.

When they were both settled in the car, the doors and windows closed but for a slight gap at the top for some air, Kristine, whose mind was completely focused on what she had planned to say, came straight out with it.

"Dad," she said before he could start up with a flurry of questions. "Have you still got your flat in town?"

"My flat?" he said quizzically. "I don't know just what you mean. As you are aware, I've moved out."

"...I know you have. But do you still have the rental on the flat?"

"Are you asking if my lease has expired?"

"Yes...I think that's what I'm asking."

"It runs out tomorrow. The owner's redecorating before the new tenant comes in. Why do you want to know?"

"So they've already got somebody lined up for it?"

Still absorbed in her own train of thought, she failed to notice her father's query.

"That's right. But why are you asking me about it?"

"Well, it's irrelevant if the landlord's already signed up somebody else."

"Kristine, you're not making any sense. Do you know of somebody who's interested in it?"

"Yes."

"...A friend of yours?"

"No."

"Well who, then?"

"...Me!"

22

Royston's jaw dropped in surprise.

"...You? ...But why, for goodness sake?"

"...Because I'm sick to death of living at home. Mum is driving me insane, and I can't wait to leave. Sometimes it seems like she's got serious psychological problems. ...Dad, I need a place of my own!"

Royston rubbed his chin, and groaned in support of his daughter's plight.

"I'm so sorry it's come to this," he said, taking hold of her hand. "I do understand how you feel, though. I was in the same position not so long ago."

"I knew you would, but I was hoping for a bit more than just understanding from you."

"You were?"

"I thought I could take over your flat...but obviously I'm too late."

Royston sighed disconsolately. He had picked up a hint of sarcasm in Kristine's remark, but sensed it was born of frustration rather than insolence, and ignored it.

He sat thoughtfully for a moment; then said, "But even if it was still free, there's no way you could afford to pay a weekly rent on a flat like that one. They don't come cheap, you know – especially so close to town. And anyway..." he added hesitantly, "...you're much too young to live in a flat by yourself."

Kristine saw red. "Dad, I thought you were on my side. You said you understood!"

"I am on your side! ...And of course I understand where you're coming from! But Kristine, please don't get heavy handed with me. If you want to come to me for help, I'm afraid this is not the way to go about it!"

Kristine calmed down. He was right. For her to get what she wanted – what she felt she needed – she would need to be more courteous in her approach.

"I'm sorry...I shouldn't have been rude."

And then she remembered saying the same thing to her grandmother not all that long ago.

"I don't know what has come over me lately. Everything is stressing me out so much..."

"...Don't worry about it," said Royston. "I recall only too well how irritating your mother can be. But as for living by yourself...I'm not so sure about that."

"I don't have to be by myself completely; I could board with one of my school friends!" said Kristine as the idea suddenly popped into her head. "You'd be willing to pay for me to do that, wouldn't you? Then the two of us could study in peace and quiet, and generally hang out together. I'm sure I wouldn't have to pay much by way of board. It would be so neat..."

"...Darling, just stop. Please!'

"Why? Don't you think that would be a brilliant idea?"

"Yes. In actual fact I do..."

"...Then what's the problem?"

Royston sighed again. The pressure was getting to him, and he had started to perspire.

He reached into his shirt pocket for a handkerchief to wipe his brow; then opened his side window to let some more fresh air into the stuffy car. His daughter's relentless pursuit of her dream was causing him to feel decidedly hot under the collar.

Up until now Royston had been listening sympathetically to Kristine's lament, and would have liked to help her. He wanted more than anything to see her settled into her last term of schooling, preferably in a happy environment.

Yet, the truth of the matter was, he could not help her financially for, known only to him, his rent and payments on Fiona's house had drastically depleted his resources.

24

Furthermore, out of necessity he had reduced his working hours from a full week in the office to barely part time at home in order to look after Emily, thereby as good as halving his income. This in itself was reason enough to give up the flat; although he had stated it was primarily to act as Emily's live-in companion.

At the time, Royston could not bring himself to admit to Emily that his decision was really based on the fact that living with her would not cost him anything.

...And these facts he would never be able to divulge to Kristine or Alicia.

Royston remained silent. While he cleaned a peephole in the misted up window, he tried to work out just what he should say to her.

At length he decided to tell her a partial truth.

"I meant it when I said I like the idea of your boarding in the home of a friend," he said, "but the truth of the matter is, I would not be able to pay for it."

"Why not? You're my father. It's what fathers do for their children! Don't you want me to do well this term?"

"Of course I do! Kristine, don't give me that! I won't be bullied. Just listen to me, if you don't mind."

"Alright," said Kristine petulantly.

She closed up the window on her side of the car, as a through-draught from the driver's window was making an irritating whistling noise. While she did so, Royston briefly explained his financial predicament to her, omitting only the part about wanting to live rent free with Emily.

Kristine remained with her head turned away from him, annoyed by what she heard, but also not in a position to dispute any of it.

In truth, she did not realise he'd given up full time work in order to look after her grandmother, and certainly it did not occur to her that he still owed mortgage money on the house she and her mother occupied.

Throughout her childhood she had always been able to go to him when she needed some cash, and her school fees were paid automatically. She never once thought to question the source...until now.

All at once Kristine felt ashamed. She looked across at her father's flushed face, and clearly recognised that her arguing had given him grief.

She opened up her window again to ease his suffering; then she said, "Don't worry about it, Dad. I understand the situation now. I won't pester you again."

"I'm so sorry, love. You know I would do anything for you if I could."

"I know. Thanks for hearing me out, anyway."

Kristine flicked the door handle and pushed it, ready to get out; but then an idea came to mind.

She turned back to face him and said, "I suppose I could always get a job."

"What! With all your school work this term?" remarked Royston jovially to ease the tension.

"Ah well. It was just a thought."

When Royston got home, entering the house nervously in case he found Emily behaving strangely, he received both a shock and a surprise.

Never one to leave anything in a mess, Emily had tided Royston's remaining belongings and neatly stacked them to one side of the lounge.

"I have taken the rest of your clothes upstairs and laid them out on the bed for you," she said with pride; hardly noticing the astonished look on his face.

"Well, thank you – I think," he said in good humour, and glanced over the remaining items.

The amount seemed a little too diminished.

"You didn't throw anything out, did you?" he asked.

"Good gracious me, no," Emily replied with a chuckle. "...Except for some bundles of old papers. They're just in the laundry, ready to go out in the rubbish. Do you want to do that straight away?"

"...Maybe later," he stated, while alarm surged through him as to which papers she meant.

Instead, he made for the kitchen.

"Right now," he said; "I need to get something to eat. It's been a long day, and I'm feeling a bit seedy."

Emily followed him and opened the fridge door.

"There's some cooked chicken in here. I've been saving it for Arthur, but you can have it if you like."

Uh-oh, thought Royston, eyeing it suspiciously.

"How long has it been here?" he asked.

"...Not very long. Only a few days..."

Royston grunted silently; reminding himself to check everything else in the fridge, and to consign the ageing carrion to the rubbish bin in the morning.

He closed the fridge; then opened a cupboard above the kitchen bench where he spotted a tin of baked beans.

"This will do," he said. "Have you eaten, Emily? There's plenty here for two."

"No, I haven't yet...but you go ahead if you're hungry. I'll have something later with Arthur."

With a heavy heart Royston set a couple of places at the table, then prepared two portions of baked beans on toast for Emily and himself.

Come and sit down," he said when the food was ready; and guided Emily to the table.

He was relieved to see that she acquiesced without hesitation and noted, from the speed at which the baked beans disappeared, that she must have been very hungry.

27

I bet she hasn't been eating well, he thought and then added, "She's probably been waiting for Arthur!"

A few days later, Royston and Emily were weeding in the front garden, when Alicia drove past.

She tooted, causing them both to look up and wave to her. Then she pulled over, performed a U-turn, and drove back to them on the opposite side of the road.

"I couldn't resist turning around," she called through her open window. "You two look so industrious."

"Why, thank you, dear," Emily called back.

She removed her gardening gloves and deposited them, along with her secateurs, on the steps. Then she walked purposefully up the path and out to the kerb.

"Don't come across!" shouted Alicia urgently when she saw how quickly Emily was heading towards her, and that a car was approaching at speed.

In a flash, Royston was at Emily's side. He, too, had seen the car and was unsure if Emily would have the presence of mind to wait before scurrying across the road to Alicia.

"I wasn't going to cross over!" Emily insisted when she felt Royston's restraining hand on her elbow.

"I know," he responded kindly; then he called out, "It's good to see you again, Alicia. Are you in a hurry, or can you come in for a minute?"

"Actually, I'm a bit rushed," she replied. "I have a client waiting and am running late – but I'm very glad I saw you."

"Oh, why is that?" Royston shouted; his voice raised as a succession of cars approached and then passed by.

"I think I'll go back in now," Emily told Royston above the noise of the traffic.

"Okay," shouted Royston in response; then added, "I'll be in shortly. I just want to have a word with Alicia."

Then, when the road was quiet, he crossed over to her.

"I tried to ring your number," said Alicia, continuing her train of thought; "but it sounded like it was disconnected. Did you know about that?"

"Ah...yes! Sorry; I never got round to telling you... I've moved out of the flat. I'm living here now."

"...With Emily?"

"Yes. It seems to be working out quite well."

"I can't say I'm surprised." remarked Alicia.

"Why do you say that?"

"It seemed to me like a logical solution to the problem of looking after Emily. Look, I'm really sorry but I need to keep going. I would like to ask you something before I do, though – if that's alright."

"Ask away!"

"Next weekend there's an organics festival in the town square. I thought I might go to it, and wondered whether you'd like to go with me; perhaps on Saturday morning."

"Organics? Do you mean organic foods?"

"Yes. I thought it would nice to see what's grown locally and sample some. What do you say?"

Royston thought briefly, warmed by the prospect of spending some more time with Alicia; then he said, "Okay, but I'll have to see if Kristine can baby-sit for me."

Alicia chuckled. "Did you say 'baby-sit'?"

"Oh dear," muttered Royston self-consciously. "Did I really say that? ...How insensitive of me. It's as well Emily didn't hear me; she would have been quite offended."

"There's no harm done; though 'granny-sit' might have been more appropriate!"

Royston joined in with her gaiety. Alicia had that effect on him. She handled everything so well. Accompanying her to a fair would be a pleasure.

He told her, "I'll let you know when I've asked Kristine."

Royston arranged for Kristine to be at Emily's by nine the following Saturday morning.

It actually suited her to leave the house at that time. Saturday was the day of the week she dreaded the most in the company of her mother.

Never the most enthusiastic housekeeper, Fiona usually managed to commandeer Kristine into doing most of the housework. She insisted it was in lieu of the board Kristine should be paying at her age; the contribution to household expenses Fiona was certain most of her friends would be making to their parents. So consequently, when Saturday came around Kristine was always on the lookout for a plausible means of escape; and on this particular Saturday her father's request came as a something of a godsend.

"Take as long as you like," she told Royston after kissing him goodbye. "Nana and I have some catching up to do."

CHAPTER TWO

Royston picked Alicia up at her home address.

It was the first time he had seen her house, and he was surprised by its simplicity.

Alicia had struck him as someone whose elegant tastes and demeanour would be reflected in her residence. Yet this, as it turned out, was not the case. Even from the outside he could tell she lived quite modestly. The address and surrounding houses suggested affluence, but Alicia's rented home did not fit that mould.

In fact, the house did not fit any identifiable mould; for the building, he discovered later, was not erected on that particular site, but was transported there by one of its former owners.

It was a tastefully refurbished period cottage, and wore the unpretentious grace with which Royston had come to associate Alicia herself.

She ran out to him when he tooted; dressed casually in jeans and a tee shirt. Royston's initial impulse was to wolf-whistle his approval; for he had long-since noticed that Alicia's trim form looked its best in the slim fitting clothing that now covered her.

On this, only the second occasion he had met with her socially, he recognised in no small way that he was really rather smitten with the district nurse.

Dreamily, Royston felt excitement for the day ahead, and could only imagine the possibilities thereafter...

"I won't be a minute," Alicia said. "I just need to change out of these old duds. I got involved in a chore and lost track of time. Do you mind waiting?"

"Of course not," he said, and started to get out of the car, but Alicia stopped him.

"No, please wait here...I will really only be a minute," she emphasised.

What a shame, Royston thought to himself; she looks great just like that. Yet, he refrained from commenting.

In the short time it took for him to get over his wishful sentiment, Alicia had gone back inside, changed into a long silky skirt and colourful blouse, and was already slamming the door on her way out to him.

It rained while they were at the fair. The stalls, though covered, did little to protect the visitors from the weather, and there were plenty of them needing shelter.

Nevertheless, Alicia would not leave the site until she had examined every stall, picked up pamphlets of interest, and sampled a range of preservative or gluten free home made products.

After a while, Royston began to shiver; not because it was especially cold but for the reason that he allowed Alicia the cover of the stalls at his own expense. Instead, he stayed in the background while waiting for her and the hoard of other women to make their plenteous selections. Then, not being particularly interested in organics as such, when boredom began to set in along with the shivers, he soon realised he was in trouble.

It was a fit of uncontrollable sneezing that drew Alicia's attention away from her browsing and onto the plight of her companion. She turned around to see Royston looking bedraggled and forlorn as he searched in his pockets for something on which to blow his nose.

"Oh you poor thing. You're absolutely saturated! I'm so sorry. Let's get you out of this rain."

To Royston's relief, she led him off through the crowds and back to the car.

"You really need to change out of those wet things," she insisted when they arrived back at her house.

Once inside, she disappeared into the spare room and re-appeared carrying a box containing men's clothes.

As soon as she opened it, a strong smell of mothballs triggered another fit of sneezing in Royston.

Yet, Alicia was more concerned for his wellbeing than the sorry state of his sinuses and. holding out a couple of pairs of trousers, she informed him, "Yes, these should fit you. They belonged to my father. I didn't have the heart to throw them away when he died a few years ago. They've been in storage…"

Royston screwed up his nose, not just at the thought of wearing clothes from a dead man's wardrobe but because he felt another sneeze coming on. However he was also chilled to the bone now, so meekly took the trousers Alicia held out to him and then picked out a warm jersey.

"Yes, please take it. …Anything to get you warmed up. I'll get a hot drink ready…or would you prefer a brandy?"

Royston perked up at the thought of the latter.

"A brandy would be nice," he said, and retreated to the bathroom to get changed.

When he returned, he entered a room that was at once warm and cosy – its instant warmth provided by an electric fan heater; the cosiness a result of the warm toning in Alicia's choice of décor.

A bottle and two brandy glasses sat on the coffee table.

"What shall I do with these?" he said, holding up his own, very wet clothing.

"Here, give them to me."

Alicia gingerly took the dripping bundle from him and slipped out into the kitchen.

Soon she returned carrying a plastic grocery bag, now containing Royston's clothes.

"I'll drop this in the hallway," she said. "Now, let me see how you look in Dad's clothes."

Royston turned around as though modelling them, and laughed. "I think they're a bit baggy on me, but at least they're dry!" he remarked, enjoying the moment.

Alicia giggled. "Yes. I'd forgotten how portly Dad was. It's funny how some memories fade in time. Now Royston, come and get some of this down you."

She handed a glass of brandy to Royston. He remarked comically on the amount she had poured.

"My goodness, Alicia! There must be the equivalent of a double! How am I supposed to drive home afterwards?"

Settling for only a few sips of the warming liquid, Royston began to feel much better.

His shivering had long since abated, thanks in part to the jumper posthumously loaned to him by Alicia's father, and to his modest consumption of brandy.

He would have liked to stay longer, he admitted to himself. Alicia's presence was becoming addictive; alluring, even. He felt a degree of confidence that they were slowly growing more in synch with each other.

Maybe one day he will be able to get even closer to her; maybe the next time he comes to her house she might allow him to take their relationship to another level...

...Abruptly, he put down his glass. Without realising it, his moment of reflection had also seen him take a couple more sips of brandy, and now he was feeling not only warmer but also a little too mellow. If he was not careful he might blow this whole relationship with Alicia; and that was the last thing he wanted to do. Alicia was just about the most important person in his life at the moment; apart from Kristine, that is…

…Aaagh! Kristine!

He had forgotten all about Kristine. She was minding Emily as a favour to him, and he hadn't given her so much as a thought. It was inexcusable to take her for granted.

Shakily he pulled himself to his feet.

"Is anything wrong?" asked Alicia in alarm. "You seem agitated all of a sudden."

"I'm sorry, Alicia. I've been very selfish, staying here…"

"…Why do you say that?"

Royston was now trying to lose the effect of the mind-numbing brandy.

"I need to go home," he struggled to say. "Kristine will be wondering where I've got to. She's looking after Emily."

"…Of course. I'd forgotten, too. It's a shame you have to leave just as we're getting to know each other."

Alicia stood up and slipped her arms around his waist, taking him by surprise. For a moment he wondered what to expect next, but it was only a hug.

She showed him to the door.

"Have a safe drive home," she said with affection. "I'll look forward to the next time."

Royston bent over and kissed her on the forehead.

"Goodbye, my love," he said; then picked up the bag of wet clothes and walked out.

It was not until he had reversed out of the driveway and with a toot driven down the road that Alicia realised what he had said to her.

"He called me 'love,'" she said to herself, and smiled as a flutter of satisfaction warmed her heart.

"Dad, what on earth have you got on?" Kristine shrieked; bemused by the sight of her father in oversized trousers.

"It's a long story," he told her.

Royston disappeared into the laundry with his grocery bag of wet things.

"How was the organics fair, then?" she asked when he came back.

"It rained and we got wet," he said succinctly. "In fact, we got extremely wet! That's why I'm dressed in these... these jodhpurs." He pulled out the trouser pants at each side to demonstrate their bagginess on him. "...The latest fashion, don't you think?"

Kristine eyed him suspiciously. "You didn't buy them at the fair, did you?"

"Heavens, no," he said with indignation. "Alicia loaned them to me. They were her father's. Mine got soaked from standing in the rain. I had to change out of them before I caught pneumonia."

Kristine was about to make a remark that Alicia might have helped him out of them, when Emily appeared.

"Hello Royston," she said. "Did you have a nice time?"

"No," he said emphatically. "I got drenched."

"Oh dear... I hope you didn't catch a cold... I see you have some new clothes. Were they from the fair?"

"...It's a long story," Kristine said cheekily and winked at her father.

Royston winked back.

"So where was your father going, that you were needed at Nana's?" asked Fiona on Kristine's return. It had not gone unnoticed that Kristine was away for most of the day.

By her reckoning it could not have been another game of golf that lay claim to Royston's time and attention. She felt sure he would not want to set foot on that hazardous turf again; not after what happened to James...and it could not have been work-related either. In all of their years together she had never known Royston go to the office at weekends. If need be, he would bring work home instead. It must have been another form of social pursuit that had occupied him for a whole day.

"Mum, I've already explained to you why I was wanted at Nana's," said Kristine.

She did not appreciate her mother's obvious nosiness.

"Oh, that's right. I remember now: some kind of a fair," said Fiona, trying to recall when Kristine gave more details about it. Then she added, "The only one I know of for this weekend is the annual organics fair. I can't believe he'd want to go there!"

"Whatever you say..." muttered Kristine.

She couldn't be bothered with underhand comments from her mother; and there was no way she would discuss where Royston spent the day; or who with...

...That is, until Fiona put two and two together herself.

"He went with that Alicia, didn't he," she said, making a statement of assumed fact.

There was no point in denying it. Kristine could not lie any more than she was willing to tell the truth.

"Where's the harm in that?" she said defensively. "They are friends, after all. Dad doesn't need to consult you!"

"Come on now, Kristine. He's obviously found himself another girlfriend, so my trying to reconnect with him will just be a waste of time."

"Mum, they're only friends. If you want to think there's more to it, that's up to you. Just talk to him!"

Emily had not given her estranged daughter even a passing thought lately; so insignificant were Fiona and her attitude over the last few months.

Certainly, a long time had passed since her comments had any effect; so it was with an unforeseen gasp of surprise that she recognised Fiona's voice on the phone.

"Hello, Mother," said Fiona casually. "I bet I'm the last person you expected to hear from!"

"Fiona…is that really you?"

Emily's marked scepticism became obvious to Fiona.

"Of course it's me!" she barked with impatience. "How many daughters have you got who sound anything like me? …Anyway, are you keeping well these days?"

Emily went quiet. Fiona was right in that she would not have expected to hear from her. And now that she was actually on the phone, Emily did not know how to respond. After all, Fiona had already rejected her more than once…

"…Mother, are you still there?" Fiona asked cautiously; "I asked how you are keeping nowadays."

Devoid of emotion, Emily replied, "I'm very well thank you. What did you ring for, Fiona?"

"Well, if you're going to be like that, I won't bother again. I was hoping to speak to Royston. Kristine tells me he's living with you now. Is he there?"

"Yes. …Just a minute."

"I don't want to talk to her; she's out to cause trouble," said Royston when Emily located him in the garage."

"Royston, dear. She is still your wife. And she has taken the trouble to contact us…"

"…Lowered herself, more like. She must be on a fishing expedition, but what for: that's the question."

"You certainly won't find out unless you talk to her."

"Alright," he said, tut-tutting. "I suppose I should."

Royston put down the tool he had been using and went through to the laundry to wash his hands. "Tell her I won't be a minute…please."

The message delivered, Emily laid the phone down beside its cradle and returned to the magazine she had been reading; though when she picked it up again she couldn't remember which article it was.

For a moment she thought she was losing her memory; but then she recalled exactly what she was doing before the phone rang – certainly not reading.

She had been communing with Arthur.

His gossamer form had presented itself before her eyes; not as an image, but in person. So close had he been to her, in fact, that she could have reached out and touched him; as she could touch him now. A smile crossed her face as the glow of reassurance in her heart intensified.

Oh how she still loved the spirit of that man. And how grateful she was for his continuing presence in her life...

"...Emily?"

Royston's sharp tone of voice broke into her reverie.

He had come into the room and witnessed a strange scene: Emily with her arms outstretched, her eyes tightly closed in meditation...and a smile on her face such as he had not seen in a very long time.

Emily blinked herself back into full consciousness. She groaned as the pain of sudden disconnection from Arthur's spirit gripped her.

"I'm sorry I startled you," said Royston. "I didn't realise you were... You were..."

Emily looked at him blankly, her heart beating wildly.

"...What were you doing just now, Emily? It looked very weird from where I was standing."

"I wasn't doing anything, dear – just talking to Arthur."

"Oh no, not again!" exploded Royston; then turned and strode from the room.

Back in the garage he tried to regain his composure; not just from Emily's hallucination, but also as a result of the brief, irritating phone conversation with his ex-wife which he regarded as an intrusion into his life.

"I still don't know what she wanted!" he muttered in frustration.

Fiona had greeted him cordially enough when he came to the phone. She even asked after his health citing, as the reason for the enquiry, the fact that Kristine told her he was caught in the rain at the weekend. And she also commented on the fact that he was now living with Emily. But that was pretty much it, he reflected worriedly. Was she just trying to touch base with him again after all this time; or was she, as he had suggested to Emily, fishing for information?

Fiona, he recalled, usually had an ulterior motive...

The following week, while Kristine was visiting Emily and her father, Alicia arrived for another check-up.

"I do think you look nice in that crisp uniform," Emily told her while having her pulse taken.

"Doesn't she just," remarked Royston who sat watching the proceedings. He winked at Alicia as she counted heart beats against her watch.

She grinned, and a moment later said, "Royston, don't be naughty. You almost made me lose count. You wouldn't want me to have to start all over again, would you?"

If it meant you had to stay here a bit longer, I would," he said mischievously.

Kristine looked on, bemused; she had not seen Alicia and Royston together before now.

There were no formal pleasantries such as she would have expected between health profession and client; or in this case, the client's son-in-law.

Quite clearly, these two were more than that.

As Kristine viewed the camaraderie that flowed naturally between Alicia and her father, she recognised the extent to which a friendship had already developed in the few short weeks since Alicia came into their lives.

She glanced at Emily to see if she had noticed it too. But Emily, who was now examining the stethoscope Alicia left on the couch, appeared to be indifferent to the cosy chat taking place on the other side of the room, or the look of curiosity on Kristine's face.

Laughing at Emily's clumsy attempt to listen to her own heartbeat, Kristine joined in with her antics.

For a few minutes both isolated groups were oblivious of each other. But then, when Kristine heard her name being mentioned, she pricked up her ears.

For some reason, Royston and Alicia were talking about her in lowered voices...

"I'm still in the room, you know," she said to them with feigned indignation.

It reminded her of how, all those years ago, her parents used to talk behind her back as though she was not there; which made her realise that the indignation she now felt wasn't really feigned at all.

"What are you whispering about?" she asked touchily.

"We aren't whispering," said Royston in their defence. "I was just telling Alicia that you showed an interest in my little flat. Alicia said she knows the new tenant."

"I'm surprised you would want to take on the expense of a flat while still at school," said Alicia kindly. "There's nothing cheaper than living at home!"

Kristine cringed inwardly. She objected to being offered free advice by somebody she hardly knew.

"There was a reason for it," she responded in a manner which emphatically told Alicia the subject was now closed.

Yet, Royston failed to notice her intonation.

"Tell Alicia why you wanted the flat," he said insistently.

"Dad! If you don't mind!"

Kristine had no intention of citing her mother's attitude as her reason even when it was the truth; so she chose a tactful way of changing the subject.

"I just needed some peace and quiet to study" she said with her back to them. Then, to terminate the discussion, she added, "It's not an issue now, anyway. Things at home seem to be improving..."

In reality, though, Kristine quickly found she had spoken too soon; for the situation at home was not improving at all; in fact, quite the opposite.

That evening, Kristine once more incurred her mother's wrath for nothing worse than forgetting to empty the dish-draining rack. Demoralised by the needless outburst she retreated to her room, and tried to rationalise the change in behaviour. She had been under the impression that they were co-existing peaceably in the last few days.

Then before bed-time, when the need to re-establish some stability between them superseded all else, she went in search of her mother to see if she had calmed down.

Yet, Fiona, it seemed, was still angry.

Kristine found her sitting at the dining table reading the evening paper. ...Except she wasn't reading it as such, but rather flipping over each page as though her mind was on anything but the paper.

Unnoticed, Kristine briefly stood back and watched her; until Fiona suddenly realised she was there.

"Don't stand there gawking. What do you want?"

Kristine suddenly lost her temper. "Mum, I know you're in a bad mood with me for not finishing the dishes, but I can't figure out why you're so cross over something that trivial. I wish you'd tell me what's going on."

"It's got nothing to do with you."

"Well don't take it out on me, then!"

All at once Fiona realised what she had been doing, and softened. She pushed the newspaper away, sighed deeply and turned to face her daughter. It was obvious to Kristine that she had recently been crying.

Instantly, her annoyance subsided.

"For goodness sake, Mother, what's wrong?" she said with only slightly more compassion than she actually felt.

She fetched the tissue box from the kitchen and pushed it across the table.

"I feel so alone," she said bitterly as she pulled out a couple of tissues. "Even members of my own family have deserted me."

Kristine screwed up her face with puzzlement. Wasn't it that Fiona deserted her family; even after she caused her husband to leave home?

"I don't know what you mean," she said. "You're the one who has kept away from Nana and Auntie Ruth. What has happened to bring all of this on?"

Fiona paused, reluctant to talk to her daughter about anything personal.

In an instant, Kristine knew something specific must have taken place. Moreover, it must have happened that very day to cause such an upheaval in Fiona's demeanour, for her moods had been much better lately. But what it could be remained a mystery. It certainly wasn't because she had stopped off at Emily's on the way home from school, as she told her mother beforehand that she would be doing so...

Flummoxed, Kristine waited for Fiona to blow her nose and compose herself; and hopefully to offer some kind of justification for the outburst.

The explanation, when it came, was like a bolt out of the blue for Kristine.

It was earlier this afternoon," Fiona eventually told her. "I knew you would be at Nana's, and thought it would be a nice surprise if I broke the ice with her and popped in for a visit when you were all there; rather than just call when only Royston and Nana were home. It would have been a new beginning for all of us."

Kristine was touched by her mother's gesture towards reconciliation after all this time.

"That was good of you, Mum," she said. "It means a lot to me that you're prepared to make the effort...and you did the right thing, waiting till I was there. So what has happened to cause this upset? You obviously didn't come in, because none of us saw you..."

Kristine paused as something came to mind.

However, before she could say anything, Fiona went on, "You didn't see me because I decided not to stop. In fact, I drove right past."

"But why would you do that when you went over with the intention of calling in?"

"That's obvious, isn't it? You were already there, so you must have known what was going on."

The bitterness in her voice had returned.

Kristine sighed. She already had suspicions over what had upset Fiona, but had no intention of bringing them up in case she was wrong.

"Mum," she said as calmly as she could. "I think you had better explain."

"Don't be naïve. I know the three of you had company by the number of cars. Dad's was parked in the driveway, and third one – a district nurse's car – was right behind it. That Alicia has been visiting your father, hasn't she?"

"No...!"

44

"...Don't lie to me, Kristine! I saw it with my own eyes! You said she and Dad were just friends, but she wouldn't be visiting him in the middle of the afternoon unless there was more to it. I didn't come down with the last shower, you know. It's obvious to me there's been something going on between them!"

"Mum, now you're being absurd. You have overlooked a couple of factors. Firstly, I was there, too. Even if they were more than friends, they wouldn't have been horsing around with me in the house as well. And secondly, Alicia was there only to give Nana a regular check-up for her back. She goes every month. I've told you that before. You are letting your imagination run away with you. Perhaps it would've been better if you'd not gone round on spec, but phoned beforehand."

"And what sort of reception would that have received?" barked Fiona; unwilling to back down.

Although she now realised she had misinterpreted the situation, she was not yet willing to admit her mistake and apologise to Kristine.

As one who had always sought personal satisfaction by venting her wrath on her family, she needed to feel that same sense of gratification now; in this instance, at her daughter's expense.

However, Kristine saw things differently.

"Well, I think you owe me an apology," she said sternly. "You are taking your frustrations out on me; not because I deserve it, but because I'm always your nearest punching-bag. ...So much for happy families! I won't forget this in a hurry," she declared, and walked off.

The following day, she told her father what had happened.

"Fiona was here? How strange," he said; more puzzled than concerned. "What is she trying to achieve by it?"

"Goodness knows. All I do know is, Mum hasn't really got anything in her life except for that little part time job, and it's getting to her. Maybe she's turning to her family again because she's lonely. What should we do about it?"

"I wouldn't have a clue. There's a lot to consider..."

"...Like what?"

"Well, everything...and all of us! If your mother started coming round, how would it affect Emily and me? I don't think I, for one, could handle it."

"She suspects you and Alicia are having an affair..."

"...An affair? You're joking!" cried Royston. "We are just good friends!"

"That's not how Mum sees it..."

"...Anyway, your mother and I have gone our separate ways now, and she knows it. She must have accepted it, too, because she didn't get upset over Sylvia."

"She didn't regard Sylvia as a threat..."

"...And she does Alicia?"

"I reckon!"

"But how could she? She doesn't know her...does she?"

Kristine shot him a glance as though she harboured an interesting secret.

Royston read her thoughts.

"Is there something you're not telling me, Kristine? Has your mother met Alicia?"

"No not that I know of...although I have mentioned her once or twice in her capacity as Nana's nurse. There was no harm in that was there?"

"No; but I ask you, please do not talk about Alicia with Fiona. I don't want her to come between us..."

"...So you are serious about Alicia?"

"I think so; but I'm just taking things slowly. After what I experienced living with Sylvia... Well, let's say I've learnt my lesson."

"Your secret's safe with me, Dad."

…Yet in other ways, Royston's secret was far from safe; for the same could not be said for Emily who, though giving the impression of being asleep in her chair, heard every word the two had discussed.

The next few days saw Kristine and Royston engaged in some serious thinking about how to reconcile Fiona with her family; assuming, he pointed out, that her intentions were sincere and not just another means of furthering her own self-serving ends.

Fiona, he reminded Kristine, caused nothing but trouble for quite some time after her father died, and to his way of thinking it would be perfectly understandable if the family was sceptical of her motives.

After some deliberation the two decided it might be an idea to bring about reconciliation on neutral territory…at a café or restaurant rather than at either party's house. That way, Fiona was more likely to behave herself.

"…However," he added with concern; "if your mother does agree to meet us, what do we do with Emily?"

"She will come with us, of course!" remarked Kristine in surprise. "Mum wants to reunite with the family, and that includes Nana!"

Royston frowned pensively. He did not want to open up a can of worms by having everybody together straight off.

"I'm not so sure it would work out very well," he said.

"Why not? We've already agreed that Mum is more likely to behave herself in a public place…and as for Nana, it might just prevent her from talking about Grandpa. She only does that at home, doesn't she?"

"Yes, as far as I know; not that Emily has given me much opportunity to find out. I haven't even taken her with me to the supermarket in case she behaves oddly."

"What about the Copper Urn in the Arcade? That would be nice and quiet – and secluded. I can't see Nana causing any problems there…or Mum, for that matter."

The decision made was that, with Fiona's approval, they would meet at the Copper Urn the following Saturday, and take it from there.

It fell to Kristine to catch her mother in a good mood and tackle her about the family gathering…

"…As you're the worthiest person for the task," Royston joked with a measure of guilt.

Although, as Kristine later reflected, she was actually the only person who was likely to pull it off.

When she went home for her meal, she discovered that Fiona was in a particularly cheerful frame of mind and, it seemed, chafing at the bit to share her good humour with her daughter.

Fiona was inclined to do that.

The people closest to her, whether at home or at work, were always the ones most affected by whatever kind of mood she was in. If she felt bright and happy everyone benefitted, and if the opposite was the case…

Kristine knew only too well what would happen under those circumstances!

So it was with relief that she struck Fiona in a vibrant mood on the very day she had been given the unenviable task of sounding her out.

In fact, Fiona was so chirpy on Kristine's arrival that she as good as sashayed up to the girl and spun her around as though at a dance.

"Mum, what's going on?" asked Kristine, dumbfounded.

It had not yet sunk in that Fiona's vibrant mood might settle conveniently into an opportune moment.

"I'm just happy," was Fiona's ambiguous reply.

"...But why?" asked Kristine with guarded curiosity, and then wished she hadn't.

Fiona instantly ceased her merriment.

"What's the matter; aren't I allowed to be happy?" she said in an accusing voice.

Sensing a mood swing coming on, Kristine immediately shifted into crisis mode to dissipate it before it took hold.

"Of course you are, Mum," she replied with fabricated sympathy. "I'm very pleased something has caused you to feel happy. You deserve to be after all this time..."

"...Okay; don't overdo it! I know what you meant...and I'll tell you what has cheered me up."

It turned out, according to Fiona, that she had received a promotion at work.

She explained to Kristine how the Manager had called her into his office just before lunchtime that very day, and asked if she would consider taking on more responsibility in her position.

'Business has been so good,' he told her; 'that we have decided to take on an extra employee, and we would like you to take her – or him, to be politically correct – under your wing. As our most senior member of staff you will, of course, receive a modest increase in your hourly rate, and three additional hours' work per day; if that suits you, and works in with your home life.'

If that suits me! Fiona had thought. You bet it suits me! It will get me out of that damnable house and into the real world a bit more! So, armed with a heightened sense of self-worth she had rushed home to wait for Kristine.

Fiona could not wait to tell her the good news.

"Well, that's...great," came a further forced response. "It's about time something positive happened for you. I'm sure you'll do very well."

49

Although she did not consider the amendment to her mother's job description as much of a promotion, Kristine nevertheless could see how enthusiastic Fiona was about it, and would not run the risk of bursting her bubble by telling her so; especially as she had by now realised how she could capitalise on her good humour.

"Mum," she said a few minutes later when the euphoria had settled. "You know how you wanted to meet up with Nana again..."

"...Actually, it was your father I wanted to connect with; but you're right. It's about time I arranged to go and see that mother of mine, too – though properly this time. No more silly misunderstandings."

"Good for you, Mum. ...And it's funny you should put it that way because we...um...I had an idea as to how you can achieve it."

What's that then?" asked Fiona, still in a good mood.

"Oh, just a way of bringing you together again," Kristine answered casually.

Fiona gaped at her. "Am I supposed to understand what you are talking about?" she mumbled. "Why don't I just go round to Nana's house...what other way is there?"

"We could go out for morning tea or lunch. It would be nicer, don't you think?"

Fiona nodded, absorbing the idea.

"Yes, I suppose that would be a harmless way of going about it – to begin with anyway," she said; then added with enthusiasm, "It could be my treat in honour of my promotion. Yes. That's what we'll do. Now, where shall we go for our morning tea?"

"We thought... I mean...I thought the Copper Urn would fit the bill. Do you know it?"

"Oh, yes; indeed I do. It's very comfortable...and they do lovely Devonshire cream scones."

Kristine breathed a sigh of relief. It looked like the plan was going to work.

"That's great!" she exclaimed with excitement, thinking how her father would congratulate her success. "...So, how about next Saturday morning, then?"

"Perfect! There is one question I have for you, though," said Fiona, looking Kristine squarely in the eye.

"A question? What did you want to know?"

"Twice just now you said 'we,' but corrected yourself. What was that all about?"

Kristine fidgeted self-consciously. She thought she had got away with her blunder.

"Oh that?" she said, giving herself an extra moment to work out what to say. "I might as well tell you, Mum. I've already run this by Dad and he thinks it's a good idea, too."

"Well, thanks very much for talking about me behind my back!" Fiona growled, the happiness bubble bursting; but then she had a change of heart. "...Though come to think of it, I suppose I should be flattered that your father is taking me seriously at last."

"Yes, he's all for it. He's just..."

Kristine tailed off.

"Go on. What were you going to say?"

"Oh, nothing important," said Kristine hastily.

She had been on the verge of confessing that her father was worried about Fiona causing trouble if they went to Emily's, but then thought better of it.

No point in stirring up ill feelings in her mother, she decided – even if there was a legitimate cause for concern.

And so it was all arranged.

Arriving independently, the two households entered the tearooms at roughly the same time. Ever the consummate gentleman, Royston held open the door for Emily to pass through; then when he noticed Kristine and her mother coming up close behind, he stayed at his post.

"Nice to see you again, Fiona" he said courteously as a host might say to his guest.

"Likewise," came Fiona's static reply, taken by surprise that Royston had come, too.

"You didn't tell me your father was going to be here," she hissed at Kristine as they searched for a table with four empty seats.

"I assumed you realised he would be," she retorted. "Wasn't that the whole purpose of the get-together?"

It was too late to change the arrangement now.

Fiona approached Emily who had found a suitable table. "Hello, Mum," she said. "It's been a long time."

"Oh, hello dear," Emily replied casually, and gave her a peck on the cheek as though there had been no falling-out between them.

Emily busied herself straightening the chairs, which had been left untidily by the table's previous occupants.

"Fiona, why don't you sit here, then you won't have the bright light from the window in your eyes. And I'll pull up another chair in case Arth…"

"…Nana!" Kristine called urgently to silence her before Fiona's instincts kicked in.

She had watched the reunion between her two family members, and suspected what Emily was about to say. The look of curiosity on her mother's face could quickly lapse into one of scorn if she did not step in to prevent it.

Nana," she said again. "We have to order before we can sit down. It's a self-service café. Why don't you come with me and see what they have to eat?"

Kristine took her hand and led her over to the counter. She picked up a couple of plates and a tray, which she then slid along the shelf.

52

"What do you fancy, Nana?" she asked, scrutinising the contents of the food cabinet.

"Nothing to eat for me. I'll have something with Arth..."

"...Then how about a cup of tea?"

Kristine started to lose her nerve.

Was Emily incapable of making conversation without the mention of dear Arthur?

Maybe this whole experiment of hers was a mistake. They hadn't been seated for a minute and she was already trying to avert disaster.

With shaking hands, she led Emily back through the tables to where Royston had been holding on to theirs.

Fortunately, Fiona was still at the counter awaiting her coffee, so Kristine seized the opportunity to have a private word with Emily.

"Could you please not talk about Grandpa while we're here?" she said with a hint of insistence.

"But why, dear? He could walk in at any minute..."

"...I know! Nana, please!" Kristine was frantic. "I beg of you; please don't talk like that in front of your daughter. She wouldn't understand..."

"...What wouldn't I understand?" said Fiona coming up behind her.

"...Nothing you need be concerned about, Mum," she said with a feeling of despair. Then, to discourage further questioning, Kristine added; knowing it to be untrue, "I just told Nana that Auntie Ruth wouldn't understand why we are doing this, that's all!"

From then on, Kristine could not look her father in the eye.

Avoiding his glare, she handed over his morning tea off the tray, returned it to the counter and self-consciously sat down next to her mother.

53

Whatever must he think of me? she wondered while the others engaged in small talk. ...But how could she have told Fiona the truth?

For a few minutes she tried to justify in her mind the pathetic attempt at deception. It was only a little white lie, she protested inwardly; voiced with the best of intentions and under the most difficult of circumstances. Surely he wouldn't think too badly of her?

Kristine felt deeply ashamed that she had needed to lie in front of her parents; and not a very convincing lie at that, as she was sure Royston had recognised.

For a while she sat mainly in silence, speaking only when questioned. With eyes focused on her drink, she failed to notice the interest her grandmother was taking in their surroundings.

Emily was beginning to remember that she had been to the Copper Urn café before – and the circumstances under which she was last there.

Lapsing quietly into nostalgic memory, Emily's thoughts drifted back in time.

She held in her mind's eye the vision of a large woman sitting at the table she was sharing with one other. The woman had been very coarse, of that her recollection was sound; but the identity of her companion in that instance escaped her...that is, until the recollection of an intensely personal conversation she was having with him abruptly came to mind.

Yes, it was definitely a man she had been talking to; a man wearing a black tunic and a dog collar...Reverend Bill Marriott. Of course!

She looked around the room again. Everything was just the same, except for the company she was keeping – and their topic of conversation.

Then she remembered what she and Reverend Marriott were talking about before the rude woman interrupted them. She had been on the verge of telling him about Arthur's subliminal visits...

All of a sudden Emily felt trapped. This place was special to her. It held profound meaning that could never be divulged to any of the others in her company at present. Kristine had said not to...that Fiona would not understand.

Overcome now with confusion and a sense of great loss, Emily allowed a tear to slowly form on her eyelid.

Only when the tear glistened and then ran down her cheek did Kristine became aware of it.

"Are you alright?" she mouthed.

Fiona, deep in conversation with Royston about her job promotion, did not seem to notice.

Emily looked across at Kristine. She smiled and, wiping away the tear, mouthed back, "Yes, thank you."

Then Kristine, who now perceived a developing sense of anguish in her grandmother, decided it was time to change the subject. As far as she was concerned, her parents had monopolised the conversation far too long.

She spoke directly to Emily.

"Nana, have you been to this café before?" she asked to try and lift her spirits.

Emily sniffed and cleared her throat, hoping the other two did not notice her attempt to camouflage her distress.

"Yes...as a matter of fact I have."

Then she turned her attention to Royston, the need to get back to normal overwhelming her.

Without thinking what she was saying, Emily blurted out, "Royston, why don't you bring your lovely new friend here for a treat?"

For a moment the café seemed to go quiet. Certainly, the other occupants of Emily's table did.

All three stopped what they were doing and stared at her in disbelief.

It was Fiona who spoke first.

With a little cough, and looking at nobody in particular, she said, "What lovely new friend would that be, Mother?"

All at once, Royston saw a need to take control before Emily said anything else to compromise his situation.

While he and Kristine searched Fiona's face for signs of annoyance, he said, "Your mother is referring to the new district nurse who comes to see her…."

"…Yes," Emily cut in. "This one only started a couple of months ago. She's very…"

"…Very professional," said Kristine in a hurry, realising what Emily was about to say; for it would not have been a comment about her new nurse's reliability. Both Royston and Kristine were well aware that Emily had become quite fond of Alicia.

"Is this the woman you told me about, Kristine?" asked Fiona with aroused suspicion.

She had not yet recognised a cover-up, but was starting to put two and two together.

"Yes," said Kristine and Emily at the same time.

"Alicia…isn't that her name?" continued Fiona. She was on a roll now.

"That's right; but why the questions? She's just Emily's nurse," said Royston, beginning to get worried.

Fiona ignored him.

"I see," she said pensively.

The picture was becoming clearer to her now; revealing some hidden and very interesting truths: they were talking about the legendary Alicia.

"...And Kristine, didn't you mention to me that Alicia is also a friend of your father's?"

"Mum, what are you driving at?" Kristine retorted with no intention of answering any questions on the subject.

Royston sprung to her defence; after all, the allegation was aimed at him.

"Fiona, please don't pick on Kristine. She's not trying to deceive you. It's true Alicia and have become friends – but that's all. Anyway, as long as she's attending to Emily as a client, there's no way she'll compromise her professional ethics. ...Isn't that right, ladies?"

"Of course," said Kristine on the offensive.

Emily refrained from commenting. She recalled only too clearly the cosy chat Alicia and Royston engaged in the last time she had her check-up. Yet, she also realised that she may have spoken out of turn in mentioning it.

If only Arthur could have been there to back her up...

"I see," said Fiona again; an image forming in her mind.

As nobody seemed prepared to fill her in about what was really going on, she had no choice but to draw up her own conclusions. And although those conclusions did not as yet include the possibility of an actual affair, from now on she would be more vigilant.

While Royston and Kristine continued to regard Fiona cautiously, Emily recognised a chance to redeem herself in their eyes.

"I hope you get to meet Alicia soon," she said to Fiona. "Maybe you could come round the next time she visits me; I have the date in my diary. Then she can be your friend, as well as ours."

Kristine pulled a nervous but slightly bemused face, and glanced at her father to gauge his reaction.

She could see that he, too, was trying to camouflage an apprehensive chuckle.

"Don't hold your breath," Fiona rasped. There was no way she wanted to meet that particular woman! Then she quickly added, "Anyway, I have to get going now. It was nice seeing you both. We must do this again some time."

With a flourish she pushed her chair back and walked out of the café.

For a moment stunned silence followed her exit.

Emily waited quietly for somebody else to speak; and when after a second or two neither of her companions did, she took the initiative.

"Well, that was very nice, wasn't it?" she said brightly. "Fiona seems to be much more cheerful than she was the last time I saw her."

"Not for long..." Kristine muttered under her breath as each prepared to leave.

Then a thought came to her.

"Dad, sorry to ask this... Would you mind dropping me off at home? Mum seems to have forgotten that I came to the café with her."

"Of course, love. I expect your mother has other things on her mind right now."

CHAPTER THREE

A few weeks later, Emily was pottering in the kitchen when there came a knock on the front door. Without hesitation she opened it; then stepped back in alarm.

Silhouetted against the intense daylight was the bulky frame of a man.

She could not see his face, but felt sure she recognised him in another way: a familiar, unpleasant odour invaded her senses. In an instant she knew who it was.

"Oh, my goodness!" she shrieked. "It's you!"

Frozen with fear, Emily waited for the man, whom she now recognised as her upstairs assailant, to strike again. But instead he spoke softly to her.

"Don't be afraid, Mrs Thompson. I mean you no harm."

At the sound of his calming voice, Emily relaxed a little. It did not seem possible that the oaf who had given her so much grief was the same gentle mannered person who respectfully stood before her now.

"Who are you?" she asked in a tremulous voice. "...And why have you come back here after what you did to me; and in my own home, too?"

She squinted, trying desperately to make out his face against the light.

"May I please come in? I owe you an explanation – and an apology."

"No! Of course you're not coming in! I would be a fool to let you back into my house..."

"...Emily? What's going?"

Royston appeared at the kitchen door.

Having heard Emily's shriek from the back garden, and not knowing what it could be or even if it was coming from their house, he took no chances and raced up.

The man in the doorway caught his breath when he saw Royston appear. Taken aback by the hostile reception from them both, he muttered an apology and made to leave.

But Royston pushed in front of a distressed Emily and stopped him.

"Not so fast, please" he said, while grabbing the man by the shoulder. "You have some explaining to do: Who are you, and what do you want?"

It was only when he stepped back into the sunlight again that Emily made out the man's features.

Instantly she knew who it was; though with a moment of hesitation in identifying him, as he looked different.

"Michael?" she said with a degree of uncertainty, and inched forward for a closer look.

With Royston's presence as a prop, she felt safe enough to confront her unwelcome visitor.

The fact that she now recognised the young man as her ex-gardener removed the unknown element. However, it did not confirm that he was the one who broke into her house the night she fell, although it certainly seemed that way: his unpleasant body odour was something she would never forget.

Neither did her identification of him offer a reason as to why he had come to see her now.

These two remaining questions needed to be answered; if not to satisfy her and Royston, then definitely for the benefit of the police case against him.

"Do you know him, Emily?" Royston asked in surprise at her mention of his name.

"Yes. He was once our gardener…and he broke into the house the night I had my fall…"

"…I didn't break in. I used a key."

"Alright, I think that's enough," said Royston, his hand still securely on Michael's shoulder. "This is now a matter for the police…"

"…No, sir! Please! You don't understand! I didn't mean any harm to Mrs Thompson."

"You caused serious injury to an old lady."

"Yes… I admit that, and I'm truly sorry about it. But it wasn't intentional. It was an accident. I panicked."

Emily could now see that Michael was remorseful for what happened that night.

Even though it all took place months ago, she sensed it had been preying on his mind. Maybe he had come to the house today; not to cause more trouble but to apologise for past transgressions.

"Royston," she said calmly. "I would very much like to hear what Michael has to say about it. I don't think he is a threat to us anymore."

"But the police still have a case against him for breaking and entering…and grievous bodily harm! You can't ignore what he has done!"

"I know…and I understand your concern. That night has haunted my dreams ever since it happened. But still I want to hear his explanation. That's what he's come here to give me. Is that right, Michael?"

"Yes…"

"…Don't assume that telling your story will absolve you from your crimes young man," said Royston roughly.

Then, letting go of Michael he stood back to allow him inside the house.

Emily put out her hand to stop him.

"No, not in here, please. Round the back if you don't mind," she said; and cupping her hand round her mouth she whispered to Royston, "...He smells."

Royston walked Michael round to the rear of the house, while Emily locked up and went out through the back door to join them.

Michael looked over the garden he once tended.

It was immaculate, with the rose bushes in full bloom.

"Wow!" he said. "Somebody's done a good job with the garden. I always loved those roses."

In actual fact, Royston had been doing all the gardening since he moved in to Emily's. It was his way of making up for not paying any board; but he did not feel inclined to respond to Michael's praise.

Instead he commanded him, "Sit down over there, if you please," and pointed to the garden seat. Then he and Emily perched on an adjacent wall.

With two pairs of eyes fixed on him, Michael began his lengthy explanation.

It was all to do with his uncle and Emily's husband, Arthur Thompson, he told them.

"Arthur?" said Emily at the unexpected mention of his name. "What about Arthur?"

"Twenty-odd years ago," Michael went on, "Uncle Ken contacted the local district council regarding the condition of the soil on a property he bought off them. He claimed it was still contaminated from an old landfill, and he sought compensation from the council.

"Arthur Thompson was the council member he dealt with, but declined the request; stating he must have known what he was getting into when he bought it. Uncle Ken tried to sell it, but nobody would touch it. So he had no choice but to keep and maintain it.

"Then about ten years ago he contracted lung cancer, even though he had never smoked. He died leaving a debt on the property for my mother – his sister – to pay off. Mum never forgave your husband. She always maintained her brother paid the ultimate price for Mr Thompson's insensitivity, and has suffered ever since."

Emily listened in abject horror.

This did not sound like dear Arthur at all. He was a benevolent man. He would have been sympathetic to their cause. ...He would have done whatever he could to help Michael's family, of that she was certain.

...And she should know!

Michael continued.

"...Anyway, as a result we ran out of money. A few years ago Mum's landlord evicted us from our flat. Then an old friend of Uncle Ken offered us the use of a house he owns just up the road from here.

"When Mum discovered that Mr Thompson lived only a few doors away, she started to think of how she could get back at him for the way her family has had to suffer."

Royston looked across at Emily with growing concern. He could see she was visibly alarmed now.

Was Michael trying to imply that she became liable after Arthur died...that she even deserved to be hurt?

"Now just a minute," he said. "There's no need to hold Emily responsible for any of this. Surely you can see you're upsetting her."

"I'm alright; really. I just can't understand what Michael is talking about. It's all so new to me. Arthur would most certainly have mentioned it. He isn't an underhand sort of person... He's a lovely man..."

Royston cut in; Emily's mind was wandering again.

"Michael," he said quickly. "What made you think it was okay to take it out on a defenceless old lady?"

63

"I didn't. ...Not at first, anyway. When Mum found out you were looking for a part time gardener, she told me to accept the job.

"I was a bit sceptical about her motives as she was still so mad about it all back then. I suspected that given the chance she would have administered poison! ...Not to you, of course, but to your husband; she hated him that much"

Suddenly Royston was confused.

"I'm having trouble following you. Let me back track: You said you and your mother moved up the road only a few years ago..."

"...That's right."

"...And you found out Mrs Thompson lived here more recently than that?"

"Yes."

"Then why did you still hope to do harm to Arthur Thompson? He had already passed away. Mrs Thompson later remarried. James Forsythe, the man who was living here while you were working as the gardener, was Emily's second husband."

"I know that now...but we didn't at the time. We still thought he was Mr Thompson. Mum never saw the man from the council who Uncle Ken dealt with. We only had a name to go on."

Emily's strained features affirmed that she had just about had enough.

All this talk of her beloved Arthur's alleged misdeeds, and now he was bringing James into it... She was not sure she could take any more.

Michael noticed it at once.

"I'm so sorry about the pranks we pulled. I had no idea you were on the receiving end of them and not your...the late Mr Thompson."

"You said pranks, as though there was more than one," said Emily, a thought coming to her. "Was it you who cut through my telephone wires?"

"Yes. That was just my idea, I'm ashamed to say. There seemed to be no harm in it; just a prank to worry you, or rather, to unnerve Mr Thompson. Then when he fired me from the job…"

"…It wasn't Mr Thompson who gave you notice; you do realise that, don't you?" said Royston.

"Yes, I do now. I told my mother about the wires. She was angry and said it wasn't enough; that I should trash the place in retribution. She noticed you'd gone out one night, and told me to let myself in…"

"…With my key?" asked Emily.

"Yes. It was the one you kept by the shed."

"Well, that explains it all," she said to Royston, without realising he would not have known about everything which took place that night.

Royston, however, assumed she was informing him the episode was over.

"Emily, I do hope you're not going to let the matter rest there!" he said critically. "What this man and his mother have done to you is criminal."

"I'm not trying to excuse my behaviour," Michael went on; "…but we didn't actually do any damage – except to the phone wires…"

"You must be joking!" exclaimed Royston; incensed by his attitude. "You put Emily in hospital and subjected her to months of hardship…"

"…And nightmares," added Emily.

"Yes!" Royston added with indignation.

"…And I can't emphasize enough how very sorry I am about that."

Michael was close to tears by now.

65

"I really didn't intend to knock you over. You must have lost your balance on the stairs when I brushed past you. It was dark, and I panicked because you'd come home. Then I just had to get out of the house. I didn't know what had happened to you until quite recently.

"Sometime later I heard that Mr Thompson... No...your second husband, that must have been...had also died... Oh dear...this is so confusing! Anyway, I started to feel badly. Mum said to forget about it; that you had got your just desserts. But I didn't agree.

"In the end I couldn't stand the strain, and came round to speak to you."

Michael wiped away a tear, and then brushed his nose with the back of his hand.

Emily's maternal instincts kicked in.

"Royston, dear," she said. "Could you please fetch my box of tissues from the kitchen? I think we could all use one at the moment."

Then, while Royston did as Emily asked, Michael said to her, "Mrs Thompson. I really am very sorry about all of this. I...we had no right to take it out on you. I would do anything to make amends."

"There's no real harm done, Michael," she replied. "I'm physically okay now. ...And from what you told us, we have done more harm to your family than you did to us!"

When Royston returned, Emily said to him, "What do you think we should do now?"

"Do? That's obvious, isn't it?" Royston exclaimed. "We need to take the matter up with the police!"

"No!" Emily cried. "I won't hear of it! On account of us, these good people have suffered unspeakably. Pursuing it with the police would be immoral."

"Do you mean you want to drop all previous charges?" asked Royston in disbelief.

"Yes, Royston...that's exactly what I mean. And I want you to arrange it, please!"

Royston had no choice but to accept the decision; like it or not. However he did have to concede that Emily seemed to know what she was doing – which certainly had not been the case in other areas of her life. Furthermore, he recalled, he was not actually around when the burglary took place.

The details of what happened back then had only been sketchy at best...and the general consensus amongst the members of her family at the time had been that she was imagining it.

Oh Emily, he thought ruefully. How we have misjudged you over this!

The following day, he and Michael called in at the police station. With statements taken and the file on the case finally closed, the two men went their separate ways.

"There is one more thing I would ask you to do for me though," said Emily on Royston's return.

"What's that?"

"I would like you to follow up on the business of their family's plot of land. It is so unlike Arthur to do something like this – I have trouble believing he could be that callous. And if it really was his doing, then maybe it's not too late to remedy the situation."

"But it's nothing to do with us now."

"I know and I understand how you might feel about it," said Emily with concern. "I would consult with Arthur, only he retired from the district council ages ago; and I know he would rather not interfere with their workings now."

"Alright...I'll make enquiries tomorrow," he promised.

For some reason, Emily's comments about Arthur did not irritate him this time.

Later that evening, he reflected on it.

"Surely I haven't started believing Arthur's still around, too?" he thought, and inwardly cringed.

The young girl at the council offices took so long to locate the file on Michael's uncle that Royston began to give up on her finding it at all.

Having waited for more than an hour and thumbed his way through every magazine he could find, he asked if he should come back later; to which she replied that it would be better if he stayed in case she needed to ask him a few questions about the case.

"...To question me?" he mumbled after she disappeared again. "I don't know enough about this wretched case to answer any questions!"

He was about to abandon his efforts and leave, having roughly worked out what excuse he would give to Emily for doing so, when the girl returned with some papers.

"Here we are at last," she said triumphantly. "I'm very sorry you had to wait so long. The council brought in a new computer system a while ago, and as this stuff is pretty old I had trouble finding my way around the filing cabinets. I'm new here, you see..."

"...I might have known," Royston muttered under his breath while he stepped up to look at the information she had copied for him.

It turned out that the girl's knowledge of the council's filing system was much better than she thought; for the photocopied letters and minutes of meetings covered all the council's dealings with Michael's uncle.

Mr Kenneth Smith, according to the papers, had applied to the local council for the purchase of the land in question a few years before he actually bought it, but had been warned by Councillor Arthur Thompson that it was the site of an old landfill, and that the quality of the ground could not be guaranteed.

However, Mr Smith aggressively pursued the purchase; eventually persuading the council to sell it to him at a vastly reduced price.

Sometime later Mr Smith discovered firsthand the level of contamination when he began to suffer the effects of it. In order to rally support, he approached the local media, and thereafter maintained through their exposure that the council should compensate him.

Once again, on behalf of the council Arthur wrote to him, reiterating that he knew what he was taking on when he bought the land.

In other words, so it seemed, Uncle Ken's predicament could be blamed on nobody but himself.

Although Michael's version of the story was compelling, it was Emily's simple statement that Arthur was incapable of being unscrupulous that proved to be correct...and Royston again applauded her for it.

As he made his way back home, though armed now with a truth that could not be refuted, Royston wondered how he could broach the subject with Michael, and whether or not he should do so.

Emily, he knew, would be delighted her faith in Arthur had born fruit. She never for one moment doubted him. But should he tell Michael and his mother? It might look to them as though he and Emily were just trying to vindicate Arthur; a move that would have been perfectly defensible. But that would not have been their intention.

If justice was not served at the time of the purchase, then Emily wanted only to see if it could somehow be restored now.

However, of one thing Royston was sure: he could not doubt what was clearly stated in black and white.

Emily was amazed by what she read; although, with more than enough information to wade through, Royston chose to show her only the relevant parts.

After affirming in her mind that Arthur was innocent, Emily told Royston, "I really think we should show Michael this report."

But Royston thought otherwise.

"I'm not so sure," he replied. "It might be better to just leave well alone. We both know that Arthur did nothing wrong – and we have the written proof here to back it up. Michael's mother seems to have received her sense of gratification from what he did to you…"

"…So what are you telling me?"

"That perhaps we should call it quits, and forget the whole thing happened at all."

"I think maybe you're right," said Emily thoughtfully. "Michael is a decent sort of boy, really. It's obvious to me now that his mother put him up to it. I don't want to embarrass him by confirming that his uncle was solely to blame for his and his family's misfortune."

Royston gave Emily a hug.

"That's my girl," he said affectionately. "Tell Arthur I'm still proud to have him as a father-in-law."

"I will," said Emily; responding with equal warmth. "I'm sure he'll be thrilled to hear it."

Later on, Royston thought over everything that had come to light.

Yet, the issue remaining uppermost in his thoughts was not Arthur's innocence, but that he, practical Royston, had begun to acknowledge Arthur's presence in Emily's life.

"It must be catching," he told a surprised Kristine, after filling her in on the most recent occurrence. "I've even got myself talking about him in the present tense!"

"I know what you mean," Kristine replied.

In fact, she knew exactly what he meant; for Arthur had already proved that he was still around by appearing to her in the rose garden, whereas Royston seemed to be accepting it on blind faith alone.

"Doesn't this put a new complexion on our relationship with Nana?" she asked him after some thought.

"In what way?"

"Well, to all appearances Nana has pretty much flipped her lid where Grandpa's concerned. But now we as good as believe it, too. ...Certainly we seem to be going along with her. Does that mean we've flipped our lids, as well?"

Royston laughed. "If we have, then I'm quite happy to admit it...although with me it's more a case of 'go with the flow.' Your grandmother seems to be fully recovered now, with the exception of her flights of fancy with Arthur. You should have heard the way she handled Michael the other day. She talked to him normally; completely in control of the situation – except when she tried to mention Arthur. That was what made me realise I should accept it; if only for some peace and quiet! It's quite frustrating, trying to correct her whenever she talks about him!"

Royston was used to Emily's banter by now. He found life so much easier when he tolerated the inclusion of Arthur and occasionally James in conversation with her, although he avoided in-depth discussion about them.

Emily's relationship with her departed husbands was one thing, but he had no wish to be part of the cosy little group; especially if someone else was around, and most especially when Fiona happened to be present. She was

71

the last person he would want to have witness the almost daily mention of the illusive Arthur.

But there was one other he felt would not understand about Arthur's presence as well; that is, if she were ever to stumble across the banter in full swing: Alicia.

Royston's apprehension was not in respect of Alicia's professional opinion, but rather her reaction to his own acceptance of something she might regard as fantasy; for he had not yet confided in her on the topic. So far, he had managed to circumvent all reference to it.

However, there would soon come a time when he could no longer keep it from her; when it may become too difficult to camouflage some of Emily's remarks.

Reluctantly, he decided to enlighten her.

"But I think it's just wonderful," Alicia responded sweetly, when he chose the right moment to broach the subject. "If somebody of Emily's age and disposition can keep alive the memory of her husband and soul-mate as beautifully as that, it gives them something precious to live for. No wonder Emily is so cheerful!"

"Don't you think it's more like giving them false hope, by encouraging them to live in the past?" asked Royston.

"No, not really..."

"...Not even when they view their spouse as more than just a memory?"

"How do you mean?"

Here goes, thought Royston nervously.

"I mean...when somebody like Emily behaves as though the husband is actually still present – still alive in the flesh, even; when she believes he understands what is going on and converses with her. Would you regard that as normal behaviour, or bordering on senility?"

"If you are talking about Emily, then I would not like to use the word 'senile' to describe her. She's far too with-it for that. Do you think she's imagining things?"

"I don't know about imagining things... I would say she believes he's there. She talks about him in the present tense...and now she's got me talking along those lines, too. Recently I've been questioning my own sanity!"

"I wouldn't worry about it. You're doing what you think is best for Emily, and for her future happiness. Have you made any plans for her yet?"

"No. Why do you ask?"

"I wondered how long you were planning to maintain your present arrangement of living here; especially after the check-ups finish."

"Are they due to finish?"

"Yes. The next one is the last."

"Oh, that's a shame," said Royston with a worried look on his face.

Alicia saw the look, and laughed. She understood what he meant, and it had nothing to do with her client.

"I guess it will be a test of our friendship if I'm not coming here to check on Emily anymore," she said.

"Or..." Royston added as something came to him. "...It might give us more freedom to see each other socially! I have been a bit concerned about the doctor-patient aspect of your visits. After Kristine told Fiona we were just friends I started to feel a bit guilty about it."

"Why, for goodness sake?"

"...Because I regard you as more than a friend!"

Later, Royston wondered whether he had overstepped the mark in speaking of his feelings for Alicia, and having her become aware of them. He reminded himself that he still needed to take things slowly. On the few occasions they had met on a social level, he had found it difficult to keep his emotions reined in.

Perhaps it will be easier, he determined, when she is no longer Emily's nurse. He had hoped that time would be soon in coming, and rejoiced that with Emily's rapid rate of recovery it was not now far off.

A man needs a good woman in his life, he maintained; and it was quite some time since he last shared his life and affections with one...

The final school term flew by for Kristine. As exam time approached, she began to panic that she had not applied herself to studying as much as she should have...and she was not the only one to worry.

In order to share their common anxiety, Kristine and her friends met regularly at one another's houses, and studied in pairs. Their hope was that this might inspire them, or at least help them to remember what they had actually learnt during the school term.

On one such study session, Kristine and her friend were working in her room when they became aware of feverish activity outside.

It was dark by this time, and Kristine peered through her curtains to see a number of cars drawing up, followed by slamming of doors and excited chatter as the occupants made their way up to the house.

Startled and annoyed by the disruption to their studies, Kristine emerged from her room in order to investigate; just as Fiona was showing the visitors into the lounge.

The commotion raised such incredulity in Kristine that she sidled up to her and angrily hissed, "Mum, what's going on? ...We're trying to study!"

Fiona turned briefly to Kristine in between gestures of welcome to her guests.

"Sorry...didn't I mention I was having a soiree for the people at work tonight?" she replied.

By now the noise of chatter was indescribable. It seemed to Kristine that a swarm of bees had invaded their house, although the number of people present was a lot less. But she didn't care how many her mother had invited. Even one noisy person in the house would have been too much at this critical time of the term.

She dragged her friend back into her bedroom, and told her to gather up her things.

"Come on," she said to her. "We can't stay here. Let's go to your place."

The next morning, Kristine tackled her mother on the disturbance of the previous night.

"You know how crucial it is that I get down to some hard study," she complained. "How am I going to get good grades if I have to put up with something like that?"

"It was only a one-off," replied Fiona with indignation. ...And I did apologise for not mentioning it to you. I don't understand what all the fuss is about."

Even so, Kristine was far from appeased, and from then on she checked beforehand that the coast would be clear before arranging to host another study session.

She did not want the humiliation of having to bundle her study partners out of the house again just because of an inconsiderate parent.

When the exams were over, Kristine came to a conclusive decision based on her growing need:

If she was to seriously consider pursuing tertiary level education, it was imperative that she not risk a repeat of the previous school term. University was serious stuff. For one thing, her studies there would not be gratis, as was secondary school. With an expensive student loan to cover her costs she would need to make every minute count, otherwise it was money wasted.

Unless she could make that kind of commitment right from the start, she might as well not bother applying for a university course at all.

So, with determination tinged with nervousness in her heart, Kristine resurrected a scheme she had mulled over some months previously.

Her decision had consisted of two measures: the first, she decided, was that she should get a little job; then later on, when she had saved up enough money, she would look for somewhere else to live – on her own.

Her mistake, though, was in telling her mother.

"You must be mad, thinking you can afford to live out in the world!" Fiona said explosively when Kristine aired her decision. "Don't you know anything about the cost of living these days?"

Kristine hesitated, feeling deflated. She had thought the whole thing through, dreamt about it and as good as set it in motion, if only in her head...and now her mother was treating her idea as insignificant.

...How dare she!

The following day, Kristine called in at Emily's to consult her father about the latest blow to her self-esteem.

When she arrived, she was disturbed to see Ruth's car parked outside and hoped her aunt's visit would not rob her of the chance to talk privately with her father.

What's more, Kristine had not even been in touch with Ruth for several months; an oversight that now induced a twinge of conscience. She sighed dejectedly, all thought of being able to air her grievances dissipating.

Once inside, she discovered Ruth was talking not to Emily, but to Royston.

"Hello, everybody!" she said cheerily, expecting Emily to appear from the kitchen at the sound of her voice. But only the two seated in the lounge responded.

"Kristine, what a surprise!" said Ruth brightly. "I wasn't expecting to see you here today!"

"How are you?" asked Kristine, now wondering where Emily was. Royston certainly did not seem concerned about her absence from the scene.

"I'm fine, thank you," said Ruth as she stood to give her niece a hug.

"...And Uncle Wilbur?" Kristine put in, remembering her manners; then without waiting for a reply she mouthed at her father, "Where's Nana?"

"Uncle Wilbur is much better these days," replied Ruth, unaware of Kristine's aside. "In fact, that's why I came to see Nana and your father – except Emily isn't here!"

"Oh!" exclaimed Kristine, and looked questioningly at Royston while Ruth sat down again. "Where is she, then?"

"I dropped Emily off at the bowling club before lunch," said Royston, answering both of her queries at once. "She was invited to the Ladies' Day luncheon. I saw no harm in it as she's doing so well."

Kristine laughed approvingly.

It astonished her to realise that she agreed with him. Emily was fine now – certainly in a physical sense. Her grief over James was well past, so why not give her free rein once more? And as for Arthur...if she did start talking about him at the bowling club, the ladies there were more likely to think it quaint rather than odd.

"Good idea, Dad," she said happily. "I bet she'll have a whale of a time. It will do her good."

"I am so pleased Mum is coming right at last," Ruth said to them both. "It has been a worry to me that I've not been in a position to help out. When Wilbur was very sick I really couldn't leave him...but he's fine now, and raring to go. In fact, he barely sits still for more than a few minutes at a time."

"Don't worry about it, Auntie Ruth; Dad and I manage. Nana, as you say, is coming right. ...And it's great having Dad here with her!"

"Yes. Emily is a lucky woman to have such a dedicated son-in-law – and granddaughter," she added with a grin.

Kristine smiled in appreciation.

"You mentioned something about Uncle Wilbur 'raring to go.' What was that all about?"

"Yes, that's right...I wanted to tell you what your Uncle and I have decided to do."

"This sounds interesting!" remarked Royston, listening intently. He had always liked Ruth; she was more sensible than Fiona...

"Wilbur has had the all clear from the hospital, I'm very glad to say."

"That's marvellous!" exclaimed Royston. "It's been such a long time...you must come over and have lunch with us one day soon."

"Well, that's what I wanted to tell you both. We won't be around for a while."

"Why, Auntie Ruth? Are you going somewhere?"

"Yes, Kristine. Your uncle and I are doing something we haven't been able to do for quite a long time now. We are taking a trip...a round-the-world trip, at that."

"Wow," said Kristine, astounded. "Are you sure Uncle Wilbur is up to it?"

"Oh, yes – he's fighting fit! I've had to supervise the formulation of our itinerary in case he includes climbing up Mount Everest!"

"I'm very happy for you," said Royston. "How long will you be away?"

"...About a year. I would have to look up the schedule, but I'm pretty sure it will take the whole twelve months. We're exploring parts of every continent."

"A year?" said Kristine, trying to take it in. She had not been away for more than a fortnight before. "A whole year on holiday! Some people have all the luck!"

Ruth laughed. "You probably don't recall how we liked to travel during the long summer holidays."

"I remember you were always going away..."

"What will you do about the house?" asked Royston, the practicalities of such a long absence coming to mind.

"We're going to advertise for house-sitter. I don't want to leave the house empty for a whole year, and it would be too much of an imposition to ask family or friends to keep an eye on the place for such a long time..."

Kristine's eyes lit up. "...I'll do it!" she cut in, surprising even herself at the spontaneity of her comment.

Royston scowled at her. "Kristine, don't be ridiculous. You can't keep going all the way over there, just to check up on the house!"

"I wouldn't need to; I could live there. University is over in that direction anyway! Will you let me house-sit for you, Auntie Ruth?"

Ruth and Royston looked at each other quizzically; Ruth thinking why not, Royston with more of a fatherly concern, which Ruth recognised at once.

Embarrassed for the fact that she actually knew little about her niece's future plans, she asked, "Kristine, it's a brilliant idea, but are you sure you could manage, what with all your studies and everything?"

"Absolutely!" replied Kristine without giving the matter any serious thought.

She saw the possibility of house-sitting as a perfect way to escape her mother's control. How could she pass it by?

Whether or not it was an appropriate action for someone in her position was beside the point. The details, as far as she was concerned, could be worked out later.

"And what on earth do you think your mother will say about your suggestion?" Royston asked with a measure of sarcasm in his voice. "She's bound to veto it. There's no way she'll let her seventeen year old daughter occupy a big house all by herself on the other side of town."

Suddenly Kristine lost her temper.

"Look, Dad," she shrieked. "I don't give a toss what Mum thinks! I'm sick of her ruling my life and not giving a hoot about my needs. I want to get away from her – you know that! I told you as much when you moved out of your flat. Nothing has changed in the meantime. And whether you like the idea or not, I'm going to do it!"

Ruth looked on, aghast; in two minds now whether to accept Kristine's offer. If it was going to cause a rift in the family, then maybe it was better to stick with the original plan, and advertise for a house-sitter.

Kristine noticed the look of concern on her aunt's face.

"You're not changing your mind, are you Auntie Ruth?" she asked in alarm. "I really need to get away from Mum, especially when I start university. I don't think I could cope living at home with her any more. Please say I can come!"

Ruth was caught in a quandary.

She was beginning to like the idea of having a relative stay in her house rather than a stranger, and she wanted to help Kristine out, too. As the sister of volatile Fiona, she understood perfectly what Kristine must be going through.

A young child might put up with a mother's irrational behaviour without question, but a girl of Kristine's mature disposition surely should not have to. However, despite her willingness to invite her niece to stay in the house, she also knew that in order to do so she needed to have her mother's permission. After all, Kristine was still a minor, and Fiona would no doubt demand the right to have her say on the matter.

She could be an uncompromising madam at times...

"...Auntie Ruth, are you listening to me?" asked Kristine with impatience.

"Yes, dear. Sorry...I was thinking."

Ruth went quiet again for a moment; there was much to consider.

At length, she went on.

"I can't just say yes, because I don't have the right to. It has to be your mother who gives the okay, not me."

"What? ...Go to Mum? You must be joking! She's bound to say no! And then I'll have to go against..."

Just then, a gentle knock on the front door, cut Kristine off mid-sentence. Royston peered through the window.

"It's Emily; she must have forgotten to take her key," he said, and went out to let her in.

A moment later Ruth and Kristine heard her ask him, "Is that Ruth's car parked outside?"

Then before Royston could answer, she saw for herself.

"Ruth, dear! ...How wonderful of you to come and visit us. We haven't seen you for ages!"

Ruth could not believe her eyes.

The sight of the fully recovered Emily standing in the doorway brought back memories; not just of her recent loss, but also of an earlier, happier time when she took on Kristine's role at Emily's wedding.

A lump formed in her throat, and she fought to tame the unfamiliar emotion. Ruth had always been the more stoic of the twins. In this instance the feelings surprised her...but did not take control. In a matter of seconds, as she stood to greet her mother, her demeanour reverted to its normal cheerfulness.

"Mum! You look great!" she exclaimed with delight. "Royston tells me you have been high-tailing it with the ladies of the bowling club again!"

"Yes, and we all had a wonderful time," cheered Emily in triumph.

"I'm so happy for you, after your recent tragedies."

"Tragedies?" asked Emily, a look of confusion crossing her face.

Knowing Emily's quirks better than Ruth, Royston leapt in to save the moment; for Emily, who currently lived in a slightly different world from the real one, would not now regard the last few months as tragedies, nor possibly even remember them.

Quickly he told Ruth, "Your mother has come along in leaps and bounds since her fall. She is just about back to normal now."

"Yes, look at me," said Emily, doing a twirl, her cheeks flushed from the couple of shandies she consumed at the bowling club; her balance not quite as it would normally be at that time of day...

"...Watch out, Mum!" cried Ruth as Emily animatedly steadied herself. "Come and sit here with me. I think you might be a bit safer."

Ruth and Emily appreciated being in each other's company once more.

Emily realised just how much she had missed all the regular outings to see her favourite twin. ...Perhaps, she thought to herself, they could pick up from where they left off and resume their fortnightly visits...until Ruth excitedly told her about the planned tour, and Emily's face dropped.

"That's such a shame," she said.

Ruth looked puzzled. "Why did you say that? I thought you would be pleased for us."

"Oh, I am! Don't get me wrong. I'm just being selfish. It occurred to me that you and I might be able to visit with each other again. But then you mentioned your trip."

"I see," said Ruth thoughtfully. "Yes, it would have been nice... There's nothing to prevent us from continuing when we get back, though!"

"When will that be?"

"...In about a year."

"A year! Oh my goodness... Are you going to be away as long as that?"

Ruth laughed uncomfortably.

"Unfortunately it's a big world out there, and it takes quite a long time to see it all! And now," she said, getting up. "I have to leave. Wilbur's meeting me in town. I need to go over the itinerary again with the travel agent – just to make sure it doesn't include Mount..."

"...But Ruth, you've only just got here," said Emily with dismay. "We've a lot of catching up to do, yet."

"Actually, Mum, it's you who has only just got here. I arrived over an hour ago. Royston has very kindly kept me abreast of the goings-on in this neck of the woods. ...And I'm so sorry," she said, looking at her watch, "but I really must be going."

"Will you come to see me again before you leave?"

"I'll try; although, as we fly out at the end of next week, I might be a bit pushed for time."

Emily watched through the window as Ruth drove away; mixed emotions accompanied by the after-effects of drink beginning to take their toll.

She dabbed her eyes with her handkerchief.

Kristine stood beside her, an arm around her shoulder.

"Don't worry, Nana. They'll be alright. Air travel is very safe these days, you know. Everybody does it!"

"You don't understand," said Emily, blowing her nose. "We've just caught up with Ruth after all this time, and now we're going to lose her again – for a whole year."

"You've still got Dad and me!"

"I know. And I'm very grateful for everything you do for me – and for what you both mean to me. But Ruth is our daughter. Arthur and I will miss her terribly."

Emily tucked the handkerchief away and walked over to the door.

"Where are you going, Emily?" asked Royston.

Her cheerful mood seemed to have been crushed by Ruth's unexpected news. It appeared to him now that she did not quite know what she was doing.

"I think I'll go to my room and lie down for a while," she said wearily. "I could do with a rest."

Alone with her father, Kristine took stock of her situation and realised she could not have planned it better herself.

When Emily had gone upstairs she said, "Do you know, Dad; this could work out quite well for me."

"...The house sitting?"

"Of course!" retorted Kristine.

"It's not a foregone conclusion your mother will allow you to do it. Don't forget that she still has an element of control in your life."

"I know. At least, I know she should be consulted, but I don't have to obey her. I've disobeyed her before!"

"Is that your priority – disobeying your mother?"

"No! ...Although I have to admit," Kristine added with a chuckle; "it's fun knowing when I've outwitted her."

"I'm sorry, love," said Royston, mystified. "I don't know what you are talking about."

"No, I don't suppose you do. It's not the sort of incident Mum would want to share with you. She was furious with me at the time…"

"Are you going to tell me what happened then, or keep dancing around it?"

"It was the day of Nana's wedding. Mum had arranged for us to go on holiday at the same time. I wanted to stay here and be part of the wedding, but Mum insisted I go on the train with her…"

"…Yes; I remember that day like it was yesterday, too," interjected Emily.

She stood in the doorway of the lounge, smiling at them both with the recollection of it.

The two exchanged puzzled glances; each wondering why Emily had not followed through with her intention of having a nap.

"I thought you wanted to rest," said Royston.

He got up and, concerned for Emily's stability, took her by the elbow.

"Is that why I went upstairs?" she said in amusement. "When I sat on the bed, I couldn't quite remember what I was going to do, so I came back down again. That'll teach me to have more than one shandy!"

Emily had a strangely vacant look on her face, as though her mind was somewhere else.

With Royston's assistance she walked in and sat beside Kristine. Then she continued with her train of thought.

"…That's right; you two were talking about the wedding ceremony which was held in this very room. As I recall, Arthur and I were saying our vows when Kristine suddenly turned up…"

"…Did you say, Arthur?" queried Kristine, thinking Emily must have made a mistake. "Don't you mean…"

"…Never mind, Kristine," said Royston, silencing her.

He was more interested in Kristine's appearance at the wedding than Emily's mistake.

"If you were going somewhere with your mother, how did you finish up here?" he asked.

"I gave Mum the slip at the station," Kristine explained after quickly deciding how much of the incident she should divulge to her over-protective father.

But Emily, whose recollection had returned completely, saw a need to fill in some gaps.

"This brave granddaughter of mine – I was so proud of you," she said, patting Kristine's knee. "Did you not know, Royston, she jumped off the train and ran all the way back here to be with me on my wedding day?"

The pride and admiration written on her face briefly gave Kristine a lift.

...Yet Royston was horrified.

"...You jumped off a train?" he said to Kristine, in a tone more accusing than enquiring. "I hesitate to ask whether it was stationary or moving..."

"...Oh, it was moving alright; wasn't it, Kristine," Emily said somewhat cheekily.

She failed to notice the look of alarm on Royston's face.

"What a harebrained thing to do! You could easily have been killed!"

"Dad, don't be so melodramatic. The train had only just started to move. I was perfectly safe."

"Didn't you fall over and hurt your knee?" Emily asked; more as a reminder to herself than Kristine. Then, before Kristine could make response, she told Royston, "When she got here the poor lamb looked like she'd been dragged through a hedge backwards. Her trousers were all torn and bloodstained, and..."

"...Okay, I've heard enough!" cried Royston. "If this is an example of the ways in which you disobey your mother, you are hardly mature enough to look after Auntie Ruth's house for a whole year!"

"But Dad, doesn't it also demonstrate how desperate I have been to get away from Mum? She's a control freak! And anyway..."

Kristine paused to draw breath.

She was becoming agitated; her father, of all people, should understand how she felt. Did he not put up with the woman for years before finally leaving her?

"...And anyway, what?" asked Royston, ready now for a full-scale argument with his daughter.

Kristine sighed. Why did parents have to be so difficult?

"I was going to say..."

"...Well?"

"Oh, this is so frustrating. Why can't you just accept how I feel? I was going to remind you that I am much older now than when Nana married James, and at the age of seventeen I think I know my own mind, don't you?"

Kristine didn't wait for an answer.

With a garbled, "Sorry, Nana, but I can't stay here any longer," she headed out to her bike.

There's only one way to handle this, Kristine decided.

She would not to seek her mother's consent to housesit for Auntie Ruth, but to tell her she was going to do it; with or without parental permission.

"If I ask her and she refuses," she reasoned with herself as she furiously cycled the distance home; "then I will be left with the choice of staying at home, or going against her wishes. By telling Mum of my decision, it will give her a few days to get used to the idea, and then I will be free!"

By the time Kristine got home, she had it all mapped out in her mind.

Not unexpectedly, Fiona was sceptical when she made her pronouncement.

To justify her sudden decision, Kristine added tactfully, "Admittedly, it will be difficult not having the comforts of home, but I have to bear in mind that I will be going to university soon. The campus is closer to Auntie Ruth's than here. ...And," she added emphatically, "I'm a big girl now and it's time I learnt to look after myself!"

"I quite agree," replied Fiona submissively, for once at a loss to know what else to say.

"That was too easy," Kristine pondered; back in her room.

She was confused now. There had been no opposition, no ranting and raving as in the past.

In fact, her compelling declaration of independence had been received so placidly that Kristine was now left with a sense of anticlimax. ...What on earth was going on?

Throughout the long hours of darkness Kristine floated between the sensation of high expectation and a feeling in the pit of her stomach that some kind of bombshell was yet to fall on her.

Maybe, she speculated, her mother didn't quite grasp what she meant...or was quietly hatching a plot of sorts in order to prevent her from fulfilling her wishes. After all, she reflected a couple of times during the night; she had come on quite strong about her decision the moment she walked in the door.

Fiona may have been caught off-guard at the time or had something else on her mind, which prevented her from absorbing what Kristine was trying to tell her...

"It will be interesting to see what Mum has to say about it in the morning," she said to herself before falling into a dream-filled sleep.

Yet in the morning Fiona's position was still the same.

"I thought you'd be sure to object," said Kristine when she and Fiona sat with their breakfast coffees to mull the whole thing over. Her mother's passive air seemed natural enough, but Kristine was all too familiar with her volatile temperament.

Something must be up, she concluded.

"I really don't know what's got into her," she told Royston on the phone after Fiona had left for work. "She's just too nice about it."

Royston listened intently to her account; dumbfounded that Kristine had taken the initiative and told her mother about the housesitting.

Like her, he had assumed she would put her foot down.

After digesting the update on his ex-wife's most recent inconsistency, he said half-laughingly, "It does seem like she's got a hidden agenda, doesn't it?"

He was curious to know what that might be.

CHAPTER FOUR

Alicia's final check-up on Emily would have been described as a fond farewell, had Royston been there to witness it.

Emily gave her a tearful send off more in keeping with that reserved for a favourite relative – such as she would have heaped upon Ruth and Wilbur before they left on their trip, if they had taken the time to come and see her first. Yet in this case, as the object of her affection stood right in front of her, she hugged her tightly.

Then she kissed Alicia with a tear-stained face, and when she was replete from her outpouring of emotion, words of undying gratitude for everything Alicia had done for her gushed out in torrents of superlatives.

"...But I'm not going anywhere." Alicia insisted when she managed to get a word in edgeways. "...And if Royston was here now, he would confirm it."

Thus, in his absence, Emily had no choice but to accept what Alicia was telling her.

"So you don't need to worry, Emily," she went on. "Old Alicia will always be a regular visitor to your home – with or without this," she said, plucking at the badge pinned to her lapel. "...At least," she thought playfully, "I presume I'll be coming here often!" She did not want to tempt fate by making a rash statement.

In truth, she hoped her visits would carry on as before, and even develop into something more than her laidback friendship with Royston...

Meanwhile, Kristine became immersed in preparations to change her place of residence.

"Shall I take just a suitcase, or completely empty out my room?" she asked her mother at the weekend.

"I don't care," Fiona replied with complete indifference; "but whatever you do, make it snappy. Your father's only got this morning to help you move your things."

With her aunt and uncle now on the other side of the world, Kristine's excited anticipation of freedom on top of Fiona's enthusiasm to see her go, had resulted in a very tense week leading up to it.

"I don't suppose you'll bother to come and visit me when you're out on your own," said Fiona grumpily.

Although she had definite plans once she had the place to herself, Fiona also remembered how lonely it could be on her own in the big house.

"Why wouldn't I come for a visit? You'll always be my mother! As soon as I get my car..."

"...Your car?"

This was news to Fiona.

"Yes, I've decided that as soon as I can, I'm going to get a job. Then, when I've got some money together I'll buy a car. I think it's time I did, don't you?"

Fiona suddenly went quiet.

For a moment she wondered just who this person was. What had become of her precious little girl? This young woman, about to go out into the world, seemed not only to know her own mind, but also appeared to have the next year or so mapped out already.

She hoped, for Kristine's sake, that she was not biting off more than she could chew. After all, she had not even started at university yet.

'...And I know what it's like to bite off more than I can chew,' Fiona recalled with regret.

"Don't make the mistake I made," she said to Kristine as a piece of advice.

"Which mistake are you referring to?" Kristine quipped.

Fiona missed her inference and went on, "Don't think in terms of going into debt to get the things you want. Your first year at university is going to be pretty expensive, and already you're talking about buying a car."

"You're a fine one to talk, Mum – after the problems you gave Dad, clocking up all that credit..."

"...I know...I know! ...But maybe I've learnt my lesson from that! You haven't seen me make any new purchases lately, have you?"

"No, I suppose not, but..."

"...Well then, you'd do well to learn from my mistakes. And the first one is not to apply for a credit card. Save up for what you want and use cash. That's the only way to keep out of debt. Mark my words girl; one day you'll thank me if you take my advice on board."

"Yes, Mother," said Kristine sarcastically.

She now had the resolution to her uncertainty about what to take with her to Ruth's. The sooner she got out of this house completely, the better. And with that, she set about packing up everything she had accumulated in her room since childhood.

However, when it came to sorting the junk from the knick-knacks, Kristine found it harder than she had imagined.

"How can I throw away the little keepsakes I've had all my life?" she said to Royston when he came to pick her up.

The look of alarm on his face when he saw that only half of her belongings had so far been packed into boxes said it all.

"Didn't your mother tell you to be ready?" he snapped. "I haven't got all day, you know."

"I'm sorry Dad, but this is so hard. Look at this picture," she said, holding up a photograph of a pet budgie she had once lovingly looked after, until it escaped and was never seen again. "If I threw this away I would have nothing to remind me of Cheekie!"

"Oh, for goodness sake Kristine! That bird disappeared when you were five years old. Does it matter if you don't remember it from now on?"

"It does to me!"

"Well, put the photo in a box along with all your other stuff, and let's get going. You can sort out what's rubbish and what's not when you've settled in at Auntie Ruth's. There'll be plenty of time to do it then. Now, please hurry! I've got a very full day ahead of me. I thought your mother would have told you that!"

Alone at last in her new abode, Kristine closed the door and surveyed her domain.

It was much quieter at Ruth's than in her old home. The road there had always been a problem for her, with noisy cars waking her up at all hours of the night. But this house was in a cul-de-sac, and the only traffic around belonged to the neighbours.

She breathed in the quietness as though it was manna from heaven.

But the thought that sneakily sprang to mind next had nothing to do with quietness, or the amount of study she could get done in that quietness. It was something else: an idea she had not been able to entertain before.

She suddenly remembered an account she once heard about the antics of university students; of wild parties and general hi-jinx. Could she one day throw a party of her own at Ruth's?

Would she dare to?

Abruptly she shoved the idea to the back of her mind. It was too early to think along those lines...university wasn't due to start for another month, yet.

"I've got a whole year ahead of me here," she reminded herself. "There will be plenty of time for partying, and anything else I feel like doing!"

Later in the evening, when night had fallen and it was impossible to envisage what could be at large beyond the curtain of darkness outside, Kristine found herself slipping into a state of heightened alertness.

"It's strange," she thought while checking all the lights were switched on; "that when a place is generally silent, there are an awful lot of disturbing little noises around."

This was something Kristine had not considered when she lived at home.

She was hearing for the first time in her Aunt's house the creaks made by woodwork as it contracted with the chill of night, the occasional drip from the showerhead, and the normally imperceptible trickling sound from water pipes at the back of the fridge.

The quiet little noises were unnerving for the girl who was used to background noise from passing vehicles, her mother's incessant chatter, and the television. ...So much so, that after only a few hours of needing to identify each sound, she decided that quietness was something she needed to reserve only for studying and for sleep. The rest of the time she wanted noise, and plenty of it.

Her first night in a different bed from her own – and in a house that was unfamiliar if not strange to her – went by slowly; especially as those same inoffensive noises seemed magnified in the early hours of the morning.

"I don't think I'll ever get used to being by myself!" she moaned; wearied from lack of sleep.

By mid-morning the next day, Kristine had had enough of her own company.

Once her unpacking had been done, with her cosmetics arranged around the bathroom vanity and pictures from her old bedroom hung in the new room, she found herself with nothing much to do.

"I suppose I could do some cleaning," she said, thinking what Auntie Ruth might expect of her. After all, she was housesitting, not on holiday. But then she remembered the chores her mother coerced her into doing at home; and with a chuckle dismissed the idea forthwith.

"No!" she declared categorically. "I'll do the housework when I feel like doing it!"

However, there was one chore she needed to address, and quickly; for Ruth had left very little by way of fresh foodstuffs in the house.

A trip to the local superette was in order.

In the afternoon, after a casual stroll to the shops and an exhausting struggle back to the house; exhausting because she had underestimated the weight of the bags she would have to carry home – Kristine flopped down on the couch, promised herself that she would put the groceries away in a minute, and promptly fell asleep.

It was teatime when she woke up again; momentarily forgetting where she was.

Then it all came back to her.

"Good grief," she said when she saw the time. "I've been asleep for hours!"

She hauled herself to her feet – slowly, as her legs, her back, and especially her arms, were all sore from the walk home from the shops.

Once she had paid a visit to the bathroom and splashed water on her face, she reminded herself that she had not yet put away the groceries which had been deposited, still in their bags, on the kitchen bench.

Back in the kitchen, an unwelcome sight greeted her. One of the grocery bags sat in a puddle of creamy goo that slowly leaked through a hole in the bottom.

"Bloody hell!" she cried. "I forgot to put the ice-cream in the freezer!"

Kristine timidly peered into it. The tub of ice cream lay on its side, the lid dislodged as a result of the rough way in which she had dumped the bag on the bench. Only a few of the other items remained untouched by the mess.

Kristine again swore loudly, annoyed about the clean-up task ahead of her, about the bread and other groceries that had been spoiled, but also extremely cross with herself for neglecting to put the ice cream away when she first came home.

Was this an indication of how the rest of her year of independence would progress?

One day in the future, she felt sure she would laugh about the incident. But right now she was upset, hungry, and slowly getting covered in the substance she was trying to clean up.

When she came to the offending tub of ice-cream she delicately lifted it out of the bag with both hands, carried the dripping object over to the bin, and dropped it into the plastic liner.

Afterwards, she changed her clothes, placing all the sticky ones straight into her aunt's washing machine. Then she made herself a sandwich from the unspoilt end of the loaf and some tinned salmon she found in the cupboard, and sat down again; exhausted and demoralised.

"It wasn't supposed to be like this!" she wailed, and burst into tears.

The following day, Kristine decided it was time she pulled herself together.

In actual fact, she had given herself another option, too; one that she soon dismissed as out of the question. During a moment where melancholy overtook rational thinking, Kristine contemplated going back home. But it did not last more than a few minutes and she came to the conclusion that her disastrous first couple of days had merely been part of a settling in period.

Even so, she still became overwhelmed by her sense of isolation from the normalcy of her life.

With neither school nor university to occupy her time, her family living on the other side of the city, and with little interest in household upkeep just yet, she decided that what she really needed was company.

"What's the point of having your own place if you can't hang out there with friends?" she reminded herself while she looked for her address book.

Yet, what Kristine did not take into account was the day of the week. The weekend now finished, she had forgotten that many of her school friends would be starting to make inroads into the workforce.

Their daily activity would soon revolve around earning a living from whichever means of employment they could secure; whereas Kristine's working life was still more than a year away, depending on the university course she might choose to take.

Then, when each telephone number she tried yielded either an electronic request for a message to be left, or a parent telling her the friend was away at a job interview, Kristine dismally recognised her true situation: that until such time as she met new people at university, she was alone and, during the week at least, friendless...

...Though not abandoned, as Kristine soon discovered; for that evening, her father and Alicia turned up.

Kristine spontaneously rushed to let them in.

She was so pleased to see them she did not consider the fact that the place was in a mess, or that she had not tidied herself up since her shower that morning; but rather she hugged them both earnestly as though they were long lost friends.

"I thought it was time I looked in on you," said Royston, extricating himself from a bear hug.

"And not a moment too soon," exclaimed Kristine with feeling, while reluctantly letting him go.

"Welcome to my pad," she said to Alicia, and beckoned her in with a flamboyant gesture.

"We decided we should give you time to get established before invading your privacy," Royston remarked.

He looked around at Kristine's initial steps to claim the house as her own.

It certainly looked different from the last time he visited Wilbur and Ruth.

"I can see you've started making yourself at home! Wasn't the couch over by the window before?"

"Yes, but I like it better here," Kristine answered with a grin; and posed on it as if to emphasise her point.

"Have you invited any of your friends yet?" asked Alicia, showing an interest in Kristine's new surroundings. She wandered over to a wilted pot plant in the corner of the room; instinctively touching the soil to see if it needed watering. Then she said casually, "I'll give the plants a bit of a drink if you like."

Kristine turned to look at the one Alicia was examining, and suddenly realised she hadn't given the pot plants a second thought since she moved in.

"Thank you, that would be very helpful," she said in an embarrassed tone. "...And no, I haven't invited any friends round yet."

Royston called through to the kitchen where Alicia had gone to fetch some water. "Give the girl a chance, Alicia; she's only just moved in."

"I know..." Alicia replied. Moments later she returned with a jug of water. "...But I remember when I first moved into a flat. I couldn't wait to show it off to my friends!"

"It's not that I don't want to," said Kristine, needing to redeem her newfound status in front of Alicia. "It's just that... Well, I actually tried to ring some this morning, but none of them were home. I think they must have got jobs or something. I'm feeling a bit left out at the moment."

Kristine leant back on the couch so Alicia could reach the plant beside her.

"Have you ever thought of looking for a part-time job yourself?" she asked; then said, "Oh, sorry," when she realised she had dripped water on Kristine's knee.

Kristine brushed the drops away. "Yes, I'd love to get a little job. But while I was at school Mum wouldn't let me."

"...And what about now?"

"I don't know. I haven't really thought about it. I want to get started at university first."

"You will need extra cash while you're at university," Alicia stated with authority. "It's a very expensive exercise, you know."

"I'll have my student loan when it comes through. That will see me through..."

"...But you don't want to depend on it. A student loan is just that – a loan. It's not free money like a grant. You'll be forever paying it off – with interest – even after you have finished your studies. Which course will you be doing, by the way?"

"Don't know...I haven't decided yet. I'll go in next week to sort it out. My father will help me with the course fees. ...Isn't that right, Dad?"

"What?" said Royston at the mention of his name.

He had seen some of Wilbur's travel magazines under the coffee table and was thumbing through them when it clicked as to what Kristine had said.

"Fees? ...For university? Oh, gosh; have I got to pay for that, too?"

"Not if you don't want to!" snapped Kristine petulantly.

The whole business of university, complicated by the unhelpful attitude of her guests, was becoming confusing and somewhat frustrating.

At once, Royston regretted his remark.

"I was only joking!" he said in haste; and then quickly added, "Of course I'll pay your fees – or at least, I'll help you out with them."

"Well, there you are," said Alicia. "You've got nothing to worry about! With your student loan, help from your father, and a little job to provide you with some spending money, you'll sail through your university year."

"That's easy enough for you to say," said Kristine under her breath. She was becoming agitated now. Why did Alicia keep harping on about a job?

She decided to ask her.

"Well...apart from providing you with extra cash, it will introduce you to the workplace and to what's expected of an employee these days. Don't forget, you haven't had a job before. You don't yet know what it's like to go out and work for your living."

Kristine went quiet. She was starting to feel resentful of Alicia's interference. Well-intentioned the advice may be, but as far as she was concerned the strain of the last few days was more than enough for her to deal with just now.

100

Suddenly she wished Alicia and her father would leave.

Unaware of Kristine's musings, Alicia went on, "At the moment you are lucky that you can live away from home without cost. But a year from now you'll be faced with the decision of where to go after Ruth and Wilbur return from their holiday. Will you go back home to your mother?"

Kristine reacted strongly at the idea. "Not on your life! Now that I've made the break there is no way in the world I would go back and live with her. I'll just have to find a place of my own..."

"...Which will cost a great deal of money!" said Alicia to reinforce her point.

Then, while Kristine tried to digest all the advice – for despite Alicia's rather pushy manner she realised what she said was actually true – Alicia added, "My dear Kristine, a little part time job now will give you a bit of a nest egg for later on. And I have an idea for a job which might suit you down to the ground..."

As it happened, Alicia did not initially plan to talk about a position for Kristine during their visit; it just seemed to slip out in conversation.

Yet, it was something Alicia had already been thinking about; and not for the benefit of Kristine's bank balance, but because of a need in the local community.

During their conversation she had begun to see a way in which Kristine might be able to earn some money and also contribute to the need...namely, as a member of staff in a rest-home and retirement village for the elderly that was currently under construction.

Alicia had long been impressed by the close relationship between Kristine and her grandmother. She felt confident that this particular girl was a natural, and would make a wonderful worker with elderly people in general.

101

A colleague in the nursing profession who had secured a senior position in the rest-home, recently told Alicia of her readiness to advertise for nursing staff, and Alicia was sure someone of Kristine's calibre would turn out to be an asset. So trying to push Kristine into a job was born more out of enthusiasm for the idea than conspiracy to see her paying her way.

However, of this fact, Kristine was unaware.

"I'll think about it," Kristine replied without commitment.

Still traumatised by all that had taken place in the last couple of days, the idea of considering something else just now was too much.

"Don't you want to know what I have in mind?" asked Alicia, desperate to encourage an interest.

"Not right now," said Kristine bluntly.

She just wanted her father and his nice but pushy lady friend to go away and leave her alone. Their company she had enjoyed...their interference she could do without; but then she remembered her manners.

"Can I get back to you about it?" she asked. "...Maybe in a week or two?"

"Of course," said Alicia, assuming Kristine was actually interested. "I'll look forward to discussing it with you."

Yet Kristine was in no hurry. She sought nothing more than to enjoy her independence and begin living the life of a university student; even if she had not yet commenced at the university...and even though she was yet to decide which course to take.

The following week, with heart in mouth Kristine cycled over to the campus to select and enrol in a course. With no friends to accompany her she felt very alone and devoid of any guidance.

102

Really, she had no idea what career path she wanted to take. Certainly, the cares of the last few years had drawn her away from any serious consideration on the subject. And her mother had not helped. With someone constantly flying off the handle in the background, as her mother was inclined to do, Kristine had found it impossible to gain a sense of direction while living at home.

As she rode her bike into the campus grounds, Kristine wondered why she was even bothering to apply for any courses at university. Was it all just a pipe dream? Would she not have been better off just leaving school like most of her friends?

She felt completely useless and lacking inspiration.

The campus was swarming with students now. For fear of causing an accident, she dismounted from the bike and pushed it the rest of the way.

Many of the students looked quite old to her – as old as her parents, even – while others thankfully seemed to be more her own age.

She decided to follow a group of the younger ones; then spotted a male student up ahead who was also pushing his bike towards the main building. For a moment he stood and looked at it as though he was not sure what he should do.

Kristine moved up beside him.

She said, "I think we need to put our bikes over there," and pointed in the direction of a bicycle stand at the far end of the car park."

The young man turned to face her.

Kristine drew breath sharply.

She recognised him.

"Hello, Kristine," he said in instant recognition. "Fancy meeting up with you here…"

"...Richard!" she exclaimed to the school friend she had not seen for months.

Yet he looked different now. Richard's fine features seemed distorted. Then she could see why. In an instant it became apparent that he had sustained some kind of injury to his face.

A recently healed scar across his cheek had left the features on that side of his face misshapen.

"Good grief," she said, more to herself than Richard. The shock of seeing him like that took her breath away.

"Don't mind me," he said; clearly embarrassed. "This is something I have to live with for now."

"What happened?" Kristine asked with great concern.

It seemed only a few months ago that Richard was her dearest friend; until Fiona put an end to their association, citing his fondness for motorbikes and the fact that he was a couple of years older than her.

"I'll tell you about it some other time," he replied. "We really should get moving here. It's going to take all day to enrol as it is." Then, while they made their way to the bike stand, he asked Kristine, "What have you been doing lately? I haven't seen you for ages."

"I know. I've been involved with... Well, I suppose you could say...I've been caught up in family matters," she said with an element of resentment, but then brightened up. "I'm free of all that now. I've got my own place."

"You have?" he said with interest. "You're lucky. I'm still stuck at home with my folks. ...But I'm hoping it's not for much longer, with university this side of town."

"Me too...I lived at home until just last week, as well. My aunt and uncle went on an overseas holiday for a whole year, and I'm house-sitting for them."

"...By yourself?"

"...Why, yes."

Richard seemed impressed.

"How are you finding it?" he asked.

"A bit lonely at times, but better than..."

All of a sudden their conversation came to an end. Kristine and Richard were back with the multitude heading for the main building.

They found themselves being herded like sheep up the front steps and into the foyer, along with what was now an immense crowd of students; all in a hurry, and with the same objective.

"Move along there," shouted a burly man, who should have been a night club bouncer rather than an employee of the university.

He waved the mob through to an auditorium, where trestle tables had been set up for enrolment into each of the courses the university had to offer.

"I guess this is where we'll split up," Richard shouted above the amplified din of chatter. "Which course are you enrolling for?"

"I haven't decided yet," Kristine yelled back.

She was beginning to panic; suddenly aware that if Richard had not been with her she would have probably turned tail and fled; never to return. She did, however, have the presence of mind to ask Richard which course he was planning to take.

"I'm going for the physiotherapy course," he replied with obvious pride.

"Oh! Why?" asked Kristine in surprise, for he didn't really look the type; but then she realised it was a stupid question to ask him just now.

This was not the environment to get into conversation with a long-lost friend on anything. With all the pushing and shoving it was far too busy, and incredibly noisy.

Just then, Richard, spotted a noticeboard next to the physiotherapy enrolment desk and, hoping to learn what he needed to do, moved over to it.

Unwittingly, Kristine followed.

It was with great surprise that, moments later, Richard discovered she was standing behind him.

"I didn't realise you were enrolling for this course, too," he said in confusion. "You told me you hadn't decided..."

"...I have now!"

Nobody was more taken aback by Kristine's decision, than Kristine herself.

Later that night she phoned her father and told him what happened at the campus, and about the course she had chosen.

"I think that's an admirable choice love," he said, and meant it.

The physio work done with Emily after her fall helped enormously towards her recovery; of this he was certain. That Kristine wanted to get into the health sector came as no surprise. She'd had enough exposure to it recently...

"I'm sure you and your friend will do very well," he said.

Royston remembered Richard from Kristine's schooldays. Although he met him only once, he was quite taken with his strength of character.

It reminded him of what he was like at that age – young and a little bit rough round the edges, but with a sound mind and a good heart.

However, after he put the phone down to Kristine, he wasn't so confident.

He also remembered what young male students can get up to at university – and that his daughter was presently living alone...

Alicia laughed when he told her of his concerns. "Don't you remember your university days?" she asked.

"Yes, I do. That's the trouble!"

"I wouldn't be concerned. Kristine's got a sensible head on her shoulders. I don't think she will let you down."

Kristine enjoyed the first full day of her university course. Having a friend on the same one made all the difference to her self-confidence.

When they broke for lunch, the pair headed out into the grounds, and Kristine pulled out a bag of snack foods that she had taken from the fridge at home.

She bit hungrily into an apple. Then she noticed Richard didn't have anything to eat.

"Here, help yourself," she said offering him the bag.

He thanked her and took something out. She could see that he was hungry, too.

"I was going to stop off at the campus shop on the way in, but I ran out of time," he explained.

"Never mind. I've got plenty here. If you like I can bring enough for two every day..."

"...Oh, I don't think so. People will start to think we're an item if we keep hanging out together."

"What's wrong with that?" Kristine asked flippantly.

"They'll wonder why you hang out with someone who looks like this."

Richard pointed at his cheek. The scar showed up more clearly in the sunlight.

Kristine cringed. "That looks sore," she said, feeling for him. "You were going to tell me how it happened."

Richard flinched in surprise.

"I was?" he said.

"Yes...the day we came to enrol. Don't you remember?"

"Oh, yes I do...alright then."

Richard paused for a moment; his silence signalling to Kristine that he was reluctant to get into it.

"If you'd rather not discuss it with me, I'll understand," she said with compassion, but wondered what on earth could have happened to cause such an ugly scar. Had he been in a fight or something?

"I don't mind talking about it," he said quietly. "It's just that I'm not very proud of what I did."

"That sounds serious."

"It was... It still is. You may have noticed I haven't got my motorbike anymore."

"No...I haven't given it much thought," replied Kristine, telling only a partial truth.

The absence of the motorbike she had indeed noted but not yet considered a possible reason for it. His scarred face was by far her greater concern.

"I might as well be straight with you," Richard went on. "This," he said, pointing to the scar, "was the result of an irresponsible act on my part."

Now Kristine was mystified. It looked like he would not be giving her an explanation so much as a confession.

"Go on," she said cautiously.

"It happened a few months ago. I'd been to a party, drank too much; thought I'd be okay to ride the bike – you know how easy it is to be blasé about everything when you've had too much to drink..."

"...Well actually, I don't," mumbled Kristine, who rarely touched alcohol.

In fact, she recalled, the last time she had any alcohol was the day Emily married James. ...Whatever was Richard going to tell her next?

"...Anyway," he went on. "It turned out I was not okay that night. According to the police report, I crossed the double yellow line rounding a bend and swerved, narrowly missing an oncoming car. Fortunately the driver stopped to see what had happened to me. They found me in a ditch on the side of the road. My helmet had come off, so I was concussed with a ripped open face and other injuries."

Kristine felt a shiver run down her spine.

"But you seem to be alright now – apart from the scar on your cheek," she said.

"I am; glad to say. They took the plaster off my leg not long ago."

"...The plaster?"

"Yes. My leg was broken in two places. And then I had physiotherapy..."

"...On your leg?"

"Yes. The physio people were great. Without them I might have been on crutches for the rest of my life."

"So that's why you're doing this course?"

"Yes...that, and the fact that doing the course is part of my punishment."

"You were punished on top of everything else? ...But why? It was an accident, wasn't it?"

Then Kristine remembered what Richard had said about the drinking.

"The police didn't see it as just an accident. They threw the book at me for being over the limit. Although, having said that, they were probably more lenient because of my injuries. They held the trial when I was well enough to attend, and the judge reckoned I had already served part of my sentence by way of the suffering. So he only disqualified me from driving or riding a motorbike, fined me enough to keep me poor for a very long time, and sentenced me to community service."

"My God!" said Kristine.

She was horrified that her old friend had been through so much just lately.

Richard sat in silence; reflecting on the incident and its repercussions.

"There's something I can't understand though," Kristine went on.

"What's that?"

"If you have to do community service as part of your sentence, how come you are also able to go to university?"

"...Because I had an idea. When my appeal came up, I suggested to my lawyer that instead of doing meaningless community service for a finite period, that I do something to help the community and keep me on the straight and narrow for the rest of my life."

"What was that?"

"I told him how grateful I'd been to the physio people in the hospital and suggested, with the new university year coming up, that I be allowed to do a physio course instead. And the judge agreed! You can't imagine how relieved I was. The only problem is, I have to commute to and from university on a bicycle, as the bus stop is too far away for me to walk. So I'll be looking for digs somewhere close to the campus soon."

Kristine watched him for a moment while he slipped broodingly into private thought. To look at him she would never have guessed that his leg had been badly injured; his walking seemed almost normal. But on his bike, the action of pedalling must still be very painful...

She tactfully asked him.

"Cycling is good exercise for my leg," he replied. "It's just so slow when I've been used to a motorbike for all these years...and it's also quite embarrassing to see the reaction of people who know me."

"I'm not a bit surprised!" said Kristine, enjoying his openness. "I can just imagine how you must feel!"

Kristine returned home in a state of euphoria; amazed that her first day there had been so productive.

How different everything seemed now, compared with the uncertainty with which she approached her initiation into the ranks of university student. The girl who only a matter of hours ago was apprehensive about entering this new phase of her life now knew exactly where she was headed...and possibly who with.

So enthused was she about the new direction her life would be taking, she decided to set all the old grievances aside, and go to see her mother. She had not forgotten the insistence with which she assured Fiona she would keep in touch. Passing on the good news about her course would enable her to follow through on the promise, and also give her an outlet for her excitement.

Yet, she almost changed her mind.

Much to her dismay, Kristine realised that she no longer had the luxury of being driven across town; the days of calling on her father to pick her up were over. In order to visit her mother she would now need to either cycle or take the bus. And, she decided regrettably, it was really too far to cycle there and back.

She recalled her grandmother once saying how much she enjoyed the fortnightly bus ride to visit Ruth. Maybe she could give it a try. Her old home was not all that far away from the stop.

Surely it wouldn't take too long to get there?

Yet, Kristine was mistaken.

One thing Emily failed to mention about her trips to see Ruth was the fact that she changed to a different bus at the city terminal.

The journey, which Kristine envisaged should take only a little longer than a twenty-minute car ride, turned out to be a double bus journey of well over an hour. By the time she arrived at her mother's house it was almost midday. She was hot, tired and feeling very annoyed at how long it had taken to get there. For not only did her late arrival reduce the time spent with Fiona, it also meant the same arduous journey awaited her for the way home.

"The sooner I'm in a position to buy my own car," she declared; "the better I will like it!"

Kristine did not intend to tell her mother about Richard. In fact, during the bus ride there she decided emphatically that she wouldn't.

Fiona had disliked the boy from the start...and Kristine suspected at the time that Fiona looked down her nose at him; solely because of his motorbike.

Nevertheless, somehow the conversation veered in that direction, and before too long, Kristine unwittingly found herself mentioning him.

Immediately she regretted it. If it were possible to suck words back in once they had been voiced she would surely have done so.

And neither did Fiona fail to spot her slip-up. With a reputation for picking up the juiciest titbits of gossip from a mere whisper, Fiona immediately homed in on the familiar name.

"Richard," she mused, as though searching the ethers for more information. "Would that be the same Richard you went out with against my wishes?"

Kristine could hardly lie to her mother; she would quickly see through it. The truth was bound to come out sooner or later anyway. ...Best to get it over with.

"Yes," she said, and then added hastily, "...but he has changed. You wouldn't recognise him now. He had an awful accident a few months ago, and is still recovering."

If that doesn't appeal to Mother's compassionate side, nothing will, she thought.

Kristine breathed a sigh of relief when Fiona took the news without making a critical comment. ...Yet even if she did object, Kristine decided, it would be water off a duck's back now.

How could she be forbidden from seeing Richard now? As a university student living away from home, it put her in an entirely different league from before.

If she wanted to continue seeing him, then she would...

"...You must bring him over one day," said Fiona, as if recognising the need for a conciliatory response.

"Do you mean that?" asked Kristine with a spontaneous air of mistrust.

"Of course! I think it's rather nice that you've linked up with someone you already know; especially as you will be at university together."

This was better than Kristine could have hoped for. She decided to capitalise on it.

"I haven't told you the best part, yet," she said.

"...Don't tell me you're doing the same course!"

Kristine could hardly believe her ears. Had the woman become psychic?

"How did you know that?" she asked.

Nobody could have told her; certainly not her father.

"It was obvious what you were going to say; but are you doing the same course by coincidence, or did you choose to take it together?"

"It's a bit of a long story really," Kristine replied. "In a nutshell, I suppose you could say Richard inspired me to take the physiotherapy course..."

"...Physiotherapy? Why on earth would you want to do physiotherapy?"

Fiona's old sarcasm was beginning to show again.

Kristine reacted accordingly.

"Mum, if you're going to be like that, I'm not discussing it with you anymore," she said in a raised voice. "Just be pleased for me. I won't bother coming all this way if you're going to be critical. The only reason I came was to prove to you that I haven't cut my ties with..."

Just then, Kristine heard something close by that made her abruptly stop what she was saying.

In the background she heard a familiar sound; a sound that could not have been made by either herself or her mother. It was the sound of a toilet flushing.

"Is somebody else here?" she asked in alarm when she noticed a distinct lack of concern in her mother.

In fact, the look on Fiona's face appeared to suggest that she not only knew who it was, but that she was also slightly embarrassed about it.

Kristine guardedly asked, "Mum, have you got someone hidden away upstairs?"

Then, as if to answer her question, a man considerably younger than her mother looked round the door.

"Hi!" he said with a wave to Kristine; then, winking at Fiona, he disappeared into the kitchen.

Kristine gaped in disbelief.

"Who's that?" she whispered hoarsely.

"He... Um... He's my...boarder," said Fiona, yet more embarrassment coming over her; especially when a stifled snigger could be heard coming from the kitchen.

"What's going on, Mum?"

Kristine was also starting to feel uneasy; her suspicions about the situation mounting.

The young man appeared again. "Coffee, anyone?" he asked with a cheeky look on his face.

Kristine regarded him critically.

As she did so he smiled haughtily at her.

It made her skin crawl.

"I'll have a cup, please," said Fiona brightly, trying to break the obvious tension in the room.

Then she said to him, "By the way, this is my daughter Kristine;"...and to Kristine, she said, "This is..."

"...I don't want to know!"

Kristine squirmed and leapt to her feet, anxious now to get away from the awful place.

She turned on her mother.

"Mum, how you live your life is your business. ...But I don't want anything to do with it!"

Then she shot a resentful glance at the condescending male, and rushed out.

'Boarder, my arse!' was the comment that occupied her mind during the journey home. By the time she arrived, it became clear what had been going on.

"No wonder Mum was supportive when I told her I was leaving home," she cried as she pulled Ruth's door closed behind her.

In the stillness of her own abode she let out a tormented groan, which reverberated around the empty house.

"How could she do it?" she wailed; her tears not very far away. Yet, she felt more like vomiting than weeping. The thought of her own mother sleeping with a creep like that made her physically ill.

She vowed there and then that she would never have anything to do with either of them again.

Meanwhile, across town Alicia was getting desperate in her desire to persuade Kristine to apply for a job.

The rest-home complex was nearing completion, her colleague had begun advertising for staff...and Kristine as yet did not even know the place existed, let alone show an interest in getting a job there or anywhere else…

At length, she decided it was time to take action; albeit very diplomatically if she wanted to make some progress in her quest.

The trouble was, the last time she brought up the subject, Kristine made it quite clear she did not like being manipulated into doing something she was not ready for.

"There's only one thing for it, then," Alicia declared. "I need to get her on her own…but how can I accomplish it without her smelling a rat?"

She tackled Royston about her dilemma.

"It would be far too obvious if I just went over there by myself," she said.

"I don't understand why you feel the need to push her into a job," remarked Royston.

So far, Alicia had not discussed the rest-home with him, or Kristine's suitability for work there; but she had already told Emily, who now sat listening to their conversation; an idea formulating in her mind.

To be of help she suggested, "Why don't you take her on a shopping spree? Poor Kristine hasn't had much in the way of new clothes for a long time. …And while you're out, you could ask her about the job."

"I think that's a great idea, don't you, Alicia?" Royston remarked; himself devoid of inspiration for such matters.

Alicia grunted. "…If she'll go with me, that is. She might think it odd if I suddenly suggest it out of the blue."

"I know exactly how to persuade my granddaughter to go with you. Just leave it to me," said Emily with a wink.

Alicia chuckled, "Emily, what have you got tucked up that sneaky sleeve of yours?"

"Be patient, and you'll see."

116

Emily rang Kristine early the following morning, hoping to catch her before she left for university.

"Nana, but of course I would love to see you," Kristine replied when Emily asked if she could come over for a visit.

"Excellent!" said Emily in triumph.

"...But how will you get here?" asked Kristine and then added, "I suppose you could ask Dad to bring you over."

"No...I'll just catch the bus."

"...The bus? Why would you want to do that if you've got Dad there to ferry you around?"

"Yes, I know your father could bring me over..." replied Emily, trying to stay calm despite Kristine's wilful remarks; for she was on a mission now; one that she hoped might be successful.

She had as good as promised Alicia that it would be, so infinite patience was a must.

"...However," Emily went on insistently; "I would prefer to come over on the bus."

"Well, I guess that's up to you. But I hated it the other day when I went over to Mum's. By the way, did you know she's got a toy-boy?"

"Kristine...that's disgusting!" Emily cried. "Don't talk like that, please! Your mother had a decent upbringing from Grandpa and me; she wouldn't lower herself..."

"...Well, she has. Anyway, that's another subject, and I don't really want to talk about it. ...When would you like to come over?"

"That rather depends on when you have your university classes. Are you free tomorrow at all?"

"I've got a morning lecture, so you could come in the afternoon, if you like."

"That would be wonderful. I'll see you tomorrow then."

"I'll look forward to it!"

For the first time since she moved, Kristine actually felt like doing some housework.

Her grandmother's visit and the fact that she felt guilty for not keeping the house clean, was just the stimulus she needed to get motivated.

When she had finished, she felt relieved that she would not now be subjected to criticism. After all, she reminded herself, it was Auntie Ruth's house she was supposed to be looking after, so Emily would have her daughter's interests at heart as well as those of her granddaughter.

Yet, Emily did not even notice.

Much to Kristine's disappointment, her housekeeping efforts received neither critical inspection nor enthralled acclaim on her grandmother's arrival.

Instead, she was given no more than a cheery, 'Hello, love," as Emily stepped inside.

Kristine remained bewildered.

How could she have been so wrong in her assumption? And why, therefore, had she worked so hard in cleaning the place up when a quick flick with a fluffy duster would have been enough?

Kristine had no idea that Emily was not there to check on the upkeep of Ruth's house, or that during the second leg of her journey she thought of little except how she could persuade Kristine to accept Alicia's invitation to go on a shopping spree.

"I suppose you are well into the university semester by now," Emily remarked when Kristine brought in some tasty store-bought snacks.

"Oh yes...and I love it!" Kristine replied while handing Emily a plate, which was accepted with respectful thanks.

Then, while the two ate quietly Emily devised a strategy on how to broach her subject.

Kristine became increasingly uneasy: something didn't feel right about this visit. To the observant girl it was obvious: politeness was not Emily's style...not towards her, anyway.

The two of them had always enjoyed such an effortless rapport that anything awkward seemed odd.

She wondered if Emily was harbouring something. Maybe she had been drifting away with Arthur a little too often, or perhaps the ride over had tired her out; it was quite some time since she last came here – not since her fall, in fact...

"Are you alright, Nana...you've gone quiet?" she asked.

"Yes, darling, I'm fine. I'm just enjoying my snack – and your company, of course."

"If anything was wrong, you'd tell me, wouldn't you?

Emily looked at her, puzzled.

"I'm sorry, love. Do I give that impression?"

"...Not really. It's just that you are unusually quiet."

"Oh...I must have been thinking," said Emily knowingly.

She was ready now to launch into her mission.

"Actually, there is something I would like to talk about with you, but it can wait until we've had our refreshments. Tell me about your course. Your father said you've chosen to do physiotherapy."

"Yes...thanks to you."

"...To me? How is that?"

"After the problems you had with your back. I know you were impressed with the physio treatment you received at the hospital."

"Of course! Well, fancy you making your decision on the strength of that! I feel quite honoured. And I wish you all the best with it."

"Thank you. Now, what was it you wanted to mention to me, Nana?"

"Um...it's about your father."

"Dad? Why? What's going on?"

"Nothing; I just wondered what you wanted to do for his birthday next week."

Kristine did a brief mental calculation.

"...Oh, you're right...it is next week. I had forgotten all about it...thanks for the reminder. Would you like us all to go out for dinner, or something?

"That would be very nice. But I need to ask something else of you first."

"What was that?"

"Alicia told me she hasn't a clue what to get him, and it gave me an idea."

"Go on..."

"I wondered whether you might ask her to go birthday shopping with you; then she'll see the sort of things he likes. What do you reckon?"

Kristine frowned; thinking hard. The idea did not appeal to her at all. ...Not with Alicia, anyway.

"Oh, I don't know, Nana. I would say Alicia knows Dad's current tastes better than me. She's the one who spends a lot of time with him. What makes you think I could help? ...And anyway, why don't you go with her?"

"Because I believe Alicia is going to be an integral part of this family, and it would be a good bonding exercise for the two of you. But as for me going with her... I don't have enough energy for a shopping expedition nowadays."

Kristine continued to pull a face.

"If I know Alicia, she will start going on about that job again. She's got a thing about it..."

"...Not necessarily. Don't judge her so harshly; I think she has learnt her lesson about not pestering you. She's more interested in finding something nice for your father at the moment. And I'm sure she would like it if the two of you got to know each other a bit better. The only time you

120

ever connect with her is when Dad is there – and when she was looking after me, of course!"

"I suppose you're right. Is that what you came all the way over here for – to ask me?"

"In part, yes. Certainly I did want to ask you. But also, I haven't seen you for ages and have missed you. I don't want us to drift apart; it wouldn't be the first time..."

Kristine did not know what to make of it.

Here was Emily making absolute sense, when not long ago they were all questioning her sanity.

Yet right now she was not sure that Emily was being entirely open where Alicia was concerned. It all seemed a bit fishy... But there was no point in making an issue out of it. The important thing, as Emily had stated, was the continuing relationship between the two of them, and her father's birthday. ...And as for bonding with Alicia: they had their whole lives ahead of them in which to do that, so where was the hurry?

"So, what do you say?" asked Emily.

"...About what?" said Kristine; her mind still elsewhere.

"...Going shopping, of course!"

"Oh, Nana!" said Kristine in a huff. "I don't particularly want to, but if it will make you happy, then I suppose so."

"Really? That's excellent. Alicia will love you for it."

"Nana, are you sure that's all there is to it – Alicia and me shopping for Dad?"

"Yes, of course! What else could there be?"

On the way home, Emily was plagued both by a feeling of triumph that her mission seemed to have succeeded, and one of intense guilt that she had misled Kristine.

In her desire to succeed she had kept from her precious granddaughter the fact that, despite an assurance to the contrary, her request did have something to do with a job.

121

She just hoped that Alicia would not dive in at the deep end, but rather ease very gently into the subject; if at all. Otherwise, not only would Alicia's faith in Kristine come to nothing, but she might risk losing her granddaughter's trust forever. And that was something Emily wanted to avoid at all cost.

"Of course, I had to make out Alicia just wanted to shop for your birthday," she told Royston over dinner. "It was the only way I could deal with it on the spot!"

"Don't worry, Emily. Alicia can be the soul of discretion when she really wants to achieve something. But if you're worried about it, I'll have a quiet word with her. By the way, Mum; does Alicia really want to buy me a present for my birthday?"

"I've no idea! I only used that as my reason for speaking to Kristine. For all I know, Alicia's not even aware it's your birthday next week!"

"Well, you'll have to enlighten her, won't you? What's that expression – 'Oh what a tangled web we weave when first we practice to deceive?' Take care, Emily dear, lest you get tangled up in this particular web!"

After that, Emily found no peace until she had briefed Alicia about the plot and the part she should play in it.

Alicia found the whole scenario alarmingly fascinating, but at the same time was indeed grateful to Emily for letting her know about Royston's birthday.

"The sly old fox," Alicia said merrily. "He hasn't said a word to me about it!"

"No…I don't suppose he would," said Emily, laughing. "You know what men are like! I'm very concerned, though, that Kristine doesn't suspect we've been conning her over this birthday shopping trip."

"Don't worry. She won't suspect a thing."

"But how will you handle all of this?" asked Emily, her apprehension about it lessening only slightly.

"Well, as you have started the ball rolling with the notion of gift shopping, I'll go along with that and take it from there. After all, I do have to get the man a present. And you are right in that I will need some pointers from a member of the family. So in that respect, Emily, yours was not a ruse but an excellent idea! As for my own objective... Well, I guess I'll just have to play that one by ear."

Kristine took Alicia to her favourite department store in the city centre.

As Royston's birthday was looming fast, it seemed more appropriate to go one evening rather than leave it till the weekend. "He might wonder what's going on if we both disappear at the same time on Saturday," Alicia had said; and Kristine was inclined to agree with her.

The pair enjoyed their leisurely look around the store's various departments.

Kristine rarely browsed when she went shopping, but generally knew exactly what she wanted to buy and where she would find it. On this occasion though, circumstances dictated a thorough inspection of everything that might make an acceptable birthday gift for the most important man in both of their lives.

At long last, and pleased with their purchases, they left the store confident that Royston would appreciate their selection of birthday gifts.

Although Emily's aspiration to see Kristine and Alicia get to know each other had been realised, there still remained the other issue to be tackled – and Alicia had certainly not forgotten about it.

"Would you like to get a drink," she asked Kristine when they were back out on the main street.

Up ahead she could see a roadside café that appeared to be open.

"Good idea...I'm parched after all that shopping," said Kristine in good spirits.

Settled into a corner table of the brightly lit café, each with a chilled bottle of fizzy drink and a straw, the two shoppers quenched their thirst.

"I suggested to Nana that we go out for dinner," said Kristine. "Is that okay with you?"

"Dinner? What...now?" asked Alicia.

She had already moved on in her thinking; away from birthdays and onto her main reason for undertaking this evening's exercise...and time was slipping by.

"No, not for you and me! ...Dinner for Dad's birthday, of course!" said Kristine with a muted chuckle. "We've got to celebrate it as well as give him presents!"

"Sorry, I was miles away just then," said Alicia, her mind snapping back to her companion. "You must think I'm a bit dense. But you are quite right. Of course we will go out for dinner – all of us."

"Nana included?"

"...Naturally. If it wasn't for her unfortunate accident, your father and I would not have become the good friends that we are today."

"It must have been fated for you two to get together."

"Oh, Kristine!" said Alicia sheepishly. "Don't speak too soon! Officially your father and I are still only friends..."

"...Not for long, if I know Dad," came the cheeky reply.

"What do you mean?"

Kristine held her tongue; realising she was in danger of speaking out of turn. Her father had already divulged to her how he felt for Alicia; but in confidence.

She hoped she had not said too much, especially as Alicia seemed to be unaware of his feelings.

Yet, that was not the only reason she went quiet.

In that same instant she had caught sight of something on the wall above Alicia's head.

It was a notice which read, 'Help Wanted', and it held Kristine's attention.

"What's wrong?" asked Alicia. She was still waiting for an answer to her question. But then she realised Kristine was staring at something behind her.

"Nothing's wrong," Kristine replied; her eyes transfixed.

Alicia turned round in her chair to see what had caught her attention.

"Are you looking at that notice?" she asked.

Kristine would not answer. She had indeed been looking at the notice. ...And not just looking at it, but also digesting every word it said.

Alicia had been after her to get a job, and in all fairness she had given it some thought; although not seriously. But that was then. Right now, she needed to find work in order to buy her car, and at the sight of the notice she actually felt motivated to do so.

Furthermore, the prospect of working in the delightful café suited her down to the ground.

Yet, she had no intention of mentioning it to Alicia; not after the way she had been pushing her to find work.

Alicia, though, had other ideas.

Taking note of Kristine's interest in the notice behind her, she saw it as an opportunity to introduce the subject she desperately needed to get into.

"Are you interested in working here?" she asked, holding off from voicing the question she really wanted to ask. She was hoping Kristine's answer would be in the negative...and that would give her the opening she sought.

"I don't really know," said Kristine.

She shrugged her shoulders, unwilling to get into it with Alicia. Yet when something inside of her seemed to take over, she blurted out, "Do you think if I applied for a job here as a waitress I might have a chance?"

Alicia was crestfallen. Had the window of opportunity closed on her proposition before it even opened?

"Well, you won't know the answer to that if you don't ask," she reluctantly conceded.

Kristine, she had to admit, would probably make a good waitress, too.

Kristine got up and nervously approached the counter, yet nobody was in attendance.

She looked around the café which was empty but for her and Alicia, and wondered whether she should call out. Maybe the waitress was in a room at the back.

Then she spotted a tiny bell by the cash register. She picked it up and was about to ring it when a girl appeared.

"Can I help you?" the young waitress asked.

Kristine replaced the bell and nervously said, "I was just looking at the notice over there."

"...About the job?"

"Yes."

Kristine's mind went blank.

She had never enquired after a job before and did not quite know what to say next.

"Can I talk to someone about it?" she stammered.

"...Now?"

"Er...yes... Is that alright?"

"No, it's not alright!" the waitress retorted sharply. "I'm working this shift all by myself, and don't know anything about a job. You'll have to speak the owner."

Kristine hesitated.

"Do you know when he'll be here again?"

126

"...He? You mean, she!" said the waitress. "Her name is Lynne, and she'll be here in the morning."

"Thank you."

Kristine turned swiftly on her heels and hurried back to the table.

"When do you start, then?" asked Alicia flippantly, and looked at Kristine.

Her face was ashen.

"Kristine, are you alright?"

"Yes. I'm fine," she said tersely. "Can we go now?"

"Of course," replied Alicia; then when Kristine made for the door, she called out, "Don't forget your parcels!"

Kristine was shivering as they returned to the car.

Alicia became concerned.

Something must have occurred when Kristine spoke to the café assistant that clearly left her shaken. ...Unless, she surmised, it was because the evening had turned cold.

In actual fact, Kristine was feeling ashamed. She had as good as flunked her first introduction to a possible job, and embarrassed herself in front of someone who, from the appearance of the girl, was obviously her junior.

The realisation of it made her feel quite sick.

Alicia chose to say no more about a rest-home job.

Apart from their successful shopping expedition, the evening had finished badly; and yet she did not know why; for Kristine said nothing about it on the way home.

Later on, Alicia wondered if it was something she had said. If that was the case, then she really should apologise before any more damage was done to their relationship.

She contacted her again the following evening.

To her surprise, Kristine was in a good mood, and even seemed pleased to hear from her.

"Alicia, I can't thank you enough," she said when Alicia was poised ready to apologise.

"Why..?" exclaimed Alicia; caught off guard.

"...For putting me on to that job!" said Kristine.

Now Alicia was baffled.

Was Kristine referring to the café? ...Or had someone been talking to her about the rest-home positions?

"If it wasn't for you," Kristine went on, "I would never have had the courage to apply for it."

"Do you mean the café job?" asked Alicia tenuously.

"Yes, of course – what else!" Kristine replied with a hint of sarcasm in her voice.

"Now I'm confused, Kristine. Last night you were upset about something when we left the café. I thought it might have been what I said..."

"Oh, no! It had nothing to do with that! It was... Well...it doesn't matter now. The thing is, this morning I'd got over my collywobbles from last night and rang the owner of the café. She had me in for a chat, and gave me one or two little chores to see how I managed them. Then after lunch she asked me how I felt about working there, and I said okay. So, in a nutshell, I start there next Monday with a shift in the morning; then an afternoon one on Tuesday...."

"...That's wonderful!" said Alicia trying to mask her own disappointment. But it had been Kristine's choice. She did not have the right to try and influence her any more.

"There is a catch, though. ...Well, there's two actually." said Kristine with a note of displeasure.

"Oh dear. What are they?"

"Firstly, it's only a temporary job for six weeks while the regular is on leave, and secondly, they were really looking for someone full time."

"Then how come they gave you the job? I presume you told them you are at university as well?"

128

"Oh yes! But they needed somebody immediately, and until now there have been no willing applicants. Everyone else who applied was looking for a permanent position, so Lynne told me."

"Who is Lynne?"

"She's my boss!" said Kristine proudly.

Alicia laughed with pleasure at Kristine's zeal.

To be sure, she was sorry it didn't work out with the rest-home, but the important thing was that the girl had found some paid work, albeit for a short time.

At least, it's a start, she thought.

Alicia could not help but he happy for her.

CHAPTER FIVE

Emily revelled in her return to full health.

The rigours of the past few months, once a drain on her vitality, had now dissipated; to the extent that she felt fully capable again, and completely well.

She would never have discussed it with Royston, but she believed sincerely that her recovery was due in no small part to Arthur's presence in her life. He was both a saving grace and a helpmate to her. Arthur's attention – a regular part of her everyday life now – had continually buoyed her up during the more troubling situations; although, she did have to admit, there had really been nothing to drag her down of late. Not even irrepressible Fiona could burst her bubble of contentment at present.

At least, that was how Emily saw it...

With Royston for company, Emily considered herself to be truly blessed; especially when, one day, he came home from a date with Alicia bearing some exciting news.

"We are now officially a couple," he announced.

"...And about time, too," was Emily's response as she hugged him vigorously.

She never doubted for a minute that one day soon they would take that step.

"So where do you go from here?" she asked, with no idea of what he might say.

"Actually, that is something I still need to get into with her," he replied.

"Oh," said Emily. "Haven't you discussed it yet?"

What Emily alluded to was her assumption that he would now plan for his divorce from Fiona and eventual marriage to Alicia. Yet Royston was referring to something entirely different.

"We've touched on the subject, but that's all," he said casually. "The thought that's been going through my mind is that Alicia should come and live here."

Emily frowned in puzzlement.

"Both of you live here – with me?" she asked. ...That did not seem very appropriate for newlyweds! "Surely, you will want a place of your own when you are married?"

"What?" asked Royston; suddenly confused.

Did he misinterpret what Emily said? There had been no talk of marriage between him and Alicia. How could there be? He still had a wife!

"Emily, I think we are talking at cross purposes here," he said. "You've got us married already, and we have only just become a couple. Marriage between us – if that's the path we decide to take – is a long way off yet."

"I'm sorry, dear," said Emily with embarrassment, while wondering just what he did mean. "I do seem to have got the wrong end of the stick, don't I? Perhaps you'd better tell me exactly what you had in mind when you suggested Alicia come and live here."

Royston was starting to realise that Emily might not regard his intentions in quite the same light as he did.

To him, it was natural that he and Alicia would want to live together. It also seemed wise, in view of the excellent relationship between Alicia and Emily, that they live in her house while they saved up for their own home. Yet, to his reckoning Emily seemed not to grasp that he intended to bring Alicia over straightaway; that is: to share his home, his life...and his bed.

131

Would Emily even be able to accept the concept of them living together in her house...and not as legitimate man and wife?

And then there was the fact that he was still married to her daughter...

"Oh dear," he thought uneasily before attempting to answer Emily's question.

Perhaps it was not such a good idea after all.

Emily was more than a little surprised by her son-in-law's cautious explanation.

Certainly it had not for one minute occurred to her that he might want to live there in sin with a mere lady friend; charming though she was.

"I have to say," she remarked. "Although it's not for me to dictate how you conduct your love affairs, it is unfair of you to involve me; especially as I come from a background that honours the sanctity of marriage. I didn't allow James to stay here until after we were married!"

"I understand what you mean," said Royston; feeling the need to justify himself. "But we're living in a different world now. De facto relationships are considered normal."

Emily grunted. "I do hate that word," she said.

"What word?" Royston was becoming impatient now.

"De facto. It sounds so... So... Oh, I don't know!"

"Immoral? Is that what you wanted to say?"

Emily sighed despondently.

She loved Alicia, and owed a great deal to Royston, but to have them both living in her house – in her and Arthur's house – in a relationship that seemed both immoral and illicit, for he was still married to Fiona, was totally out of the question, as far as she was concerned.

"I'm sorry, Royston, but I really can't allow it. ...Not in our house, anyway."

While Royston quietly absorbed what she was saying, Emily continued undeterred.

"If you and Alicia want to live together, that is your own business. If you want to live together at her house you will have our blessing. However, Arthur and I can't allow you to do so under this roof. What if Fiona decided to pay us a visit? It's quite likely that she will, now that we have made up. Have you thought about that?"

Royston had not. Admittedly, he realised, when he and Alicia pledged their love for each other, the euphoria that enveloped them obscured all considerations of a practical nature. They could see no harm in sharing their happiness with Emily. She was more than a mother-in-law to them both. The fact that she was now turning them down flat left him speechless.

Emily noted his subdued demeanour and capitalised on it. She had not quite finished with him yet.

"I suspect," she went on, "that you have overlooked something very important to Arthur and me – that you are still bound in marriage to Fiona. What do you intend to do about that?"

Now Royston felt deflated. Extricating himself from his marriage to Fiona had been the last thing on his mind.

Off the top of his head he said, "I suppose we'll have to apply for a divorce."

Emily roared with laughter.

"Do you seriously think my darling daughter will let you go – especially when it involves another woman? You may have your work cut out for you there, my boy!"

"Emily," said Royston, the adrenalin starting to pump round him again. "I don't know why you are adopting this unhelpful attitude. I've done nothing to offend you, except suggest Alicia comes to live with me here. There's nothing wrong with it in this day and age; but it is your decision, and if you decline, then I suppose we will have to make some other arrangement."

In the back of his mind, Royston was hoping that a firmer hand might cause Emily to give in; yet her opinion remained resolute and she said nothing.

Emily's scruples actually weighed heavily in her breast. They held far more sway than the sense of gratitude she otherwise felt towards Royston.

In response to his coercion, all she could say was, "If that is your wish, then good luck to you both. Naturally, I will miss you and will always be grateful to you..."

Emily sniffed back a tear as the reality of her situation hit home. Royston was actually going to leave her. But she still had Arthur to think about. There was no way he would agree to an arrangement such as the one Royston was suggesting for himself and Alicia.

"I'll pack up a few things for tonight and collect the rest of my stuff some other time," he said dejectedly.

"You don't have to leave right now, do you?" asked Emily in alarm. This was not what she wanted at all. She had just hoped he might come to his senses; that he would wait until he could marry Alicia before living with her. That was how it should be done. That was what she and Arthur had to do all those years ago...

Yet Royston replied, "There's no point in my staying here any longer. Under the circumstances I don't see how I can, do you?"

Royston went to his room, and came out a few minutes later with a holdall.

He paused as the enormity of his decision sunk in.

With an air of disbelief he said calmly, "Goodbye Emily. Take care of yourself, won't you?"

"Will you still come and visit with me?" asked Emily awkwardly as she showed him to the door.

"Of course we will. But now that you are well again, our visits probably won't be as often as in the past. I wouldn't like you to be offended by our presence."

"Royston, now you're being unreasonable! I've nothing against you and Alicia living together – just not here!"

In frustration, Emily averted her eyes.

Immediately, she heard the door clicking shut and when she turned to look, he had gone.

"Did you really think she would accept your suggestion; the way you broached the subject!" Alicia exclaimed.

Royston's reappearance on her doorstep, a bag in hand, had caught her off guard.

She had expected his next communication with her to be a report on Emily's joy that they had finally made a commitment to each other. It certainly was not part of the plan to drop a bombshell on her by proposing they both live in her house.

That possibility, according to Alicia's understanding of the situation, was a long way down the track.

Alicia followed him in, picking up the bag which he had dropped in the hall. He looked, to her, like he could tear his hair out, so furious did he seem about the outcome of the discussion with Emily.

Yet, in reality, Royston was embarrassed that he had blown an opportunity that would have served them all very well for the future.

"I'm sorry, Alicia. I seem to have stuffed everything up," he said with remorse.

"But why did you ask her there and then? I thought we were going to wait. ...And did it not occur to you that Emily might refuse?"

Royston walked over to the glass cabinet where Alicia kept her modest amount of alcohol. He pulled out each bottle in turn and checked the contents; then he selected one, opened it up and poured himself a drink.

"Do you want one?" he asked, and took a sip.

"No... No thanks," she said; still stunned by his blatant lack of sensitivity.

Alicia drank very little. The alcohol in the cabinet was for just Royston.

It looked like he would be availing himself of it more often from now on.

Suddenly it all became clear. The overnight bag was not just the reaction of a man who needed to get away for a while; Royston was making a statement.

"Are you thinking of moving in here?" she asked, while he allowed the warming liquid to soothe his emotions.

This was a far cry from the time he needed brandy after catching cold in the rain. That occasion made Alicia feel wanted. She felt close to him. But right now she regarded his presence more as an encroachment on her privacy.

She waited for his answer.

"I don't know...what to do," he stammered.

Alicia's tone had not been particularly welcoming. Yet, prudence now dictated that he not put his foot in it twice in one day.

...Perhaps he should have waited to be invited.

"Would it be all right if I stayed here just for tonight?" he asked timidly.

Alicia softened. Now that the alcohol had mellowed him slightly, he looked more like a helpless child in need of a hug than a tactless male.

She responded appropriately.

"Of course you can, my love. After a good sleep you will be able to see things more clearly. Family disagreements are always upsetting."

What Alicia had in mind was that the morning Royston should go home and repair the damage with Emily; for she had her own schedule to stick to, and moving in with Emily was not part of it.

Despite her protestations, Alicia hoped that sometime in the future she might be the one to approach Emily with that same enquiry. But this could not take place for a while, and for good reason: Alicia was not in a position to give up the lease on her rented cottage.

The long-term lease on her home was negotiated down to a manageable rent because she intended to stay there. If she were to break into the agreement before it had run its course, she would have incurred a penalty; which she was not prepared to shoulder.

But that was not the only reason she wanted Royston to make peace with Emily: Alicia did not actually want to live with him just yet; either in her house or at Emily's.

She was not ready for that step in their relationship.

It was too soon.

The pain of her divorce still grated on her emotions, and although she loved Royston and was very happy with the commitment they had made to one another, she was not yet prepared to bring it onto such a personal level as sharing a home together.

Royston, however, was thinking along completely different lines now, and going back to Emily with cap in hand was furthest from his mind.

In walking out on her he had, from his point of view, given up his role as Emily's live-in companion; for she no longer needed him – certainly not in the way she did after her accident and the death of James.

Emily was back to her old self…better than her old self. If her arguments with him earlier were anything to go by, then clearly she was firing on all cylinders again; or maybe Arthur was the one doing the firing.

And that was another thing...

Royston was exhausted from living with an old lady who continually imagined the presence of a husband she buried years ago – even if that lady was their dear Emily.

...So why would he want to go back to her?

As each contemplated their own perspective in the time it takes to groan under the weight of indecision, a stalemate situation developed between them.

It was Alicia who recognised this first; although she was actually the only one to recognise it.

The more perceptive of the two, Alicia knew without doubt that Royston's pride would not now permit him to go back home; not to live there, anyway. As far as she could see, the only options available to him were to find another bachelor pad or to go back to Fiona for a while.

...But then she had another idea.

"If you won't go back to Emily's to live..." she said; "...why don't you keep company with Kristine?"

Alicia felt sure she had hit the nail on the head with this new suggestion.

She stood back, confidently waiting for his response.

Royston looked at her sideways.

"I take it you don't want me living here, then," he said.

It was not a question, and Alicia knew it.

She sighed disconsolately.

"Oh dear; Royston, I think you and I have very different expectations of our relationship at the moment."

Kristine knew nothing of the mix-up across town. ...Not because she hadn't bothered to keep in touch, but for the reason that she was too busy.

At the request of her employer at the café, Kristine had handed over a copy of her university timetable. That way, Lynne had advised her, she could include Kristine in the weekly roster, and she would also know when her newest recruit might be available to work extra shifts at short notice. And Kristine, too new an employee to recognise when she was being exploited, found herself working all hours of the day and often into the evening.

The fact that Kristine had university lectures to fit in did not seem to matter to Lynne.

In her opinion, the workplace came first.

"Thank goodness it's only for a few weeks," Kristine wailed as she hurried out of university one day, and went straight to the café for an evening shift.

At about teatime, she was working in the back room of the café when Lynne came in and said, "Kristine, there's somebody here to see you."

"Oh really!" was the surprised response.

As she removed her disposable gloves and threw them into the bin, she thought, 'I wonder who that could be,' and peeped round into the café.

It was Alicia.

"Don't take too long will you?" said Lynne. "We're very busy, you know."

At a loss to know how to deal with the unexpected situation, Kristine self-consciously mumbled, "Sorry about this. I'll only be a minute;" fully intending to tell Alicia, who she presumed to be paying a social call, that she could not possibly chat now.

Yet the serious look on Alicia's face told her there was more to it than just a social visit.

"What's the matter?" Kristine gushed; anxious to send Alicia packing and to find out what was going on.

A multitude of questions swarmed through her mind, as she quickly pulled out a chair and perched on the edge of it to hear Alicia's response.

Out of the corner of her eye, she could see her boss hovering by the counter to keep an eye on her.

While Alicia briefly explained what had happened the previous day, and how they were all at something of an impasse, Kristine's apprehension grew.

At last she cut in on Alicia's onrush of concerns.

"Look, Alicia," she said in frustration. "I'm sorry there seems to be a family crisis at the moment, but I need to get back to work. Would you please get to the point? How does this affect me?"

Alicia gulped nervously; then came out with, "We think your father should come and stay with you at Ruth's."

Kristine's mind went blank. ...In fact, she was later to reflect that at that moment she was actually in shock. As it was, she did not have even a second to absorb what Alicia suggested, for Lynne was now at her shoulder.

"Kristine...if you please," she said, while at the same time smiling at Alicia in the interest of courtesy; for she could not afford to have a potential customer spreading it around that she was impolite.

Kristine leapt to her feet awkwardly.

"Sorry, Lynne; it won't happen again," she said.

Then, offering Alicia neither response nor comment of any kind, she hurried back to her rightful place.

Disappointed in Kristine's reaction to yet another of her practical suggestions, Alicia could do nothing except stare after her; in the hope that she was able to talk to her again before her uninvited guest settled in for another night.

Even one night with Royston in the house had been too unsettling – for them both.

When Kristine eventually arrived home, exhausted and not wanting to think about Alicia's proposal, she rang the one person who she thought might be able to shed some light on the fiasco.

While she waited for the phone to be answered, the effect such a move would have on her hit home.

She realised, as Emily's cheerful voice came over the phone, that if her father moved in she would relinquish all her newfound freedom.

With the recognition of it fresh in her mind and a lump forming in her throat, she struggled to say, "Hello, Nana. It's Kristine! Can you talk?"

"Yes, of course," said Emily. "...But it doesn't sound like you can? Are you ill?"

By now Kristine had swallowed back the restriction, and spoke normally again.

"No. I'm not ill! ...Nana, would you please tell me what's going on over there? Why on earth did Dad move out in such a hurry? And why is it so important that he come to live with me?"

"What do you mean? I don't know anything about that arrangement."

"I just found out from Alicia, while I was at work, that you kicked Dad out and now he's got to move in with me! And I'm not very happy about it. Can you please tell me what it's all about?"

Emily could not believe her ears.

Something very strange must have gone on somewhere between her disagreement with him the night before, and Kristine's frantic phone call.

"Calm down, Kristine," she said, while trying to remain calm herself. "I don't know what you are talking about. I certainly did not kick your father out. He left here of his own accord."

"But why? And why did you say he had to come and live with me? Are you trying to ruin my life?"

Kristine was beside herself now. Her dream of living as an independent university student was fast turning into one more family nightmare.

"Darling, you are not making any sense. Where did you get these ideas from? I think you have been misinformed somewhere along the line. Alicia and your father are going to live together; that's all. None of us are trying to ruin your life, Kristine!"

"Well you might not be, Nana, but Alicia is. She as good as told me so."

Emily was beginning to catch on now. The way Kristine was talking – especially about dear Alicia – suggested one thing to her: Kristine was reacting irrationally, and whatever happened to upset her wasn't nearly as terrible as she was trying to make out.

"Kristine, dear, why don't you tell me what you've been hearing; then we can talk about it."

So Kristine explained to Emily that Alicia had barged into the café, interrupted her at work and then dumped the proposal on her lap.

For her part, Emily told Kristine what happened at her house the night before.

"I have to be honest," said Emily after giving the matter some thought. "It doesn't sound to me like anyone is trying to lay down the law to you, but rather that Alicia is trying to find a solution to their problem. What I don't understand though, is why they would want you to take Royston in if they are planning to live together."

"I don't know!" exclaimed Kristine in despair. It had been a long and frustrating day. All she wanted to do was have a shower and go to bed.

"None of this makes sense to me," said Emily, trying in vain to make reason out of mayhem. "I tell you what, love; you go to bed now. I will ring Alicia right away and find out exactly what is going on...you don't need to fret about it anymore. I'll ring you back after I've talked to her."

"No, please don't! I've had enough of it! Sorry, Nana. I didn't mean to yell. I'm just extremely stressed about all of this. If you could possibly handle it, I'd be very grateful. There is just one thing I need to ask of you, though."

"What's that?"

"Would you please tell Alicia that I can't have him here? He'll just have to find somewhere else. I'd rather jump off a cliff than have one of my parents living with me again."

"Goodness gracious! I hope it doesn't come to that!"

"Why not? He's lived in a flat before!"

"No, I didn't mean that! I meant, you jumping off... Oh, never mind! Goodnight Kristine. I'll get to the bottom of it. You go and rest."

Emily's heart was thumping wildly when she put the phone down. The whole episode had distressed her far more than she expected.

She made a mug of tea, and without thinking put in a whole spoonful of sugar instead of the half she usually took. Then she sat in the unlit lounge trying to gain some perspective on the situation...and find the momentum to take it further.

For a while, she sat in the darkness, her drink grasped between both hands; hardly noticing her own reflection in the window, for the curtains had not yet been drawn. Moonlight danced on the liquid in her cup, making her realise that her hands were shaking.

"I'm too old to get involved in family problems," she said, with the tremor also in her voice.

143

But then, as the sweet tea refreshed her, she realised something else. In taking a tough stand with Royston and Alicia, had she also caused insurmountable difficulties for the whole family?

She was pondering this when the phone rang again, and she got up to answer it.

Presuming it to be Kristine with another request, she said without wavering, "Kristine, I said I would deal with it. Just leave it to…"

"…Emily," said a woman's voice. "It's not Kristine; it's Alicia. I've been trying to reach Kristine, myself."

"Oh no!" mumbled Emily out of earshot. "…Must I wade through all of this again?"

After a lengthy discussion with Alicia, Emily eventually accepted that all the parties involved had had their wires crossed right from the start. Nothing had actually occurred as it seemed at the time, and the solution, it transpired, was far simpler than anyone could have envisaged.

Once Alicia explained that Royston had misunderstood her about the issue of their living together right away, it all came clear.

As far as Emily could make out, there was no reason for Royston to move. He could just pack up his few bits and pieces and bring them back to her house.

Then, she supposed, Alicia would feel more at ease, Kristine would be relieved, and Royston…

Emily was not too sure how Royston would feel about it just yet. He was a man, after all, and men are not as ready to capitulate as women.

Besides, she thought; if Royston had not misunderstood Alicia in the first place, none of this mix-up would have happened at all.

As Emily had rightly guessed, it was only after gentle persuasion on Alicia's part that Royston did capitulate, and decided to return to his place of residence.

And there was nobody more pleased with his decision than his daughter.

Emily's family were now collectively of the opinion that she had recovered from all her recent misfortunes.

However, there still remained one as yet unresolved concern: Kristine and Royston were the only close family members who knew about Emily's continued association with Arthur.

Even though they both accepted this benign peculiarity in her behaviour, neither had any intention of mentioning it to the others; for in the family's eyes she was just back to being her old self: wise and capable Emily.

Yet, Emily did not feel the same.

Now that she had spent a couple of nights alone in the house, she began to realise she was not quite as confident as in the past.

Acutely aware that age and her recent experiences had unnerved her, she bore emotional scars that were often troubling when she was alone for any length of time, and especially at night. Not even the knowledge of Arthur's presence helped her through those restless night hours.

It was reassuring to have him there, she conceded, but even he could not dispel the dark thoughts and persistent sleeplessness that, but for her prescribed sleeping tablets, were almost companions in themselves.

After her second night alone, Emily decided she could not wait to see if Alicia convinced Royston to come home.

She phoned through as soon as she was up, using the excuse of catching them before they left for work to justify the early intrusion.

Much to her surprise, Alicia announced, "He's already on his way there!"

"My goodness that was quick work! Well done! You did the right thing in sending him back. ...Oh, I hear him now," she said hastily. "I'll talk to you later."

A moment later, Emily let him in.

Shamefaced, he said, "I'm so sorry about all this."

"Don't worry, Royston," she responded gently. "I'm just pleased to have you back. I had forgotten how lonely I get in this house on my own."

Kristine found it easy to be reconciled with her family once she learnt about the misunderstandings.

Emily phoned to give her the good news, while Royston settled back in.

Relieved that she would not now have to put up with her father, Kristine immediately contacted Alicia.

"I just wanted to welcome you to the family, and to apologise for my rudeness," she said after Alicia remarked that she was in a bit of a rush.

"Thank you Kristine...apology accepted," Alicia replied. "...And I feel like I'm part of the family already."

Unfortunately, while she proffered her words of welcome, Kristine overlooked the fact that her front door was open.

Consequently, she failed to hear somebody step inside and pause briefly to eavesdrop on her phone conversation with Alicia.

Only when, a moment later, a hesitant knock on the door announced the visitor's arrival, did Kristine realise someone was there.

In horror she looked round to see her mother standing in the doorway.

"My God, Mum! What are you doing here!" she cried.

With her hand cupped over the phone for privacy, she hurriedly whispered into it, "Alicia, I'm sorry but I have to go now."

Without waiting for a response, she hung up.

Meanwhile, Fiona had walked on into the lounge. She looked critically around it.

"Ruth's place hasn't changed much over the years," she said nonchalantly when Kristine came through to her. "By the way, who was that you were talking to on the phone?"

"That's none of your business, Mum! This is my home now. You can't barge in without knocking and interfere..."

"...I did knock; and you haven't answered me yet. Who was on the phone? It sounded like you were welcoming somebody into the family. Would you care to explain?"

"It's got nothing to do with you!"

Kristine felt violated. Her mother was the last person in the world she wanted to have learn about Alicia and her father. But it was too late now.

While Fiona made wild speculations, mentioning Alicia's person if not her name, for she had momentarily forgotten what it was, Kristine deliberately kept silent. She felt badly that she had let slip a secret so personal to her father. And now her conscience plagued her.

"Well, are you going to tell me?" Fiona asked.

"I believe phone conversations in this country are still private," Kristine said in defence of her position. "You really have no right to keep hounding me."

"Is that all you have to say?"

"Yes. Now, if you don't mind, I've got things to do."

"It sounds like you're kicking me out."

"You said it!"

Fiona relented.

"Kristine, what has happened between us? Not long ago we were getting on so well."

147

"You're asking me? You should really be asking that of yourself, Mother!"

Kristine was in no mood to indulge her mother's peace offering, especially after the incident with the boarder.

Yet, Fiona was quick to retort.

"...And what is that supposed to mean?"

"If you can't figure it out on your own, I'm not going to waste any more of my time trying to explain! By the way, you haven't told me what you're doing here. You weren't exactly invited!"

With both mother and daughter in a heightened state of agitation, sensible discussion between them was now out of the question.

Fiona; still troubled by Kristine's phone conversation when she came in, refused to give way on her rage until she had obtained an explanation.

...And, although desperate to retain her secret, Kristine was struggling to steer clear of the subject.

"Look, Mum..." she said a little more calmly. "I know you want to keep tabs on everything I do – and everybody I talk to," she said, pointing to the phone; "but you can forget it. My life is my own now. I'm a university student, not a child, so you no longer have any jurisdiction over me. And incidentally," she added. "Speaking of affairs, haven't you got somebody waiting for you at home?"

"What are you talking about?" asked Fiona indignantly.

"As if you didn't know!"

Disgust began to filter into Kristine's tone of voice as well as scorn.

"I mean that creep you've been keeping; your toy boy... your lover...your boarder. Whatever you want to call him; I don't care. Please tell me he's a has-been. It makes me sick just thinking about it."

Fiona's face, flushed with embarrassment, looked like it was about to explode; for taking a young lover had been a mistake she would regret for the rest of her life.

Once he had fleeced her of every cent she possessed, he had walked out one morning and not come back. That, some weeks ago now, had slipped into the background of her mind, and to remember it sickened her.

Having Kristine resurrect it in such a coarse way was more than she could bear.

With a howl of frustration, Fiona grabbed her bag and made to leave. But the need to retaliate overpowered her, and she turned on Kristine.

"I'll have you know, I selflessly stopped off on my way out of town to try and patch things up with you. I didn't have to; I wanted to. I could have continued my journey, not given you a thought, and enjoyed a pleasant day out. But I wanted to connect with you. ...And in answer to your disrespectful question: Yes, my boarder has gone. So don't talk to me in that insolent manner. I am still and always will be your mother!"

Fiona stormed out of the house; then briefly returned to fire a parting shot.

"By the way, I've figured out who you were talking to on the phone. It was Alicia, wasn't it? You were welcoming Alicia into the family...and that can mean only one thing. Well, you can tell your father from me, that if he wants to marry the woman any time soon he'll have a fight on his hands: a hell of a fight!"

When the resonance of the slammed door had faded away, a refreshing silence descended on the house. For a moment Kristine expected the barrage of hostility to return; that the echo of her mother, too, would sneak back and start up all over again.

Alarmed by the prospect of it, she quickly ran to the laundry and locked the outside doors.

Kristine was not taking any chances.

As she headed back to the lounge, she made a detour through the kitchen to get a drink of cold lemonade; she needed it. She was parched, hot and very much in need of a boost to her sugar level, for she found she was shaking uncontrollably.

Giving herself a few minutes to get over the distress a confrontation with her mother always seemed to evoke, she then made a decision.

It was imperative her father was made aware of what just happened.

On the phone to him she said, "Dad, can you come over here – now? It's urgent!"

"That woman is nothing but a witch!" Royston hissed after Kristine had delivered her side of the story; even though her tendency to exaggerate had coloured Fiona's remarks more than was warranted.

Yet, justification aside, in this instance Kristine was not about to be lenient with her mother. Already in her short life there had been too many crises in their relationship, and this was just one more.

As far as she could determine, there was no chance of reconciliation now or ever.

"What do you think she might do?" asked Kristine; still very much aggrieved.

"Nothing, I hope. Anyway, what could she do? She can't prevent me from living with Alicia. And if I decide to file for divorce she has no choice but to accept it."

"...Or fight it. She did indicate to me that if you wanted to marry Alicia you would have a fight on your hands – and those were her exact words!"

"I don't really care what the bitch does. She's not going to spoil our chance at happiness."

"I would like to see you happy," said Kristine sincerely. "You deserve a bit of good fortune in your life, especially after the rough time you've had in recent years. Nana was very lucky to have your help when she needed it."

"What do you mean by 'was'? I'll be living with her for quite a while yet."

"...So Alicia really does want to delay living together until you're married?"

"Not necessarily. We're quite happy to live in sin..."

"Dad! That concept went out with the dodo!"

"I know. But that was what your grandmother calls it."

"I guess Nana wasn't accepting of your suggestion that you both live at her house, then."

"No; and neither, I take it, was Arthur. At least, that was what she said."

"Good grief; does she still see Grandpa's phantom? I thought she would have moved on from that long ago. She looks so much better these days."

"And so she is. But I suspect it's more because of Arthur than in spite of it."

...And I can understand why, thought Kristine privately.

The distant memory of a certain warming glow, which once accompanied her vision of Arthur in the rose garden, would ever remain with her.

Grandpa, it seemed, was still in the picture.

Kristine's stint at the café mercifully came to an end.

Her six-week contract had been extended by a couple of weeks, much to her annoyance. Lynne, her employer, got on her nerves more and more with each passing week, and her demands on Kristine's time became progressively more intrusive, despite her other commitments.

"The woman thinks she owns my soul," she whispered to Emily when, on the pretext of stopping for coffee, she had called in at the café to see her granddaughter at work.

Kristine enjoyed acting as though they did not know each other, and when Lynne withdrew to the back room they giggled about it like a couple of schoolchildren.

However, now the interminable period was over. Lynne handed Kristine her final pay, together with a certificate of employment as proof that she had worked at the café; which released in Kristine such a feeling of euphoria that she felt like celebrating.

It was bliss, she later reflected, to be able to sleep in when her lecture wasn't until the afternoon, or to go straight home from university instead of biking into town.

She even managed to fit in the party she had been longing to have, and invited a few friends from her course, including Richard.

Yet there was also a downside to her freedom: there was no more money coming in.

While she was working, Kristine had saved as much as she could towards the car she so badly needed. By the time she finished her time at the café she had accrued more personal wealth than ever before, but it still fell short of the amount she needed for the deposit on her car.

...And she now knew which one she wanted.

On the way to and from university, Kristine rode passed a car sales yard; and right at the front of the forecourt was positioned a two-door, metallic blue hatchback.

She fell in love with it at first sight, and prayed fervently that nobody else would come along and buy it. She even approached the proprietor to see if she could put down a deposit on it and pay off the rest later or maybe take the whole thing out on credit. But he insisted almost rudely that she was far too young to utilise credit, and in any case, hire purchase was out of the question because she had no credit rating.

However, he did explain that if her parents were willing to act as guarantor, he would be prepared to reconsider. So, with cap in hand she approached Royston.

"Do you know what acting as a guarantor entails; what I would be required to do?" he asked in a serious tone.

"No, not really," she replied with naivety. "I suppose it means you will keep after me until I pay it off."

By the manner in which Royston roared with laughter at her response, Kristine realised she really had no idea what being a guarantor meant.

"You are right in that I would make you keep up with your repayments, but what you don't realise is that if you renege on them, I would have to make them instead. And, naturally, that is something I am not prepared to do. So, I'm sorry love, but hire purchase is out of the question at the moment. Anyway, you're not earning now, so how could you possibly afford it? You would be much better off to find yourself another job and keep saving until you can pay cash."

"That's more or less what Mum once said I should do," muttered Kristine dejectedly.

"...Your mother? Good grief; she's a fine one to give you financial advice. Fiona is well-practiced when it comes to buying on credit..."

"...I know. But I must admit, at one time not very long ago, she seemed to realise how stupid she had been to do it, and advised me not to follow suit."

"I'll take my hat off to her for that, then. ...For nothing else, mind you – just that!"

Not long afterwards, Alicia learnt of Kristine's dilemma.

This brought back memories of a certain quest she had embarked upon a few months earlier.

Since Kristine took the job at the café, Alicia had given up on pursuing her for a position in the rest-home. It did not seem fair to pressure her further while she had so much to deal with. And even though Kristine was now no longer working there, it still did not register in Alicia's mind that she was once again free and looking for another job; and therefore open to suggestion...

...Until Kristine herself brought up the subject.

Really, she had no choice. Once Royston had turned his daughter down for the money to buy a car, and especially when he refused her the means of purchasing it on credit, Kristine began to panic.

She searched diligently for work through newspapers, the university noticeboard and adverts stuck to the corner shop window. It was not until her search led her nowhere that she remembered Alicia's persistence, and realised she never did find out what it was all about.

Kristine had no idea back then, that Alicia had singled her out for a very special type of work.

At that time, she assumed Alicia's determination was because she wanted her to experience a workplace first hand and learn to be financially accountable.

So, with an element of nervous curiosity, she asked her why she had been so pushy about the job.

"It's funny you should ask me," remarked Alicia when the shock of coincidence had waned. "I was on the verge of contacting you about it!"

"You were?"

"Yes. Your father told me about the car you like, and how you need the cash to buy it. It made me think about a job that would have been ideal for you."

"I wondered why you kept pressuring me – it wasn't the money so much as the kind of work."

"Oh, I see...somebody's told you about it, then."

Kristine looked at her quizzically.

"Told me what?" she asked.

"...About the rest-home."

"Rest-home? I don't know anything about a rest-home. I thought you were just being bossy with me."

"Kristine! I wouldn't do that! No; when I spoke about it before, I had something very specific in mind; something I thought you would be good at; but you weren't interested in any sort of job at all at the time. Then, when you went to work at the café..."

"...You dropped the idea," said Kristine, remembering that Alicia had not mentioned it recently. But then she put two and two together. "Were you going to tell me about the rest-home, only I didn't give you the chance?"

"Yes; that's it in a nutshell!"

"...But why a rest-home? What makes you think I'd be any good in a place like that?"

"Because I've noticed how well you interact with your grandmother; because I have a friend who is the manager of a new rest-home that has just opened up...and because I would still recommend you to her, if you are interested."

"Really?"

"Oh, yes!"

"Wow!" said Kristine; taken aback to think that Alicia had sufficient faith in her abilities to actually recommend her for a position there.

After a moment to collect her thoughts, she went on, "So the question is: do I want to do that sort of work."

"I suppose so," responded Alicia; still in a daze that they were talking about it after all this time.

"...And what sort of work would I actually be doing?"

155

"I'm not sure...but if you are interested I could arrange an interview for you with my friend."

Kristine recoiled.

This was all happening too quickly for her; yet, she did so want that car...

"Could you?" she found herself saying. "I really would appreciate it."

"Certainly. I'll give Grace a ring in the morning."

"Grace?"

"...My friend. She's in charge of the rest-home. There is one thing I should mention about your car."

"What's that?"

"Have you got your driver's licence yet?"

"...Driver's licence?"

In an instant, Kristine's hopeful demeanour changed.

"Oh, shoot; I forgot about that." she said grumpily. "I'll need one to drive the damn thing, won't I?"

"I'm afraid so."

At long last Alicia was able to contact her nursing associate about Kristine.

Grace, the rest-home's manager, received the call with interest; however, her response was far from encouraging.

"I'm sorry," she told Alicia bluntly. "Applications for the various positions here closed a while ago. We are currently fully staffed, and also have a list of relievers. Now, if you'd had told me about this girl when we were still advertising, I would probably have snapped her up."

Disappointed, Alicia broke the news to Kristine.

"Oh, well. I suppose it was worth a try," Kristine replied.

With her focus of attention on a copy of the road code in readiness for her written test, Alicia's discouraging news did little except wash over her.

Accepting, now, that her plans to buy the car must be put on hold, Kristine began to pour all her energy into applying for a driver's licence.

Once she had passed the written test – on her second attempt, as anxiety caused her to make mistakes – she registered with a driving instructor and for the first time in her life, sat behind the wheel of a car.

A month and ten lessons later, she sat her practical test.

Royston drove her to the test centre; then waited in the car park opposite, while the examiner put her through her paces. Afterwards, he watched as she walked towards him; trying to gauge from her expressionless face whether or not she had been successful.

Hesitantly, he opened the passenger door for her.

"Well, how did you get on?" he asked, not expecting her reply to be positive. Fiona passed her test only after several attempts, and he had unconsciously assumed it would be the same for Kristine.

Thus, when she wafted a piece of paper in front of him with as straight a face as she could manage, he presumed it meant she had failed.

"Never mind, love. There will always be another time," he said, and started the car; but then Kristine stopped him.

"Dad? What are you doing?"

"I'm taking you home, of course."

"Oh no you're not!"

"What do you mean?"

"We're going out to celebrate!"

"You passed, then?"

"You bet I passed! You're looking at a fully-fledged new driver! ...Well, maybe not fully fledged yet," she added, forgetting an important factor. "But I've got my restricted licence, which means I could drive to the university – if I had a car of my own!"

Kristine fluttered her eyelashes at Royston; her mood so buoyant that all thought of how she might acquire the car vanished. And Royston, not wishing to spoil such an exciting occasion, could not bring himself to remind her.

"Congratulations, love," he gushed; patting her on the knee. "I'm very proud of you."

"It's such a shame we're not in a position to help Kristine with the finances," Alicia remarked to him later on.

"Yes...an awful shame," responded Royston pensively. "I felt terrible when she dropped the hint, especially as she had passed her driving test! I would have done anything to be able to deposit a set of car keys in her palm there and then. The look on her face would have been priceless. We'll just have to help her find work, and carry on saving."

Just then, Alicia came up with an idea.

"Hang on a minute, though. I think there is a way we can help her buy that car after all."

"How on earth can we do that?"

"Well... At the moment the problem is that she doesn't have enough cash for it..."

"...And she can't get credit. Don't forget that."

"Yes, I know. That's where we can help."

"In what way?"

"By taking out the credit for her!"

Royston looked at Alicia as though she had gone mad.

"I don't like the sound of this," he said warily.

Alicia settled cross-legged on the floor in front of him, ready to expound her theory.

"Here's my idea," she began in earnest. "I'd like you to tell me what you think..."

The frustration in Kristine mounted. It had been weeks since she first saw her little blue car, and it was still there.

She felt sure by now that fate must be waiting for her to claim it. But there was nothing she could do. The car might just as well have been sitting on the moon for all the use it was to her.

Then, one afternoon as she rode home from university, she noticed that the car had gone. In a state of panic she propped her bike against the wall of the car yard's site office and asked the manager what had happened to it.

"We sold it, of course," he said in none too courteous a tone of voice.

The girl, he had long since decided, was becoming a bit of a nuisance, hanging around the yard, sounding him out about finance when she must have known she didn't stand a chance. He was glad to be rid of the car. At last it meant she would no longer pester him.

Disappointed, Kristine took her frustrations out on her feather pillow.

She had rushed home and thrown her backpack onto the bed in anger; then lunged at the pillow as though to slay it and sobbed her heart out, lamenting all the passion and expectation she had placed in that little blue car.

When all her disappointment had been expelled, she fell into a deep sleep.

The sun was just going down, when the doorbell rang.

It rang twice. The first ring blended into her dreaming, but the second woke her up with a start.

She leapt off the bed in fright.

"Who on earth can that be?"

Quickly checking her appearance in the mirror in case it was somebody important like Richard, she straightened her clothing and answered the door.

"Oh, it's you, Dad...what are you doing here?" Kristine stammered when she saw who was there.

"That's no way to speak to your father," said Royston in good humour. He could see Kristine had been crying and suspected why.

"Sorry, Dad. I'm really not in a very good mood at the moment. Come in if you must."

She stood back to let him pass, but Royston remained where he was.

"Oh, this isn't a social visit," he said. "I've come to show you something."

Kristine screwed up her nose.

"What are you talking about? And for goodness sake, come in, will you? It's cold with the door open."

"Don't you want to know what it is?"

"Not particularly. Dad, stop playing games; I'm not in the mood. My car's been sold and I'm very upset about it!"

"Which car do you mean? ...This one?"

Royston moved out of Kristine's way, and pointed in the direction of the road.

Curious, she followed his gaze, and let out a gasp; for parked right outside the front gate was her blue car.

The look of amazement on her face made Royston burst out laughing.

"Well, say something," he exclaimed.

"I... I don't know what to say," she uttered.

Then she lost her temper.

"Dad, how could you be so mean? You bought my car! You knew I really wanted that one, and you've gone and bought it for yourself!"

Kristine rushed back inside the house and slammed the door, leaving Royston speechless on the doorstep.

"Whoops," he said self-consciously. "That didn't work out too well. I'd better try again."

He reached for the doorbell and rang it once.

"Kristine!" he called through the door.

Back in her room, Kristine responded distantly.

"Go away! I hate you,"

Royston knocked again; loudly.

"Open the door, Kristine. I think there's been a bit of a misunderstanding..."

Then before he had a chance to explain, the door was wrenched open and Kristine, now at the end of her tether, confronted him ready to kill if necessary.

"Well?" she said, her eyes flashing.

"These aren't for me," he said timidly, holding out a set of car keys.

She stood for a moment staring blankly at them.

"I bought the car for you...silly!"

Kristine burst into tears. It was all too much for her.

"Do you want it, or not?" asked Royston, teasing her.

"Oh, Dad..." Kristine replied sheepishly.

She took the keys off him and kissed them; then she reached forward and wrapped her arms around his neck.

"I'm so sorry," she said with passion. "I didn't mean any of those horrible things. ...And thank you very, very much for buying me the car!"

Kristine pulled back from him and fingered the keys; her heart ready to burst, her mind in a whirl.

"Get your house key," said Royston with authority.

"Why do I need that?" she asked.

"You'll want to get back into the house again."

And then it dawned...

With a cheeky grin, she rushed to the kitchen, returned seconds later with her key, and purposefully shut the door behind her.

"Come on, then," she said to her father. "Let's take my new car for a spin!"

Later on, her cheeks still flushed with nervous excitement, Kristine baled Royston up in the kitchen while she waited for the kettle to come to the boil.

As far as she was concerned, her father still had some explaining to do.

"I don't understand," she said. "The last time you and I talked about financing my car you said you couldn't help me. ...And now you've actually bought it! Did you win the lottery or something?"

"...Don't I wish? No, it's nothing like that. In fact, it was an idea Alicia came up with that started the ball rolling."

"Go on...this sounds fascinating."

Kristine peered out of the kitchen window to where she could just see the shiny new occupant of her driveway. Its metallic surface glinted in the light from the window.

She chuckled with delight.

"Well," Royston went on; "Alicia hoped you would get this car. It was important to her as well, for some reason. She wanted to help you out, so..."

"...What...financially?"

"Yes."

"My goodness! I couldn't let her do that!"

"Kristine, please let me finish. There's more to this than you realise."

"Okay."

Kristine picked up the two mugs of coffee she had made and took them through to the lounge; then sat down to wait for her father's explanation.

Royston took a sip, pondering where to begin.

"I suppose the idea really got moving after we talked about it to Emily..."

"Nana? Where does she come into this?"

"Wait...just let me explain, if you don't mind. I insist you listen to the whole story without commenting."

"Alright. I'm sorry. ...Carry on."

Kristine put her coffee down. Then she leant back in her chair, ready to act out the role of captive audience.

"The plan Alicia and I had originally hatched up was to approach you..."

"...Me?"

Kristine!"

"Sorry! I'll shut up."

"Thank you. ...Now, where was I? Oh yes. Alicia and I were going to suggest you put the contents of your savings account down as deposit on your car, and we would jointly take out credit on the balance of the purchase price. Then, when you were in a position to contribute..."

"...When I get another job?"

"Er...yes. When your funds had built up again, you could take over the payments."

"That sounds like a good idea. Is that what you want me to do – take over the payments?"

"... I haven't finished, yet. It's quite a long story."

"Sorry."

"Anyway, as you must by now have realised, we didn't actually approach you for the deposit..."

"...That's right; you didn't or I would have known about it! So how did you get the money – borrow it?"

Royston gave up on having the floor to himself for his explanation. Instead, he sighed and reluctantly answered her question.

"No...well, not exactly. Your grandmother joined in..."

"...How? She didn't buy it for me, did she?"

"Not outright... Kristine, will you please let me finish!"

Royston was beginning to feel angered by the constant interruption. He drew breath and tried to continue.

"To cut a long story short, she's loaned us the money."

"Do you mean to say she's loaned the money to me?"

"Sort of... We bought the car in our name, initially with her money. But now you must play your part and pay her back as and when you can. Then, when you have done so, the car will be transferred into your name."

"That's wonderful! I really must thank her!"

Kristine's enthusiasm for her new car was tempered only by a rising panic about being able to pay for it.

To start everything off, she withdrew the money she had saved and took it as deposit to Emily. Then, content with the way things it had all turned out, she sat down to reconsider her options with regard to earning, and paying off the rest of the loan.

Alicia had told her that the rest-home job fell through because they were fully staffed. However, desperate now to get a foot in the door, Kristine began to wonder if she could perhaps go in on a voluntary basis and then slot into a position when one became available.

She decided to ask Alicia's opinion.

"People are bound to need time off occasionally. I could help out to start off with, and learn the job while I'm at it," Kristine ventured to suggest.

Alicia nodded, but held back from reminding her that the rest-home also had a list of relieving staff.

"That's not a bad idea, Kristine. Why don't I give Grace a ring and see if she can fit you in? The place is up and running now, so she should be on duty."

Later on, Alicia contacted her with heartening news.

"I've arranged an interview for you at two o'clock the day after tomorrow..."

"Really! That's brilliant... Except... I'll need to check my university timetable."

"Oh, bother. I forgot about university. Can you find out as soon as possible and let me know?"

"I'm looking at the timetable right now. Could you hang on a minute?"

Kristine flicked on the light to better see her highlighted list on the wall, and with relief told Alicia that 2pm Friday would be fine.

"You will need to take a copy of your reference from the café with you."

"What's a reference?"

"Oh!" exclaimed Alicia. "Didn't your employer give you a document to prove you worked for them?"

"Yes, Lynne gave me something when I left, but it was called a 'certificate of employment'."

"That will be it. ...And also take your driver's licence with you for identification."

With nervous hope, Kristine set off in persistent drizzle for the new Everglades Retirement complex.

The name of the street had sounded familiar when Alicia read it out to her, but once she was on the road and still needing to concentrate on her driving, Kristine's mind seemed to go blank as to where it was.

"Why didn't I check the map before I left home?" she said, reprimanding herself.

While she waited at traffic lights, Kristine racked her brain to remember which way she needed to go.

A loud toot from behind informed her that the lights had changed, and with a start she bunny-hopped forward; her distracted mind trying to revert to her driving.

Then out of the blue she recalled where the street was.

She cried out, "Of course...it's off the ring road!"

The windscreen wipers played intermittently as Kristine negotiated a short cut to the ring road. She had cycled in that direction many times before, although the experience was nothing like this.

Entering the dual carriageway she drove extra carefully, glancing at first one street sign and then another, until she came to the exit she was looking for, and turned into it. Moments later she saw the complex away in the distance.

Kristine drew up opposite a wide frontage, where a tarmac driveway sloped away from the road.

As she cautiously steered into it and drove down the slope, she noticed young shrubs that had been planted to line the driveway; so new was the development.

Soon she caught sight of a large single storey building standing at an angle to the driveway.

Its modern appearance indicated a facility that was as up to date as any of its kind. But Kristine was oblivious of that, for just then she was intent only on finding an available space in the car park.

With her car's central locking clicked into place, Kristine walked up to the main entrance. Its door silently swished to one side as she approached. Through the opening she could see a large office, and headed for it.

Inside the building, a lingering smell of fresh paint and new carpet greeted her. It was a strange atmosphere; very different from the cold and clinical one she encountered while visiting Emily in hospital.

This was a far more homely environment. ...And by the look of it, very busy.

A lady dressed in a pale blue uniform asked her if she needed some help.

"I've got an appointment to see Grace," Kristine said nervously, caught off guard by the frenetic activity and the fact that someone had spoken to her.

There seemed to be people everywhere; whether staff or patients she could not tell. But all of them looked to be so much older than her...

"Would you wait for her over there, please," said the lady, pointing to a couch opposite the front door.

An elderly woman sitting nearby gave her a funny look, and Kristine assumed that this one might be a patient. She smiled in return. Then, when the woman looked the other way, grunting an obscenity, Kristine's confidence left her.

It suddenly hit home that she was applying for a job in a line of work that was completely foreign to her.

"Surely, they won't want me here?" she cried inwardly, and was about to sneak back out of the front door when another lady came up to her.

"Don't mind Molly," she said kindly. "Her bark is worse than her bite!"

Kristine looked up at the face of another staff member whose uniform was navy blue with a white trim, and she saw emblazoned across her smiley-face badge the name, 'Grace, Clinical Nurse Manager'.

Kristine leapt to her feet. "...Oh hello. I'm Kristine," she said. "I've got an appointment at two o'clock."

"I'm pleased to meet you, Kristine. ...And you're right on time," said Grace, looking at her watch. "I have some forms for you to take home and fill out...and there'll be a police report, of course. Come in my office where it's quiet. It can be noisy in this part of the building at certain times of the day. Our residents are getting ready for their occupational therapy session, as you may have noticed."

Occupational therapy...what's that? Kristine wondered as she mindlessly followed Grace into a room next to the main office.

...And did Grace say something about a police report?

"Whatever am I letting myself in for?" Kristine grumbled out loud during her drive home. The whole idea of working somewhere like a rest-home was ludicrous.

Later in the day, she related her harrowing experience on the phone to Alicia.

"Don't worry," came her response. "It's bound to be a strange environment for you to begin with. And as for the police report... They just want to make sure you are who you say you are. Would you like me to come over and go through it all with you?"

"Oh, yes please! Would you mind?"

"I'll be right there!"

Kristine felt like a weight had lifted from her after she had signed the application form.

"Well, that's the first part done," said Alicia. "What else do they want you to do?"

"Grace asked me if I was prepared to do a four-week course. I was too frazzled by everything that was going on to tell her about my university lectures, so I just agreed to do it. But I must have been soft in the head. How can I be in two places at the same time?"

"Just be sure and talk it over with her when you return the application form. ...And ring first to check she will be there, or you might have a long wait."

Kristine suddenly sighed and went quiet.

"What's the matter?" asked Alicia.

"I'm still not convinced I want to work somewhere like a busy rest-home, with lots of different things happening all at the same time."

"I understand how you must be feeling at the moment, but you'll make a fantastic caregiver. Believe me; Kristine, you really have got what it takes."

Kristine was not convinced.

"But I don't know anything about rest-homes! Spending time with Nana is one thing, but that place is so huge! And there was this weird patient who swore at me..."

"Oh dear," Alicia chuckled. "That wasn't a good start for you, was it? ...By the way, they're called residents: hospital patients; rest-home residents. Can you understand that?"

"I'm not sure. I can't even tell the difference between a rest-home and a hospital..."

"...You'll learn!"

The course, Kristine found out, was not as intrusive of her time as she had previously feared. All she had to do each week was to view a film on various aspects of rest-home care and, working from a photocopied manual, complete a question sheet. Then, at the end of the course she would be judged. If the assessment proved to be satisfactory, she would be eligible to join the staff, and wait for a position to come up.

By the time she had watched her first DVD she began to feel more familiar with the idea of rest-home care, and more confident about her prospects as a whole. And once she had worked through the entire course, especially as she passed it with flying colours, she felt she was finally getting somewhere with her new profession.

At long last she could take on paid work, and start to pay off her grandmother's loan.

In the meantime, alone and with plenty of time to think, Fiona was having some misgivings about her reaction to the news of her husband's latest fling.

She now began to realise that Alicia was not like Sylvia. It was not just a matter of Royston finding someone else to keep him warm at night, for he was genuinely fond of Alicia. Furthermore, the family thought she was a gracious and helpful person, too.

And yet, it annoyed her that her husband had found someone else when she had no-one.

169

The thought of this made her feel abandoned, and so angry that at times she suspected she might actually need a session of counselling.

Yet, rather than make an appointment with a therapist, she opted for a less demeaning approach, and sought her mother's opinion.

"At least Emily will be objective; I'm still her daughter!" Fiona assured herself. ...After all, the last time they talked, they were almost civil to each other.

It would certainly be worth a try.

Emily welcomed her warmly; albeit with some uncertainty. Having Fiona come to see her was a routine she had long since got out of.

To her surprise, though, she did not feel too suspicious about a possible reason for the visit this time. Moreover, the anticipation of a chat with her previously estranged daughter gave Emily a buzz of excitement.

Fiona dived straight in.

"Mother, I would like to talk to you about Royston and that Alicia woman."

Emily tightened.

"What do you want to know?" she asked guardedly.

"I was wondering what you make of Alicia," said Fiona, noting the caution in Emily's response. "Do you think she's a good person?"

"Yes; most definitely!" Emily replied with enthusiasm. "Royston would not be so smitten with her if she wasn't a good person."

Then she added in defence of her opinion, "Kristine and I think the world of her."

Fiona paused to absorb her mother's remarks.

"Why do you ask?" asked Emily patiently. She could see that Fiona was bothered by it.

170

Ignoring the question, Fiona continued.

"...Did Kristine tell you about the row we had over her father's new affair?"

Fiona was stabbing in the dark now. She could only guess at the half-truths her daughter might have divulged.

"Yes, she did," replied Emily; then added diplomatically, "She said you weren't too happy that Royston and Alicia were thinking of living together..."

"...She didn't tell me that! ...Are they living together?"

"No! Not yet, anyway. Royston is still with me. But they are officially a couple. And I think it will only be a matter of time before they do move in together."

"So they're serious?"

"Oh, yes. They are in love."

"Huh! ...Whatever love is. I wouldn't know. Royston and I were never really in love."

"You must have been at one time, or you wouldn't have had Kristine. ...And if I remember correctly, Royston swept you off your feet when he eventually proposed to you."

"Mum; that was ages ago. I was still in my teens. I was infatuated with the attention of an older man. ...And, if you recall, I was pregnant."

"...How could I ever forget?"

Emily chuckled with the recollection.

Then she said, "...Anyway, Royston isn't all that much older than you. Your father and I accepted him into the family, once you were engaged. You twins both married older men...and you did have a beautiful child."

Fiona chuckled inwardly, enjoying the trip down memory lane. But then she also remembered how everything had changed in recent years...how she had changed.

Was it because she had fallen out of love with her older husband?

171

Had she in fact lost interest in her marriage, giving rise to her irrational behaviour in recent years? If this was the case, then why would she want to hold on to husband who had no interest whatsoever in her?

"Do you think Royston and Alicia will ever want to get married?" she asked tenuously.

Fiona suspected she knew what would come next.

"I believe so; that is, when they have sorted out their living arrangements. And when..."

"...What do you mean by living arrangements?"

"There has been talk of them coming to live here. Alicia is in a rented house. Their finances are a bit stretched at the moment, and Royston asked if they could live here with me to save money. But I said they could not..."

"Why? You all get on well, don't you?"

"That's got nothing to do with it. Of course I'd enjoy the company, but they would not be living here as friends, if you know what I mean."

Fiona sighed. "Ah...yes. I do know what you mean."

"Anyway, I told Royston that Arthur would not permit them to live here unless they were married..."

"...Arthur? Which Arthur?"

"Your father, of course! I consult him over everything."

Suddenly Fiona went quiet. This was something new.

Why was her mother talking about her deceased father as though he were still alive?

"Mother, what are you talking about?" she asked, her old cynicism emerging again.

Emily failed to notice her about-face.

"Have you forgotten already, dear? We were talking about Royston and Alicia. ...And I thought I was the one with a bad memory!"

Emily could barely wait for Royston to come home. She was sure, after her curious conversation with Fiona, that he and Alicia would soon receive his ex-wife's blessing on their relationship.

"I couldn't believe it, either!" she exclaimed when he appeared to be dumbfounded by her news. "It seems our Fiona wants only the best for you."

At last Royston was able to speak. "Did she say anything about giving me a divorce?" he asked.

"Oh, no! It's a bit soon to think along those lines, don't you agree? Just be thankful for small mercies. Fiona's gone from being extremely negative about it to almost happy!"

Royston was indeed grateful for Fiona's small mercies; so much so that he decided to thank her personally. Yet, his decision was not based only on gratitude. He also wanted to sound her out about the prospect of getting a divorce; if only tentatively for the time being...

This was the first time he and Fiona had been alone in their own house since the break-up of their marriage.

A strange feeling overwhelmed Royston, coming back to the house he had lived in for so long; a house that he still owned. It had changed very little in that time.

"Well, to what do I owe the pleasure?" Fiona asked in a formal manner.

Fiona had been expecting him; Royston deemed it wise to confirm he would be welcome.

To Fiona, it was a foregone conclusion that he would come; for there was no doubt, after her chat with Emily, that the gist of their discussion would go round the family in less time than it takes to boil an egg. And now, here he was, right on cue; but as for his motive in coming...

This she was yet to find out.

173

However, instead of politely enquiring what might have brought him to her home after all this time, she jumped straight in with a question that had haunted her ever since she left Emily's earlier in the day.

"What do you know about Arthur?" she asked without mincing words.

Royston hesitated.

"...Arthur? Do you mean Arthur, as in...your father?" he said; and when Fiona nodded knowingly, he felt a sense of foreboding creep through him.

Without a doubt, he deduced, Emily must have spilled the beans. But what did Fiona make of her eccentricity?

He assumed she was going to tell him.

"Oh...Arthur..." he said slowly; thinking on the spot how he could respond.

If he said too much, it might affect Emily's situation. Yet if he said too little, Fiona would become suspicious that he was keeping something from her.

To take the edge off a potential crisis, he answered with, "Emily has recently gained a great deal of comfort from your father's living memory."

Fiona was ready with her repartee.

"It's more than that and you know it. Come on Royston; she's hallucinating, isn't she?"

Royston felt deflated. He had not come to have Emily's sanity questioned, but for a friendly discussion with his ex-wife about the possibility of a divorce. However, in order to hopefully achieve his objective before the night was out he needed to accommodate her probing.

"I wouldn't say she is hallucinating," he said, regretting the need to talk about it at all. "She just misses him so much that she needs to keep his memory included in her daily life and activities – you know how close they were. ...I'm sure you can understand that!"

"Well, naturally I understand, but it's not normal for an old woman to go around imagining things. In fact I would say it's a worrying sign. You hear about old people getting senile dementia and that sort of thing. I hope my mother isn't heading that way."

"...No of course not, Fiona!"

Royston was struggling to retain his composure now. He desperately wanted to get off the subject, but his wife seemed to be obsessed with it.

"Emily is as sane as you or me. She just has a crutch that helps her cope with each day. We all have that, don't we? If you remember, your crutch was to go shopping all the time..."

"...If it was a crutch, I certainly don't need it now."

"No, indeed you don't. You've made great strides lately, and I'm very proud of you."

"Thank you, Royston. I appreciate that...it's better than being regarded by the family as an ogre. Anyway, what did you come over for? I haven't really given you the chance to get a word in, have I?"

"I just wanted to thank you..."

"...Thank me? ...Whatever for?"

"Emily said you spoke to her about Alicia and me. She said you were more tolerant in your attitude towards us. I wanted you to know your acceptance of our relationship means a lot to me."

Fiona grunted. "I'm not that saintly," she said. "I'd been doing some thinking, that's all. The old me would have dug her heels in and made your life difficult, but the new me... Maybe I'm growing up in my attitude. If you and Alicia want to tie the knot one day, I won't try and stop you."

With relief at Fiona's unexpected compliance, Royston gave her a hug. "Thank you, love; you're a gem."

Fiona responded to him in kind.

"I don't recall you saying that to me before," she said.

Then she remembered something Emily told her.

"By the way, where do you and Alicia intend to live? Mum tells me you are still living at her house."

"That's right. I don't know what we are going to do just yet. Emily is adamant we can't live together in her house until we are married..."

"I know; she told me. She said Arthur wouldn't like it."

"Um... Yes...Emily has some old-fashioned ideas about modern relationships. But it's her house, so I guess she can do what she likes."

"What about Alicia's? Couldn't you move in with her?"

"Not really. It's a rental property, which means that if we lived there I would be paying twice over."

"What do you mean by that?"

"I would be paying a contribution to Alicia's rent and, as you know, I am still paying the mortgage on this house and will be for a long time to come."

Suddenly Fiona felt weak-at-the-knees.

"Good God, I forgot all about the mortgage here..."

She flopped down on the couch in a state of shock.

Royston retorted, with just a hint of sarcasm in his tone, "Did you think it was mortgage free now?"

"I guess I didn't think about it at all. I'm so sorry."

Fiona was troubled now. She felt like a proverbial kept woman; except that this one was developing a conscience which would not ease until she had made amends.

"There's only one thing for it, then... If you're paying the mortgage on this house, then you have the right to live in it; don't you agree?"

Royston looked at her agog. He had not considered the possibility; yet now he thought about it, Fiona's suggestion made perfect sense.

When they first split up, Fiona retained the house solely because of Kristine. But now...although their daughter was still a minor, she had moved out of her childhood home and would probably never live there again...

Taken aback by Fiona's statement, Royston suddenly found himself at a loss for words.

"What's wrong, Royston? Has the cat got your tongue?"

"I think it must have!" he replied. "This is so generous of you, Fiona. I really had not considered bringing Alicia to live here. ...But what about you? I presume you would not think of staying on here if we were to move in;" this last remark made with mounting apprehension.

"Goodness me, no. Why would I choose to stick around while my ex-husband cosies up to the new love in his life?"

Royston breathed freely again. He was beginning to have a new respect for Fiona; but not to the extent of the three of them cohabiting.

"I appreciate your gesture more than you can imagine, Fiona, and I am tempted to accept it. But this now brings up the question of where you will live. Could you afford to finance a place of your own?"

"Oh, I wouldn't need to go to the expense of getting my own house – or even a flat. ...Not yet, anyway."

"What, then? You have to live somewhere."

"Well, yes, of course. ...But I have the perfect solution; and I'm surprised you haven't suggested it. I'll double-up with Kristine until my sister returns from her trip. What do you think of that?"

CHAPTER SIX

Kristine left the rest-home with a package containing her uniform proudly tucked under her arm.

As she crossed over to the car park, she smiled with relief that the long wait was over. She was now officially on the staff at Everglades Retirement Village and Rest-home. Soon she would be working; which meant that soon she would be earning again.

The thought of it inspired her.

As yet her only training for the job had been from DVDs and manuals. She had received no practical training in the actual role she was to fill as caregiver to the elderly. That, Grace had told her, would come when she was called in for her first shift with a buddy.

"What do you mean by 'buddy'?" Kristine had asked.

"It means that you'll be teamed up with an experienced caregiver, who will show you the routine for that particular duty. We call it 'orientation'. ...And you will also have your first experience of working with an elderly person – other than your grandmother, that is."

At home, Kristine hurried into her bedroom to try on her new uniform.

She held up the smock in front of her wardrobe mirror, but rather than feel pride in the sight, she shrieked, "I can't wear that! I haven't worn a frock since I was little!"

Then she quickly relegated the uniform to a hanger and shoved it in her wardrobe.

Not long afterwards, Kristine received a phone call from Grace asking if she was available for a duty the following morning. Having already told Grace about her university course and given her a list of the times when she would be free, Kristine felt obliged to accept.

"Yes, that's alright with me," she replied with cautious enthusiasm. "What time do you want me to come in?"

"The shift is from seven in the morning till three in the afternoon..."

"...Seven? You want me to be there at seven o'clock in the morning?" said Kristine in horror.

She wouldn't even be awake by seven in the morning!

"Yes, of course. That is when the morning duty starts. ...But the girls usually arrive ten minutes early so they can receive handover report from the night staff before they go off duty. I take it you are happy with that?"

Grace's remark was voiced as a question, but to the astonished Kristine it sounded like an instruction.

She said, but did not mean, "Yes...quite happy, thanks."

Throughout the rest of the day, Kristine was in a daze.

As the evening wore on, she began to worry that she needed to pull her socks up and get a few things ready for the following morning. But what should she take with her? She really had no idea. Nobody told her what she might need...and what about lunch? Was there somewhere she could buy a sandwich and a cup of coffee?

Why, she grumbled, did she not think to ask when she was in there for her course, or collecting her uniform?

Before she got ready for bed; far earlier than she had ever gone to bed before, she reached for her alarm clock. One thing Kristine had never needed to do in the past was to set an alarm; yet, with a sense of urgency she felt the need to do so now.

Then she agonized over how much time she should allow to wake up, get up, shower, have breakfast and head off to the rest-home.

"My God!" she cried out in anguish. "I'll have to get up in the middle of the night to do all that!"

But then she guessed a more reasonable time to get up would be six o'clock; and If she was late arriving, too bad; she could adjust the alarm setting for next time.

That night, she could not sleep.

Without meaning to, she went over and over in her mind everything she learnt in the course, panicked about the fact that she never did get round to trying on her uniform, repeated her mental check-list for the morning, and every now and then reminded herself she had to wake up when the alarm went off.

Consequently, no sooner had she managed to drift into asleep than she would jerk awake again. By the time the alarm did go off, she felt like she had not slept at all.

Even a quick shower did not dispel the drowsiness that was clouding her mind at a time when she needed to have all her wits about her.

The uniform she was reluctant to try on proved to be baggy around the top and far too long. She desperately hoped no-one from the university would see her in it...

Exhausted, Kristine dragged herself off to work. As she did so, she started to think she had died and gone to hell.

"This is the worst day of my life!" she cried out when forced to brake hard at traffic lights just as they changed.

Feeling like a fish out of water, Kristine floundered her way through her first duty as a caregiver. At the end of it, and thinking back, it seemed to her that she continually made mistakes rather than learn anything constructive.

On the way out, Grace called her into the office and asked how she got on.

"Oh alright ...I think," Kristine replied; yet was too tired to really know.

In truth, Kristine had never worked so hard in her life.

She spent a good measure of the eight-hour shift on her feet; both of which were now too sore to walk on. The caregiver assigned to her was not in the least bit helpful, but utilised her to ease her own workload; and to cap it all off, some of the sights, sounds and smells round the place made her feel quite sick.

The elderly people in the rest-home were nothing like her Nana. An old man she had been asked to assist was heavy, demanding, and repulsive in some of his personal habits. She dreaded the time when she might have to shower him or take him to the toilet...

"Alicia must be mad if she thinks I'll be good at this job," Kristine thought dismally, while Grace showed her how to sign off after her duty.

"Of course, it would be better for you to work several consecutive days," Grace went on, replacing the pen in its holder. "That way, you'll improve your skills; otherwise you are in danger of forgetting what you've learnt. Are you able to come in again tomorrow morning?"

As Kristine was almost in shock after her exhausting duty and did not have a photographic memory of her timetable, she replied, "I'm not sure when I'm free. I'll have to get back to you. Is that alright?"

"Yes, that's fine. But don't forget to ring, will you?"

"I won't."

When Kristine got home and the trauma of the day hit her, she thought no more about the promise she had made, but instead collapsed on her bed, still in her uniform, and went straight to sleep. When she awoke two hours later, she remembered she was supposed to let Grace know about the following morning's shift.

In despair, she burst into tears.

"I wouldn't be needing this stupid job if it wasn't for the car," she wailed as she picked up the phone; knowing full well that by now Grace would have left for the day.

But then she noticed a message had been left on her answer phone: it was from Everglades.

The message stated, "Kristine; this is Grace. I'm calling to let you know we won't need you tomorrow after all. But give me a ring to arrange for your next duty. ...Oh, by the way, everyone says you did a great job today. I know it would not have been easy for you."

"Thank God!" Kristine gasped. "I don't have to go in to that accursed place again just yet." The fact that Grace also complimented her for her efforts went unnoticed.

She replayed the message to make sure she really had been given a reprieve.

After a decent night's sleep, she determined, she might be able to evaluate her situation there a little bit better.

Alicia had great difficulty grasping what Royston was trying to tell her. Knowing Fiona's reputation, she could hardly believe that his wife might willingly offer to relinquish the house. It was just too absurd a notion to take seriously.

"There must be some kind of mistake," she said to him; none too kindly. "You and I both know Fiona is embedded in that house for life!"

"...Not anymore, apparently! My ex-wife seems to be a changed woman. It was she who suggested it!"

"But you must have dropped a hint, surely. How did the subject come up?"

"I told her I would be paying double if we lived at your place: a contribution to your rent and the mortgage on my house. Fiona had overlooked it; but once she remembered that I still owed on the house she has been occupying, she seemed to realise what she must do. We even had a hug to seal the pact – and it's been a very long time since we felt inclined to hug each other!"

"Well I never! This must have been written in the stars! For Fiona to give up her home and hand it over to you must surely have been divine intervention."

Royston laughed. "I couldn't assume that; but she sure has done an about-turn from her recent attitude towards us. I've got no idea why."

"Do you think I should talk to her about it? ...Thank her, or something?" asked Alicia with a twinge of conscience. Fiona's gesture may have been more than just kindness; it may also have been a sacrifice."

"No way! Don't even think of getting in touch with her. Fiona could have a change of heart at any time. She may have just been in a good mood when she suggested it..."

"...But Royston," Alicia cut in, worried by a developing thought. "If we are going to take over your house, where is Fiona going to live?"

Royston chuckled. "I have to give that woman credit, you know. She can be quite resourceful when need be."

"...In what way?"

"She came up with the most obvious solution. It would be perfect for both of them, especially as they are getting on better..."

"Them? Who are you talking about?"

"Fiona and..."

"...And Emily! ...Of course! That would be perfect! And as you said, they have been getting on much better lately."

Royston was taken aback.

It was not Emily who Fiona had suggested staying with; it was Kristine. Yet, on reflection it made better sense that she live with her mother – if for no other reason than she could be on hand if Emily needed her. However, this was Fiona's decision, and she had made her choice. He would not interfere with that.

...But he did need to correct Alicia on the matter.

"Actually, you're wrong there," he said. "Fiona didn't say anything about Emily; she suggested staying at Ruth's."

"...With Kristine?"

"Well....yes. ...Till Ruth and Wilbur come back, that is."

"You're joking! Does Kristine know about it?"

"I haven't told her..."

"...No, she can't know, or she would have been banging on your door in despair by now."

"Why do you say that?"

Alicia paused, remembering Kristine's horrified reaction the last time it was implied that one of her parents might move in with her.

"Do you recall when we talked about the possibility of your going to Ruth's?" she asked.

"Yes, of course. But what does it have to do with this?"

"I didn't mention it to you at the time because you would probably have taken offence, but Kristine was quite upset at the prospect of you staying there."

"How do you mean?"

"She was dead set against it, to be brutally honest."

"I don't understand. Why would she object? We get on just fine."

"I know you do. But that's got nothing to do with it. Just think, Royston: Kristine had the opportunity to escape her domineering mother, and be independent. Then she learns her father's thinking of moving in with her. How would you expect her to react?"

"You're right! I'm glad you told me about it. ...Oh, no!"

Suddenly Royston looked aghast.

"What's wrong?"

"...Why Fiona, of course!" he cried in alarm. "If Kristine didn't want me living with her, how will she react if the same domineering mother turned up on her doorstep?"

"...Precisely!"

Kristine woke late the next morning. Still exhausted from a long shift spent on her feet, she did not feel like facing the world again. Instead, she settled back into a comfortable state mid-way between sleeping and full wakefulness.

However, the day ahead beckoned to her determinedly. There was something she had been meaning to do for some time and had been it putting off; something about which she was beginning to develop an uneasy conscience.

When Ruth and Wilbur left their niece in charge of the house, they did so with an assurance from her that not only would she look after the place, but that she would also keep them up to date by email with regard to family matters and other items of interest.

So far Kristine had given little thought to it; but time and conscience having caught up with her, she felt she now had little choice in the matter. So, while she prepared breakfast at a time when most people would be having lunch, she began to think about what, out of all that had been going on, she should tell them.

As the headmaster of a large school, Wilbur had needed a computer of his own. This still sat on a desk in the corner of the dining room, together with a monitor and an up-to-date colour printer.

Kristine, whose computer use was minimal, had never bothered with email. ...Not until now, that is. Not until the need to write to her aunt and uncle stared her in the face.

With heart in mouth, she pressed the on-button at the front of the computer box, and the machine slowly burst into life. To her dismay, she realised that it had not been switched on since Wilbur gave her a run-through before they left on their trip.

Watching the screen for signs of life, Kristine wondered if she could use her uncle's computer for her own work, too. Soon enough she would need to print off university papers in readiness for her exams...

As the screen lit up; its curser slowly converting to an arrow, she studied the icons for something that looked like it might open up email.

"...Ah, yes. This must be it," she said, and clicked on the likely-looking icon.

Then, after the dial-up network noisily connected, one message after another appeared in the Inbox.

"Good grief," she said as they all came through. She counted over twenty in all.

Then she noticed that most of the messages were from Ruth and Wilbur. She clicked open the latest email. It read, 'Kristine, it is imperative that you respond to our request. Please do so as soon as you receive this message!'

In a panic, Kristine realised just how negligent she had been in not bothering with the computer before now.

Wilbur, in showing her how to use it, had intended she communicate with them regularly, and she had failed to do so. It sounded, by the tone of the latest email; already a week old, that they were annoyed by her slackness.

"What must they think of me?" she exclaimed in alarm and full of remorse.

Kristine traced back through the emails in order to the find the one that bore the message Ruth was referring to. Her remorse intensified when each one opened revealed a similar plea, and it was not until she had worked through to the beginning of the list that she finally opened one up that gave her the all-important detail.

She was reading through it, trying to decipher what Wilbur was in the process of telling her, when she heard a knock on the front door.

"Oh, rats!" she said; more anxious to ease her guilt over the email messages than to see who was there.

But then curiosity took over, so she pushed back her chair, and hurried to the door.

"Hello, Dad...am I glad to see you," she said with relief when she realised the caller was actually somebody who might be able to help her with the email.

Royston's jaw dropped. Was he too late? Had Fiona caught up with Kristine already?

...Although, he had to admit as he followed her inside, she did not seem terribly upset about the prospect of her mother coming to live with her.

"I must say, you're very chirpy about it," he remarked; then wondered why she went straight to the dining room.

However Kristine, her mind still on the emails rather than his comment replied, "I still haven't worked out what it means. Come and see what you can make of it."

By now Royston was confused. He had, though, begun to suspect they were talking about two different things. If Fiona had got to her first, she didn't seem to mind...and if not, then what on earth was she referring to?

Kristine sat her father in front of the computer.

"I've been getting all these emails from Uncle Wilbur telling me to respond to a message he says he sent. I'm trying to find out what he's on about. Will you please have a look for me?"

Royston let out a long breath, realising he was right. They had definitely been talking at crossed purposes.

"Yes, of course I will," he said. Then, as he competently worked his way through the emails, he casually asked her, "…By the way, have you heard from your mother lately?"

"No. Why do you ask?"

"I was just wondering… Ah, here we are. I think this is the one he's referring to… My goodness, Kristine," he said in distress. "It's weeks old!"

"I know, I'm sorry," said Kristine sheepishly. "This is the first time I've had the computer on."

"Oh well. At least we're onto it now. You go and make us a cuppa, and I'll see if I can work out what your uncle wants us to do. Then we can talk."

Kristine did as she was asked. While she busied herself in the kitchen she questioned what all the fuss over the email had been about; she hoped nothing was amiss and that her slackness had not made things worse.

By the time she took the drinks through to Royston he had finished with the computer and was in the process of shutting it down.

Kristine handed him his drink.

"Have you dealt with it already?" she asked in surprise.

'Yes," he replied, and swivelled round in his chair.

Kristine sat sideways at the dining table, waiting for some form of explanation.

"Well?" she said. "What did he want?"

"Nothing too complicated; not for me anyway, although I think you might have struggled with it," he said. "There's a legal matter Uncle Wilbur needs our help with. He wants us to look up some papers. I sent him a quick email telling him I'll get on to it. He'll reply to me, not you, so you don't need to be involved with it anymore."

"Thanks for doing that, Dad. But why all the follow-up emails? He seemed almost panic-stricken. I thought for a minute that I'd overlooked something really important!"

"He was probably worried because he hasn't heard from you. Uncle Wilbur would always get in a flap over very little. I suppose that's why he finished up by having a heart attack. Mind you, who wouldn't get stressed, having responsibility for all those children, when none of them are your own…?"

"…Dad?" said Kristine, a thought coming to mind.

"Yes, love?"

Royston took a sip of coffee, enjoying its fresh flavour.

"You said just now you wanted to talk. …What about?"

Royston looked up at her. "I did say that, didn't I?"

He groaned inwardly, having briefly forgotten about his panic over Fiona. Should he still tell Kristine, or let it go in case Fiona changed her mind?

No, he decided. It was too risky to have Kristine learn about it the hard way.

"It's about your mother," he said.

"Oh, what now?" grumbled Kristine, a peeved look on her face. "What has she done that would interest me?"

Like Alicia and her father, Kristine was impressed that her mother had offered them the house; that is, the aspect of the offer Royston elected to mention.

He could not yet summon up enough courage to tell Kristine how it involved her. …Not at first, anyway.

"Wow!" Kristine exclaimed. "I wouldn't have thought her capable of doing something as generous as that! Is she touched in the head?"

Royston laughed.

"We wondered that, too. But whatever her reason, the fact of the matter is, I get my house back!"

"That's so neat, Dad," said Kristine warmly. "I'm really pleased for you and Alicia. I bet you never imagined having it to yourself again."

189

"Not in a million years! But if your mother doesn't have a change of heart in the meantime, it is going to happen; and quite soon, so I believe!"

"So, where's the old battle... I mean, where's Mum, going to live then? Some new toy boy's pad, I suppose."

Royston's heart sank.

This is it, he thought gloomily.

One thing he had always hated was women's emotional outbursts, and he knew without doubt that Kristine would become very emotional after he had given her his news.

"Dad...you've gone quiet. ...Why?"

Kristine looked at him.

Her curious glance, though only questioning, began to harbour a seed of suspicion.

Royston hesitantly returned her look; his expression of heartfelt apology revealing the fact that he had something displeasing to tell her.

"What's going on, Dad?" she asked. Then, answering her own question, she said in a serious voice, "Oh no! She wants to come and stay here, doesn't she?"

"I'm afraid so..."

"I knew it! I knew this was too good to last!"

Kristine's reaction exploded into the room.

She thumped her fist on the table while giving Royston every imaginable reason why her mother should be forced to change her mind.

Thoroughly intimidated by the verbal assault from his daughter, Royston would have crawled under the table to escape it if he could.

"It might not be so bad..." he started to say.

"...Dad! Just listen to yourself," she interjected. "I came here to get away from her. Have you forgotten that?"

"No..."

"...And don't you also remember how she used to drive me up the wall when we were living together?"

"Of course I do, Kristine."

"Then how could you consent to it; just so that you and Alicia can shack up together?"

"Kristine! It's not like that at all!" cried Royston, trying to defend his rationale. "...And anyway, when your mother offered us the house, I wasn't aware you felt so strongly about sharing with someone here. It was Alicia who set me straight. But by that time it was too late. Fiona had already made her decision..."

"...Decision! You mean it's already been decided? ...And I have no say in the matter? You and Mum are at it again: making your decisions around me just like you did when I was a child. That's all I am to you: a child you can control!"

Kristine rushed into the kitchen and grabbed her car keys. She needed to get out; to flee from yet another impossible family situation.

While Royston stayed put; desperately wondering how he could make amends, she headed for the front door.

As she turned the knob, he called through and pleaded with her not to overreact.

With one hand still on the doorknob, she yelled back, "There's no way that vixen is coming to stay in this house; not if I can help it!"

All of a sudden Kristine felt pressure on the other side of the door. Somebody was pushing it open.

Angrily she wrenched it back, and with eyes flashing saw her mother standing on the porch.

"Oh, God!" she shrieked. "This is just too much! I can't stand it anymore!"

Then she pushed past the astonished Fiona, and left.

Struck dumb by the tirade, Fiona watched her rush off.

A moment later, she poked her head round the door and, assuming Royston was inside as his car was out in the street, she called him.

"Royston, can I come in?"

Immediately, Royston appeared in the hallway.

"Talk about timing!" he said sarcastically.

Fiona ignored his remarks and walked straight in.

"You told Kristine about our arrangement, then."

Royston suddenly looked sheepish.

"Yes; I told her just a minute ago. It seemed like a good idea to forewarn her."

"But it was only a suggestion. And now Kristine's rushed off when I need to speak with her."

"Well, it's a bit late for that, now."

"You don't understand; I really must talk to her. ...And I need her to come with me."

"...Whatever for?"

Fiona slumped onto a chair with tears in her eyes.

"For goodness sake, woman; tell me what's wrong. You look a mess."

"Well, thanks for nothing," she said, and blew her nose. Then she went on, "I'll have you know I've just come from the hospital."

"...Hospital? What's this about?"

He sat down beside her, and with concern took hold of her hand.

"It's Mother," she said in distress. "I received a call from someone at the bowling club to say she'd been taken to hospital again..."

"...But why? What happened to her?"

Royston was troubled now. Had he been negligent in leaving his charge alone so much recently...and would this somehow affect his plans for the future...?

192

"Mother collapsed while she was there this morning," Fiona continued. "The paramedics found my number and rang me, so I went straight to the hospital. The doctors are assessing her now. They said something about a stroke…"

"…A stroke? Oh dear me, no! Poor Emily! This is awful. …And after everything she has been through."

"I tried to ring Kristine here, but the line was engaged and my calls kept going onto the answer phone. She must have been chatting for ages. I just couldn't get through, so I really had no choice but to come round. I had hoped to discuss my thoughts with her, but that's all changed now."

"Kristine hasn't been on the phone that I know of," said Royston, puzzled by Fiona's remark, and then he realised something. "…But we have been on the Internet. They've still got dial-up here. …That must be why you couldn't get through. I'm so sorry."

"It's alright. You weren't to know. But I do still need to find Kristine."

"Why Kristine?"

"Because she is family, of course. She's the only blood relative here just now, apart from me. …And I need her."

Royston suddenly leapt to his feet.

"Come on," he said. "I'll go with you. I don't know when Kristine will be back."

Fiona got up and hurried after him. "Is that such a good idea?" she asked.

"Why shouldn't I be the one to go with you? I am still family, too – and I do live with Emily, so that in itself gives me certain responsibilities."

He put his arm round Fiona's shoulder.

"Don't worry. I'm sure Kristine will come as soon as she can. You take your car and I'll follow in mine. Just give me a minute to lock up."

When Kristine returned sometime later she could see by the absence of parked cars that both her parents had now gone and left her in peace.

With relief, she entered the house.

She glanced at the phone in the kitchen, and noticed the light blinking to indicate that a message for her had been recorded.

Assuming the message must be from Grace calling her in for a duty, she could not be bothered dealing with it just yet, and left it unanswered.

Had Kristine taken the trouble to listen to the message, she would have heard Fiona's anxious voice informing her that her grandmother was in hospital. And, if she had even gone to the phone she would also have seen a hastily scribbled note to the same effect that her father had placed next to it before their departure.

But Kristine's spirit had received a blow and she was still smarting from it. All she wanted was to be left alone and undisturbed.

She was tired. All in all, it had been a bad day...

With a heavy heart Kristine ignored the kitchen and its urgent messages, and headed off to her room for a rest.

PART TWO

CHAPTER ONE

Fiona and her ex-husband entered the ward where Emily had been taken, and approached the desk.

A nurse pointed to a single room just along the corridor and said, "Mrs Forsythe is not to be disturbed..."

"...Her name is Thompson, not Forsythe," Fiona stated with marked indignation. "Her second husband died, and she is going by my father's name again; we're her next of kin. Is there any news on her condition, please?"

The nurse paused briefly while jotting down everything Fiona told her. Then she looked up and merely said, "Yes, your mother is resting comfortably."

"Was it a stroke?" asked Royston.

"I'm sorry, the nursing staff are not at liberty to discuss a patient's condition. You will have to wait for the doctor to give you details."

"When will that be?" asked Fiona, and glanced around as if expecting him to appear at any moment.

The nurse checked her watch. "...Probably in an hour."

"Do we have to hang around here for that long?" Fiona asked Royston.

"Do you have somewhere more important to go right now?" he asked with a hint of annoyance. "Emily is your mother, Fiona. Surely you care enough to give her some of your time."

Fiona sighed dejectedly.

It wasn't that she couldn't face having to be there for Emily, so much as she could not handle being there at all.

She hated hospitals. The memory of her father's last days in that very hospital still made her feel ill, such was the unsettling effect it had on her at the time. She hoped her mother would recover quickly enough that they could all go home and get on with their lives.

Throughout the time they waited for the doctor, Royston and Fiona spoke very little.

Royston sat alongside Emily, who floated in and out of sleep. Holding her hand, he occasionally gave it a squeeze; to reassure her, if she could recognise it, that somebody was present.

Fiona, on the other hand, found it hard to sit still. The thought of sick patients and the odour associated with hospitals in general was getting to her. So it was a great relief to her when the doctor finally walked in.

The sound of voices close by caused Emily to open her eyes and take notice.

Her normally bright features seemed sallow and drawn, and she made no attempt to speak.

Royston smiled at her; then quietly said, "Hello, Emily. How are you feeling?"

Emily made no reply.

Instead she purposefully moved her expressionless eyes from one person to another, as though trying to identify just who was in the room.

"I'm afraid Mrs...Thompson has suffered a stroke," the doctor said to Fiona after introducing himself.

"I don't really know what that means," Fiona replied. "Is she going to get better?"

"It's hard to tell just at the moment. It depends on her rate of recovery and how dense the stroke was."

"What do you mean by that?" asked Royston.

"There may have been very little permanent damage, in which case she will recover quite well. Or, as is often the case with the elderly, the damage could be more severe…"

"…Which would leave her paralysed down one side…is that it?" asked Fiona in an increasing state of anxiety.

"…Quite probably."

The doctor could see that his patient's daughter was not yet able to come to terms with what had happened, and as there was nothing further he could say which would help her to understand the situation, he excused himself, citing the need to move on to other patients.

However, as he turned to leave Emily's room, he was almost bowled over by someone rushing in through the open door.

It was Kristine. She apologised profusely.

Breathless from concern and the fact that she had just leapt up several flights of stairs, Kristine stood for a moment gasping, while the doctor made his delayed exit. Then she turned her attention to her family; in particular, to Emily.

In between gasps she said, "I've only just seen…your message. Sorry, Mum… I misunderstood…why you came to the house. I thought it was because of…"

"…Yes, yes. We can talk about that later. Right now, as you can see, we have other things to worry about."

Kristine walked over to the bed.

At the sight of her granddaughter, Emily raised a watery smile with, as Royston noted, just one side of her mouth lifting in a crease.

A tear formed in Kristine's eye to see her precious Nana in yet another predicament.

How unfair life can be at times, she thought.

"Did she have a stroke?" she asked Royston quietly, and smiled down at Emily.

"I'm afraid so. It only happened this morning. ...Here," he said, getting up. "Come and sit with her for a while. I could do with stretching my legs."

Emily's eyes followed the girl as she walked around the end of the bed and took the seat Royston had offered.

"Darling Nana... What are we going to do with you?" Kristine said lovingly.

Emily was kept in hospital for a total of three weeks, and then discharged home.

Yet again, Alicia was assigned the care of her ongoing medical needs; together with a daily home-help to attend to her showers.

Royston, too, once more found himself caught up in the all too familiar routine of looking after an invalid. Yet, this time he did not shoulder the burden of care alone.

Fiona took it upon herself to regularly call in on her way to work, and sometimes afterwards as well, to see if there was anything she could do to help. And Kristine made the trip across town whenever she had some free time, so that Royston could have a break.

Kristine felt desperately sorry for her father and Alicia. They had been so close to finally having a life together, but yet again circumstances had wrenched them apart.

"It's a silly rule that says you can't become friends with the relative of a patient," she grumbled to Alicia one day. "Can't they get someone else to do your check-ups so you and Dad can be happy together?"

Alicia had been thinking about that, too.

Though dedicated to her work, and both professionally and personally interested in Emily's recovery, she had also been looking forward to living a normal life with the man she loved.

Kristine was right...surely there must be a way around the code of ethics which intrinsically barred her from having a relationship with Royston.

"It's not like Dad's a blood-relative of Nana's," Kristine pointed out when Alicia agreed in principle that the rule was silly. "He may be my father, but he's only related to Emily by marriage, even if he is the one who's looking after her. That should make a difference, shouldn't it?"

"It might," Alicia replied; a glimmer of hope emerging. "...D'you know, Kristine, it definitely might."

The more Alicia thought about it, the more she realised Kristine could be on the right track. In fact she became so convinced Kristine was correct, that soon afterwards she tackled her supervisor at the health board about it.

"That shouldn't be a too much of a problem," he told her when she explained the situation. "...As long as you're not living with the patient!"

His last remark was made flippantly, but it cut Alicia to the quick. If she and Royston were to live together, that was precisely what they would be doing; despite Emily's original decree. There was no way in the world Royston could allow Emily to live there by herself now. She was far too infirm to manage alone. The only way in which she and Royston could share their lives from now on was if they lived together at Emily's. ...And the health board wouldn't allow it unless they were married.

"Damn it!" she said explosively, when reality slammed the door in her face yet again.

From then on, Kristine was kept busy with her university lectures, duties at the rest-home, and visits to see Emily.

In retrospect, she wondered how she managed to fit it all in. But of one thing she was absolutely certain. She could not have done so without a car. The freedom to get

201

around with greater speed allowed her to make her plans with the assurance of being able to carry them out.

...And one such plan was to confront her mother about moving into Auntie Ruth's.

As nothing more had been said about this since Emily's latest catastrophe, she assumed it had been put on hold.

During that time, Kristine's initial worry had diminished to just an occasional reflection on how ludicrous the idea was. She felt sure she could resurrect it with Fiona without blowing a fuse.

...Not that there was anything to be concerned about, she assumed; for the big swap around as originally decided upon could not possibly take place because of the stroke.

From Kristine's own perspective, the immediate future seemed quite clear: Alicia and Royston would both live at Emily's in order to look after their patient, her mother would stay where she was, and she, Kristine, would remain the sole occupant of Auntie Ruth's wonderful house.

Yes, the future, as far as she was concerned, seemed much brighter than it did not so very long ago. ...Except for one, unfortunate oversight on her part:

The reason it was working out so well for her was entirely due to her grandmother's bad luck.

Once she realised this, Kristine's conscience plagued her. In effect, she would be benefiting from the misfortune of a sick, elderly lady who was dearer to her than life itself. The knowledge of this was just too great to bear alone.

With it weighing heavily in her breast, she arranged to meet up with Fiona. She desperately needed to clear the air and find out for sure just what the situation was.

"You really hurt me with the cutting remark you made," Fiona said when Kristine broached the subject. "You called me a vixen!"

"Did you hear me say that?" Kristine asked sheepishly. She did not realise at the time that it had been overheard.

"Oh, yes. And I would very much like to know why you saw fit to use such a derogatory comment when I thought we were friends again."

For a moment, Kristine was rendered speechless by the unearthing of her faux pas. It had been uttered at the height of her frustration, and she certainly had not meant for her mother to hear it.

"Sorry, Mum. I didn't really mean it. I was just a bit mad at the time."

"Obviously! But it doesn't matter now. I take it you were upset about the prospect of my moving into Ruth's."

"Yes; I like having the place to myself. But now that Nana is ill again, I feel awful that I'm getting what I want, while Dad and Alicia will be stuck living at her house with no privacy..."

"...Who told you that?"

"What?"

"...That they will both be living there?"

"Nobody; I just guessed. I assumed that will be the plan. Alicia is usually there when I call in. ...Why did you want to know who told me?"

"Because it's not true."

"I don't understand."

"Your sick grandmother is not so sick, now, that she can't indicate her wishes. The notion of Royston and his mistress living under her roof made her very angry. She still doesn't want them living there! Apparently that has not changed since it was first brought up. All she said, when the subject was raised, was 'No... No... No!'"

"...I had no idea."

Kristine paused while the implication filtered through.

"...So where does Alicia live at the moment, then?"

"Where she's always lived, I suppose. They are caught between a rock and a hard place over this business. They can't live together at Nana's, and they can't live together anywhere else either, because it would leave Nana all by herself; which of course is out of the question."

"That's so unfair. There must be something we can do to bring them together."

"Like what, pray?"

"I don't know! If I wasn't so busy I'd have Nana with me at Auntie Ruth's! I know enough about looking after old people now to be able to do it. But it just wouldn't work."

"Why do you say that?"

"I told you – I'm too busy. I have work; and lectures..."

"...Alright, don't bite my head off. I do understand what you mean."

All of a sudden, a thought crossed Kristine's mind which took her by surprise.

Fiona noticed immediately.

"What are you thinking?" she asked.

Kristine looked up at her questioningly.

Would it be possible? she wondered. Could it work out in the long run?

"Yes; that's it!" she said to Fiona, a look of triumph in her eyes. "I have the answer!"

For the first time since her return from the hospital, Emily actually felt like getting up.

She was aware that something major had happened and that she had some kind of disability; because when she tried to, she still could not make the limbs on the right side of her body move.

Even worse, whenever she attempted to speak, strange sounds came out of her mouth instead of the words she was actually trying to say.

Emily was finding her inability to communicate with the family far more frustrating than the fact that she needed assistance with everything; for it meant that she could no longer convey her thoughts and wishes.

To compensate for this, Alicia had given her an activities chart divided into numerous small squares. Each square contained a picture relating to the activities of daily living, together with the word associated with it. So, all Emily had to do was point at the relevant square in order to put her wishes across.

"It would also be helpful at this stage," Alicia explained to Royston, "if you were to ask Emily questions that need only a yes or no answer. Trying to verbalise her wishes is too hard for her just at the moment."

Unfortunately for Emily, though, Alicia's versatile chart did not include a square that allowed her to indicate she wanted to get out of bed. And this morning, she was more than ready to get out of her bed.

The old Emily would have merely hopped out in order to begin her day; but the incapacitated Emily was not now capable of doing it.

Visualising the best way to accomplish her objective, she realised that the only way she could alert Royston to her needs was by inching herself to the edge of the bed, dangling her legs over the side and then banging on her bedside table. That way he would be able to see exactly what she wanted to do when he came in.

To Emily, this was the only way to go about it. But when in alarm Royston responded to the banging, he interpreted her actions very differently.

"Emily! What are you doing? You'll fall out of bed!"

He hurried over to her. With one arm across her back, he lifted both legs with the other, and then settled her safely under the covers.

205

Emily squawked with annoyance.

"No... No... No!" was all she managed to say, but with a look in her eye that told Royston exactly how she felt.

"Why were you trying to get out of bed by yourself? Do you want a broken hip on top of everything else?"

Emily looked at him blankly, unable to absorb his critical comment. But then Royston remembered about using the chart and Alicia's sensible advice. Swallowing his stress, he picked up the chart and studied it.

While his eyes scanned the pictures, he said, "I'm sorry, Emily. I didn't mean to shout. It's just that you gave me a fright. Were you trying to get up for...the toilet?" he said when he spotted the relevant picture. "Is that right?"

He held up the chart in front of Emily, expecting her to nod her affirmation of his choice or point to a different picture, but instead she pushed it away.

"No... No... No!" she exclaimed angrily, and wriggled to the edge of the bed again.

"Oh, Emily!" Royston cried out in desperation. "I can't understand what you want to do!"

All of a sudden, Emily blurted out, "Get up!" and then flopped back on the pillows.

Royston looked at her in amazement. This was the first time he had heard her utter anything coherent since her stroke. But he also noticed that the effort in doing so had left her feeling exhausted.

"You would like to get up; is that it?"

"Yes... Yes!"

Emily's eyes lit up with relief that she had finally got through to him. She looked expectantly at him, and began again to slide her legs over the side of the bed.

"No, not now!" he cried anxiously. "I'm not ready to move you yet!"

From then on, it was a matter of the spirit is willing but the flesh is weak; for Emily felt so much better in herself that she began to assume she was physically back to normal.

Yet, such an assumption was far from the truth. The stroke, having left her partially paralysed down one side, had also robbed her of the ability to recognise it. In effect, she saw nothing wrong with resuming her normal routine.

Emily's enthusiasm to get going was matched only by Royston's increasing paranoia each time he witnessed her trying, one-handed, to haul herself up.

"We've got to do something about this," he said to Alicia in a private moment. "I'm going out of my mind with worry that she might fall and break her neck."

"Have you spoken to her about it?"

"Of course, but she can't – or won't – take heed. Either it all goes in through one ear and out through the other, or our Emily is getting a bit stubborn."

"Maybe we need to give her some more exercise. She might just be getting bored. I'll bring her another walking frame: something more suitable for her present condition. That way, she can regain a bit of independence without putting the fear of God into you all the time. ...And also, it will help her to strengthen her stroke side."

Royston felt the weight of frustration lift from him, and gave Alicia a hug.

"My love, what would ever I do without you?" he said tenderly. "You seem to have a solution for everything."

Alicia sighed dolefully.

"Well, not quite everything."

"What do you mean?"

"There's one thing I heard about today that I've really got no answer for."

Royston held her at arm's length. With great concern, he looked into her worried face.

"Is something wrong, Alicia?" he asked.

"There will be soon," she replied. "I received notice that the lease on my house expires at the end of next month. If I want to renew it I will have to pay full rental from now on, and I can't afford it. I don't quite know what to do."

"Damn!" Royston snapped; frustration starting to settle on him again. "This is so unfair."

"What's unfair now, Royston?"

"It's as though we are fated not to be together."

Puzzled, Alicia pulled a face. "Has this got something to do with my rental?"

"Just think...if Emily had not suffered her stroke, where would we be living now?"

"In your house, I suppose."

"And if she was not so dogmatic about us living here?"

"I don't think you should blame Emily for any of this. She can't help what's happened, or the way she feels. It's not her problem that we want to pursue our relationship."

"I know. But it still doesn't solve our problem. You can't afford your new rental, and there's no way I can leave Emily. So I'm damned if I know what the solution is."

"We'll just have to hope something turns up soon."

Alicia could not have imagined that, even as she spoke, the wheels of advancement had already been set in motion.

Unknown to Royston's half of the family, the other half had been hatching a plot.

Initially, Fiona resisted Kristine's inspired answer to their problem, and as good as told her she needed her head examining.

"Do you really want me to stay with Nana from now on!" she exclaimed in disbelief. "Can you honestly see me living in peace and harmony under the same roof with my invalid, loopy mother?"

208

"Well, why not?" Kristine answered cheekily. "It is the perfect solution! It won't cost you anything to live there. Nana's got loads of money, so you can give up your job…"

"…Wait a minute, Kristine. What makes you think I'd want to give up a good job to look after her full time?"

"Because she is your mother; because she is sick and probably won't get better this time. And…" Kristine paused to draw breath. "…And because I reckon you owe her for all the years you distanced yourself from her."

"That's not a very nice thing to say."

"Maybe not, but it's true! You've finally reconciled with Nana, so this is a good opportunity for you to demonstrate your sincerity, and look after her in her old age. None of us knows how much longer she's got. She might have another stroke next week and…"

"…Okay, Kristine. You've made your point."

Fiona frowned dejectedly. She did not like the sound of it at all. She would be tied to someone who was more like a vegetable than a person, and would have to look after her like a patient rather than her mother. And then there was the fact that she had never before had anything to do with a stroke victim…

"You really are asking a lot," she said peevishly.

But Kristine was on a roll, now.

"It's not as though you'll be left to cope by yourself. Dad, Alicia and I will be helping out, and Nana already has carers morning and evening. You would just be there to keep her entertained, make her cups of tea and cook your meals. You could take her shopping and on outings when she's a bit better – that sort of thing. It would be fun for both of you."

"It doesn't sound much like fun to me."

"Will you at least think about it?"

Fiona sighed again.

209

"I suppose so...but don't expect a favourable response. I'm giving it some thought, not my consent."

With the arrival of the new walking aid, a light frame high enough for her to lean on with her elbows, Emily could now contemplate taking her first few steps.

Each passing day now saw a slight improvement in her abilities. The areas of her brain that had been only slightly affected began to heal, giving her back some use down her stroke side. Added to this was the regular exercise regime she engaged in with assistance from Royston and Kristine.

Emily's granddaughter could not have known, when she signed up for her physiotherapy course, just how useful it would prove to be. As she learnt more about the need of physiotherapy in the recovery of stroke patients, so she became enthused to put her knowledge into practice with her grandmother.

Furthermore, her caregiver work at the rest-home also paid dividends when it came to picking up more ideas on how to be of assistance with regard to Emily's needs.

One of the ideas was in respect of speech therapy. Emily's level of cognitive speech, though better than none at all, seemed to be improving very little beyond her initial attempts to make a point. She had settled into a groove of saying yes and no, with only an occasional remark blurted out when she became agitated.

Basically, the recovery of her speech still needed a lot of work. And that was where Kristine felt sure she could also help.

All in all, Kristine found the work of the various therapists at Everglades quite fascinating.

They regularly assisted residents with their exercising, occupational activities, and where necessary, with speech.

One day Kristine arrived at Emily's with something that resembled a pack of cards.

"What have you got there?" asked Royston, bemused.

"I stopped off at the toy shop after work and bought these," she said, and fanned the cards out so that Royston could see what was on them.

"But they are for young children; you had a book like this when you were a little girl," he remarked, and pulled out one of the cards.

It had on it a picture of a cat, with the word spelt out in large print underneath.

He took the rest of the cards off Kristine and began to look through them.

"Yes, I do remember," she said. "I thought this would be useful in helping Nana to speak properly again. I got the idea off the speech therapist at work, and she sneaked a pack out of the cupboard for me."

"It's a bit insulting, don't you think: giving kiddie-cards to a mature woman?"

"No, Dad. What you don't realise is that because of the stroke, Nana can no longer read, write and speak. She has to virtually learn all over again – the same as with walking. She's getting better at that, isn't she?"

"Oh, yes. With me holding on to her she's taking a few steps now. But I still need to keep a chair close by, just in case she tires."

"Have you thought of a wheelchair," asked Kristine.

"...A wheelchair? Wouldn't that defeat the purpose of helping her to walk again?"

"Not necessarily. It just means you can drag the chair along behind you when you're walking with her. Then, when she's had enough she can sit right down again. And, of course, it means you can take her out and about more. There is one drawback, though."

"...I'm afraid to ask."

"They're pretty expensive."

"Even so, it sounds like a good idea. Perhaps we can get one through the hospital. I'll check with Alicia."

The cards Kristine brought went down a treat with Emily.

While Royston took the opportunity to go out to the shops, she and Kristine sat together at the table.

Emily laughed at the cards as though she was seeing the objects on them for the first time all over again.

"What is that?" asked Kristine, pointing to a picture of a bird on the card she was holding.

Emily thought for a moment, then pointed outside but made no attempt to mouth the word. This told Kristine that Emily had no problem recognising the objects, but could not express her findings.

However, she also realised that if they were to make any progress she would need to move beyond recognition of objects alone.

"Nana," she said with persistence. "I know the birds are outside, but I didn't ask you where it is, I asked you what it is; and I would like you to tell me, please."

Abruptly, Emily's jovial mood changed with Kristine's firmness. The childish exuberance of someone showing off her abilities turned into the ordeal of searching her mind for an answer.

She slowly opened her mouth in an attempt to oblige, but no comprehensible sound came out.

"Let's try again, shall we?" said Kristine, taking a softer tone of encouragement.

She was beginning to understand how it might take a while to get Emily talking again – and that success was not necessarily assured.

As promised, Fiona reflected long and hard on Kristine's request. She did not much like the idea of relinquishing either a job she enjoyed or the house she had occupied for a long time just to look after an invalid.

Only Kristine's affront on her conscience kept her from rejecting the suggestion.

Yet, the girl was right, she secretly admitted; in that she owed Emily for the years of inattention. Even so, this was a difficult decision – and one which she would have to make before too long.

"I really need to sort myself out here," she declared; "Or I'm going to lose favour with the family again."

Once Emily had settled into her regular routine after the stroke, Fiona basically left all her needs for Royston, Alicia, and Kristine to look after. It therefore came as a shock to realise that she had not even visited her mother in that time…so how could she accurately gauge Emily's current condition?

At length, she arrived at the conclusion that before she could effectively make a big decision like this, she should at least go and see the old lady for herself.

It was Emily who saw Fiona's car pull up outside the house. She fidgeted excitedly, and in her enthusiasm to share the observation, scattered Kristine's cards all over the table.

Emily looked worriedly at Kristine; half expecting to be told off; yet Kristine was more interested in whatever had caught her attention.

"It's alright, Nana," she said, getting up from the table. "We can tidy those up later."

Kristine walked over to the lounge window; Fiona was just getting out of her car.

She slammed the door and turned towards the house. Seeing Kristine at the window, she waved cheerfully.

213

"It's Mum!" Kristine announced, and waved back.

"I...know...!" responded Emily with clarity; then gasped in surprise at her own audacity.

"Nana!" cried Kristine. "You can speak!"

"No... No... No!" came Emily's exasperated response.

She alone knew that it was a flash in the pan motivated by excitement.

However, Kristine was intent only on sharing the good news with Fiona. She rushed to the door to let her mother in; energised because she was certain Emily must have regained her powers of speech – and also because she was hoping to hear Fiona's long awaited decision.

"Hi, Mum! I'm so glad it's you!" she cried.

"Why?" asked Fiona with curiosity.

She was not used to this sort of welcome from Kristine.

"It's Nana. She can talk properly. Come in here and see for yourself!"

"Hello, Mother," said Fiona brightly. "It's lovely to see you again. Kristine tells me you are doing very well!"

"No... No... No!" said Emily, frustrated now that she had slithered back into her monotone groove.

But Fiona misinterpreted her.

"Well, if that's the way you feel when I take the trouble to visit you..." she barked crossly, and made to leave.

"Mum, wait! Nana didn't mean it like that! Up until a few minutes ago that was all she could say! Please don't take it personally. She's still very sick, you know."

Kristine could see the opportunity of reuniting mother and daughter slipping away. Frantically, she tried to claw the momentum back.

She grabbed Fiona by the arm and pulled her to where her grandmother was sitting.

Emily held out a card to her, beaming broadly.

Caught off guard, Fiona looked at it fleetingly.

"It's a fish!" she stated with disdain.

"Yes… Yes!" said Emily proudly, as though it was she who had identified it.

"What's going on here?" asked Fiona, freeing herself of Kristine's grasp. "You just said Nana can speak normally."

Kristine looked beseechingly at Emily. "I… I thought she could. Nana came out with something as clear as a bell, just as you arrived. But now…"

The disappointment overwhelmed Kristine. To have her say something coherent in front of Fiona would have been such an encouraging sign. While Emily slipped back into her own world again, Kristine felt sure that her mother was as far away as ever from making a commitment.

Yet, Fiona had experienced a change of heart. The sight of her mother, the pitiful victim with whom she kept vigil in the hospital, deeply moved her.

Immediately, she felt a great sense of remorse for her unhelpful attitude when she first came in.

Pulling out a chair, she sat down at the table and picked up the card Emily had held out.

"Can you say 'fish', Mum?" Fiona asked, a tear welling up in her eye.

As Emily watched the tear spill over onto Fiona's cheek, her focus moved away from the card.

"Cry…" she said with the same clarity as before.

Kristine looked on, overjoyed.

Fiona threw her arms around Emily's neck and kissed her fervently, tears now flowing down both their faces.

"Oh, Mother," said Fiona passionately. "I do love you."

Emily gently pulled back from her.

She wiped a tear from Fiona's cheek with the forefinger of her good hand, and said, "Love…you…too."

"I think this calls for the tissue box," sniffed Kristine; herself close to tears.

"Kristine," said Fiona when she had blown her nose. "If, in spite of everything, you want to go ahead with the little arrangement we discussed, I'm game."

"Mum...that's wonderful," Kristine stammered; her cup of happiness overflowing into a second tissue.

Now she could relax.

...Now she could still have Ruth's house to herself; this time with a clear conscience.

CHAPTER TWO

Royston would never have envisaged, when he returned with the shopping, that his life was about to change. It was a great surprise to him: seeing not only his daughter but also Fiona at the house. Furthermore, they seemed to have taken over in his absence.

After he brought in the last of the grocery bags with Kristine's help, he said to them all, "Well, this is a very nice family get together. Is it a special occasion, or something?"

"You could say that," said Fiona, amicably; "especially after what's been going on here."

"Oh, have I missed something?"

With one ear inclined to conversation while he put away his purchases, Royston heard Fiona recount how clearly Emily had spoken, how thrilled she had been to see that the invalid appeared to be recovering, and how happy she was about the new arrangement...

"...What new arrangement are you referring to?" asked Royston, showing a little more interest in Fiona's burble.

He crumpled up the last of the plastic bags and roughly stuffed it with the others in the drawer reserved for such a purpose. Then he joined Fiona and the rest of his family at the table.

"I see you've been playing with Kristine's cards, Emily," he said cheerfully; causing her to beam back at him. Then, again he asked, "What's this arrangement?"

Fiona shot Kristine a questioning glance. "Haven't you spoken to your father about it yet?" she asked.

"No, there's been nothing to mention until just a few minutes ago…"

Royston's attention inquisitively moved from Fiona to Kristine; his expression one of disbelief.

"…I have been waiting for Mum to make up her mind what she wants to do."

"Well, you know what I've decided now," said Fiona. "Will you tell him…or shall I?"

Emily, enjoying the spectacle of a family reunion, sat quietly with a fixed grin on her face.

"…Actually, I think I would like to tell him myself," Fiona went on.

Addressing Royston directly she declared, "Kristine and I have come to an understanding. After much persuasion on her part, and a great deal of thought on mine, I have decided that I should be the one to look after Mother from now on. So, I will move in here, and you two can take up residence in your own house as we originally planned. I believe it's long overdue – don't you?"

Emily's grin converted to a wide-eyed stare, indicating that at least in part she understood what was being discussed around her.

She waited for Royston to make his reply, together with Fiona and Kristine.

Though dumbfounded by the announcement, he said, "Are you sure, Fiona? It's a terrible imposition on you."

"Of course – I wouldn't have said it otherwise! "Fiona replied indignantly. "Mum and I are enjoying each other's company; we'll have a ball! You and Alicia can finally have your house back."

Royston went quiet. After a moment he said, "I…I don't know…what to say. How does Emily feel about this?"

Fiona glanced across at the still wide-eyed Emily.

"Mum will love having me live with her again after all this time apart."

I hope so, thought Royston; but said nothing.

Still in a state of disbelief, Royston and Fiona worked out a date for their changeover of residence; then, when he had waved her off, he hurried back in to Kristine and Emily.

With concern he quietly asked Kristine, "Do you think Fiona realises what she's letting herself in for? She hasn't exactly had much experience with Emily lately, what with the stroke and...Arthur."

"Well, it will be a learning curve for her then, won't it?" quipped Kristine.

Yet, deep down, Kristine's attention had been deflected by Royston's note of concern. She wondered if Emily really would be alright in the care of her unpredictable daughter.

Later in the day, Royston sat down with Emily to explain exactly what had been arranged.

The exchange was to take place in three weeks' time; a couple of days before Alicia's rental contract was due to expire. This, he assured Emily, would allow plenty of time for her to absorb what was happening; especially the fact that soon it would be Fiona living in the house with her, and not him.

Emily listened closely to his explanation, saying nothing but nodding occasionally.

Her expression gave him little indication of whether or not she actually understood. Worried that she might fret in his absence, he tried to reassure her that he would visit regularly and generally help out just as much as before.

"You do understand all of this, don't you?" he asked in a serious tone.

In reply, Emily smiled knowingly and said, "Fiona..."

On the allotted day, Royston collected up everything he brought with him when he left his flat, and packed his car up so tightly he could barely see out through the rear view mirror. Then, while Kristine kept company with Emily, he drove over to his new home to help with the changeover.

It proved to be a gruelling day for Royston; involved as he was in every aspect of the three-way shift. By the time Alicia had moved out of her house and they were able to complete the final phase of the shift, with her belongings only roughly deposited throughout his house, Royston had had enough of being a workhorse, and was exhausted.

Not until the following morning did the reality of their situation begin to sink in.

While he made a cup of tea to take to his still sleeping partner, Royston reflected on Fiona's generosity, and how coincidentally their fortunes had changed.

"I never thought I'd be saying this," he told Alicia later in the morning, "but I really owe Fiona a debt of gratitude. If it wasn't for her, I don't know where we'd be right now."

"Probably moving me into a pokey little flat like the one you lived in, I suppose." Alicia laughed at the idea. "I must go and thank Fiona for her thoughtfulness – I haven't even met her yet!"

"Well, you will get your chance very soon. Isn't Emily due for her check-up this week?"

"Oh, yes; that's right! I had almost forgotten, what with the shifting and everything. It should be a very interesting check-up this time..."

"Do you want me to come with you?"

"Of course not," Alicia retorted. "I don't need you to hold my hand; not even with the infamous Fiona!"

Emily's first night with her new live-in companion passed relatively smoothly, and she was only marginally more nervous than Fiona with the prospect of getting up to the toilet during the night.

Kristine had already demonstrated the various assisted moves required for Emily; so by the time Fiona was left to cope alone, she and her patient were both well practiced.

Once the upheaval of all the changes had subsided, daily life settled into a quiet routine. Alicia met Fiona and got on surprisingly well with her, Royston found he could spend more time at work, and Fiona, with the help of the others, was able to work out a regime that was judged satisfactory for both herself and for Emily.

The only family member to suffer was Kristine. She soon discovered that when you are responsible for a big house and have a full schedule each day, there is very little time to call your own. In fact, she was so busy that she failed to recognise a build-up in her stress level, and as a result found herself continually in a state of exhaustion.

She noticed this especially during her morning duties at the rest-home.

Kristine had never adapted particularly well to the early starts. She found it taxing, having to arrive so early and then working flat out until her late break for morning-tea. Her list of tasks for the morning, she was sure, would have kept two people fully occupied; let alone just one.

In an environment where the heaviness of a caregiver's workload tended to be overlooked by the senior staff, her sensitivity slowly felt the growing weight of oppression. The other caregivers, she had observed, didn't seem to mind. These were women who were nearer her mother's age than her own. Most of them were full timers; the rest-home their only job, and they seemed to enjoy the social side of being with friends more than the work itself.

Thus, as a reliable part-time worker, she felt left out.

Kristine was one of only a few who worked the morning shift part-time due to other commitments. Because of this, she didn't make friends as easily as her workmates. The idle banter of the older women did not interest her, and invariably at break time she sat alone in the staffroom while the rest went outside for a cigarette.

She was therefore very relieved when she was asked to take on an afternoon shift: a duty that began in the middle of the afternoon and finished late in the evening. Once she had learnt the routine, become accustomed to helping the residents get ready for bed instead of getting them up, and was used to going home late at night – she discovered that she actually preferred it that way.

It meant, though, that when she had a lecture in the morning and a duty in the afternoon she was not able to fit in a visit to see her grandmother.

This state of affairs also marked the beginning of a decline in her social life.

Just occasionally, Kristine would discuss these issues with Richard while at university; for he had already told her that his social life was just about non-existent.

It appeared that conversely he had too much spare time on his hands.

"I blame it on this," he explained, pointing to the vivid scar across his cheek. "The girls I go out with don't hang around when I try to get close to them!"

"How incredibly mean," Kristine said to him; but then realised that if she didn't know him so well she probably would react the same way.

Richard, she felt sure, was just about as nice a person as she could wish to meet. His accident had taught him a harsh lesson, and he had worked incredibly hard at his course. As far as she was concerned, he deserved to meet someone who would appreciate all his finer qualities. But there was still the matter of the scar…

One day, Kristine was telling Richard how lonely she was at work, when a thought came to her.

"Why don't you come and work at the rest-home?" she asked impulsively. "There are already two male caregivers on the books. You would fit in very well, especially with your physio experience. And I would really enjoy having an ally in my alien work environment."

Richard snorted with mock contempt.

"Even if I was looking for work, I just can't see myself helping little old ladies with their showers!" With a few weeks still left for his accident compensation payments, finding work was not high on Richard's list of priorities; yet he did not want to appear discourteous and so promised Kristine, "I'll bear it in mind…thanks for the suggestion."

"Well, how about working as a volunteer, then?" she went on, pushing the matter. "You could assist with their physio classes, if it's okay with my boss."

Suddenly Richard lost his temper.

"I said I would keep it in the back of my mind, didn't I? Just drop it please, Kristine! I don't want to work in a prissy rest-home anyway – certainly not at the moment!"

"Okay! I'm sorry! I didn't mean to pressure you! It's just that I would really like it if you were there with me, as well as on the course. I think it would do us both good. We could move ahead together…"

Richard went quiet, his face sullen; his mood hostile.

Alarmed by his reaction, Kristine apologised.

"Honestly, I didn't mean to upset you," she said with a measure of guilt.

Richard was not someone she would ever want to upset. She liked him too much. And besides, she had often noted, his temperament could be volatile at times.

She wondered if it was in some way connected with the motorbike accident; or maybe the fact that he had lost his driver's licence...

"I tell you what," she said, trying to make amends for her insensitivity. "Would you let me apologise properly and buy you dinner some time – or even cook for you?"

Richard looked at her oddly.

"You...cook?" he said with less than enthusiasm.

Caught off guard by his cynicism, Kristine immediately regretted the suggestion. While thinking up an impromptu reply, she realised that she had never actually cooked for anyone else before; her own meals usually concocted from whatever happened to be in the fridge.

"I'm no chef," she said honestly, "but I could knock up a tasty bacon and eggs."

She looked at him demurely to break the impasse.

Richard gave in...Kristine could be so disarming when she wanted to get round him. Maybe a simple meal with her wouldn't be too bad.

"What say I take you out to my favourite eatery first," he said affably. "They serve really nice pub lunches; their scampi and fries are my favourite. Then, perhaps next time I'll allow you to cook for me."

Richard was teasing her now, and with relief Kristine recognised it. The smile that spread across his face could not be misinterpreted. It looked like she was forgiven.

"That would be really neat," she said.

When she got home, Kristine could not help but prance exuberantly around the lounge.

"I'm going on a date with Richard... I'm going on a date with Richard," she sang with delight.

Emily dreamily awoke from a particularly satisfying night's sleep in the company of Arthur.

With a start, she realised she was back in her room; still incapacitated and facing yet another difficult day.

During the first few weeks after Fiona moved in, Emily's only real comfort had been in her contact with Arthur. He alone related to her as the person she had always been. And only he could draw her to a place where she was free of all limitations. She had no idea where that place was; just that it was quite heavenly...

Emily rang the bell on her bedside table to let Fiona know she was awake.

Since her return from hospital she had been utilising the commode beside her bed if she needed to get out, but still relied on help in doing so.

Although some of the strength was returning to her stroke side, she was not confident enough to manoeuvre onto the commode unaided. She was also very aware what the consequences for her might be if she tried; for as yet, she had managed to avoid any conflict of interest with her daughter, and preferred it remain that way.

Fiona came in response to the summons. She flicked a switch on Emily's automatic tea-making machine – a gift from some of the bowling club ladies on her return home. Then she helped Emily out onto the commode.

In Royston's day, he would have had a cup of tea with Emily after she had got back into bed. But Fiona, who preferred to stick with her old routine of a strong black coffee on rising, was now in the habit of making the tea for Emily and then leaving her to enjoy it in bed by herself.

Later on, when the morning helper had showered Emily and then left to go to her next client, Emily sat comfortably in her recliner chair, watching her favourite soap opera on television. At the same time, Fiona was putting a load of washing through in the laundry; this Emily knew from the distant whirring sound of the machine's spin cycle.

What Emily did not realise was, that while she slipped into a quiet doze in her chair, Fiona, still drying her hands on the laundry towel, came into the lounge to ask Emily what she would like for lunch.

However, when Fiona entered the lounge, her reaction at the sight that greeted her displaced all prior thoughts as she struggled to rationalise what she was seeing.

Emily, apparently asleep in her chair, was reaching out with her good arm in what seemed to be an embrace...as though somebody else was in the room with her.

Fiona did not know what to do. Never before had she seen anything like this from Emily, and it alarmed her.

Silently, she tiptoed back out of the room.

The sight of it took her so much by surprise that she momentarily forgot what she was doing, and rather than return to the laundry, she went into the kitchen.

At the window she stood looking vacantly out over the rose garden that had been her father's pride and joy. Still in a daze from the peculiar display she had just witnessed, she did not notice that the roses were looking especially lovely, thanks to Royston who, true his promise, regularly came round with Alicia to tend the garden.

Neither did Fiona notice an unusual glow around the bushes that highlighted the diverse shades in each bloom; the whiskey rose in particular...

Suddenly, Emily called her from the lounge; breaking Fiona out of her trance. At the same time, the washing machine beeped to let her know it had finished its cycle.

Coming to, Fiona shouted, "Won't be a minute...I'll just empty the machine." Then, moments later, she returned with a basket full of washing tucked under one arm and the clothes rack hooked over the other.

Emily made to get up and help her with the load.

"Mother, what do you think you're doing?" exclaimed Fiona, and dropped the content of both arms in her rush to prevent Emily from getting out of her chair.

Emily slumped back in alarm. She looked anxiously into Fiona's eyes, willing her to understand that all she wanted to do was help. But when she tried to speak, the only words that came out were, "No... No... No!"

"Oh, don't start up with that pointless babble again," snapped Fiona in frustration, and picked up the washing that had fallen out of the basket. "It's difficult enough having to look after an invalid without you doing foolish things like trying to get up by yourself!"

Emily swallowed back a tear that had welled up.

To her, it look like the novelty of care was beginning to wear off and Fiona was now learning the reality of looking after an invalid.

It would have been so nice, Emily thought, if their time living together could have been filled with the pleasantries of reconciliation.

Yet, life even at the best of times is seldom as simple as that. Despite Fiona's good intentions, Emily sadly realised, she is never likely to change.

She looked on while Fiona, apparently still in a rotten mood, hung the damp clothing on the A-frame. It crossed her mind that maybe having her daughter move in was not such a good idea after all. But what other option was there? Emily would be the first to concede that Royston and Alicia deserved a chance to move forward in their relationship.

Yet, she did miss having Royston at home. He was so much more patient than Fiona...

Emily discreetly reached for a tissue to dab away the tears before Fiona noticed. It was easier to camouflage how she felt than try and explain.

If only the stroke had not robbed her of the ability to speak properly, she lamented. If only Arthur were here at her side to speak for her. He would know what to say...

"Mother, you're mumbling," said Fiona when the last of the washing had been hung over the frame.

Emily groaned an inaudible "Sorry," and then sank back into her misery.

How she wanted to yell out, 'I can't help the way I am!'

Kristine's arranged date with Richard came into effect.

Less of a date and more of a get-together, their lunch at the busy local pub offered little opportunity to engage in meaningful conversation, for each remark needed to be shouted over the noise, rather than spoken privately.

Nevertheless, Kristine enjoyed his company. Away from all the pressures of the outside world, she found him to be more relaxed and therefore more congenial a companion. She did notice one thing about him, though. Whether by coincidence or intent, he sat at their table with the scarred side of his face away from public view.

Kristine also noticed how he rarely faced directly into the room, indicating to her that avoiding people's stare must now be a practiced art. She respected that, for she had noticed on many other occasions just how fickle people can be when confronted by a disfigurement.

Back at the car, she thanked Richard for the meal and asked if he would like to go round to her house for coffee.

"No thanks...just take me straight home, if you don't mind," he said, to Kristine's dismay. "You'd have to come out again to drive me back to my place...and I wouldn't want you to go to the trouble."

"I understand," said Kristine, trying to hide her feelings.

She refrained from telling him that it would have been no trouble at all.

Before he got out of the car, Richard leaned over and gave her a peck on the cheek in appreciation of the ride home. Then he said, "There's something I want to discuss with you. It was too noisy in the restaurant to bring it up."

Kristine's heart skipped a beat. Did he want to arrange another date?

"The other day you asked if I was interested in working at that rest-home. Well, I've been thinking about it."

Kristine's level of expectation fell sharply.

"Really?" she said with only cursory interest. "I thought you weren't going to consider it."

"I wasn't. But then I got to thinking some more about it and rang the Accident Compo people as to whether I could work while I'm still receiving compensation. They told me it could be arranged, but subject to certain limitations."

"So what have you decided to do?" asked Kristine.

"Would you think it weird if I changed my mind and took you up on your suggestion?"

"Do you mean...to work at the rest-home?"

"Yes."

"Wow! I think it would be really neat having you work there with me!"

"What do I do about it, then?"

"I've got a shift on Monday morning. If you like, I could mention it to Grace, my boss, and see what she says. You'll have to fill in an application form and the police report..."

"...Police report? What do they want one of those for?" he asked uneasily; the suspended sentence he was still working out coming immediately to mind.

"It's nothing to be concerned about. They just need to check your background – to make sure you are who you say you are, as I was told, and that you're not wanted by the... Oh dear! I'm sorry, Richard...I forgot about your conviction. I didn't mean to bring that up."

229

"Well, that's that then, isn't it?" said Richard dismally. "...So much for my ever finding a job!"

"I really don't think it will matter very much," Kristine remarked hopefully. "As long as you explain everything to Grace before she gets you to fill out the police report. I'm sure she will accept your explanation. I believe you are a decent sort of guy, and I will certainly guarantee that when I speak to Grace."

Grace, however, was not so sure that his conviction should be taken lightly.

"We have to be very careful who we employ in a place like this," she said with concern. "There are some strange people out there, and the residents need our protection as well as our care."

Kristine started to panic; for when she talked it over with Richard she had as good as promised him that Grace would be amenable.

"What if I were to vouch for his character?" she asked; employing her last resort. "I believe Richard to be a good person who has learnt from his mistakes."

"Well, if you have confidence in him..." Grace broke off in thought and then added, "I suppose the fact that he is a student on the same course as you could act in his favour. It certainly implies he can't be all that bad!"

"Does that mean you will employ him?" Kristine asked enthusiastically. She was anxious for Richard to have some positive feedback from her.

"Wait a minute, Kristine. I think you are being a little bit presumptuous here. I'll grant him an interview...and we'll take it from there. How does that sound?"

Kristine curbed her enthusiasm.

"It sounds great. ...And thank you. Shall I get Richard to phone you?"

"No, that won't be necessary. Just tell him to ring our number – you'll have a note of it somewhere – and the receptionist will make an appointment for him."

Kristine was on duty when Richard came in for his initial interview.

As she carried out her tasks, she would pass the office where she could see him talking to Grace. But when she looked a short time later, the office was empty.

"Rats!" she exclaimed privately.

She had hoped to catch him before he left the building, and was disappointed he did not think to hang around long enough to let her know the outcome of the interview.

The moment she got home from work, Kristine rang him to find out.

"How did it go?" she asked excitedly.

"It went well – of sorts," he said guardedly.

"What do you mean? Did Grace make something of your conviction after all?"

"No, it wasn't that..."

"...What then? I can't imagine what else might put them off hiring you!"

"Oh, they hired me alright..."

Now Kristine was confused.

"...But not as a caregiver!"

"You must be joking!" exclaimed Kristine. "After all your physio involvement, you'd be wonderful with the oldies. And it's not as though they don't hire men, because they already have a couple of male caregivers. The old ladies love having them around..."

"...It's not because of my gender."

"Well...what?"

"It's because of my scar!"

Kristine was astounded. How dare Everglades judge him solely on his scar! Surely they weren't that bigoted?

She decided to tackle Grace about it right away, and phoned her before she left the rest-home for the day.

"It's not that we don't want him," Grace explained. "...Like you, I was able to see beyond his misdemeanour; after all, none of us is perfect. And, as you say, he has learnt from his mistakes. It's just that I have to take the feelings of our residents' into consideration."

"What has that got to do with it?" asked Kristine, her annoyance showing in her voice. She could see her dream of working with Richard slipping away.

"We don't want our clients to be offended by a staff member's appearance. You didn't warn me about the scar on his face. It really is quite... Well... Let's say..."

"It's ugly, is that what you're thinking?"

"In a word, yes – not that it will always be like that. In the fullness of time, and with cosmetic surgery, I see no reason why he shouldn't get his good looks back again. But just at the moment..."

At an impasse, Grace tailed off.

Obviously Kristine saw beyond the scar as well. But that was no reason why she should subject the ladies to the sight of it. Some of them would be repulsed, and even complain about it to their relatives...

"Between you and me, Kristine," she went on. "I really think that if Richard worked as a caregiver just yet he would frighten some of our sensitive ladies. A few of them don't like having males work with them as it is..."

"...But Richard said you hired him."

"We did! There are other employment opportunities at Everglades that would suit his abilities."

Kristine spoke a little more calmly now.

"Am I allowed to enquire what he'll be doing, then?"

"Certainly. We've employed him as a trainee cleaner."

"...A cleaner!"

"Yes. It will be useful to have an extra male cleaner on a casual basis. Richard seems to think it might work in well with his work restrictions...and also his studies, of course."

Kristine was not happy about the outcome of Richard's interview. She complained bitterly to him at university the following day.

"Why did you let them give you such a menial job?" she said in frustration. "I was really looking forward to working on the wards with you. ...And if those old ladies don't like the look of your scar, then I don't think much of them!"

Richard listened to her ranting unperturbed.

"It really doesn't bother me," he said with humility. "Of more concern was the possibility of being refused because of the conviction. I'm used to my scar offending others. At least as a cleaner I can avoid the residents and get fit in the process," he added jokingly.

With the passage of time Fiona was discovering that life as a carer meant her own wishes had to be put on hold.

She acknowledged, during a spare moment in which to reflect on her situation, how different looking after an adult was compared with bringing up a child.

For one thing, she moaned to herself, a toddler can be picked up and carried, and generally told what to do. In her day, she expected and received obedience from her own offspring; not that Kristine needed to be prompted all that often: in the main she was a delight to have at home.

Yet, with Emily...it was more like trying to take care of a chimpanzee than a human being, she thought bitterly. The woman can't even feed herself without dribbling!

She told Royston of her difficulties during one of his visits, stopping short at suggesting that they should never have swapped houses.

In reality, she wanted more than anything to ask him if they could revert to the way things were beforehand, and hoped fervently that he might offer of his own accord...

Yet, if Royston was sympathetic towards her regarding Emily, he certainly had no inclination towards changing places of residence again.

Instead he merely suggested, "Probably all you need is some time for yourself once in a while. Would you like me to sit with Emily tomorrow so you can go off for a bit of retail therapy?"

That was not the response Fiona was hoping for. She said, "No thanks...I shouldn't let it get to me, that's all."

"Don't forget, looking after an elderly person, especially one who is as incapacitated as Emily, takes a lot out of you. Most of the time I was living here, Emily was okay. She had recovered from the fall by then, so all I had to deal with was her eccentricity."

"What do you mean by that?"

"...Her conversations with Arthur, of course!"

"...My father? Where does he come into all of this?"

Suddenly Royston realised he had said too much.

He assumed that Fiona must have by now encountered and come to accept Emily's interaction with Arthur. It was only after he mentioned Arthur's name that he realised she may not have had that pleasure yet.

Recently, he had only spoken with Emily in such a way that she needed to nod or shake her head in response, for she still could not make reasonable conversation; so how did Fiona know?

Oh dear; what have I done? he groaned inwardly.

234

Emily's little secret had been safe from Fiona, and now he had set the proverbial cat amongst the pigeons. She really did not know that the spirit of her dead father was present in the house!

How on earth could he worm his way out of this pickle without giving her a full, truthful and totally unacceptable explanation?

As it happened, Royston's plight was saved by the bell: that is, by Emily's bell.

Having learnt not to incur Fiona's wrath by attempting to get up by herself, Emily was now in the habit of ringing and then waiting patiently for her daughter to come and help her out of bed or the recliner chair.

Though still waiting for an answer to her query, Fiona automatically rose to her feet to respond; and Royston instinctively followed.

Together they went in to Emily.

Emily was thrilled to see her favourite son-in-law again. She reached out to Royston, inferring that she wanted him to be the one to help her.

He smiled apologetically at Fiona.

"Be my guest," Fiona responded, and stepped back to give him room. "Mother seems to prefer having you to look after her, anyway."

Then, when Emily had been settled in her chair, Fiona tackled Royston again.

"You said something about my mother talking to Dad. What was that all about?"

Royston glanced at Emily to gauge whether she heard Fiona's question. If she had, he deduced, she certainly did not show it; but seemed more interested in arranging her bits and pieces around her where she could reach them without having to lean or use her stroke arm.

However, when he looked away from her, Emily slowly raised her eyes and turned her head towards him; for the mention of her beloved had not escaped her.

Discreetly, she strained to hear what they were saying about him.

Royston hastily considered what to do. Maybe it was time to come clean about Arthur; for like it or not, Fiona was Emily's carer now.

As Emily's condition improved, there were bound to be occasions when Arthur's name would slip out in general conversation with the family. Royston had already told Fiona that she still held him fondly in her memory.

Yet, looking on the bright side, if she did not regain her speech completely, then Emily's talking about Arthur – and presumably, with Arthur – might never arise again. And that would keep the secret secure...

Royston's confidence returned.

"I thought I explained to you that Emily still thinks fondly about Arthur," he said after only a moment's hesitation; hoping it would satisfy Fiona's curiosity.

"Do you think Mother hallucinates about him?" Fiona asked; recalling the worrying spectacle she came across recently; for it definitely seemed to her as though Emily was reaching out to somebody.

"Hallucinates? Why do you say that?" asked Royston in alarm. ...Whatever had Emily been up to in his absence!

"The other day, she was sitting in her chair, and I saw her trying to hug someone when there was nobody in the room but her. At first I thought she was asleep, but she couldn't have been. It was really weird."

Royston quickly thought how to respond and recalled a similar incident during his time as her carer.

"She might have been dreaming," he said feebly.

Could Fiona be having suspicions already, even though Emily was not able to speak?

"How did you react?" he added in a casual tone.

"I tiptoed out of the room," Fiona replied. "It startled me to see her doing it. She seemed to be away with the fairies. ...I didn't quite know what to make of it. One thing has come to mind, though."

"What's that?"

Fiona looked through to Emily, who had now grown bored with trying to grasp what they were talking about, and stared blankly at the television.

She turned back to Royston, and spoke to him in little more than a whisper.

"I'm wondering if my mother's becoming senile." Then, when Royston's pause indicated an unwillingness to give reply, she gasped, "My God, I'm right, aren't I? Mother has dementia, and you already knew!"

Royston sprung to his and Emily's defence.

"That's not it at all! We don't think she has dementia..."

"...You don't think she has? What sort of remark is that? It's my mother we're talking about!"

Fiona's tone was animated now. Furtively she checked if Emily was looking, and expressed relief to discover that she had drifted off to sleep.

Royston sighed; the task of maintaining such an evasive response too onerous to continue.

He decided to use another approach.

"It's very hard to determine exactly what Emily's mental state is. Before the stroke she would come out with the most logical remarks. Even when she'd recovered from her fall she seemed completely in control again. Anyone else would have flipped their lid if they were attacked like that, but not Emily. She's a tough nut to crack, that one. There's no doubting she's been affected by the stroke though, and not just physically. But as for her having dementia...I really don't know."

"Well, it's quite clear to me..." Fiona began to say, but Royston butted in abruptly.

"...I hope you're not going to assume she has dementia just because she can't express herself very well!"

"What else am I to think? I can only gauge her state of mind by what I see. I'm the one who is with her all the time now, so I'm in the best position to judge!"

"Fiona, you're not an expert. You can't accurately judge her state of mind; you can only guess at it. Until recently Emily was as normal as you and me; except for..."

"...Except for what? ...Her odd behaviour? So we're back to that? Exactly what was she doing before the stroke?"

Royston capitulated. He had no choice, now.

With a deep breath to give him courage, he began his explanation.

Yet again, as he began to mention Arthur's name, Emily jerked out of her slumber and took notice.

"Arthur!" she said abruptly. "...My Arthur?"

Royston looked plaintively at Fiona.

"See what I mean?" he whispered.

Kristine was not at Everglades when Richard reported for his first day of work. She had been rostered on for an afternoon shift, which meant that as he was finishing his working day she was just beginning hers.

However, she did manage to catch him before he left, and asked him how he had fared.

"I felt like a fish out of water," he said candidly.

Kristine laughed. "That's how I felt after my first shift!"

Richard smiled in acknowledgement of her remark; then said, "Otherwise, it was okay; apart from these..."

He glanced down at his hands, now reddened around the knuckles from wearing the thick gloves the cleaners were required to use.

"I look like I've got dishwasher hands," he jested.

"You didn't find it too much, what with your injuries from the accident? This was the first time you've done something strenuous, isn't it?"

"Yes. ...But they had me observing more than anything, so I haven't really done all that much today. It felt quite strange – working, and yet not working."

"When are you on again?"

"I've got another orientation the day after tomorrow."

"That's brilliant!" exclaimed Kristine. "I'm on duty that morning, too! We'll be here together!"

Kristine sailed through her afternoon on cloud nine. At long last her best friend would soon be working with her, albeit in a different capacity.

The following morning Kristine called on her grandmother before university.

"It's really practical," she told Fiona while waiting for Emily to wake from her morning nap. "Richard and I will be able to coordinate shifts, because we are free of lectures at the same time."

"Don't forget you are there to work, not to fraternise with your boyfriend!" Fiona retorted.

"Mum! Richard's not a boyfriend. We're just colleagues; buddies, friends. It is possible for a girl to have an ordinary friend who happens to be male, you know."

"Well, make sure it stays that way," said Fiona sternly. You're too immature for anything else with him."

"What is that supposed to mean?"

"You know how I feel about boys who ride motorbikes, and I'm not likely to change my mind."

"I'm sorry, Mum, but I'm not too concerned how you feel. Richard is a nice guy, and he has been through a lot, so lighten up on him!"

"Alright, but just you be careful; that's all I'm saying."

"...For crying out loud!"

Kristine's visit to her grandmother was not going well. She had gone there with the intention of spending time with Emily, so was resentful that anger over her mother's remarks was driving her away before she had done so.

Yet, before she could make her escape, Fiona cut in with, "Oh, by the way, Kristine..."

"What now?" Kristine responded with impatience. This was too much like the old days. Her mother's benevolence seemed to have come to an abrupt end.

"Well wait and I'll tell you," said Fiona; beckoning her through to the kitchen – and out of earshot of Emily.

Then, when she had closed the door for some privacy, she asked in a lowered voice, "Have you ever noticed any odd behaviour in your grandmother?"

"What do you mean – odd? Nana has had a stroke. She's bound to behave oddly."

"Yes, I know that! ...I mean...before the stroke? Did you ever hear her talking to herself – about Grandpa?"

Kristine's hackles rose. She knew exactly what Fiona was referring to, and where this impromptu grilling would lead. Her instincts warned her not to get into it with her mother; now or ever.

If necessary she would have to lie, or at very least, skirt around the truth.

"Nana often used to talk about Grandpa. He was the love of her life...you know that! Even James knew it. You're not thinking of taking it from her, are you?"

"No! ...And you are missing my point. Have you ever heard her talking to herself when she is by herself?"

"For goodness sake, Mum! What on earth are you going on about now? When I am with Nana, she talks to me; not to herself. Am I also supposed to know what she does when she's alone? Now...if you don't mind, I really need to leave. You're forgetting I have lectures!"

At last, Kristine managed to escape.

Exhausted from yet another verbal assault, she needed to stop for a moment to catch her breath.

Would her mother's onslaughts never end?

...And what of Emily? Would she be safe from Fiona's tantrums now?

CHAPTER THREE

Emily had always looked forward to her monthly check-up appointments with Alicia.

No longer just her healthcare professional, Emily treated her like a daughter-in-law now. The fact that Royston was still married to her biological daughter appeared to have slipped her mind since the lovebirds moved in together.

Fiona, on the other hand, was no more than one of the carers to Emily; for very little affection passed between them when they were alone together. Only when Royston, Alicia or Kristine turned up did Fiona attempt to behave as though her charge was still her own dear mother.

Alicia had the kind of rapport with Emily that brought out the best in her. She managed to encourage her both with speech and in her activities; something Fiona failed to do; not that she tried very hard.

To Fiona, Emily was merely an invalid who needed to be looked after. To Alicia, she was a much-loved member of her extended family, who deserved to be given back her independence.

This quality Fiona had come to recognise in Alicia and, to a certain extent, she resented it.

One thing Alicia liked to do when she came round was to go into the back garden and cut a few stems of roses.

She had noticed that there were never any flowers in the house, despite their colourful garden. Knowing Emily's love of roses as she did, this gesture became her way of giving pleasure to someone who was now unable to pick them for herself.

No such consideration ever occurred to Fiona. When Alicia habitually arrived at the back door holding a bunch of the flowers, Fiona barely acknowledged the effort she went to on Emily's behalf.

...Except on just one occasion; and it came about not long after Fiona's probing conversation with Kristine.

Fiona was now determined to find someone who would support her theory that Emily had dementia. If she could get this verified by a member of the medical profession, she would feel much better about the situation; and she would know for sure that her estimation was right.

...And Fiona always liked to be right.

True to tradition, Alicia left her car in Emily's driveway and went straight into the back garden.

Fiona watched from the window as she snipped blooms with secateurs out of the shed; then she timed an exit through the back door to coincide with Alicia's entrance.

"Alicia!" she said, feigning surprise. "I didn't realise you were here!"

Fiona stepped back inside in order to allow her possible collaborator to come in, and quickly closed the door.

Then, ingratiating herself, she added, "What a gorgeous selection of flowers. Mother will love them!"

"Yes, the roses are magnificent at this time of the year. Emily does enjoy having freshly picked blooms in the house. They remind her of Arthur."

"...My father?" Fiona exclaimed. "So you know all about him, as well?"

This was more than she could have hoped for.

Alicia pulled out a vase from the kitchen cupboard and carefully placed the flowers in it.

"Oh yes," she said, filling the vase from the tap. "Emily frequently speaks about him. Theirs was one of life's great romances, from what I hear."

Fiona was disappointed. Alicia appeared to be talking in the past tense. She decided to try a different tactic.

"Have you been aware of anything connected with Dad in recent times?" she asked.

Alicia stopped what she was doing; her suspicions well aroused. Royston had mentioned a discussion that Fiona initiated with him not long ago; one in which she seemed to be fishing for information. He thought at the time her motives were rather dubious, and Alicia now understood what he meant.

She turned to face Fiona; a hint of distrust in her eyes. "What do you mean by that?" she asked.

Sensing the wariness Fiona avoided eye contact with her. It was obvious Alicia knew something, too...and it was far more than she was willing to discuss. Was her entire family deliberately keeping a secret from her?

Alicia heard Emily attempting to call out, and hurried to her in the lounge.

"A..li..cia!" Emily stammered in her enthusiasm, and then exclaimed when she saw the flowers: "Lovely...roses! ...Arthur's roses?"

"Yes, they're from his garden," said Alicia.

She bent to give Emily a kiss on the forehead.

Then, when she saw Fiona coming up behind her, she said, "I'll just put the vase on the dresser, where you can see them. They will be safer, and you won't be so likely to...to get scratched on the thorns."

Alicia was remembering a previous visit when she left flowers beside her chair. Emily, absorbed in the memory of Arthur, appeared to be talking to them; as though Arthur himself had brought them to her. It had been a disturbing observation at the time; one which confirmed to Alicia that her patient was imagining things. She did not want to risk it happening again – certainly not in front of Fiona.

Later on, Alicia relayed her growing fears to Royston.

"I'm really worried about this," she told him. "It looks like Emily is definitely becoming delusional. You, Kristine and I are all aware of it; and now Fiona of all people has noticed her special little eccentricity. ...And as Emily's legitimate next of kin, Fiona has power of attorney over her; and it could spell trouble for Emily."

"Do you think she's on some kind of witch-hunt?" asked Royston pensively.

"What kind of witch-hunt?"

"I don't know for sure. Fiona never had a great deal of patience with her mother. When she suggested our present arrangement, especially as she seemed keen to look after Emily, I thought she had changed her tune. She suddenly became compassionate. But right now all of that seems to have gone out of the window, and I'm concerned that she may have reverted to her old conniving self."

"Perhaps Fiona's just not cut out for the responsibility she's taken on. It isn't easy, looking after someone as infirm as Emily seven days a week."

"Alicia, you're not telling me something I don't already know," chuckled Royston. "Surely you haven't forgotten the various parts I've played in Emily's life during the last couple of years."

"No, my darling, I have not forgotten," replied Alicia in a playful tone. "It's just that you are a different type from Fiona. You're of sound character and naturally kind. But, going on all that you have told me, and from my own observations, Fiona on the other hand seems to be self-serving rather than self-less in her dealings with Emily."

245

Royston laughed. "You're right there!

Then he went quiet; and frowned as a worrying thought crossed his mind.

Alicia noticed it at once.

"What are you thinking?" she asked with concern.

"I was just wondering..." he said slowly.

"Wondering what, Royston?"

"...About Fiona's motives. We are assuming she's just looking for an excuse to be critical of Emily, but there may be more to it than that!"

The Everglades retirement complex opened the first of its village facilities amid great fanfare.

The consortium's managing director, accompanied by several of his executive officers and members of the local media, ceremonially cut the ribbon to open the serviced apartment buildings.

This done, the distinguished party walked through an apartment which had been tastefully furnished especially for the occasion.

Kristine and Richard covertly watched the spectacle from a discreet distance.

"I hope they wiped their feet before they went in," said Richard dubiously. "...Or I will have to shampoo that brand new carpet afterwards!"

Although members of staff were officially invited to the formal opening, only Grace and the registered nurse stayed for the whole function, which included speeches and an afternoon tea.

The two caregivers on duty were required to look after everything in the rest-home while this took place, as well as attend to their own responsibilities.

Richard commented on it as he and Kristine went off to complete their respective tasks.

"The registered nurse here must have very little to do if she can take time to socialise while she's supposed to be working," he said with feigned sarcasm.

"...Tell me about it," said Kristine, assuming his sarcasm to be genuine. She had made a similar observation not long after she joined Everglades. "It seems to me that the busier we caregivers are, the less we see of her. I'm sure she just doesn't like hard work, because she deliberately keeps out of the way. I only ever see her when Grace wants to chat, and when the doctor comes on his rounds."

"You're really not joking about this, are you?" remarked Richard in alarm. Had he opened a can of worms with his flippant remark?

The look Kristine gave him answered his question.

However, the fact that they were now within earshot of other people prevented further discussion on the matter.

But Richard had nonetheless made a mental note of the situation. He decided that from then on he would watch out for unfair practices, especially ones that disadvantaged either him or Kristine.

The following day, Everglades' management sent out a memorandum scheduling a staff meeting for the following week, and requesting that all the employees be contacted. The meeting, they were told, was compulsory, and if they attended while off-duty they would receive an additional hour's wage in recompense.

Kristine and Richard touched base with each other as soon as they received the news.

"Are you going?" Kristine asked.

"We have no choice but to go – it's compulsory. If we don't attend, it might mean a black mark on our records, and I'm not going to risk that at such an early stage of my employment here!"

Kristine checked her university timetable. To get to the meeting promptly and stay for even one hour meant that she and Richard would be late for their afternoon lecture.

"I suppose that won't matter quite so much," remarked Richard. "I'll ring the university office and see if we can send in an apology in case we are a bit late. You never know, the meeting might not last very long."

The all-important meeting was to be held in the rest-home's tiny staff room. Kristine sensed, from the number of people who turned up, that she would start to feel claustrophobic very quickly in the confined space, and opted to sit by the ranch slider that led out to the staff smoking area.

She looked over the spacious area outside and at the fine weather, and wondered why they could not have had the meeting out there.

Ten minutes into the start time, the regional supervisor for Everglades' arrived, and offered a hurried apology for keeping everyone waiting. To make amends for it, he complimented Grace and all the staff for giving the facility a head start over their rivals in the city.

"Thanks to all of you," he added, "we have produced a quality service for the local community. And I am sure you are all dedicated to continuing this praiseworthy trend."

Kristine smiled, appreciating his comments, and joined in with the senior staff and others as they applauded the supervisor.

Then she glanced at Richard who seemed, from his slouched demeanour, not to share in the moment.

Instead, he looked thoughtful, as though his instincts were trying to tell him something.

Kristine tried unsuccessfully to catch his eye.

The regional supervisor continued.

"As the village complex expands," he said, "it naturally means that the responsibilities of staff will be constantly changing, and your cooperation during this period will be very much appreciated. I want you to be on the lookout for revised task lists and also give Grace your feedback on how it all works out. Every couple of months I will come in and we can discuss any issues that arise."

What does he mean by that? Kristine thought.

She looked at Richard again.

He was now staring directly at the regional supervisor. Suddenly he spoke.

"Will you be putting additional staff on to cover our extra workload?" he asked bluntly.

He already had in mind the cleaning of the new serviced apartments. As yet there had been no indication as to who would be responsible for those.

The supervisor coughed self-consciously, and looked not at Richard but to Grace.

It was she who responded.

"Of course, we will revise staffing requirements as more facilities are opened," she said with authority; then added, glancing back at the supervisor as if for confirmation, "But in the meantime, we will be looking to you all to go the extra mile if the need arises. Remember, the important issues are the comfort of our residents and the success of Everglades. We are confident that all of our staff here will rise to this worthwhile challenge."

"I suppose it won't be too bad if everyone pulls their weight," Kristine remarked afterwards.

She and Richard had dashed to the car, conscious now that they would be horribly late for their lecture.

"It's alright for you," he replied as he waited for Kristine to open up. "You have a team-mate to call on if you are overloaded. There's only one cleaner on at a time. ...And

I'm not busting a gut for an outfit that pays minimum wage but expects maximum output!"

Fiona dropped Emily off, complete with wheelchair, at the bowling club. She was well enough now to attend again.

The chair, though the lightest of its kind, was unwieldy to stow in the back of the car, and Fiona struggled with it.

Emily had been invited for lunch by the members of the ladies' club; longstanding friends who insisted on keeping her in the fold. A stroke, they maintained, should not stop people from enjoying themselves.

And so, an excited Emily greeted her associates in the only way she knew how as Fiona once more placed her in the wheelchair.

"Thank you; we'll take over now," said one enthusiastic lady, and whisked Emily off to a gathering that seemed as secretive to Fiona as anything behind closed doors could ever be.

However, she was not in the least bit envious of her popularity, but quite the opposite.

With Emily safely in the care of her friends at the club, Fiona breathed a sigh of relief that at last she had some time to herself.

Fiona had given herself two options of equal appeal to fill in her free time that day.

She was torn between enjoying the luxury of going for a long invigorating walk, or paying a visit to her favourite shopping centre. But after only a short deliberation, she opted for the former.

Incurring even more debt on her credit card would not be a good idea.

A walking route she once took circled an entire housing estate, and led her right back to where she left the car.

She headed for it; then parked and changed into the walking shoes she kept in the back of the car.

The cool air felt good to skin used to spending most of the time indoors.

As she walked along, she happened to glance up at a small sign attached to a lamp-post. It pointed down a side road, and read, 'Everglades Retirement Village.'

The name sounded familiar.

Wasn't that the rest-home where Kristine worked?

It shamed her to realise she had paid so little attention to her daughter's recent activities that she wasn't sure just where Kristine did work.

Fiona was about to walk on past the side road when something stopped her, and instead she headed down it. Curiosity had taken hold. She wanted to take a look at the premises because, she thought with parental smugness, she would then be able to boast to the family that she was showing an interest in her daughter's workplace.

However, when she saw the sprawling complex with its numerous and diverse buildings, all in various stages of construction, she could not figure out just where Kristine's workplace might be.

But then she noticed an imposing building, standing back from the main car park, which appeared not only to be finished, but actually in use.

"That must be their rest-home," she said out loud. "I wonder if Kristine is there today..."

Fiona's eyes scanned the car park for her daughter's distinctive blue car, but to no avail. Though disappointed, she turned away and continued with her walk.

Later in the day, she phoned Kristine and told her of the detour she had made.

"I had hoped you might be there at the time," she said.

"Why? You weren't thinking of coming to see me, were you?" asked Kristine cynically.

Since their last falling-out over Emily's eccentricity, she had remained sceptical of her mother's intentions.

"No, of course not. I just think it would have been nice: to be so close to you while you were at your place of work. Can't I be proud of my grown up working daughter?"

"For goodness sake, I'm over eighteen and a university student. You're treating me like a child again!"

"I'm sorry. But I am proud of you. I love the way you are forging ahead with your life."

"Thanks, Mum!" she said, sounding surprised.

In fact, Kristine was very surprised; compliments didn't often escape from Fiona's lips. She felt a reciprocal gesture might be in order.

Thinking quickly she said, "Would you like me to show you over Everglades some time? You might be interested in all the facilities they're installing, like a bowling green, a day-care centre and even an indoor swimming pool."

"It all sounds fascinating. ...And yes, I would love to take a look round – if it could be arranged."

"I'll ask Dad to stay with Nana one day next week, and give you a guided tour if you like..."

Royston arrived promptly on the arranged day; much to Kristine's relief.

Although she had no duty at the rest-home, there was a university lecture straight after lunch which she needed to attend, so her spare time was at a premium.

As a courtesy to her employer, Kristine had seen fit to ask permission for their exploration of the village, for most of the complex was still little more than a building site. Not even Grace had ventured into the most distant areas, although she knew every detail of the complex by heart after pouring over the plans from time to time with site officials or guests.

As a member of staff Kristine, too, had been required to familiarise herself with the plans.

"Be sure to take a copy with you," Grace insisted. "And for goodness' sake, keep out of trouble. I don't want any complaints from the building contractors on account of your guided tour!"

Kristine parked in her usual place in the staff car park. While Fiona got out, she extricated her copy of the site plan from the glove box.

"I'll show you the rest-home where I work first," she said before locking the car. "You may be able to meet Grace. She's my boss. She's also a friend of Alicia's."

"Alicia? How come?" Fiona asked as they walked across to the main building.

"Alicia said they did their nursing training together. It was through her that I got this job. She recommended me to Grace as a caregiver."

"That was nice of her. I like Alicia; she's very sensible."

Kristine looked at her in amazement while they waited for the main door to swish open.

The last thing she had expected was to hear something complimentary about Alicia.

But then Kristine's train of thought was broken as the noisy life of the rest-home once again flooded her senses.

"There's Grace!" Kristine suddenly exclaimed. She had spotted her coming down the corridor with the registered nurse. "Let's wait here. I might as well introduce you."

Kristine pulled her mother aside while the flow of foot traffic hurried by with its usual efficiency.

"Hello, Kristine," said Grace, halting briefly. "...This must be your mother."

She reached out a hand to Fiona, who took it warmly.

"Hello, I'm Fiona," she said cheerily. "It's good of you to let us look over the rest-home. I didn't realise how busy a place like this can be!"

"I'm afraid there's nothing restful about a rest-home at this time of day," Grace said humorously. "And now, if you'll excuse me, I must get on."

"Of course. ...And thank you again."

"Sorry to hold you up, Grace," added Kristine.

"No problem," she replied. "Enjoy your tour!" And then she was off down the next corridor.

Now that they were free to wander, Kristine made a quick calculation as to where she should start her itinerary of the site. It was far too busy right now to show her mother round the rest-home. Perhaps she could bring her back in half an hour or so when the residents were in the dining room for lunch; it would be quieter then.

"Come on, Mum," she said, guiding her back outside. "I'll show you the village first. ...Now; where's my plan."

The two stood looking over the tiny diagram; then at the immense site it represented, which stretched out before their eyes.

It was hard to envisage the complex in its finished state from the sketched illustration, as only a few of the villas had so far been completed. But the network of avenues meandering through the site had already been surfaced, and provided a point of reference.

"We should begin over there," she said, indicating the skeleton of a building that, according to the tiny printing on her plan, would ultimately serve as the village's main restaurant and recreation centre.

When they returned to the rest-home, the smell of cooking greeted them.

"Hmm, what's for lunch?" asked Fiona frivolously.

"I don't know what's on the menu today, but lunchtime is their snack meal. The main meal is at teatime."

Kristine was becoming accustomed to talking like a tour guide now.

She walked her mother through to one of the corridors and said, "Come this way, Mum. I'll show you what their rooms look like. They all have their own ensuites."

Fiona hesitated.

"Would that be alright? I don't feel comfortable going into someone's private room."

"This one's empty at the moment," Kristine replied. "A new resident is due to come in next week. ...Ah, here it is."

Fiona halted outside the bedroom door.

"What on earth is that awful smell?" she said, screwing up her nose.

She looked critically at Kristine as a pungent aroma of soiled carpet caught her nostrils.

Kristine pulled a face, too.

"Oh dear. They haven't shampooed the carpet yet. The last resident was incontinent. He needed to be reassessed for hospital care as we couldn't manage him anymore."

"I don't think much of the way you keep the place clean, if a smell like that is allowed to linger."

Fiona tip-toed across the carpet to look at the ensuite.

Kristine suddenly felt annoyed by her mother's insulting comment; for Richard and the other part time cleaner did their best under the most difficult of circumstances.

She said in defence of them, "You have to remember, Mum, that the residents are old – some of them a lot older than Nana. Incontinence goes with the territory in a place like this. And we don't have enough cleaners or caregivers to cover the workload. It's a sad fact of rest-home life, I'm afraid... Mum... Mum, did you hear what I said?"

Yet, checking out the adjoining ensuite, Fiona was no longer listening.

"Look at this," she said with delight. "They've got warm-air hand-driers – how quaint!"

Back at the car, while Kristine searched for her key, Fiona took a last look at the complex; content now that she was familiar with her daughter's place of work.

But there was one more building, standing to the right of the rest-home, which she had failed to notice earlier on. It appeared to be nearing completion.

"What will that building be for?" she asked, pointing to it. "I don't remember seeing it on your plan."

"It's the new day-care centre...like a crèche. It's due to open soon, I think."

"Day-care...for older people," mumbled Fiona; thinking out loud. "Now that's very interesting..."

Apart from the smell in the vacant room, Fiona was quite impressed with the rest-home.

Back at home, she carefully explained to Emily how the village was laid out and jovially told her about the warm-air hand-driers.

"You'd really like it, Mum!" she insisted. "They have their own bathrooms!"

Emily listened closely. She understood everything Fiona was telling her.

Retirement villages were not unfamiliar to Emily. She and James had been to a function at another village when they both played for their bowling club team.

As she sat listening, a fond memory came to mind of getting lost in the maze of streets as they tried to find their way out again.

Had she been able to speak properly she would have recounted this amusing tale to Fiona.

Yet, Emily suspected that if she did try to talk, nothing intelligible would come out, so she just smiled and kept her reminiscences to herself.

Throughout the days that followed, Fiona could not help but reflect on her visit to the retirement village.

It seemed the perfect place for elderly people to spend their sunset years in a safe, supported environment.

The rest-home, with staff on duty twenty four hours a day, made her realise just how fortunate their local elderly community were to have somewhere like that close by; especially those who had nobody else to look after them.

She empathised with working sons or daughters who had an infirm parent at home to look after as well as their own children. Somewhere like the rest-home, she decided, must surely be a godsend for those who can't afford to stay at home in order to look after their elderly relatives.

Yet, Fiona also counted her own blessings that Emily's financial situation was substantial enough to support them both; that she no longer needed to earn a living, and that she would never have to consider such a drastic course of action as utilising the services of a rest-home.

"I wouldn't do that!" she declared with conviction. "She is still my mother!"

Even so, she did miss the contact with her colleagues at work. In many ways it had been a welcome change of pace to stay at home with Emily; but having the responsibility of it resting on her shoulders all the time...

"...There's no point in my dwelling on it," she sternly reminded herself.

However, it was not long before the issue resurfaced.

There were only so many activities suitable for someone in Emily's situation. What's more, her general condition, now that she had reached a plateau in her recovery from the stroke, was not as good as Fiona first expected.

It looked, to her, that Emily would now be permanently disabled, and therefore a long-term liability.

"I'd really hoped she would come right," she confided in Alicia during a check-up. "It's so hard to know what to do with her now. We've exhausted all the possibilities. Mum is as bright as a button on the inside, but she obviously is not going to be able to talk normally, or walk without someone holding on to her. And the way she fantasizes about my father... It's a great disappointment to me, I can tell you. My mother will always be an invalid now."

Alicia listened warily. What was Fiona trying to tell her? That she had had enough of being a nursemaid?

"Actually, I think she is doing rather well," Alicia said, then smiled sweetly at Emily and received a beaming grin in response.

"It's alright for you," Fiona went on as though Emily was not present. "She's not living with you. Thanks to me, you and Royston don't have to deal with this all of the time. I never have any freedom these days!"

Alicia turned and looked at her aghast.

Whilst she appreciated Fiona's sacrifice in a way she could never repay, it worried her to think the arrangement was not working out – either for Fiona, or for Emily.

And then she had an idea.

"Fiona, Kristine tells me she took you to see Everglades recently. What did you think of it?"

"It was very nice – and much grander than I imagined. Why do you ask?"

"I was just thinking. My friend Grace is the manager of the rest-home..."

258

"…Yes, I met her."

"Oh! That's good! It makes what I am going to suggest a bit easier."

"…Which is what?"

"You will have seen all the new buildings going up when you were there. One of them is a new day-care centre for the elderly. It has just opened. You may have noticed the advertisements in the local paper."

"I hope you're joking! I don't have time for reading the paper, let alone looking through any adverts. I tell you, an adult invalid is more time-consuming to look after than a newborn baby!"

"Yes, I can well imagine that."

The professional in Alicia sighed, as the friend of the family sympathised with Fiona's plight; for she considered herself to be responsible for them all, not just her client. After all, if she and Royston had not become an item, this situation might never have arisen.

But right now Alicia needed to shake off those feelings. The district nurse had something to suggest to the client; or rather, to the client's daughter – if she could get Fiona to listen. And she was sure it would be of help to her.

"Look, Fiona," Alicia went on. "Would you be interested in taking Emily to a day-care session occasionally? It will give you a break and Emily a bit more stimulation."

Fiona went quiet. She looked enquiringly at Alicia, and then glanced across at Emily who had been paying close attention to their conversation.

The sound of her name being mentioned always drew a response from Emily. She knew of old that it could mean they were devising something behind her back; something she probably would not like.

"I don't really know anything about that sort of thing," responded Fiona. "Kristine said it's like a crèche?"

"Yes; it's something like that...except they have an organised programme which is devised specifically for the elderly in order to keep them active. What do you think?"

"I reckon it would be perfect. ...Don't you, Mum?"

Emily was staring at both women now, her eyes wide in anticipation of a bombshell she suspected was about to be dropped on her. Was Fiona concocting something again?

She wanted to say she didn't like the thought of being regimented; of being treated like a child. However, she also knew how Fiona hated it when she tried in vain to talk...so she waited in suspense for further comment.

Yet Fiona's question had been more of a statement than an enquiry. Without seeking her mother's consent, she had already decided that sending Emily to a day-care facility was the ideal solution. With a bit of free time she might even be able to go back to work for a couple of days per week.

"Do you know what their hours are?" she asked Alicia with increasing enthusiasm.

"...Probably nine till three. Are you interested?"

"Yes, I believe so. I might give Grace a ring tomorrow and see if I can arrange something. Thank you so much, Alicia. I think the day-care is a great idea."

Emily could stand the tension no longer. Had Fiona and Alicia taken the trouble to consult her over it, they would have realised that she was not happy with the gist of their conversation.

As it was, with Alicia bidding her a brief, "Bye-bye Emily; see you again soon," before dashing off to her next client, and Fiona ignoring the "No... No... No!" that burst from her lips after Alicia had gone, Emily was left with nothing but a feeling of dread that the rug was about to be pulled out from under her – and without so much as a 'by your leave.'

My life is still my own, she wailed inwardly; silently lapsing back into her silent world of fantasy, where there was no manipulation by those entrusted with her care, and where she found the solace lacking in her real world.

She had long since arrived at the conclusion that she had nothing better to do with her days than spend time with Arthur and the roses Alicia brought for her.

With great surprise, a couple of days later, Kristine saw her mother enter the front door at the rest-home.

From the dining room opposite, where she had hastily finished setting the tables for lunch – hastily because she and the other caregiver were running late – she glanced up at Fiona's silhouette; then looked again to confirm her observation...and suspicion.

For a moment she hesitated in her task, but the need to prepare for lunch overruled any desire to speak with her mother. Instead, she made do with a quick wave from a distance, which was returned along with an expression that stated, 'Can't you even come over and say hello?'

Later on, Kristine promised herself that she would go round and apologise for seeming rude...and to find out just why Fiona had gone to the rest-home.

...Surely she wasn't there after a job? That would be just too much...

What Kristine did not observe was that Fiona had Emily with her that day, and that when she went into the rest-home Emily was still in the car.

Furthermore, Kristine could not have known that while she and the other caregiver were serving the lunch to their residents, Fiona and Grace took Emily over to see the day-care facility where lunch was also being served.

But of these activities Kristine was as yet unaware.

The sight of so many elderly people, some of whom were severely incapacitated, caused Emily pain.

It alarmed her to witness people of her own age in such a state. She was used to seeing her peers living out in the community, pursuing normal activities with vigour. And her reaction on sensing such melancholy was to turn away; not just because the sight troubled her, but also because she suspected that before long she would be expected to join them.

Satisfied that her decision to enrol Emily at day-care was the right one, after lunch Fiona wheeled Emily around the centre's large communal lounge.

It looked, to her, as though the room served as both dining room and recreational area; for the trestle tables and chairs set out for lunch were being moved back to the walls and the centre of the room made ready for their afternoon's entertainment.

"The local ladies' choir will soon be arriving to sing to them," Grace explained; then added, "By the way, there is one thing I need to know. Is Emily continent?"

Fiona looked at her agog. It was rather too personal a question to be asked with so many people around, and she felt uncomfortable that she was required to answer it.

"Of course!" she whispered with indignation. "I don't allow my mother to be incontinent!"

Grace chuckled knowingly. She wanted to tell her guest that one day she would have no say in the matter; but refrained from doing so. Instead she asked her, "I take it Emily can be managed in the toilet by only one helper?"

Fiona found herself becoming impatient. With a sigh she responded, "Yes! I manage just fine by myself."

"That's excellent then. Would you like to give me your decision now, or talk about it with Emily first?"

"Talk about what?" asked Fiona innocently.

"...Why, Emily joining us at day-care! I presume you've discussed it with her."

"There's nothing to discuss. ...And yes, I have made my decision. I would like her to start as soon as possible."

During their drive home, Emily sat beside Fiona in near panic. She had gathered, from the visit, the environment and the conversation between the two women that there was to be a major change in her daily routine, and she did not like the notion at all.

Emily was comfortable in her own home, with her own belongings – and her wonderful memories. She could not imagine being without her roses, her favourite television programmes, and her beloved husband.

It was the thought of losing the company of Arthur that finally pushed her over the edge, and while Fiona pulled away from an intersection – pausing in her description of their exciting new routine in order to concentrate – Emily seized her opportunity to object.

Using her good hand, she repeatedly thumped Fiona's knee, crying, "No... No... No!"

Shocked by the outburst while she was driving, Fiona swerved unintentionally, narrowly missing the kerb.

"Mum!" she shrieked "What do you think you're doing? Are you trying to get us killed?"

Then, when Emily refused to stop the attack, she said sternly, "Okay, that's enough of that," and pulled over.

Emily was sobbing now. Her anger vented, she felt only anguish, and although she had stopped hitting Fiona, the meaningless words still tumbled from her mouth in a vain attempt to convey her point of view: that she felt hurt and betrayed...and there was no other way she could complain to Fiona and nothing she could do about it.

The purpose of Fiona's visit to the rest-home continued to haunt Kristine.

Surely the woman would not have gone there purely on a social visit...and anything more than that did not bear thinking about.

So, curiosity having driven her mad throughout the rest of her shift, Kristine could not wait to hurry round and find out what was going on.

"What on earth are you doing here?" Fiona said to her in none too friendly a manner.

"Well, excuse me for caring!" retorted Kristine.

Surely her mother realised why she was there!

Slighted by the strange reception, she said with a hint of sarcasm, "Am I allowed in, or what?"

Without a word, Fiona spun round and returned to the kitchen where she had been preparing their evening meal. She was still indignant over Kristine's rudeness at the rest-home among other things, and had no wish to chat with her on a social level.

Kristine went straight in to her grandmother; anxious to make amends for ignoring her the last time she came over. But for some reason, she noted, Emily was clearly agitated and barely responded.

Instinctively, Kristine knew it must be connected with her mother's rest-home visit.

"What's going on, Mum?" she asked outright.

"I'm afraid I don't know what you're talking about?" replied Fiona, taking her frustrations out on a carrot she was peeling.

"Oh, come on. I'm not stupid. I can see something has happened. You're mad as hell and Nana is obviously upset about something major. I know you were at the rest-home for who knows what reason, so I have to assume it has something to do with that. Am I right?"

"Have you been talking to Grace?" snapped Fiona.

"...About what? Mum, I'll say it again: what on earth is going on?"

Fiona sighed and threw what was left of the depleted carrot into the sink. She picked up a tea towel to dry her hands and then turned to Kristine.

"It's nothing very terrible," she said; capitulating. "I've just arranged with Grace for your grandmother to attend the day-care centre three days a week!"

Kristine laughed out loud. "Is that's what it's all about? You had me worried. I think it's a great idea!"

Fiona stared at her in astonishment. "You do?"

"Oh, yes. It will be wonderful for Nana! She must be stagnating just sitting in the lounge here day after day – no offence to you, of course. She will be able to meet lots of new people, and be stimulated. They will probably even get her talking again... Oh, Mum, I'm so thrilled!"

And with delight, Kristine threw her arms around her bewildered mother.

She had for some time now been concerned for Emily's mental state, stuck at home with only Fiona for company. When Grace initiated a day-care facility, it had crossed her mind that Emily might benefit from something like that; only she dared not suggest it to Fiona in case she accused her of interfering. Yet, now it appeared Fiona had been thinking along the same lines...

"There's one thing I can't figure out, though," Kristine said when Fiona extricated herself from the unexpected embrace."

"What's that?"

"If you and Nana have arranged something so exciting, then how come she is upset and you seemed to be angry when I came in?"

"That's obvious, isn't it?"

"Not to me, it isn't!"

"Well you had better ask Nana, then. ...And keep your voice down, if you don't mind."

Kristine was mystified. "I don't understand what you're saying. ...Anyway, how can I ask Nana? She can't respond!"

"No, but she still hears perfectly well and understands every word you say; so please lower your voice!"

"Alright... But what is it you don't want Nana to hear? Is there something more to all of this?"

Fiona pulled her out into the laundry.

"I don't want Nana to hear us talking about her – she's agitated enough as it is."

"But why not? Is it because of this arrangement you've made with Grace?"

"Of course! She doesn't want to go."

"Oh...I see... So that's why Nana is so agitated," Kristine responded. She broke off in thought for a moment and then said, "Leave it to me, Mum. I'll soon bring her round to our way of thinking."

During her months of working at the rest-home Kristine had come across some residents who could be difficult to motivate. Out of necessity, she had learnt a few tricks as to how to get around them. She hoped Emily would be easier to win over than some of her headstrong residents.

Kristine hurried back to the lounge and quietly closed the door for privacy. This conversation must definitely not be overheard, she determined.

Emily had nodded off to sleep, yet when Kristine came back in she awoke with a start.

"Sorry, Nana," Kristine said in a whisper. "I didn't mean to make you jump!"

She dropped onto her knees beside the recliner chair. One glance at the sorrowful face told her Emily's skittish reaction had been due to an upset far more overwhelming than merely being startled. And when she looked closer, she noticed that her eyes wore the trace of recent tears.

It seemed to Kristine just at the moment that Emily was more in need of support than any form of persuasion.

"Dear Nana," she said, wiping away a salty tear stain on Emily's cheek. "You're having a bad day, aren't you?"

Emily looked into Kristine's eyes, smiled and pressed her hand against a damp cheek before kissing it tenderly.

Suddenly Kristine sensed what the problem might be. If her estimation was correct, it was not that Emily balked at the idea of becoming involved with a day-care group, but rather that she was being pressured into going.

The situation bore all the hallmarks of her mother's usual heavy hand. And what made it worse was the fact that Emily could not express an opinion or defend herself except by way of her emotions.

No wonder she was so upset, reflected Kristine.

However, this now left Kristine in a quandary.

She had as good as assured her mother that she could be persuasive; but that was before she understood what had happened to make Emily so annoyed.

Even so, she still felt the motive behind Grace's day-care suggestion was a good one. And in truth, she felt sure that once Emily got used to being there she would enjoy it.

Perhaps she could use her powers of persuasion after all. Certainly it was worth a try.

"Mum tells me you went to have a look at our new day-care wing today," she said candidly; a remark that instantly evoked a furious glare from Emily.

"I think it would be wonderful for you," Kristine went on, undeterred by the glare.

"No... No... No!" was Emily's annoyed response; for she had assumed her granddaughter was on her side.

Kristine immediately sprang into action.

"I take it you weren't too keen on the idea, then?" she said sympathetically.

Again Emily found her voice.

"No... No... No!" she shrieked frantically.

Oh dear, thought Kristine. This is not going to be as easy as I had hoped.

Kristine waited quietly while Emily simmered down; then patiently continued on her quest.

Emily was in many ways no different from the residents she worked with. In fact, the only significant difference lay in their family connection.

As such, Kristine decided to draw on her experiences at the rest-home in order to converse with her grandmother; at very least, to help Emily understand the purpose of a day-care facility.

"I'm sorry you feel so strongly about it," Kristine said sincerely, trying to avoid Emily's fixed glare. "For the life of me, though; I can't fathom why you don't want to go. Take it from me, Nana; it would be fun for you!"

Then Kristine decided to be blunt in her questioning.

"Were you upset because Mum didn't consult you?"

The response was immediate.

"Yes... Yes!" Emily replied; the look now deepening to one of amazement that Kristine had read her feelings.

Spurred on by a bit of progress, Kristine continued.

"How did you feel when you were there?" she asked; then remembered Emily would not be able to answer her.

Thinking quickly, she tried to imagine what she would have encountered.

It would have been crowded and probably very noisy. It would no doubt have seemed like an alien environment for a quiet soul like Emily to be thrust into.

Therefore, Kristine deduced; under such circumstances Emily would have replied that she didn't like it all.

Kristine questioned her accordingly.

Emily responded by flinching, as the recollection of her day from hell returned.

There was so much more Emily could have told Kristine; so many reasons why someone like her might not want to go to a place like that. And, as far as she was concerned, her main reason had more to do with Arthur than anything she was likely to encounter there.

It would have meant that she could not sit and quietly commune with him, as she so liked to do. The recliner chair in her lounge was not just somewhere comfortable for her to while away the hours, it also provided her with a means of escape from her reality so that she could be with Arthur. ...For every time she slipped away in consciousness to join her departed husband, her bossy daughter always assumed she was asleep and left her alone.

Every fibre of her being recoiled at the thought of being deprived of that escape. Her trysts with Arthur were all that kept her going; that kept her sane. At least, that was how Emily viewed it.

But how could she express this to the family without them considering her to be senile; even though she knew her granddaughter would understand...?

Kristine was at an impasse. She had not picked up even a hint of Emily's real opinion.

"Nana," she said kindly. "I won't try and convince you that you'll enjoy day-care to begin with, because I know you probably won't. But if you give it a go for a couple of days to get used to the place, I'm sure you'll soon start to feel at home. I know the staff will really make a fuss..."

"No... No... No!"

Emily was adamant.

"No... No... No!" she repeated, and cried out plaintively, "Arthur...not there!"

Suddenly the penny dropped. All Kristine's recollections of encounters with Grandpa came flooding back, and she realised exactly why Emily did not want to go.

She whispered, "Nana, are you still seeing Grandpa?"

"Yes... Ye-es!"

Emily's words erupted as a heartfelt sigh. The relief that Kristine now understood was immense, and at last she felt a heavy weight lift from her heart.

The pieces began to fall into place for Kristine now. Emily's primary concern was as much in connection with what she was leaving behind, than in what she would be going to.

She wanted only the quiet of her own home, not noisy, unfamiliar surroundings...and she wanted Arthur.

This revelation meant that Kristine now needed to re-evaluate the situation – something she found herself doing quickly, as she could hear Fiona serving up their meal.

Kristine looked anxiously at Emily.

"I'll be back in a minute," she said, and hurried out to prevent her mother from going into the lounge.

"Well?" said Fiona.

She turned resolutely to Kristine; a look of expectation on her face.

"Have you managed to get through to her," she asked.

"...Not quite," Kristine replied; although she knew it was far from the truth. "Nana found the day-care centre very noisy today. She probably would, as the stroke has made her extra sensitive to noise. But more than that, she values the peace and quiet of home..."

"...You told me you were going to persuade her to go," Fiona hissed, realising that Kristine was hedging.

"I know! You don't need to go off the deep end at me! I'm just trying to work out the best thing to do!"

"Kristine, it's not exactly your decision...and I've already made arrangements with Grace; starting tomorrow."

"Mum, did you ask Nana what she wanted?"

"Why should I? I'm the one who looks after her, so I'll be the one who decides what she does, if you don't mind!"

Fiona was shouting now.

From the other room Emily's distraught voice could be heard conveying, as only Emily could, just how she felt about it:

"No... No... No!"

Kristine was desperate. Caught between two viable points of view, she knew she had to come up with something that would appease both her mother and her grandmother, or Fiona would become even more annoyed than she was, and Emily's anxiety level might bring on a further stroke...

"Look, Mum," she said, her heart beginning to race. "You can't just railroad Nana into doing this. It would be cruel. I insist we take her feelings into consideration."

The assertive manner in which Kristine delivered this decree surprised even her.

Even more surprisingly, the abruptness of the directive brought Fiona to her senses.

On the verge of tears, she said plaintively, "Kristine, you don't understand. It's not you who has the responsibility of looking after an invalid all the time. You don't know how much of a strain it is. I am just about at my wits' end these days. Nana can be so stubborn..."

"...Mum, I work with people like this – and some are far more difficult than Nana. Don't you remember the awful smell in that bedroom at the rest-home? That's what they do, you know. You're lucky if Nana's okay that way."

271

"But why should I be the only one in the family who has to deal with everything around here? It's very waring, you know. I never get a decent night's sleep because Nana has to get up in the night. And I would really like to go back to work or spend time with my friends now and then. I bet you and Dad don't think of that!"

"Have you forgotten that Dad looked after Nana all by himself before you took over?"

"No, I haven't; and I am very grateful for that. But it was different for him."

"Why?"

"For one thing; he's a man. He's stronger than I am and I bet Nana didn't give him as much flack as she gives me. ...Alicia knows how I feel."

"What does Alicia have to do with it?"

"It was she who suggested day-care."

"Oh..! Sorry, I didn't realise that..."

Kristine paused to draw breath; then slowly a solution came to mind.

"Mum," she said cautiously. "Instead of throwing Nana in at the deep end, why don't you take it a day at a time?"

"What do you mean?"

"You've made some arrangements with Grace, haven't you? What are they?"

Fiona stopped and reflected.

"I take her in three days a week to begin with..."

"That's too much. It needs to be no more than one day a week. Did you plan to leave her or stay there with her?"

"...Leave her, of course."

Kristine flinched. The thought of her beloved Nana being dumped into a strange place was a little more than she could bear. ...How like her mother to be so insensitive! But this was not the time for criticism. The new strategy still needed to be decided upon.

"Okay," she said. "I have an idea. For a couple of weeks; or even a month, why don't I take Nana one day per week, stay with her and bring her home again? I could probably fit it in with all my other activities. That way she will be with someone she knows, and I can look after her and talk her through everything that's going on. Then, when she's got used to being in that environment, we can start to leave her there by herself for a few hours, and so on..."

"...Like when you started at kindergarten?" said Fiona.

"Kindergarten?"

"Yes; when you were little. You won't remember how I stayed with you for the first couple of days?"

"Of course! Well, actually, I don't remember; but that's what I mean for Nana. Good thinking, Mum!"

Kristine left the house feeling much happier than before; and for more than one reason.

She now had an excuse to give Emily a break; but more importantly, she had finally convinced her that a couple of hours at day-care with her granddaughter and the other ladies would not be such a bad thing after all.

"...And when you get back," Kristine had whispered in Emily's ear, knowing that it would clinch the deal, "You can spend all the time you like with Grandpa!"

A day was arranged that fitted in with Kristine's schedule.

She arrived at Emily's house early, and took over from the morning helper before she had quite finished.

"I'm taking Nana out this morning," Kristine told her in a matter of fact way. "So I'll pretty her up, if you like."

With Emily strapped safely in the passenger seat of her car and the wheelchair folded flat in the back, Kristine attended to just one more thing before they headed off. She hurried round to the back of the house and plucked a single, perfectly formed whiskey rose from the garden, which she then carefully slipped into the buttonhole of Emily's jacket; much to her delight.

A finishing touch," she said, patting it gently; then as an afterthought she added, "It will remind you of what you can look forward to when you get home."

Emily looked across at her quizzically.

"Why, Grandpa, of course!" responded Kristine, reading her thoughts. "...And he'll probably be with you in spirit at the day-care centre as well!"

Predictably, Emily was glad to get back home after her first session at the centre, despite Kristine's attentiveness.

Even the mid-day meal, served to her at a separate table so that she didn't feel too claustrophobic, was tastier than she had anticipated.

Nevertheless, the excursion still wore her out, and left her in need of a nap on their return.

While Emily rested on her bed, Fiona insisted Kristine give her a full report on the session; then eagerly enquired when her original idea of a three-day week could begin.

"Be patient, Mum! Surely you can see the need to take it slowly? I kept a careful eye on her, and she seemed okay with everything. But we can't push her."

Kristine gave a chuckle as she recalled something that had happened during one of the morning's activities. She told her mother about it.

"It was so funny," she said. "A woman came round with aromatherapy oils to massage the ladies' hands. When she got to us, Nana held out a hand to her. She didn't look at what the woman was doing, but just stared into her face. It was all I could do to keep from laughing. Then, when the therapist had finished, Nana reached out and put a dab of oil on her nose, as if to say 'thank you'."

Yet Fiona was not impressed by the amusing tale. She saw the experiment in a different light from Kristine.

This was merely a means to an end as far as she was concerned; and the sooner she was able to achieve her objective with their arrangement, the better.

"So, when are you taking her again?" she asked without remarking on Kristine's anecdote.

Kristine noted her mother's indifference but chose not to respond. It was up to her to help Emily accept the new regime. She would get no support from home.

"I've booked the same time next week," she replied.

Fiona groaned as though under a heavy burden.

"Is that all?" she snarled. "How much more of this do I have to put up with?"

Then she stormed off in frustration.

Annoyed by her mother's comments, Kristine rued the day her father accepted the offer to exchange houses.

It had been a big mistake to assume Fiona's desire to be with her ailing mother was more than a flash in the pan; for just lately she had been demonstrating that it was not.

Kristine suspected that the tension in the house might severely compromise her grandmother's situation there, and was worried about her. Would the attempts to ease Emily into a different routine alienate Fiona even further, rendering it impossible for her to ever get used to the new weekly schedule?

If only her mother had not reverted to her self-serving ways! Having even one selfish person in the family makes it hard on everyone else...

Yet, unknown to Kristine at the time, she was wrong to think so harshly of her mother. Fiona had done the best she could manage for an elderly, dependent person who, though her own mother, was not the most cooperative of people to deal with; thanks to her stroke.

Emily just wanted to be left alone. If she could speak properly she would have informed Fiona as such right from the start. But she could not express herself except through her emotions.

What's more, Fiona's volatile personality showed little patience for Emily's emotional outbursts, especially when all she sought from her charge was cooperation. Like a leopard unable to change its spots, she could not become easy-going just because the situation in which she found herself demanded it.

With Kristine gone and Emily still asleep from exhaustion, Fiona poured herself a glass of wine and flopped down in front of the television. Slowly her attention drifted from the screen to the faraway place she would go to when the first sip of alcohol caressed her mind, and she slipped into a shallow sleep.

All of a sudden, a shadowy figure appeared before her as though in a dream.

It was someone Fiona recognised: a reality in her life she had almost forgotten about; and he was extending his arms towards her in supplication... It was Arthur.

With a gasp of shock she came to; abruptly recognising that she must have drifted off. But what was the image of her dead father doing in her dreams? She hadn't given him so much as a thought for ages; except where Emily's day-dreaming was concerned.

Instantly Fiona shook it off, putting it down to tiredness and the effect of alcohol on an empty stomach; for it was a long time since she had eaten lunch.

She looked up at the clock.

"I must have been napping for a while," she grumbled.

Then she quickly got up, went into the kitchen and flicked on the kettle; still warm from the drink she made for Kristine. Emily would need to get up soon anyway, she decided with authority. A cup of tea was always a relaxed way of waking her.

As she climbed the stairs, it surprised Fiona to realise that she had in fact made two drinks instead of the one she would normally make.

She gently sat her mother up against the pillows and handed her a mug; then, without thinking what she was doing, sat down on the edge of the mattress and leant against the bed-head next to Emily.

Together they drank their tea.

Emily took a sip, and smiled.

"Nice..." she said, raising the mug as if in a toast.

"Yes," said Fiona passively. "I think we were both ready for a cuppa."

CHAPTER FOUR

Richard let out a long sigh of exasperation.

For the second time during his shift he was being pulled up for something he supposedly had omitted to do.

The first complaint, from a male resident, was that the floor of his ensuite had not been cleaned the previous day. The second was from the registered nurse on duty that for two days in a row the waste bin in the nurses' station had not been emptied.

Richard had argued in his own defence: "Don't blame me for someone else's oversight. I wasn't here yesterday!"

"Well, you are here now," she retorted.

Kristine caught sight of the annoyance on his face.

Also frustrated that she had failed to make headway with her tasks, she approached him and said, "You, too?"

Then she placed a hand reassuringly on his arm.

Yet Richard was in a bad mood.

He shrugged Kristine's hand away and strode off to fetch his cleaner's trolley; for rather than respond to her gesture of friendship, right now all he felt like doing was emptying the contents of the waste bin on the registered nurse's head.

"What is it with the staff here?" he said to Kristine during their break, having released some of his frustration on the vacuum cleaner.

"Who precisely are you talking about?" asked Kristine, immediately understanding what he was referring to.

"Oh…just…staff. Why can't they accept that I'm very busy and am doing my best, instead of looking for excuses to be nasty? It's almost as though they get a kick out of it."

"It must make them feel important."

"…I suppose so."

Kristine sipped her orange drink; enjoying its coldness, and also appreciating the fact that she and Richard had the staff room to themselves.

Outside, the older women on duty sat huddled under the veranda, trying to keep out of the wind while they lit up their cigarettes and gossiped loudly.

"Look at them all…they're so full of themselves," said Kristine, indicating those of her colleagues whose work ethics she found questionable. "They treat the place like they own it. I've seen them…wasting time chatting, while the likes of you and me rush around like nut cases…"

"…And get stuck with picking up their slack. Yes. Tell me about it. It wasn't my fault the damn rubbish bin wasn't emptied yesterday. That stuck-up registered nurse should have a go at the other cleaner, not me! I've a good mind to make a written complaint about it."

"Is there any point?" Kristine remarked. "Grace would side with the registered nurse, for sure. They are thick as thieves those hierarchy types. If your complaint was only over a rubbish bin, she would probably have a go at you for making a mountain out of a molehill."

"It was more like the straw that broke the camel's back, but you're probably right. By the way, do you know when they are holding another meeting about our task lists and staffing in general?"

"D'you mean, a management meeting?"

"Yes. Didn't they want an update on how the changes are working out? I've got a few things to update them on, I can tell you…"

"...Oh! Are you not happy about the changes they've made to your schedule, either?"

"No way. The hierarchy here expect us to fit a quart into a pint bottle..."

"...A what?" Kristine laughed at the strange expression.

"It's a saying – 'You can't fit a quart into a pint bottle'. In this case it means we can't fit two hours' work into one hour. But that's what they expect us to do around here..."

"...Because they won't put on extra staff?"

"Yes. They gave us the impression at that first meeting that they would review the staffing situation in a couple of months, but I haven't heard any more about it. Personally, I think they were just paying lip service to us, and have no real plans to keep their promise."

"Richard, are you suggesting they just told us what we wanted to hear?"

"Well, you know what they say about companies and the like – profits before people!"

"Shouldn't that be the other way round in a place like a retirement village?"

"It should be, but apparently not at Everglades!"

"I hope you're joking. I really wish they would come up with something helpful; and soon. I'm tired of having to work my tail off every time I'm on duty, especially when I suspect I'm the only one pulling her weight..."

"...Shush, Kristine. The women are coming back in..."

"...After their own bitching session, no doubt," Kristine laughed mockingly.

Kristine regretted having got onto such a touchy subject while she was still at work.

Her conversation with Richard, though on a topic they both felt strongly about, left her feeling so disturbed that she found it hard to wear her professional smile with the residents or be courteous to staff for whom she had little respect. The only ones she felt comfortable talking to were Richard, and Grace. ...That is, until Grace called her into her office for a chat later in the day.

After inviting Kristine to sit down, Grace pulled out her own chair and addressed her directly.

"Kristine," she said in a serious voice, "I am afraid I have received some negative feedback about you."

Startled, Kristine answered back.

"...About me? You must be joking! What have I done that would cause negative feedback?"

"I received a letter from the sister of a resident. I won't mention who it was..."

"...Am I not allowed to know who has been complaining about me?"

Kristine's hackles were beginning to rise now. ...She was the one with legitimate complaints!

"Just let me explain what happened," Grace said calmly. "Then you can tell me your version of the story."

Kristine capitulated.

"Okay, I'm sorry, Grace. What did the relative say in her letter to you?"

Grace reminded Kristine about an incident a few days previously, when a gentleman asked her to do something for him and she refused.

"Yes, I remember the incident," Kristine retorted; "but it wasn't like that at all."

"Hang on, Kristine; you'll have your chance to speak."

The resident, according to Grace, complained about the incident to his sister; who in turn became indignant that a mere caregiver – whose sole purpose in being there was to assist the residents – should refuse a reasonable request. As a result, his sister felt duty bound to report the incident in writing to management.

When Grace stopped to draw breath, Kristine jumped in with a caustic response.

"I'm not surprised they made a fuss over it, especially when you consider who these people are!"

"Kristine! Just remember your position here, please."

"What...a mere caregiver'?"

"Well...yes, I suppose we should look at it that way in these circumstances."

Kristine groaned under her breath.

"If you insist, Grace... Now, can I explain to you what really happened?"

"Alright...but I expect honesty from you."

"Of course! My God! What is it with everyone around here? I may only be a caregiver in your book, but I am still an intelligent and responsible person!"

Kristine then went on to explain the sequence of events which lead up to the criticism:

She told Grace how she had been rushed off her feet during the morning, because the other caregiver on duty, who seemed to shirk her responsibilities, was not around when she should have been working. Consequently, when one of her residents rang his bell and demanded Kristine help him, she had no choice but to turn him down...

"...And do you know what he wanted me to do for him? Did his sister tell you that?" she asked Grace in a furious tone of voice.

"No, she just said that you refused a direct request..."

"...Well I'll tell you, then! He just wanted me to see why he couldn't get a certain channel on his television! ...As if it really mattered!"

"It mattered to him, Kristine. And it matters to us when the relatives lay a complaint about it."

"I can't help that!" said Kristine, exasperated. "My job is to attend to the needs of my own residents; not to their whims and fancies and certainly not to the whims and fancies of the other caregiver's residents, especially when she disappears! Mr 'You-know-who' was her responsibility, not mine. Did you take it up with her, too?"

"No. It was you they complained about."

"...That's because I was the only one doing any work at the time! With all due respect Grace, I really think you should challenge the other caregiver about why she wasn't doing her job. Oh, and by the way, do you know where I eventually caught up with her? She was out in the car park talking to her boyfriend right on the residents' lunchtime. I'm sorry, Grace, but I do think it's a damn cheek pulling me up for something that was not my fault!"

Taken aback by the offensive from her caregiver, Grace said, "Kristine, I appreciate that you must feel cross, but I still need to remind you that the residents are our primary concern. If the gentleman in question had a problem that needed attending to and you couldn't help him at the time, then you should have explained your situation to him. I'm sure he would have understood. What did you say to him, anyway? His sister told me you were quite rude."

"Rude? Me!" cried Kristine in disbelief, and leapt to her feet. She had had enough now, and just wanted to get out. "I'll have you know, I have never been rude to a resident. It was because I was stressed out. Maybe whatever I said to him came out wrong because I was exhausted – and getting frantic, because lunch was about to be served. But caregiver feelings apparently don't matter around here."

Grace scratched her head; caught between appeasing a client and giving a staff member the benefit of the doubt.

"...I tell you what," she said at length. "If you could quietly explain this to the resident and apologise for your rudeness that day, I'm sure that would do the trick – just to keep the records straight..."

"...But why should I have to?" Kristine retorted, nearing the end of her rope. "I didn't do anything wrong – except be human. I say again, Grace, it is the other caregiver you should be reprimanding, not me. Now, can I please go? My residents are waiting for their afternoon tea!"

Richard cheered when she told him of the confrontation with her boss.

"Good for you, my girl! It's about time someone stood up for us!"

"I probably shouldn't have said anything, but I was still worked up after our griping session this morning," Kristine admitted with remorse. "I'm not usually outspoken, unless I'm incensed about something, and I do hate being at work with a bee in my bonnet. It makes the duty so tedious."

"I know what you mean. ...Although, in my case, I finish up by working even harder."

"Really? I think I would be more inclined to opt for a go-slow or something, on principle."

"Oh, I wouldn't say I work harder out of a sense of duty, but more out of frustration. When the adrenalin kicks in I work like a Trojan; and feel better afterwards."

Kristine laughed. "It's alright for you. You can take your frustrations out on a mop and bucket. I can't very well take mine out on a resident!"

With the ice broken, Kristine managed to finish her duty in reasonably good spirits.

In retrospect she could see Richard's point – she did stand up to the hierarchy for a just cause. The question now was: would it earn her respect or a black mark?

"I guess only time will tell," she thought afterwards.

But of one thing Kristine was now certain. She did not want to work the morning shifts if she could help it; even if it meant being separated from Richard.

The thought of working alongside the older women any longer was more than she could stomach.

Caregivers on afternoon duty were generally younger people; students who, like her, opted to work shifts after their school or university day had finished. Unfortunately though, they were also students who sought to fill in as many duties as they could, leaving fewer that could be offered to Kristine.

"Oh dear," she moaned. "Why is my work becoming so frustrating? All I want to do is earn enough money to pay for my car."

To compensate for her difficulties at work, Kristine threw herself into the task of getting Emily used to being at the day-care centre.

It became something of a mission for her, as though the role had been entrusted to her by a power greater than herself; to the extent that after a couple of weeks her zeal started to drive her mother mad with its intensity.

From Fiona's perspective, it was as though Kristine had nothing in life except Emily's adjustment to the regime.

"I'm getting sick and tired of you and Nana's day-care," said Fiona one day. "It's all I hear about these days."

"But Mum, I thought you wanted her to go more often. You made a lot of fuss about it when she started."

"It's not that... In fact I am very relieved she is getting used to it, thanks to you. I just don't like the way you keep harping on about it. Good gracious, Kristine, at your young age there should be more in your life than just babysitting an old lady; even if she is your grandmother!"

Like the resonance from a bell, Fiona's words continued to ring in Kristine's ears long after they were uttered. Her comment brought Kristine back down to earth with a thud, and she realised to her horror that if she had little by way of a social life beforehand, she had even less of one now. Her year of complete freedom in Auntie Ruth's house was being wasted. In only a few months they would be home, and it would be too late to take further advantage of such privileged liberty...

In the meantime, while Emily slowly adjusted to changes in her daily routine Fiona, with projects she was anxious to implement, decided to speed them up.

Although she appreciated all that Kristine had done to ease Emily into accepting hubbub over solitude and noise over quiet, it was not long before Fiona began to feel that the gentle approach was far from meeting her own needs.

Without consulting Kristine or Emily, she arranged with Grace for a second day to be added to the weekly regimen.

"The time for babying Grandma is over," she declared emphatically. "Both Kristine and I have our own lives to lead, too. Emily is used to her new schedule, so from now on I will drop my mother off at the centre, and then pick her up at three o'clock!"

The first Kristine knew of this arrangement was when Grace directed a staff member to find her and send her into the office. Then Grace rushed into an explanation for the summons, preventing Kristine from commenting on the fact that she had been dragged away from showering a resident, and needed to get back to her.

"It's about your grandmother," Grace explained.

"Oh, no..." Kristine remarked with dread. As far as she was concerned, this could mean only one thing.

Kristine dropped onto a chair by the desk, all thoughts of her resident gone.

With heart in mouth, she feared the worst and hastily sought confirmation of it.

"So Nana has...passed away, then?" she asked sadly.

"Passed away? Do you mean...died?"

"Yes. Isn't that what you are telling me?"

"Goodness me, no! Your Nana is very much alive – and firing on all cylinders from what I hear," Grace added with a disguised chuckle.

Kristine breathed a sigh of relief.

"Thank God for that! So what is the problem with her; and what's it got to do with me?"

"She is currently at day-care! Your mother dropped her off this morning. ...I assumed you knew!"

"No...it's news to me."

"Emily has been allocated another day with us, at your mother's request. But unfortunately..."

"...Uh-oh. What's she been up to?"

As yet, Kristine could only guess at the reason why she had been called into the office.

"...Unfortunately Emily has decided quite categorically that she doesn't want to stay with us; so will you please go over and pacify her."

Just then, Kristine remembered about her resident; and more importantly about the kitchen girl sent to fetch her who Kristine had asked to remain with the resident until she got back...and who even now would be awaiting her return so that she, too, could continue with her tasks...

Kristine looked at Grace with consternation.

"I can't go over there at the moment," she said limply.

"Why not, pray?"

"Because I was in the middle of showering my resident, so cannot rush off and leave her with a kitchen hand."

"Oh! I see..."

"...Anyway, Nana isn't my responsibility today; I didn't even know she was coming. If Mum decided to bring her, then she should be the one to come and pacify her!"

Once again, Kristine felt exasperated.

The unreasonable situation in which she kept finding herself was becoming perplexing. Yet, her annoyance was not directed towards Grace for making such an impossible request, nor at Emily for causing a problem over at the day-care centre. Rather, her angst was placed squarely at the feet of Fiona for deceitfully altering their arrangement and not telling her about it.

"I tried to phone your mother, but there was no reply," Grace informed her.

No, she's probably out somewhere spending Nana's money," Kristine hissed under her breath.

"What did you say?" asked Grace, having failed to catch the allegation; but still, she understood the dilemma her caregiver was facing and advised her: "Don't worry about the shower; I'll attend to it." Then she added, "...Now, will you please go over and sort out your grandmother!"

Kristine found Emily in a distressed state; sitting alone in her wheelchair in the glass-partitioned office assigned to the day-care supervisor.

Emily, so Kristine was told, had been too disruptive to remain with the others.

As soon as Kristine entered the facility Emily shrieked, "No... No... No;" the volume of which conveyed to Kristine just what she was thinking.

Emily was hopping mad about something, and Kristine suspected what that might be.

"Mum dumped you here, didn't she?"

Experience had now taught Kristine that the only way to effectively placate her grandmother when something had upset her, was to empathise with her.

With the realisation that Kristine understood her plight, Emily calmed down; but then she burst into tears.

Oh dear, thought Kristine. What do I do now?

Her mind flicked back to the situation at work; to the resident she had been forced to leave with a kitchen girl; to Grace allowing her to deal with Emily even though she really had no choice in the matter.

With a sense of despair for the impossible predicament in which she found herself, Kristine felt like crying, too.

"Nana," she said quietly, while Emily rummaged in her bag for a tissue. "I don't finish work for another hour or so. Could you possibly stay here till then and I will take you home straight afterwards? Would that be alright?"

"Go home...now!" Emily stated with authority.

Kristine looked through the office's glass partition to see if the commotion had been noticed by anyone else in the centre. It was obvious from the many pairs of eyes now cast in their direction that it had.

The supervisor walked over and opened her office door.

"Is everything alright in there?" she asked in a tone intimating annoyance that the problem was not resolved.

"We seem to be in a bit of a jam," Kristine responded. "Nana doesn't want to stay, and I don't finish my shift until three o'clock. Have you or Grace managed to get in touch with my mother yet?"

"No. She's still not answering her phone."

Kristine groaned under the weight of responsibility. She wanted to appease both her Nana and her boss, but could not be in two places at the same time.

The supervisor recognised her dilemma immediately.

"I have an idea that I'd like to suggest to Grace." she said. "Wheel your grandmother out of there while I use the phone." Then, when her call had been made she said, "Yes, Grace is quite agreeable to it;" as though Kristine would know what she was talking about.

"Agreeable to what?" Kristine asked with Emily looking on uneasily.

"...To my suggestion. She is quite happy to have Emily over at the rest-home until you've finish your duty."

Kristine was flabbergasted. "You're joking!" she said in near panic. "How can I possibly look after Nana and do my work at the same time?"

"You won't need to. Emily can socialise with the other residents, and you can pop in to see her in passing."

"Oh!" responded Kristine; astounded by the simplicity of the solution. Yet, one detail still needed to be taken into consideration, and Kristine felt the need to mention it.

"That's a really good idea," she responded politely; then added in a half whisper, "But what if Nana behaves badly over there, too?"

The supervisor was becoming impatient now. She had done everything she could to accommodate the needs of a caregiver and her unruly grandmother, and was anxious to have the problem off her hands so that she could get back to her other clients.

Clearing her throat purposefully she said, "Let's not be cynical about this, shall we? You will just have to persuade Emily that this is in her best interests."

It felt strange to Kristine, going back to her workplace with her grandmother in tow – like the convergence of her two worlds, as she later reflected.

After explaining to Emily why she had been taken there, Kristine introduced her to some of the staff.

Grace greeted her courteously.

"Hello, Emily. It's good to see you again."

Emily grinned broadly, enjoying both the attention and her granddaughter's company.

Kristine wheeled her into the communal lounge where the occupational therapist was holding a session on flower arranging with a group of residents.

The therapist glanced up from her work to see who the latecomer was, and not recognising Emily as one of her regulars, looked enquiringly at Kristine.

"This is Emily, my grandmother," said Kristine, as much to the other ladies present as to the staff. Then, for the therapist's clarification she added, "Emily is going to enjoy your company for a while, if that's alright."

"Welcome, Emily" said the therapist without question. "Come and join us. We are just making some table centres for the dining room. Do you like roses?"

The therapist handed her a bloom she had prepared for the arrangement she was working on.

"...Rose?" said Emily; her eyes lighting up. She showed the flower to Kristine. "...Look!"

"Yes," said Kristine, and explained to all present, "Emily loves roses. She has a whole garden of them at home."

"Then you must take her to see the new garden that's been laid out in the back courtyard," the therapist insisted.

Kristine looked puzzled.

"I didn't know we had a rose garden here."

"We have now − it's brand new. The gardeners put the finishing touches to it just this afternoon. I'm surprised you haven't seen it yet."

"I guess I've been too busy to look," Kristine responded sheepishly, and then said to Emily, "Isn't that wonderful, Nana? These ladies have a rose garden, too."

Emily ignored her. She was absorbed in her flower; a familiar sight to Kristine now, with the many occasions that Emily had been lost to a rose bloom when she visited her at home.

Kristine always knew what that meant, although she never confronted her over it. She silently prayed that Emily would not start talking about Arthur now. This was not the time to air her eccentricity. ...However, Kristine noted, she

291

did seem more settled now than at the day-care centre, and for that small blessing she was grateful.

At the completion of her shift, Kristine breathed a sigh of relief that nothing troublesome had occurred during the disruption to their afternoon.

Emily seemed to be at peace with the ladies in the flower-arranging group. ...Or maybe, Kristine reflected as she wheeled her out of the building, the roses contributed to her passive demeanour more than anything.

Just then, she noticed Fiona's car parked at the main entrance to the day-care centre.

Kristine cringed. "Oh rats," she said to Emily. "Mum's looking for you. She's not going to be very pleased about any of this."

As if responding to Kristine's hunch, Fiona hurried out again, her look of displeasure clearly visible. Straightaway she saw Kristine with Emily, and stopped in her tracks.

For a moment, both stood rooted to the spot.

It was Kristine who acted first when she realised that Fiona's car was in fact holding up other people waiting to collect their relatives.

"I'll see you back at home!" she called out cheerily.

Then, without waiting for her reply, Kristine continued towards her car.

"Hey, wait a minute!" Fiona called back.

She made to go over to them, but was quickly reminded by the tooting of a horn that she was indeed blocking the day-care entrance.

With a grunt of displeasure, Fiona got into her car and aggressively drove off.

The familiar throaty sound of the car's engine caught Emily's attention, and she pointed after it. A look of alarm crossed her face.

The euphoria of her afternoon with Kristine and the lovely roses gave way to the recollection of why she had been taken to the rest-home. She suspected she would be in trouble with her daughter when they got back.

"Okay, Nana; let's go home," said Kristine, oblivious of Emily's fears.

She unbuckled the wheelchair's lap belt and helped her to get out. Then, when she had secured her into the car and loaded the awkward chair, she added with a wry grin, "We'll go and face the music, shall we?"

"I know what you're going to say," she said when Fiona met them at the door.

Kristine eased the wheelchair backwards up the front steps and into the house.

Fiona responded with feigned indignation.

"I wasn't going to say anything; although admittedly I was annoyed to hear your grandmother created a scene in front of everybody. But it appears you and the supervisor dealt with the situation adequately, so I've no complaints."

Kristine pushed Emily into the lounge, whispering in her ear, "Do you need to go to the bathroom, Nana?"

Emily looked up at her.

Cheekily, she mouthed back, "No...thank you!"

She had enjoyed the afternoon with her granddaughter. Kristine was much better company than Fiona.

With Emily settled in her recliner chair, Kristine bent over and kissed her on the forehead.

Much to Emily's dismay she said, "I'm sorry Nana, but I must get going. I've something planned for this evening, and will need plenty of time to get everything ready."

"What have you got planned?" asked Fiona.

Kristine looked around disapprovingly. The information had been for Emily's ears only.

She ushered her mother into the kitchen and said, "I'm just having a friend round for dinner;" hoping Fiona would be satisfied with her flimsy explanation. Then she added quietly, "By the way, we can't leave Nana at day-care by herself anymore. She's obviously not going to settle there. And besides..."

"...Besides, what?" asked Fiona curtly. The snub had not gone unnoticed.

Kristine responded accordingly. "You don't need to be so huffy about it, Mum. If you hadn't dumped her there in the first place it might not have come to this."

"For goodness sake, Kristine, what are you implying?"

Kristine faced her squarely; the pent up frustrations of her afternoon ready for expression.

She said cuttingly, "As if you need to ask! I wouldn't be surprised if the day-care people refuse to have her back, especially unattended. There are other clients to consider, you know...and from what the day-care supervisor said, Nana outstayed her welcome good and proper today..."

Kristine left Fiona to reflect on her comments, and hoped she wouldn't take it out on Emily.

After all, she maintained, her mother only had herself to blame for the problems that arose.

Emily was not an object to be shoved out of sight just to suit Fiona's purpose. She had her own wishes that needed to be considered, too.

From what Kristine understood of the day's events, Emily had not even been consulted about being left there by herself. It really was no wonder she reacted the way she did.

Yet, her behaviour at the rest-home, Kristine recalled, was the exact opposite. Was it because she had Kristine close at hand; or maybe something else?

While she prepared for the arrival of her dinner guest, Kristine pondered the day's strange happenings. A smile crossed her face, as the image of Emily tenderly caressing a rose provided the answer to her wondering.

Indeed, the transformation she witnessed in her Nana's demeanour had nothing to do with her or the change in their environment. It was the rose, or rather the power of her rose, that kept Emily entranced. In the rose Emily saw, sensed and enjoyed the presence of her beloved Arthur.

Kristine was putting the finishing touches to a lasagne she had made when the doorbell rang. She checked her watch. Could that be Richard already?

Curious, she opened the door.

"I'm sorry to be so early," Richard said, walking straight in. "I hope you don't mind. A friend gave me a lift. My bike is out of action at the moment."

Kristine looked at him dumbfounded. Her dinner guest was dressed to the nines; the only thing missing, according to Kristine's observation, was a bow tie.

"Wow!" she said; impressed. "Don't you look snazzy?"

Immediately she regretted the remark; especially when she saw the look of embarrassment on his face.

"A bit over the top, eh?" he replied; noticing Kristine's casual attire.

"No! I think you look great! I just haven't got out of my cooking gear yet!"

Kristine, who stood before him still wearing her jeans, had planned to transform her appearance just before his arrival. She wanted tonight to be special as there was something important she needed to ask him. ...At least, she hoped she might have the opportunity to ask him.

As it was, with the moment of embarrassment passing between them, all she could say was, "Go on in, and I'll give myself a quick makeover."

"Please don't go to any trouble just for me!" he called after her as she rushed into her room.

But Kristine did not hear him, for her bedroom door had noisily clicked shut, cloistering her in a solitude that she hoped would give her the inspiration she would need to match Richard's neat appearance.

"Why did he come so early?" she groaned anxiously, while trying to select something reasonably dressy from her wardrobe.

Meanwhile, Richard wandered around the living area of Kristine's home.

The aroma of freshly baked lasagne caught his senses.

"Something smells good," he remarked, and gravitated towards the kitchen.

Kristine had placed an assortment of snacks, a bowl of salad and the hot lasagne on the kitchen bench, ready to transfer to the dining room for her guest. The kitchen sink contained all the pots and pans from her cooking. When she emerged from her room, Richard had filled the sink with hot water, and was washing the cooking pots for her. The surprised expression on her face made him laugh.

"I have to sing for my supper," he said in jest. "...Or at least, help with the dishes."

"I don't know whether to thank you or be cross with you," said Kristine.

This was not what she expected of her dinner guest.

"Don't do either," he said, peeling off kitchen gloves that were far too small. "Just enjoy the evening as much as I intend to!"

Kristine chuckled to herself.

Never had she considered Richard to be domesticated, but rather would have expected him to flop down on the couch, switch on the television while she changed, and probably leave her to clear up afterwards.

In a way, she was relieved he had shown his domestic side to her. It would make it easier for her to put forward her proposition.

After they had finished eating, Richard exclaimed, "That was delicious, Kristine!"

"Well, thank you," she said amicably.

This was so different from the many times they would get together at the rest-home or university, when all they seemed to do was complain about work. Richard had a much nicer disposition when he was not under pressure.

While they washed up the remainder of their dishes, Kristine listened contentedly to his banter, and wondered when there would be an opportune time to bring up the subject she had hoped to raise. She did so want to sound him out; after all, that was why she invited him — apart from the fact that not long ago she promised him a home-cooked meal.

With the last of the crockery put away and their coffee made, Kristine decided that it must be now — or never...

"Richard," she said as they each walked through to the lounge, carrying a coffee mug. "There is something that has been on my mind for a little while, and I wondered what you might think about it."

"What's that?" he asked, removing a cushion from the couch with one hand while steadying the coffee mug in the other. Then he sat down.

Here goes, thought Kristine with trepidation. I might as well come straight out with it.

"What would you say to sharing this house with me?" she asked cautiously.

Richard stopped in the middle of sipping his coffee and looked at her sideways.

"Do you mean...just you and me?"

"Yes," she replied sheepishly. Then when she saw the look of concern on his face she added, "...Just as friends, of course. You know...flatmates!"

In response Richard put his coffee down, as if the very act of doing so would aid his ability to think.

"Wow! This is a bit out of the blue, isn't it? What made you suggest it?"

Kristine felt uneasy about her proposition now. Was she in over her head to even consider asking Richard?

Thinking quickly, she began:

"Two things have been on my mind recently. Firstly, I get really tired of being here by myself all the time, and secondly, I wondered if you might actually like the idea of moving in here. It wouldn't cost you anything, apart from food and things like that..."

"...But what about your folks? When are they due back from holiday?"

"Not for a while yet. I've got the house to myself for the whole year."

"And then what? My folks wouldn't take me back again if I left home now – and you'll have to find somewhere else to live in the near future... I presume you won't go back and live with your mother."

Kristine went quiet as she had not thought it through that far ahead. It looked like her proposal wasn't going to work out in her favour after all.

However, sensing the reason for her disquiet, without delay Richard said, "I suppose we could find somewhere together when your relatives come home."

Kristine gaped at him. This was even more than she had hoped for!

"Do you mean to say you like the idea?"

"Yes, I suppose so. I find it suffocating living at home, and I'm not the best of company for the oldies..."

He stood up and strode around the room, testing it for spaciousness.

Nodding in approval, he said, "Yep, I could live here for a few months, no problem."

"...With me?" Kristine asked tenuously. She didn't want him to discount that side of any arrangement they made.

"Of course! I'm not likely to try and kick you out of your own home!"

Kristine couldn't believe what she was hearing. She had presumed he would at least want to go away and think about her offer.

"Okay," she said breathlessly. "It's agreed! You will be my flatmate here until my relatives get back!"

"Great! Which is my room, then?"

Richard made for the hallway and headed off towards the bedrooms.

In a state of escalating excitement tinged with alarm, Kristine leapt up and hurried after him.

"...Not that one, it's mine!" she shrieked when she saw his hand reach towards the door of her own untidy room. "You can have the Master bedroom. I found it too big, and moved into this one. ...But you might enjoy the space."

"Gee, thanks. I'm honoured," he retorted; yet, when he looked inside the room he wasn't so sure.

"It's a bit flowery," he said, pointing to the bed with its bold colour-scheme.

"That's only the duvet. You can bring your own bedding if you like."

"I guess that would be alright."

Richard plumped down on the side of the bed, trying it out for comfort.

"This is nice," he said, and spread himself out over it. "Yes, I think I'm going to like living here."

"Here...with me," she repeated.

"Yes, Kristine...with you! That's the second time you've said that. You needn't worry. I'll do right by you. You may find it hard to believe, but although I may be a bit rough round the edges, I've actually got a heart of gold!"

"I don't doubt it at all," she chuckled, recalling the sight of him standing at the sink, wearing a pair of bright yellow kitchen gloves.

"...You've done what?" remarked Royston when Kristine happily told her father of the arrangement. "I hope you ran it by your aunt and uncle first."

"No. Why should I?" asked Kristine indignantly.

"...As a courtesy, of course."

"They wouldn't mind!"

"They wouldn't mind if your flatmate was a responsible young woman. But Auntie Ruth might have something to say about bringing your boyfriend into the house."

"He's not my boyfriend!" Kristine was exasperated now. "Dad...it's only Richard! You know him; we're just friends. There's nothing going on between us!"

Royston sighed; caught between two sets of values.

He approved the idea of his daughter having a live-in companion until Ruth and Wilbur returned, yet he was also entrenched in an old-fashioned notion that she would be too naïve to live in a platonic relationship with a man who looked like he'd been around the block a few times.

Reluctantly, he backed down.

"I suppose it would be alright till they get home, which can't be too many months off now. ...And if it doesn't work out, then you'll be leaving there soon..."

"...It will work out, Dad. We'll make it work out! Richard and I are both mature adults, despite what you think. ...And it's ages before the others come back from their trip. So you've no need to worry!"

Even so, Royston was far from happy.

His daughter he trusted; but could he say the same for Richard? Once a young man himself, Royston understood masculine desire.

Would Kristine be able to handle unsolicited advances from him?

The following weekend, Richard turned up at Kristine's house with a friend and a borrowed trailer. With little in the way of personal possessions, the car plus a trailer load completed his move with ease.

"What do you want to do with that?" asked the friend, pointing to the last item on the trailer: Richard's powerful motorbike, repaired and restored since his accident but as yet unridden.

He decided to ask Kristine.

"Where would I be allowed to store my bike?" he called inside to her.

Kristine, who was making up Richard's bed, did not hear the discussion with his friend. Leaning round the doorpost she answered him.

"Just bring it in here," she said, thinking he meant his bicycle. "You can prop it against the far wall; there's plenty of room."

Richard's friend let out a loud guffaw.

"I think your lady friend must be a bit touched in the head," he smirked. "Whoever heard of keeping a motor-bike in a bedroom?"

Shaking his head scornfully he walked back out to the trailer, ready to oblige.

With a perplexed look on his face, Richard saw an urgent need to correct the misunderstanding before they found themselves with a motorbike inside the house. He rushed after his friend to stop him.

Just then Kristine appeared.

"Where is it then?" she called after him.

Richard halted and turned around. "Where is what?"

"Your bike!"

"...There!" he said, and pointed towards the gleaming monster now being carefully unloaded from the trailer.

Kristine shrieked. "Oh, my God! You're not thinking of bringing that in here, are you?"

Richard raised his arms heavenward, and directed his friend down the driveway.

"I'll find somewhere to stow it later on," he told him.

Then he explained to Kristine what meant by 'his bike'.

That evening, the two new flatmates relived the hilarious moment over a celebratory glass of lager. Still fond of his beer, Richard had brought a crate of his favourite brew with him.

Although Kristine was not a drinker herself, she relished the fact that she was sharing in something he liked; for if they were to live together harmoniously, she knew she must accommodate his lifestyle as well as Richard himself.

She also realised that Richard had learnt his lesson over drinking to excess. Alcohol would not be a problem in the future, of that she was certain.

As Kristine had prophetically stated, Emily was no longer welcome unaccompanied at the day-care centre.

The ruling to this effect was impressed upon Fiona not long after the unfortunate incident. Yet, despite Kristine's advanced warning, the decision still took her by surprise.

Annoyed, Fiona wrestled with the dilemma throughout the weekend, barely refraining from taking it out on Emily; not because she did not feel like using her as a scapegoat for her frustrations, but for the sole reason that she knew

302

it would achieve nothing, as her mother's moods of late had been fragile and at times uncontrollable.

As far as she was concerned, with the promise of a return to work on the horizon, any proposal that she might offer to stay with Emily at day-care was completely out of the question; and that was final!

By Sunday's end, Fiona had come up with what, to her, was the only solution to her problem.

Although it had never been her intention, she saw no option now but to insist that Kristine extend her weekly commitment as Emily's day-care companion. A call to her sister's phone followed shortly afterwards.

With great surprise, Fiona heard a man's voice at the other end of the line.

"Is that Wilbur?" she asked; thinking Ruth had returned.

The voice replied, "Did you say 'Wilbur'? There's no-one here of that name."

"I'm sorry. I was ringing for my daughter Kristine. I must have misdialled."

"No...you've got the correct number. This is Richard, her flatmate. I moved in only recently."

"Richard? ...Richard who rides a motorbike?"

"Yes. ...At least, I used to."

Fiona was getting the message now.

"Well, can I speak to Kristine, please?"

"I'm afraid not. She's doing an afternoon shift."

"Oh...have her ring me when she comes home, then."

"I'll probably be in bed by then. I've got an early start tomorrow. I could leave her a message, though..."

"...Never mind! I'll ring her myself!"

Fiona hung up abruptly. She was cross now. How dare Kristine get a boarder in Ruth's house without permission? She felt sure her sister would neither know about it, nor approve of the clandestine arrangement even if she had been informed. ...And as for Kristine's choice of flatmate...

"Sparks will fly when I catch up with you, my girl," she said out loud.

It was not until later in the evening that she recalled her original reason for contacting Kristine. And when she did, she also realised that she could hardly chastise her in one breath and then ask a favour of her with the next.

"Perhaps I'd better make light of the flatmate thing," she decided prudently. "It's possible I overreacted. Kristine is a sensible girl. She may have already emailed Ruth for permission to get someone in."

She looked up Everglades in the phone book, and then reluctantly rang the rest-home to speak to her daughter.

After a few rings a polite girl answered the call.

"This is Everglades," she said. "How may I help you?"

Without hesitation Fiona asked her, "Is Kristine there? I wish to speak to her, please."

"This is Kristine speaking..." the girl said; then added cautiously, "Mum...is that you? Why are you ringing here?"

"I phoned you at the house to discuss Nana's day-care, and your friend answered..."

"...My friend? ...Oh...Richard. Yes; I was going to tell you about him..."

"...Alright, alright. We can go into that some other time. Just now I need to ask if you'll go with Nana the day after tomorrow. The day-care people won't accept her without one of us there as well."

"I thought as much. Hang on a minute; I'll check on my roster. Now...what have I got...?"

Kristine looked down the comprehensive list of duties for all the Everglades staff members. She caught sight of her own name, and traced her finger across the page till she reached the relevant column.

"Here it is… I've got another afternoon duty that day."

"Oh! Does that mean you won't be able to take her?"

"…Not necessarily. I could take her early and bring her home after lunch. …Then I'd be in good time for my shift. How does that suit?"

"Oh, Kristine, that would be marvellous. I really would appreciate it."

"Have you got something on that day?"

"Yes. I'm starting back at work. They asked me to fill in for someone who's on leave."

"What time do you finish?"

"…About four, I think?"

"Four? …Four o'clock in the afternoon?"

"Yes, of course! Why do you ask?"

"…Because I have to be at work by three. You will just have to finish early and come here!"

Fiona hesitated. "Oh, I wouldn't do that! I won't spoil my chances of getting more work by being picky about when I leave on my first day back!"

Kristine was becoming agitated now. Her mother was not only holding up the main phone line and keeping her from her tasks, she was also displaying her usual tendency towards selfishness.

Although Kristine needed to place emphasis on one or two more points – such as the fact that accompanying Emily was only a favour to Fiona not a moral obligation, and that her own employer had rules where punctuality was concerned – she thought better of pursuing the issue just at the moment.

"Mum," she said. "I can't discuss it anymore. I am still at work, you know. We'll talk about it in the morning."

"Okay," said Fiona, assuming Kristine had agreed to her request. "Thank you, love. …I'm sorry I held you up."

Kristine angrily put the phone down.

305

'I don't know why I do it!' she thought in despair. 'Why do I allow my mother to manipulate me all the time?'

However, during the night Kristine began to have qualms about her attitude. In effect, she regretted having been so harsh in her way of thinking.

Her mother's commitment to Emily had been based on an assurance of a reasonable measure of recovery. Yet, in reality the liability had become more arduous than any of them could have envisaged. Furthermore, of the two, she was the only one who understood her grandmother's state of mind and knew about Arthur as a real presence... As far as she could fathom, Fiona still had no knowledge of this, but assumed Emily was becoming senile and, out of need, had reacted accordingly.

The whole unhappy situation must be a nightmare for them both!

How, then, could she criticise the motives of someone who had voluntarily taken on such a responsibility with no sure knowledge of how it might pan out? It was too easy for her and the other family members to just sit back and allow Fiona to cope with everything alone.

Thus, when a way to solve her mother's problem came to mind, Kristine decided to make amends.

...But first, she realised, she needed to seek permission from Grace.

Later in the morning, Kristine called Fiona with her plan.

"I asked Grace if Nana could stay at the rest-home with me for my first hour of work – like she did the other day; then you can come and pick her up at four. ...How's that for ingenuity?" she remarked triumphantly.

The pause on the other end of the phone belied the look of disapproval on Fiona's face.

"Kristine, I know you mean well, but I don't appreciate you taking matters into your own hands where my mother is concerned. You should have consulted me first. I make the decisions for Nana; not you."

Kristine was dumbfounded. Had she not wasted a good night's sleep feeling sorry for her mother, and then taken admirable steps towards solving an annoying problem?

Suddenly she snapped.

"Honestly Mum, you are so ungrateful! I have bent over backwards for you recently and given up a great deal to help out with Nana. Yesterday you put me in a tight spot over this four o'clock business, and all you can say now is, 'you don't appreciate it'!"

"I didn't mean it quite like that..."

"...When are you going to accept that I am not a child anymore? I'm just as capable of dealing with matters that arise as you are. And the arrangement I made with Grace was the logical one to make. What on earth don't you like about it? ...Or is it just that you can't stand someone else stealing your thunder?"

"What's that supposed to mean?"

"It means that you want everything done according to your own wishes, of course. What else could it mean? It wouldn't hurt you to be a bit flexible. You didn't ask Nana if she wanted to go to day-care; you just took her. Neither did you consider my needs. The issue with timing the pick-up tomorrow is something I sorted out myself. Can't you just leave it at that, and be glad you've been relieved of the responsibility?"

Fiona gave up. It was true, the overlap of times was of concern to her, and it was also true that she had not yet done anything about it.

"You are right," she said with forced humility. "I really must learn to be flexible. Your plan is just great."

"Well, thank the Lord for that!" said Kristine; none too courteously. "Now why the hell couldn't you have said so in the first place?"

When Kristine hung up on her mother she noticed that the answerphone light was flashing. Quickly, she opened it up.

The message was from Everglades, notifying the staff of a meeting the following afternoon at two-thirty.

Alarmed that this might affect her plans with Emily, she rang to see whether the meeting was compulsory, and if not, to register her apology.

The thought of having to leave Emily unattended for any length of time worried her.

"Yes, I'm afraid it is compulsory," said the receptionist. "It's the meeting with management."

For a moment all thought of her commitment to Emily disappeared. This was the meeting she and Richard been waiting for. Excitement shot through her in anticipation of news that management would now resolve their workload and staffing issues.

"That's great; I'll definitely be there for this meeting," she said, and put down the phone.

Only then did she remember about Emily.

Richard had already heard about the meeting, as he was at work when it was announced.

He concurred with Kristine's belief that management would finally come through for the staff.

"It's a relief to know that Everglades are thinking of us," remarked Kristine during the university lunch break.

"Don't count your chickens too soon, though," Richard replied. "We haven't yet heard what they'll say."

"I know...but what else could it be?"

That night Kristine fretted about the day ahead. She knew it was going to be a long day, acting as companion to one old lady in the morning and then looking after multiple elderly residents throughout the rest of the day.

But it was the time in between that gave her the most anxiety. How would Emily behave at the rest-home while she attended the meeting?

During their day-care session, Kristine wondered if she should forewarn Emily of the situation; for if she found just cause to dwell on the girl's absence, problems might well ensue...and to be hauled out of a management meeting just to attend to a precocious old woman would be too embarrassing for words.

But then she decided against it.

In Kristine's opinion, her grandmother would receive enough stimulation from the afternoon's therapy activities not to give her absence a second thought.

Kristine brought Emily over to the rest-home just before the meeting was due to start.

Once inside, she instantly heard raucous voices behind the closed doors of the manager's office, and assumed the top brass were already there.

She cringed at the sound of the registered nurse's shrill giggle. It seemed that, rather than help the staff finish their work prior to the meeting, their supervisor would rather hobnob with management.

"That's typical!" Kristine muttered under her breath, and took Emily straight into the lounge.

The occupational therapist, preparing for her afternoon session, was seating the slow trickle of residents as they came into the lounge.

She grimaced at Kristine as if to say, 'I wish they could move faster; I haven't got all day!'

309

Kristine pulled a similar face back.

She empathised with the therapist; knowing how it felt to be restrained by the slow pace of the residents when she had many tasks to do in a short space of time.

But then, the therapist switched from a grimace to her professional smile and said cheerily, "Hello, Emily! I'm so pleased you have come to join us again."

Emily beamed, and glanced excitedly around the room as though looking for something.

When she appeared not to see it, she gazed enquiringly into Kristine's eyes and said, "No... flowers."

Immediately Kristine realised that she was expecting to see the roses again, and panicked. She knew of old how quickly Emily could become irrational if she felt something was wrong.

She looked at the occupational therapist who was in the process of handing out bingo sheets and plastic discs ready for the weekly session.

Kristine's heart sank. This was a game Emily would not be able to play, as her attention level was still minimal.

But then she had an idea.

With a quick, "I'll only be a minute, Nana," she darted out through the foyer in the direction of the rose garden.

On the way out, a staff member insistently reminded her that she should get to the staff room as the meeting was about to start.

Yet, Kristine was on a mission, and nothing was going to stop her from completing it.

Assuming that by now at least one rose bush would have blooms on it, she deftly plucked the choicest head; not caring if anyone saw her do it – which they did.

The gardener, himself heading indoors for the meeting, witnessed the theft and shouted, "Hey, what do you think you're doing?"

Kristine looked up in alarm.

"Sorry, but I need to do this," she called out. "I'll explain why later."

Then she dashed inside; trying not to look too rushed.

Back in the lounge, Kristine breathlessly showed Emily her flower, and was relieved to see her reach out for it.

With a broad grin, Emily said, "Thank...you."

"Nice touch," said the therapist, grasping the reason why Kristine had done it. "I'll fill up a bingo card with Emily so she doesn't feel left out...and make sure she wins at least one of the games!"

With no more time at her disposal Kristine blew Emily a kiss and hastened from the lounge.

Emily stared after her in dismay; a look noticed by the therapist, who swiftly distracted her before apprehension could set in.

"Let's join in with the others," she said, wheeling Emily over to the table. "You and I are going to have a nice game of bingo."

The staff room was already full when Kristine hurried in. Richard was seated by the ranch slider.

Although he had saved a seat for her, he was forced to relinquish it, and gave her a disgruntled look to that effect. So Kristine found herself squashed into a corner behind the door with nothing to sit on.

While the management team introduced themselves to new members of staff, Kristine snatched a moment to draw breath after her hectic day with Emily. Suddenly she realised she had not eaten lunch, and it was a long time before her next break. She was also thirsty.

She looked with envy at a fellow caregiver who was sitting next to the water cooler, and almost willed her to send over a cold drink.

311

She noticed, too, that nobody had bothered to open any windows in the increasingly stuffy room.

All at once, Kristine felt like crying in despair. She was exhausted already, with a full shift still to work. The saving grace for her frustrations must surely come in the form of good news from management.

That, if nothing else, should be enough to cheer her...

Meanwhile, Emily was enjoying her rose bloom while the occupational therapist played games of bingo for her.

With her teeth, she gleefully ripped open the bite-sized chocolate bar she was given for winning the full house on her second game, not for a moment suspecting that it was won by fraudulent means.

After messily consuming her chocolate, Emily sat back and enjoyed the spectacle of other ladies winning similar prizes, with the gentle scent of her unlawfully procured rose continually pleasing her senses.

Several minutes later, the congenial atmosphere in the lounge was suddenly shattered by the noise of shouting coming from somewhere nearby. It seemed at first that a male resident was upset; certainly, the therapist reacted as such to the ladies.

"Somebody's not very happy," she said, making light of the disturbance, and then cheerfully continued to clear up after their bingo session.

Then, not long afterwards, the shouting could be heard again; this time much louder. Furthermore, it was clearly not the voice of an elderly gentleman, but that of a much younger man.

The therapist looked up in alarm. Through the doorway she saw a male member of staff heading for the entrance.

It was Richard.

Kristine hurried after him without excusing herself from the staff meeting.

She had agreed with every angry sentiment which Richard expressed to his superiors, and which drove him to barge his way out; for the meeting had not proceeded as either of them expected. In fact, the gist of it turned out to be quite the opposite.

She caught up with him at the bicycle rack.

"Just leave me alone," he snapped as he aggressively tightened the strap of his helmet. "Nothing you could say will make me feel any differently. As far as I'm concerned, Everglades is the pits. This whole set-up is nothing more than a money-making racket! People are just a commodity to the hierarchy. They don't care about the residents, and they certainly don't give a damn about their staff! I've a good mind to resign and tell the local papers why..."

"...Oh Richard, I would hate it if you left," said Kristine in weary distress.

Although she was discouraged by the comments made by management, she had held her tongue.

Right now, she felt guilty that she didn't back Richard in his stand against their latest demands.

"Kristine, go back to the meeting; I'll see you tonight," said Richard, ready to ride off.

With nothing more she could say in response, Kristine stood for a moment and forlornly watched him go.

How disastrously the day had turned out compared with her hopes of that morning.

Not only did the meeting go on far longer than she had expected, but also it delivered unwelcome news to the overworked staff.

As she walked back to the main building, she went over in her mind everything management told them.

313

In essence, they advised their staff that from the first of the month the degree of dependency of the residents they accepted into Everglades would be increasing, and clients previously assessed as suitable for hospital would now be eligible for rest-home care.

In addition, to accommodate the extra workload, each duty was to be lengthened by half an hour...however, they added with an air of conciliation, state-of-the-art lifting equipment would be brought in so that caregivers could manage the dependent residents more easily.

Richard took the news badly. As soon as he realised that instead of taking pressure off the staff management were in fact adding to it, he could keep silent no longer.

"You don't give a rat's arse about your staff, do you?" he exploded, shocking those who were closest to him.

Grace immediately sprang to management's defence by reminding Richard that he was not actually a caregiver and that the changes did not even apply to him...

"...If it involves one of us, it involves all of us," he had shouted back, and then barged his way out of the room; unwilling to stay in the stifling atmosphere any longer.

Kristine, still conveniently tucked behind the door, had slipped out after him; cringing at the tirade of expletives that accompanied his exit from the building.

For a moment, she stood outside the entrance watching senior personnel leave the staff room; then as she moved inside, she heard a car tooting.

Turning round, she saw her mother waving wildly. Fiona had come to collect Emily.

Kristine, however, was still too incensed by what had taken place to be bothered waving back.

Instead, she wailed, "My God, is it that late? I'll never get my tasks up to date by tea time!"

314

Inside the door she was faced with a wall of bodies and loud chattering from the staff. To her consternation most people seemed quite cheerful.

Did I miss something? she thought curiously.

She had assumed that everybody else, like Richard and herself, would be unhappy about the increased workload. Yet, they appeared to be unperturbed by the prospect of having to work harder. And rather than hearing derogatory remarks, she overheard one woman suggest it might be fun stringing the residents up on a hoist.

Her colleagues, it seemed, were not taking the changes seriously. But then, she guessed, they would not be the ones to shoulder the extra workload. It would probably fall to her if past experience was anything to go by.

Suddenly she felt sick to her stomach.

Kristine headed towards the kitchen, ready to begin her preparations for the evening meal: tasks that were already behind schedule on account of the meeting.

...But then she remembered her grandmother. Emily was still in the lounge, and she had not been in to see her since leaving the meeting.

With relief she recalled that Fiona had already arrived to collect her.

...Even so, she decided; she should at least say goodbye.

Kristine turned back to the lounge, just in time to see Fiona coming in through the front door.

Immediately, Fiona reprimanded her for not responding when she tooted.

"Are you too proud in your fancy uniform to even wave to me now?" she snapped. "...And why were you outside when you are supposed to be looking after Nana?"

Kristine saw red. "Mum! For goodness sake, don't you start, too! I've had enough for one day."

Then she sidestepped her mother to look for Emily. She found her sitting by herself in the lounge; clutching her already wilted rose.

The therapist, assuming Emily would soon be picked up, had completed her shift at three o'clock and left.

Tears trickled down Emily's cheeks and onto her blouse.

At the sight of her, Kristine knelt beside the wheelchair and apologised profusely for not coming in sooner.

"We had this awful meeting, and it went on for ages…" she explained, trying to appease her; then she said, "…Oh look; Mum is here to take you home!"

Emily abruptly took control of the situation with a fierce glare in her eye.

"No… No… No!" she cried in anger, and thrust the sorry rose into Kristine's face.

"Nana, what's wrong," asked Kristine plaintively, trying to place Emily's feelings ahead of her own.

Fiona looked on in alarm.

Then Emily held out the rose to Fiona.

Morbidly, she said, "Arthur…dead."

At once, Kristine understood.

CHAPTER FIVE

At long last the university semester and Kristine's course came to an end.

With the gruelling schedule of study and exams on top of Everglades mercifully behind them, both Kristine and Richard felt a weight lift from their shoulders.

"At least we can now get out of the rest-home and look for a proper job!" Richard said, pleased that his reliance on their sub-standard wages could soon be exchanged for a decent income.

Kristine knew what he meant. The hourly rates of pay at Everglades were the lowest in town. She had struggled to make ends meet even in her rent-free accommodation, and to repay Emily for the car.

But one thing troubled her about finishing the course. Now that it had come to an end, did it mean that she and Richard would part?

At least, she conceded, for now they still lived under one roof, and were employed by the same rest-home as well. After his outburst at the staff meeting, Kristine had persuaded Richard that walking out on them just now was probably not the best idea if he wanted to leave with some kind a reference.

Her experience of working at the café had taught her the benefit of biding one's time, if not one's tongue.

She wisely told him, "Having a reference might mean the difference between being chosen for a job and it going to someone else."

Yet, there was also an ulterior motive in her suggestion to him. She had secretly thought how nice it would be if she and Richard could resign from Everglades together.

However, that was only a pipe dream. So far, neither of them had even applied for another job, let alone secured one. ...Nor could they until they had found out from their exam results whether or not they were entitled to do so.

When the day for the results arrived, Kristine and Richard nervously drove over to the university.

With their unmarked envelopes finally to hand, Kristine insisted, "Open yours, first."

Kristine was quietly confident about her results. Exams had never really been a problem for her; she always sailed through her secondary school exams. But she was worried about Richard. With all his troubles in recent years, she feared how he might react if he failed his finals.

Richard slit along the top of the envelope with his finger and pulled out the flimsy results slip.

He turned the paper round the right way, and poured over the printing.

Then his eyes lit up.

Excitedly he cried, "I don't believe it! I passed!"

Kristine joined in with his excitement.

It looked like they would be able to move onto the next phase of their careers together after all.

"Well done, Richard, I'm so pleased for you!" she said, hugging him.

"Okay; your turn," said Richard, extricating himself from her grasp. "Don't you want to open yours, too?"

"Yes, of course," she laughed, and tore the envelope open with a flourish.

But then her jaw dropped, and wide eyed in disbelief she digested the word emblazoned on her slip.

"Oh, my God; I've…I've failed!" she stammered, looking up at him helplessly.

"You're joking! There must be some mistake."

Richard took the slip from her, hoping she had misread the vital word. But there had been no misunderstanding.

"How can you possibly have failed?" he said. "You're so much better at learning stuff than I am!"

Kristine was too stunned to comment. The colour had now drained from her face, and she needed to sit down.

"I feel sick," she said in despair.

All her hopes had been pinned on passing her exams. Now she had no qualifications and no prospects.

"What am I going to do?" she wailed.

Richard took up the initiative.

"Come on, Kris; it looks like you're going into shock," he said, pulling her up. "Let's go to the campus café and get something sweet into you."

Kristine meekly allowed him to lead her. A sugary cup of tea later she felt slightly better. Part of her felt like crying; not just because of her bad news, or the fact that she had spoiled Richard's moment of glory, but because the other students in the café had obviously passed their exams by the volume of happy chatter that surrounded her.

"I have to get out of here," she said with a heightened sense of urgency.

Grabbing her purse Kristine made for the exit.

Suddenly she felt out of place in the university.

Richard followed her.

Back at home, Kristine sat hunched over in the lounge, her chin in her hands, her eyes fixed on the floor.

Her whole world had turned upside down and there was nothing she could do about it.

Richard poured them both a drink of lemonade, and sat opposite her. While she sipped intermittently he observed her with concern; he had never seen Kristine depressed before. Of the two of them, he was the one who had the mood swings; not Kristine.

He knew her as a person of strength.

She had buoyed him up; made him less conscious about his appearance, and given him back his self-esteem by caring about him. And now, here she was in the depths of despair; looking to all appearances like a different person. …Certainly not like the Kristine he knew.

All at once a surge of compassion engulfed him.

Kristine was special – the closest friend he'd ever had; and right now she was hurting.

Instinctively, he went over to her, squatted beside her chair and put his arm around her shoulder.

Kristine burst into tears.

"I'm sorry, Richard," she whimpered. "You must think I'm very selfish, concentrating on my misery and denying you the right to celebrate."

"For goodness sake, Kris; I haven't given it so much as a thought," he said kindly…and meant it, too. Since Kristine opened up her envelope and received the shock of her life, he could think of nothing except the pain she was feeling.

To ease her burden of conscience, he gently said, "Maybe, when you are feeling better about things, we can celebrate my success."

Kristine nuzzled her head against his shoulder.

How strong he seemed in her hour of need.

She glanced at him, and found herself looking directly at the scar. Up close it still looked unsightly, despite its many months of healing. Then she stroked it gently with her fingertips, causing Richard to recoil slightly.

"Why did you do that?" he asked in surprise.

"Oh, I don't know. I guess it was my way of saying thank you for being such a good friend to me."

Across town, Fiona was becoming restless again. In effect, she had had more than enough of her mother's company, despite the additional sessions at day-care.

It would help tremendously, she thought, if Emily could be a bit more cooperative, a little less dependent, and not quite so senile; particularly where the ghost of her father was concerned.

Never a day went by now when Emily did not bring his name into their rather one-sided conversations, especially when Alicia brought her roses. On those occasions Emily seemed to drift off into fairyland. Why the roses conjured up an image of Arthur she could not figure out. Sometimes it was as though he was actually present. And when Emily spoke of him in public...well, that was a step too far.

At length she decided it was time to impress upon Alicia and Royston just how much stress she felt, and gave them an urgent call.

Fiona's ex-husband and partner called in frequently these days; conscious as they were that Emily was now quite a handful for her. On the occasion of this visit Fiona, true to character, had no compunction about airing her many grievances over her mother's eccentricities – after all, they were no longer a private affair. She felt sure that half of their village must be aware of Emily's ghostly association with her deceased husband by now.

While Royston watched the spectacle of Emily enjoying her roses, Fiona took Alicia through to the kitchen on the pretext of helping her with afternoon tea. She wanted to talk in private, and Alicia was quick to realise why.

Any suspicions Alicia may have had about Fiona had long since dispersed. Once Emily's eccentric behaviour became open to public scrutiny, she witnessed firsthand that Fiona was not trying to stir up trouble anymore.

So, placing herself in the frame of mind to assist in any way she could, she smiled knowingly as Fiona recounted Emily's most recent escapades.

"To be honest," Fiona said at length. "I just don't know what to do with her anymore. Kristine has to stay with her when she goes to day-care because she won't sit quietly unattended. She's behaving more like a naughty toddler than a mature and reasonable adult."

"I think you've hit the nail on the head there," Alicia responded with a nod. "An outcome of stroke, along with other things, is the loss of maturity. Just as Emily is in the position of having to learn how to talk and walk again, so she has to re-learn how to behave in an adult manner. Unfortunately, though, it doesn't look like that is going to happen now. She will probably remain childlike..."

"...Then how am I going to manage her in public if she misbehaves all the time? In some ways it's even worse than having a little child at home. At least children actively show an interest in what's going on in their lives. The only activity Emily's interested in is her flowers..."

"...Because of Arthur?"

"I believe so. The rose garden here was his special place, and I think Emily is taking comfort from having a living part of him still in her life. But surely she should be socialising with other people as well?"

"If Emily had not suffered the stroke she would be living her life to the full again. But the stroke has robbed her of everything except the ability to remember. Memories are all she has to sustain her; nothing else matters apart from those and her immediate family..."

"...Which brings me back to my dilemma. Emily may need little more than she already has here at home, but I want considerably more than that! I'm really stagnating with just my mother for company!"

Fiona was becoming frantic now. Alicia had as good as stated there was no chance Emily would ever emerge from her childlike shell and be normal again.

"I'm sorry to keep complaining like this," she went on, "but I don't think I can take much more of it. Please tell me what I should do, Alicia!"

"Is everything alright in there?" asked Royston, peering round the doorpost. "We can both hear you in the lounge, and it sounds as though you are having an argument."

"Yes, we're fine, thanks," replied Alicia with half an eye on Fiona who, she realised, was exhibiting signs of distress. Fiona may have been selfish all her life, but right now she was genuinely suffering.

When Royston returned to Emily, Alicia went on, "I take it the day-care experiment is not working then?"

"Not really," said Fiona. "...Not unless Kristine is with her...and she's got work commitments as well so doesn't have much spare time."

Alicia frowned as she pondered an idea. "You wouldn't think of having a full-time helper to look after her at home, would you?"

Fiona paused for a moment.

"I don't think that would work," she said, "There would need to be more than one or two carers involved to cover the whole period. Mum would hate it, for sure; and to be quite honest, I don't like the idea of having a succession of strangers traipsing through what is my own private space as well as Emily's..."

"...I see your point."

Alicia again went quiet for a moment; deep in thought.

Fiona was desperate for her to come up with a solution now, and watched her face for signs of inspiration.

Then Alicia said, "As far as I can make out, there's only one alternative open to you..."

"...Which is what?"

"Have Emily assessed for long-term residential care."

"You mean, in somewhere like Everglades?"

"Yes. ...Although, now I come to think of it, she may be considered too dependent for rest-home care. She would need to be in a hospital environment where there are staff and facilities for Emily's level of disability. How would you feel about that?"

Fiona cringed. She hated hospitals. The very mention of the word brought back memories that made her shudder.

Alicia took note of her reaction.

"It will come to that sometime in the future, anyway," she said. "Emily is completely dependent now and is not likely to improve as time goes on."

Fiona capitulated. "I suppose you're right. But I do hate the idea of her being in a hospital. Those big, impersonal wards would be too much for her."

"She would not necessarily be in a big ward. They have single rooms, too. And also, the private hospitals take into account the fact that their patients actually live there, and make their surroundings homely and attractive. You might be surprised..."

"...Even so, my mother would never settle in a hospital. If they're having trouble with her in the day-care centre, think what she would be like in a busy hospital! There's only one place apart from here that she has been happy."

"Oh, where is that?"

"...The rest-home at Everglades, of course! Kristine said Mum loved it the days she took her into the lounge there. They even gave her a rose to hold. ...And I've been through

Everglades...it's lovely. They all have their own ensuites. Mum would settle in really well."

"But, Fiona, Emily's not eligible for rest-home care. She needs a hospital. They wouldn't accept her permanently at Everglades with her level of dependency, even if she was welcome; which presently she is not."

Alicia went away, feeling she had let the family down.

As Emily's primary health carer she should have been able to give constructive advice, rather than the unsuitable suggestion she came out with.

She told Royston about it later on.

Ever suspicious of Fiona's motives, he said, "You don't suppose she wants me to look after Emily again, do you?"

"Royston, shame on you! Of course she doesn't! Fiona's had some serious problems with her mother just lately; problems that none of you could have envisaged. She's not coping and really needs our help. Personally, I think Emily should go into care."

"That's a bit extreme, isn't it? ...I mean, we're talking about Emily, here – our bright and vibrant Emily. Have you forgotten what she is normally like?"

"You are referring to what she used to be like, Royston. Emily will never be that way again. The stroke has robbed her of those qualities, and also many of her abilities as well. And she isn't the only one affected here. We need to look after Fiona and Kristine, too."

"Emily will always have feelings, though!"

"Yes, and those feelings will be taken into account. But it's her physical condition that's causing problems. If Emily could express herself properly and still had a degree of independence, it would be different. But as things are, the next step is to have her assessed for residential care."

Kristine rallied only gradually from her shock discovery.

So ashamed was she of her exam failure that she kept it from her family.

After a few days, Richard backed away from his morose companion; leaving her alone in order to begin his quest to put his qualifications to good use. It was not long before he came back to her with some surprising news.

And this time, he decided, she was not going to rob him of his moment in the sun.

"I've got myself a proper job," he told her straight out; as much as anything to snap her out of the melancholy that permeated the whole house.

Kristine smiled, but also sighed dejectedly. How she had looked forward to the joint celebration when they both found jobs out in the community. All she could manage for Richard by way of congratulations was, "I'm very happy for you." But before sinking back into her dreary comfort zone she thought to ask, "Where is it, then?"

"At the general hospital," he answered. "I start off as an assistant to the physiotherapist, but there's also room for advancement, so they tell me."

"What about your scar? Did that bother them at all?"

"Apparently not; although the interviewer said it looked painful. I guess a place like that treats patients with scars that are far worse than mine."

"Yes, I suppose so. When do you start?"

"In two weeks' time: which fits in well with giving notice at Everglades."

The mention of giving notice was too much for Kristine. She burst into tears; in doing so reminding Richard of their one-time aim to resign from Everglades together.

"Oh, sorry, Kristine. I forgot about our mutual ambition. It was thoughtless of me to mention it."

Kristine sniffed back her tears.

Suddenly Richard became irritated with her. She wasn't just in shock anymore; she was feeling sorry for herself. As a male, that was something Richard could not tolerate.

He said tersely, "Look, Kristine, don't you think it's time you got over your disappointment? Wallowing in self-pity is not going to solve anything for either of us."

"It's alright for you!" she cried angrily. "You've got your qualifications, and now you've got a job. I've got nothing. Where the heck do I go from here? ...Just you tell me that, because I sure don't know!"

"It's not as bad as all that!" Richard retaliated harshly. "You've still got Everglades, and there is nothing to stop you re-taking the last semester of our course. Failing the exams last time doesn't mean you won't pass next time. And there is no way you're likely to fail again, is there?"

While he chastised her, Kristine glared at him; stunned into mindless silence.

Instinctively, Richard recognized that his words had hit home, and he continued a little more kindly; determined to bring an end to her pain.

"My friend, it's not the end of the world. Life really does go on, you know."

Then, rather than wait for Kristine's anguish to gather momentum once more, he flicked a sympathetic half-smile in her direction, and retreated to his room.

Kristine sat for a moment, absorbing what he had said. If it wasn't for the fact that she still felt depressed about the whole affair she would probably be appreciating Richard's constructive suggestion by now.

...And it had been a constructive suggestion: taking the course again. If the truth were but known, it was only her misplaced assumption that she and Richard would move on together that triggered the depression.

327

Six months wasn't too long to wait, she thought; a slight glimmer of hope making its presence felt in her somewhat deflated self-esteem. But then, with a further pang of grief she remembered Everglades. How could she cope with another few months working there, knowing that Richard would not be around for moral support? She would be left to struggle with all that hard work by herself.

Another tear fell.

She went into the kitchen for a tissue. Catching sight of herself in a makeup mirror on the wall, she gasped...what a sight she looked! Her hair might not have been brushed for days, from its appearance.

She quickly straightened it, blew her nose on the tissue, then decided Richard had been right in accusing her of self-pity. ...And yes, it was definitely time to get over it.

To make amends she would cook him a nice meal; then spruce herself up for a pleasant evening. Richard deserved his celebration, and at long last he was going to get it.

A short time later, Richard timidly emerged from his room; the aroma of hot spices drawing him into the kitchen.

"What's that you're cooking?" he asked Kristine, who was stirring vegetables in preparation for a pasta sauce.

Still holding on to the saucepan, she twisted her head round and said over her shoulder, "It's dinner...for us."

Then she put down the saucepan and faced him.

"I thought about what you said, and decided you were right... Oh, are you going somewhere?"

Richard had on the leather jacket he usually wore when he went out for the evening. He looked down at it, caught off guard; not wanting to cause her any more grief.

"Yes, I am. ...At least, I was. But as you have gone to the trouble of preparing us both a meal, maybe I'll stay and eat with you; I am a bit peckish."

"Are you sure?" she asked, embarrassed all of a sudden for putting him on the spot. "I could just save you a meal. I don't want you to miss out on your celebration."

"Yes, I'm sure... I'd like to stay here," he said, removing his jacket as if confirming his intention. "We can celebrate here; and," he said with a cheeky grin; "I'm sure your uncle won't mind us opening one of his bottles of wine!"

"He's probably forgotten what wine he's got anyway," suggested Kristine, happy now that the most recent drama in her life seemed to have abated. The tension between them of late had grown distressing.

"I tell you what," Richard said, "I'll check out the wine, and then you can serve up that delicious smelling meal. ...Let's celebrate!"

With a glass of rich red wine each, and the pasta sauce enhanced with a generous spoonful of the same, Kristine toasted Richard; and he reciprocated.

"I don't know what I've got to celebrate, though," said Kristine, the wine going straight to a head that was unused to taking alcohol.

"Okay, then," said Richard, correcting himself. "Here's to my current success, and your future success. How's that for a positive attitude!"

"I'll drink to that!" Kristine responded, chinking her glass with his; then taking another sip of the sweet and titillating beverage.

As the evening wore on, with the dregs of pasta sauce soaked up with crusty bread, and the last drop of wine drained from the bottle, Kristine felt more mellow than ever before in her life.

Coming out of the doldrums was like a great weight lifting from her. She felt happy to the point of euphoria, and yet she didn't really know why. Maybe it had something to do with the wine...or with Richard...

He, too, was in a remarkably good mood.

With the release of a few inhibitions, the two flatmates retired to the couch with their drinks; to chat about things they had not discussed before: topics of a personal nature and opinions they had for or against the people they knew.

Then casually Richard came out with something which astounded Kristine; something she had not expected to hear from him.

He told her that in their schooldays he was attracted to her and hoped they might go out together.

...But that was before the accident, he added...and then he apologised in case it sounded as though he changed his mind about her. In fact, he explained, it was only because of the accident and his resulting loss of confidence that caused him to veer away from her...

Abruptly, Kristine realised what Richard was alluding to: the torment he went through knowing he might be scarred for life; the low self-esteem that must have overwhelmed his strength of character.

Had this camouflaged what had all along been his true feelings? Was he trying to tell her that now?

As if to test her theory, Kristine moved up closer to him on the couch; however, thanks to the effects of the wine, the sleeping giant of passion was already awakening in him, and the touch of Kristine's knee against his roused it fully from sleep.

Richard looked at her with a strange and compelling gaze, as though peering into her soul.
Shifting his position slightly, he slipped an arm around her shoulder and drew her close to him.

Although it was with the scarred side of his face that he suddenly descended onto her lips she did not seem to notice, and they kissed for the first time, giving no thought to decorum; parting only when the need to draw breath necessitated it.

"I think we were ready for this," said Richard, adjusting his position on the couch; his intention of taking passion further catching Kristine by surprise.

Somehow she knew what was about to happen...

...And that she would be powerless to stop it even if she wanted to.

I've never done this before," she said nervously. "I don't know if I should..."

But Richard was in control.

He gently led her into lovemaking, taking her innocent sensitivities into consideration, and leaving her feeling like Cinderella to his Prince Charming. Afterwards, when they separated exhausted but exhilarated, Richard snuggled up beside her on the enormous couch, and brushed a stray lock of hair from her face.

To him, she looked radiant; for her eyes twinkled and her cheeks blushed with the fulfilment of a new bride.

She turned her head to him and looked deeply into his eyes. Still breathless she gasped, "I never knew it could be like this!"

"I really am your first, then?"

"Oh yes...I wouldn't lie about it!" And then she laughed. "If my aunt and uncle could see us now, they would have a fit! And as for my mother..."

But then, as if Kristine's remark had tempted fate a little too persuasively, Richard and Kristine simultaneously sat up at the sound of a key being rammed into the front door lock, and it quickly opening.

331

"Oh, my God!" said Kristine, leaping up from the couch; her face even more flushed as she frantically attempted to straighten her clothing.

Then almost immediately a voice called through the now open door.

"Kristine...we're home!"

It was Ruth.

If Kristine had thought she was swift enough to put on an air of innocence, she was mistaken; for the moment Ruth and Wilbur looked into the adjacent lounge they could see that something had been going on.

"Auntie Ruth!" cried Kristine in disguised horror.

"Hello, love...sorry we're late...the plane was delayed."

Then she noticed the shambles in her house, and the dishevelled state of its occupants.

In a critical tone, Ruth asked, "Would you mind telling me what has been going on here...and who this might be?"

She indicated and then looked directly at Richard; her other hand still clutching one of the many bags they had with them.

Kristine came to her senses with a jolt.

Abruptly she said, "Yes, of course. This is Richard, my boy..., my flatmate. We were celebrating because he's just passed his exams and got a job. But you haven't told me, Auntie Ruth, why are you here? You weren't due back for a while yet."

"I know," said Ruth, making room for Wilbur to bring in more bags. "We decided we'd had enough of travel and came home a couple of weeks early. But Wilbur explained it all to you in his email. ...You did receive it, didn't you?"

"...Email? ...Um...did I receive it? I'm not sure."

Kristine was mumbling now; the reality of the situation sinking in to an alcohol-affected mind.

In an instant, her magical evening had turned into a nightmare. She had been caught in an untenable state of affairs in her prim and proper aunt's house, and she didn't quite know how to get out of it.

In the background Kristine heard her uncle say, "I'll take the bags into our room."

With a gasp, Kristine raced for the door.

"No! Uncle...wait! You can't go in there just now."

"Why not?" asked Ruth. "Haven't you got it ready for us? We told you in the email we'd be back today. ...And now I come to think of it, you never did reply to say you'd received the message."

"I...I don't know whether I received it...or not," Kristine stammered ineffectually. "I haven't been checking emails lately. I've been very...busy..."

"...So you didn't know we were coming home early?" asked Ruth.

"Um...no. I'm sorry, Auntie Ruth. I'm really sorry."

All this time, Richard had remained in his seat; shocked into silence by what was taking place.

While Kristine conversed with her aunt, he discreetly reassembled his clothes and gathered together the wine glasses still cluttering up the lounge table. Then he slipped out to the kitchen with them, feeling it was not his place to get involved in a family dispute. The thought of being trapped between two emotional females unnerved him.

Had this not been a factor he might have stayed in the kitchen and started washing up; a token gesture he would have been obligated to make to compensate for Kristine's oversight with her messages. But the raised voices coming from the other room, not just about the email but also because Kristine had allowed a male lodger to come into their house, so intimidated him that he quietly placed the dishes in the sink and slunk off to remove his belongings before Kristine's relatives realised he had been sleeping in their room.

Somehow, Richard knew he could no longer regard it as his own room.

Without a second thought, he pulled his hold-all out of the wardrobe and began packing his clothes.

A few minutes later, having changed over the bedding and bundled up his own, he deposited everything in the only empty spot on the hall floor; the rest of the space still taken up with luggage.

At that moment, Wilbur came in through the front door with the last item from his car, and found himself face to face with the strange male.

Though in a state of panic, Richard took the initiative.

Cheerily, he said, "Hello, Sir...I'm Richard."

Instinctively, he extended his hand in greeting to diffuse what might yet turn into an awkward situation.

However, with a smile Wilbur returned the gesture and the two men shook hands like old friends.

"Have you taken good care of Kristine while we were on holiday?" Wilbur asked.

"I've tried to," replied Richard, relieved that her uncle seemed to be alright about his being there.

Then Wilbur noticed the bag and duvet dumped at the other end of the hallway.

"I hope you're not leaving on our account," he said.

"I've been using your room...I hope you don't mind. We didn't know you were coming back till now, so I've only just cleared my stuff out of it. ...My bike's still in there."

"Your bike?" asked Wilbur with a puzzled look.

334

"...My pushbike. I've been leaving it inside for security reasons. I'm dependent on it just at the moment, so don't want to risk it being stolen..."

"...Good grief," Wilbur cut in when he noticed the scar on Richard's face. "I bet there's a story behind that gash. Are you alright now?"

"Yes, Sir. Thank you; I'm fine. ...But maybe now is not the time to get into it."

"Quite right, young man. Anyway, where are you going when you leave here?"

"I'm not sure...I didn't realise I would be leaving quite so soon. I guess Kristine didn't get the message that you two were coming back early. ...It caught us on the hop."

"Oh, I see. So you've nowhere else to go?"

"Not really, no."

"Well, if you don't mind sleeping in a single bed, there's another room you can use."

"That's very kind, Sir; but I don't want to be a burden to you and your wife."

Richard glanced towards the lounge where the women were still deep in conversation.

Wilbur followed his glance and, realising what Richard was referring to, he said, "If you prefer, I'll talk it over with my wife...what did you say your name is?"

"Richard."

"Ah, yes." Wilbur pulled a face and pointed to his head. "Two much relaxation addles the brain!" he said, and then added, "Wait here. I won't be a minute."

Wilbur clambered around the pile of luggage and went into the lounge, where Kristine and her aunt still sat on the couch; deep in conversation.

Yet, their debate over Richard's presence appeared to be far less animated than before.

Wilbur interrupted them.

"Come on, ladies, there will be plenty of time for you to catch up on gossip in the morning. Right now, Ruth, I need to know if you have any objection to this nice young fellow bunking down in the spare room until he finds other digs."

By now, Ruth had recovered somewhat from the shock of learning that Kristine had been keeping male company in their absence, and that she had allowed him to use their bedroom.

"...But we didn't sleep together," Kristine quickly added; followed by a twinge of conscience when she realised that as of a few minutes ago her claim was no longer true.

Ruth looked at her husband while he spoke. He seemed a little flushed from his exertion and the journey home.

"...In the spare room, did you say? Yes, I suppose that would be alright."

Kristine gave her a hug.

"Thank you so much...both of you. Richard is a special friend of mine, and I wouldn't want to see him homeless on account of my negligence."

Later that evening, when bedrooms had been re-allocated, the kitchen tidied, and everything had generally returned to normal, Ruth and Wilbur, exhausted from their arduous day, headed off to bed.

After the travellers had said goodnight and disappeared into their room, Kristine and Richard found themselves at a loss to know what to say to one another.

For a couple of hours each had been on tenterhooks over the appearance of the house owners, especially as Kristine and Richard had almost been caught engaging in an intimate liaison; one which had been brought on by the effect of alcohol – an effect that was fast wearing off.

In retrospect, Richard could not believe that it had even happened; and Kristine, whose state of euphoria vanished the moment she heard a key in the door, was beginning to feel decidedly guilty about it.

If it hadn't been for the wine she would not have gone that far; of that she was certain.

But it was too late now.

Richard was the first to break the silence.

He said quietly, "I'll look for somewhere else to live in the morning."

Kristine stared at him, aghast.

"Why?" she asked in a hoarse whisper.

"I don't have a choice, do I?" he said in dismay. "There's no way I can live in this house, now your aunt and uncle are back for good."

"Well, if you go, I'm coming with you," she announced impulsively, taking them both by surprise.

"Do you mean you want us to flat together somewhere else?" asked Richard, not sure of her intentions.

"...After what happened tonight...why not? I think we're more than flatmates now, don't you?"

Richard nodded cautiously.

He could not dispute Kristine's logic.

"Okay then," he said brightly. "First thing tomorrow, we start looking for a place of our own!"

CHAPTER SIX

The following morning, when a welcome sleep-in and then a leisurely lunch had more than made up for their gruelling flight home, Ruth rang Emily.

Surprised to hear Fiona take the call, she assumed her sister was just visiting her estranged mother, and warmed to the fact that they must have reconciled in her absence.

Fiona's reaction to Ruth's call was spontaneous.

"Good grief, have you two actually come home?"

She held the receiver to her chest and related to Emily who was on the phone.

Emily responded gleefully.

"Yes... Yes!" she exclaimed, and reached out her hand for the phone, but then retracted it when she saw Fiona pull a face, dismissing the notion.

"Did you just speak to Mum?" asked Ruth.

"Yes," replied Fiona. "She's right here."

"Put her on, will you...I've so missed hearing her voice."

Fiona went quiet; a disturbing thought occurring to her.

"Fiona, are you there?" asked Ruth.

"Yes, of course. ...I'm afraid you won't be able to have a chat with Mum, though."

"Why not? Is she alright?"

Perhaps there was another reason why Fiona might be paying Emily a visit.

Fiona hesitated again.

Probing, she asked, "Hasn't Kristine kept you up to date with what's been going on here?"

"No, and I'm not too happy about it. We hardly heard from her at all. ...Why, what has happened?"

"So you don't know about Mum's stroke, then?"

"...Stroke? Our mother has had a stroke!"

"Yes. It happened a few months ago."

"For goodness' sake...why wasn't I told?"

"Because it didn't involve you and Wilbur...and there's been enough of us around here to deal with it. If you were informed, you would have wanted to come home..."

"...This is terrible!" murmured Ruth in distress. "I had no idea..."

But then her emotional reaction yielded to her normal style of response.

"How is Mother now, anyway – she's obviously up and about? ...On second thoughts, don't answer me if Mum is within earshot. I'll come right over and see for myself."

Emily greeted her prodigal daughter with enthusiasm.

Ruth, on the other hand, found it hard to feign joy on seeing an incapacitated Emily for the first time.

In effect, the sight of her mother looking frail gnawed at her heartstrings. Yet, still she hugged the diminutive figure and allowed Emily to caress her face while expressing her glee with unintelligible gibberish.

When Emily's short attention span drew her back to the television screen, Ruth jumped at the chance to speak to her sister in private.

"I must say, I'm completely overwhelmed by this," she said, the tone of her voice revealing her true feelings. "I just wish you could have warned me about it sooner."

"Well," said Fiona, unmoved by Ruth's discomfiture. "If you hadn't elected to take off and travel the world, you would have been here to help her right from the start."

"Are you trying to make me feel guilty?"

Ruth knew her twin well enough to recognise sarcasm when she heard it.

"Now why would I want to make you feel guilty? It's not like I've struggled with Mother's unreasonable behaviour by myself seven days a week, or done everything for her the whole time. We couldn't have you feeling guilty about something like that now, could we?"

Ruth turned away.

"I think I'd better go," she said.

The strain was too much to bear on only her first day back. She had hoped their homecoming might have been a fresh start for her and her sister, but apparently it was not meant to be.

"Yes," retorted Fiona. "Perhaps you had better leave; unless you're prepared to pull your weight with Mum from now on, and not disappear on some new venture."

Ruth ignored her, and went back through to Emily.

"Mum, I have to go now," she said lovingly; then added, "But Wilbur and I are back to stay, so we will be seeing a lot of each other from now on."

Emily smiled at her, not really understanding what Ruth was telling her.

"Bye...bye," she said clearly in a cheeky voice.

In the kitchen Fiona heard this, too; and rued the fact that Emily had spoken proper words to Ruth when she, the one who had sacrificed everything to look after her, only ever received meaningless babble...

Kristine and Richard revelled in their newfound lodgings.

When, a couple of weeks later, they transferred all of their possessions from Ruth's, Kristine little knew to what extent she would move ahead in life, as she was no longer a child nor really a teenager anymore; certainly not when it came to her level of maturity.

The fact that she had chosen to move out of her family circle altogether reflected her desire to demonstrate that level of maturity.

To her, it seemed as if fate had decreed that, after extricating herself from her mother's control, she was now ready to become an independent woman in every sense of the word. For when she and Richard moved in together they did so not as flatmates but as partners.

All the same, despite the huge change that took place so unexpectedly in her life, Kristine still did not lose sight of her immediate goal. She was as determined as ever to pass the physiotherapy exams.

For this she had the full support of both parents, who happily agreed to finance her semester at university.

However, there was one matter over which her mother, at least, did not offer her support, and that was Richard.

Fiona had never particularly liked him; of that Kristine was certain.

She had anticipated her mother would have a lot to say about them moving into a flat together, and gritted her teeth when she mentioned it.

In the interest of peace and propriety, Kristine decided not to inform Fiona about their sleeping arrangements; keeping her fingers crossed that she would not ask. And so for the time being the fact that Kristine and Richard were partners was kept a secret.

Besides, Kristine maintained with conviction:, now that she was a mature eighteen-year-old: eligible to legally drink, to vote, and even marry, what she did from now on was really none of her mother's business.

With Richard working his regular hours at the physio clinic and Kristine taking mostly afternoon duties at Everglades, the lovebirds soon discovered that they hardly ever saw each other during the week.

Furthermore, when Kristine was off duty, her time was divided between keeping house and chaperoning Emily at day-care. Thus, little time was left for strengthening their relationship or enjoying shared meals.

To make up for it, each weekend Kristine and Richard ensured they ate home-cooked meals and had some fun in each other's company.

Though still relatively new to domesticity, Kristine was very aware that if the two of them were to make a go of their relationship they needed to do this regularly. She had witnessed enough heartache between her parents to risk it happening to her as well...

In the meantime, Ruth took to heart what Fiona had said.

Shock that their mother suffered a stroke while she was on holiday soon gave way to acceptance that Fiona really needed her help where possible, and that she should make herself available. ...And when she asked her sister in what way she could help, Fiona was very quick to tell her.

"For one thing," Fiona stated without hesitation, "You can take Mum to day-care two days a week and stay there with her. Kristine has been doing it, but when she starts back at university she won't have the time anymore."

Taken aback by Fiona's insistent request, Ruth said, "Alright, I suppose I could do that for you...and for Mum."

Shortly before Kristine's first class back at university, Ruth joined Emily and her niece at Everglades for a practice session in the day-care centre. Kristine introduced her to the duty supervisor, showed her where everything was, explained the routine, and then, needing to get off to a lecture, she left them to their own devices.

Emily was thrilled to have Ruth with her.

She allowed her favourite twin to wheel her around the centre; pointing out her preferred places and activities, and generally settling in for a wonderful day...a day that, in a strange sort of way, she considered to be like old times; for the recollection of the fortnightly bus journey to spend Thursdays with Ruth came agreeably to mind.

However, whilst Emily may have been enjoying the day, the same could not be said for her replacement escort.

Ruth had never had any real exposure to infirm, elderly people. Even her own mother's plight left her somewhat at a loss to know how she should act towards them. She was used to working with bright, energetic children; not the elderly. The only patient in her life had been her husband; but he was still comparatively youthful and well over his heart attack now.

The prospect of being with so many for even one day, let alone twice a week on a regular basis, filled her with a worrying sense of dread.

Ruth suspected this would be the case almost as soon as Kristine left to follow her own pursuits.

It wasn't that Ruth had no regard for old people, but rather that she felt completely out of her depth with them. When an assistant asked her if she would like to help with one of the activities, she declined so abruptly that she felt quite ashamed of herself.

By the end of the session, during which time she had nervously helped Emily to the toilet on two occasions; a task which she found unpleasant to say the least, Ruth wondered what she was letting herself in for.

Thus, by three o'clock she had had enough.

With Kristine on hand again to help take Emily home, Ruth thankfully said her goodbyes and escaped to the seclusion of her car; then with an obligatory toot, drove off in the opposite direction from the mother she loved more than life itself.

"I was shocked by the way it affected me," she told Wilbur afterwards. "How could something as normal and natural as taking care of one's own mother cause such feelings of revulsion? I truly am disgusted with myself."

"Don't worry, Ruth," he responded reassuringly. "From what you've told me about Emily's condition, she could almost be a different person from the mother you last saw a year ago. ...And who wouldn't be affected by all those doddery old dears? They're a far cry from our lively school children. You'll get used to it, I'm quite sure. After all, if you are to honour your commitment to help out, you have no choice but to get used to it!"

"Oh, don't put it that way!" cried Ruth, still disturbed by the whole experience. "Just at the moment I'm not sure I'm up to it. I can't even chat properly with Mum anymore. And we did so like to chat!"

"Don't you think you are over-reacting?"

"If I am, it's justified. Not all that long ago we were anticipating a joyful return home. Instead, we have landed in some kind of nightmare. I'm beginning to wish we had stayed away!"

Some weeks later, after a demanding day that involved a lecture in the morning followed by a frustrating afternoon duty, Kristine arrived home exhausted and demoralised.

Once inside, she slumped down on the couch in front of a startled Richard; without speaking to him or bothering to remove her coat.

Motionless, she blankly stared out, her gaze resting on the carpet in front of the television screen, as though her mind was pre-occupied with an annoyance.

Richard watched her, at first with vexation over her lack of manners, but then with concern; for Kristine, although impulsive by nature, had not been as distant as this since her unfortunate exam result.

At last he felt compelled to say something.

Timidly, to avoid a possible backlash, he said, "Are you alright, Kris?"

Gradually life appeared to return to her blank stare, and she turned her head to look at him.

It was obvious from the dazed expression on her face that she was not angry, but rather traumatised.

"Sorry, what did you say?" she remarked casually.

Worried, he asked her, "What's wrong? I haven't done anything to upset you, have I?"

The warmth and concern in his voice melted her frozen feelings, and she smiled.

"No; it's not you. It's... It's that place!"

"Do you mean university...or Everglades?"

"...Everglades, of course! I tell you, it's getting worse by the day. Not only are they bringing in new residents who are far too handicapped for us to manage, but also the students I'm on duty with still don't know the meaning of the word, 'work'. I'm not sure how much more I can take! If only I had passed my exams, I would have been out of there a long time ago!"

Richard sighed in sympathy. He alone knew exactly how she felt. He had suffered the same frustrations and seen the kind of slackness she was referring to.

But he also knew that Kristine was way beyond talking about her grievances at the moment.

...Besides, what could he possibly say that would ease the situation for her? She needed understanding from him; not cavalier advice.

345

Without hesitation he joined Kristine on the couch and put his arm round her.

"You poor soul, I do feel for you," he said affectionately. Then after a moment he asked, "Did you manage to have a sit down and something to eat at work?"

"I had a quick break and some of the leftover tea. The call bells kept going off, so neither of us got much of a break. But it took the edge off, I suppose."

"There's leftover pizza in the fridge if you're peckish."

"Oh, did you get takeaways?" she said, showing a mild interest at last.

"No way, I made it from scratch!" replied Richard with an air of indignation. "I'm becoming a dab hand in the kitchen now," he added with a swanky expression.

Kristine giggled at his antics; her mood brighter.

She nudged him in the ribs, and said merrily, "Says who? When do you ever do any cooking?"

"...I'm learning, anyway. ...And it's a pretty good pizza. Here, I'll get you a piece."

"This should be interesting," Kristine quipped, and sat up straight ready to receive his culinary offering.

When she saw the pizza she laughed out loud.

"Well you may scoff, my dear," Richard said, feigning offense; "but just wait till you taste it. My pizza may be a bit rustic, however it is packed with flavour."

Grinning, Kristine poured over it, searching for morsels on the topping that she might recognise. Then she picked out a bit of meat and held it up to him.

"What's this?" she asked timorously.

"It's salami, of course! Stop picking at it, and just take a bite. I promise it won't poison you!"

Kristine gave in. She had only been teasing, and had to admit that the warmed through wedge of his pizza smelt quite delicious.

She took a bite, and her surprised expression met his.

"I told you it will be yummy," he said as she mumbled appreciatively with her mouth still full. "Don't ever doubt my ability to multi-task!"

With her mouthful duly swallowed, Kristine giggled.

"You've got hidden talents, alright," she said cheerily, and took another bite.

Early the next morning, Kristine was violently sick.

Richard could hear her vomiting in the toilet bowl while he was getting ready for work. When she emerged he was waiting for her; a worried look on his face.

She looked at him sheepishly, embarrassed that he had heard her retching.

"Sorry about the racket," she muttered.

"I guess the pizza was too rich for you after all," he said, trying to make light of it, but also troubled that his cooking may have had an adverse effect on her.

"...Or maybe I was just too tired to eat very much," she said as she headed back to bed.

Yet, Richard was not convinced. During the morning it crossed his mind that perhaps the salami he used from the fridge was not as fresh as he thought.

Had his offering actually given Kristine food poisoning, despite his rash statement to the contrary?

But then he realised that if it was food poison, he would have been affected by it, too. She must have been right all along: that she was just too tired to eat.

Still concerned at lunchtime, he phoned to see how she was feeling.

"A bit better, I think," she said drowsily. "The last time I threw up was over an hour ago; so I should have got rid of whatever made me ill by now."

"You may have picked up a tummy bug," he suggested.

"Could be...who knows..."

By the time Richard got home, Kristine was her usual self again, much to his relief.

On later reflection, he concluded that it must have been the food that caused her vomiting, or she would still be looking seedy.

The last thing he wanted to do was poison his girlfriend.

The next morning found Kristine dry-retching again...and by the following weekend, when severe symptoms still had not eased, she began to have suspicions as to just what was causing her nausea.

With her heart in her mouth she checked the date on her bedroom calendar.

"I don't believe it – I'm over a week late for my period!" she exclaimed.

Usually regular as clockwork Kristine had never needed to keep a record of her cycle, but waited for the tell-tale signs to alert her of a period's imminent arrival. With the changes that had lately taken place in her life, she had not given it much thought.

Yet, on making her discovery, she realised in despair, "If I'm as late as this it can only mean I'm pregnant!"

In panic she rushed off to the pharmacy for a pregnancy test kit.

Back in the privacy of the flat, with Richard mercifully at work, she looked through the instructions on the leaflet and meticulously followed them.

There was no doubting the result.

She and Richard were expecting a baby.

Later that day, when the shock of revelation had subsided slightly, a guarded ripple of excitement coursed through her; for young though she still was, she had felt like a fully-fledged married woman ever since she and Richard moved into the new flat. It seemed almost natural that the next step would be to have a child.

But then her head overruled her heart and she realised with reluctance that Richard might not feel the same way.

In fact, she thought, if he were to find out about it he might even be put off staying with her, and move out. The prospect of that, just at the moment, was too horrible to contemplate. And so she decided not to tell him. ...Not yet, anyway. Not until she had gauged whether he regarded theirs as a permanent relationship. And she was not too sure how she could determine that.

Keeping her secret from Richard was just one of the many issues Kristine now had to deal with. Preventing her family from finding out was another.

So far, her parents were under the impression that she and Richard were only flatmates. If they suspected there was more to it, they certainly did not let on; and Kristine had no doubt that if her mother had suspicions she would soon be on to her about it.

Thus, it troubled her when Fiona phoned with what she termed a 'grave concern'.

"A grave concern?" echoed Kristine.

Could she mean..? Of course not. Kristine chided herself for being paranoid. How could anybody possibly know?

"Yes, I regard it as very grave," Fiona went on. "I never thought I would hear this about my own..."

"...But Mum!"

Kristine gasped in horror. My God, she does know!

Shell-shocked, she thought quickly.

Not only had her mother somehow found out, but she was coming down on her like a ton of bricks.

This was all happening too soon!

"Don't 'but Mum' me," Fiona continued in an enraged tone of voice. "How could she do it to me – to us?"

"But you don't understand..," Kristine began, and then stopped abruptly. "...She? Who's she? Mum, what are you talking about?"

"...Your aunt, of course. What did you think I was talking about – the weather?"

"...Oh, never mind."

Now Kristine was confused...but also relieved that she had been mistaken.

However, there still remained the question of just what Auntie Ruth had supposedly done.

Still incensed, Fiona paid no heed to Kristine and, yelling down the phone, tore a strip off her sister for, as she put it, deserting the family in their hour of need.

"How has Auntie Ruth deserted you?" asked Kristine in a scornful voice; her paranoia now eased. "Come to think of it, how could Auntie Ruth do anything that might upset you? She's not like that..."

"...Well, she is now."

The tremor in Fiona's voice worried Kristine. She had never known her mother to be as distraught as this before; it seemed she was actually in shock.

"Mum, where are you now?" she asked.

"I'm phoning from work. I needed to contact you about it urgently..."

"...About what? Mum, do you want me to come over?"

"No, don't come here. Go to the café at lunchtime, and I'll explain everything there."

In the Copper Urn, Kristine found her mother sitting at the corner table; deep in thought.

Fiona looked up as she approached and sat down.

"What's this all about, Mum?"

Fiona regarded her critically.

"Don't you think you should get a cup of something, or they might ask you to leave?"

Kristine glanced around. The café was filling up quickly, with only a few vacant seats at occupied tables.

"I suppose you're right," she said, and got up to join the lengthy queue of patrons.

A few minutes later she returned to the table.

Fiona glanced at her watch.

"Good grief, Kristine – you took your time!"

"That's not my fault; there was a long queue!"

"Alright; just sit down with your drink. I've only got half an hour for my break."

"Well then, you'd better tell me what's bothering you."

"It's your aunt."

"I know that...but what has she done to upset you?"

"She has betrayed me; that's what."

"On the phone you said she's deserted you, and now it's betrayed. This sounds very melodramatic, even coming from you. Why don't you just explain what's happened?"

Fiona sighed petulantly.

"My twin has backed out of the arrangement I made..."

"...What arrangement? ...Oh! Do you mean, where she takes Nana to day-care?"

"Yes. She says she finds the whole thing too upsetting. As you can imagine, I'm very angry with her for dumping the responsibility back on my shoulders."

"But why has she pulled out? She was so keen to help you – to help us! It's been brilliant for me not having to fit day-care in as well as everything else."

"I know! It's exactly the same for my situation...and I'm really sorry, but you will have to include Ruth's two days at day-care with your routine again."

Kristine went quiet; stunned by Fiona's announcement.

It looked like she would be back on the old frenetic treadmill; and pregnant, to boot. This was an impossible situation she could not even contemplate now.

Immediately, she sprung to her own defence. There was too much at stake now for her to submissively accept.

"Why me? Why does it have to fall to me? I'm going to be heavily overloaded again. Don't you care about that?"

"Of course I care! But as you know, Nana cannot be left at day-care unchaperoned, and you are definitely the best person to look after her there."

Kristine's temper flared. It was obvious her mother was loading it onto her because she didn't want to have to deal with it herself.

"What about you? Why can't you play your part? Yours is only a part time job. You could easily come to some kind of arrangement with your boss?"

"No...no, that's not possible...I can't take time off," said Fiona, hedging.

She was eager to work full time again now. Already, it did not sit well with her boss that she had a dependant at home who might draw her away from work occasionally.

In fact, it had been on her short-term plan to have Emily at day-care for the whole working week so that she could work full time. Ruth's refusal to help out anymore had put paid to those plans. Her working future now depended on Kristine's cooperation...

"What do you mean, you can't take time off?" Kristine hissed angrily, trying to refrain from making a scene in the crowded café; but the unreasonable demand her mother had made deserved a quarrel, and Kristine would ensure that she got it.

"My boss has expectations of me," Fiona replied; not exactly truthfully for it was she who had offered herself for full time work. "...And besides, you are forgetting that I've had sole responsibility of Nana at home for a long time now. Why should I be saddled with it everything? You and your aunt are being unfair in leaving it all to me." And then she stated firmly, "I'm sorry, Kristine; you've got no choice but to fit day-care in with your other activities – and that's all there is to it!"

Fiona stood up, upsetting the table as she did so.

Kristine looked on, open-mouthed.

All at once she felt ill. Had Fiona not still been standing over her, she would have made for the café's toilets and attempted to rid herself of whatever had brought on the bout of nausea. But as it was, she could do little except suffer the cramping in her stomach until her mother had gone out of sight.

Fiona woodenly thanked her for coming and, citing the need to get back to the office, left the café without further comment. As far as she was concerned she had done what she came to do: she had issued her decree. What Kristine thought about it did not matter.

How frighteningly easy Kristine found it to vomit when she finally reached the toilet.

With her head still poised above the bowl in case it was not yet over, she hazily calculated when this added burden on her time and energy was likely to begin.

To her dismay, she realised it would come into effect the next morning!

Kristine worked out that if today was the last day Ruth would be helping, and if Emily was due at day-care again in the morning, it would mean that she would be taking her to day-care and also working her afternoon shift.

Then, the morning after that she had a university class followed by another duty...

353

As she dry-retched with anguish over the prospect of such a hard schedule, Kristine had serious concerns for her health and wellbeing during the next few days.

She desperately needed to escape the terrible workload her mother had inflicted on her. Furthermore, she urgently needed to talk to somebody about it. ...But who?

Her rescue came unexpectedly during Emily's monthly check-up with Alicia.

On this particular day, Kristine mercifully found herself with nothing more to do than take Emily to day-care, sit patiently with her throughout the session, and then bring her home again.

They had not been home for long when Alicia arrived.

"Alicia...you gave me a fright! I didn't know you were due a visit," said Kristine when Alicia let herself in through the back door, carrying a rose from the garden.

"Hi, Kristine," Alicia responded while shutting the door behind her. "Your mother rang last night to tell me Emily wouldn't be home from day-care till after three. But that didn't matter – I just rearranged my schedule."

Alicia trimmed the rose ready to take through to Emily. She glanced up at Kristine while doing so and said, "How are you? I haven't seen you for a while."

"I've been busy. Did you know...my aunt and uncle are back from their trip?"

"Yes. Royston told me. He also said you've moved in with your boyfriend. How is that working out?"

"Oh, alright, thank you," replied Kristine with a sigh.

She was so exhausted even the briefest of comments to Alicia required more effort than she was willing to expend.

"Are you okay?" asked Alicia astutely. "You really don't look very well."

"Actually...I'm not... I... Um..."

Suddenly another bout of nausea overcame her.

"Would you excuse me...for a minute," she stammered, and rushed off.

When she returned, Alicia had given Emily the rose and was watching her delighted reaction.

"Come and have a sit down, Kristine," said Alicia. "I can see something's wrong. If you'll let me, I'd like to help."

Alicia's kindness was too much for Kristine, who dissolved into tears: silently so that Emily would not notice.

She took hold of the hand Alicia offered and followed her into the dining room for some quiet conversation.

Kristine blew her nose on a handkerchief pulled out of her trouser pocket.

Alicia gave her a moment to compose herself, and then said, "I get the impression this is all too much for you now. ...Am I right there?"

Kristine sniffed back a last tear and looked her straight in the eye. Alicia was always so perceptive.

"Is it that obvious?" she said with a sigh.

"To me, it is. Why don't you tell me what's going on?"

Kristine hesitated. How much of this should she divulge to Alicia? She was not yet ready to tell anyone else about the pregnancy, let alone Alicia, so she just said, "Since Mum told me I was back on deck with Nana I've been so stressed out I don't know where to put myself."

"...And I would guess you're not only stressed, but also unwell by the way you disappeared to the bathroom just now... Are you ill?"

Again Kristine hesitated.

At length she said, "I wouldn't say I'm ill. It's probably just been too much all at once."

"In my opinion, it's all too much for both you and your mother," said Alicia thoughtfully.

355

She swivelled around in her chair and looked at Emily. How contented she seemed just now, holding the rose to her breast; and yet, how difficult the lives were becoming of those responsible for her. Maybe it was time...

She turned back to Kristine. "When will your mother be home?" she asked.

"Just after four o'clock. Why do you want to know?"

"There's something I must discuss with her. If it's alright with you, I'll stay here till she gets back. You go home now; it looks like you could use a rest."

"Thank you Alicia. I do need to lie down for a while. I'm sure Mum wouldn't mind if you stayed here without me."

Nevertheless, Kristine was curious to know why Alicia needed to talk to her mother. She was concerned it might have something to do with their conversation, and did not want Alicia discussing it with her.

"You won't tell Mum what we talked about, will you?"

Alicia patted her hand affectionately.

"Don't worry, I know what not to say to Fiona," she said with a chuckle. "You head off now...I'll see to Emily."

Gratefully, Kristine left.

She was exhausted. The vomiting had robbed her of any remaining stamina, and she was becoming dehydrated.

The relief to be free of responsibility, if only for a short time, was immeasurable.

As soon as she got home she went straight to bed, and fell asleep the moment her head touched the pillow.

Meanwhile, Alicia was faced with the task of explaining to Fiona why she was at the house and not Kristine.

Fiona reacted vigorously.

"Kristine was supposed to wait till I got home! We can't have her keeping you from your work while she ducks off somewhere else!"

"It wasn't like that, Fiona," replied Alicia. "Kristine isn't feeling very well...I told her to go. ...Besides, Emily was my last client for the day...and I wanted to talk to you."

"...Really! ...What about?"

Fiona put down her bag and flicked on the kettle.

She shot a cursory glance at Emily, whose attention was still focused on the rose.

"Hi, Mum," she said to see if she would get a response. On getting none, she gave a huff and turned back to Alicia.

"I don't know why I bother," she grumbled. "She's away with the fairies when she gets her nose into those flowers. Now, what did you want to talk to me about? I'm a bit pushed for time this afternoon, because I've got friends coming tonight, so I need to get Mum ready for bed early."

"That's what I wanted to talk to you about."

"What – my mother's bedtime? I hope you're not going to tell me my business, Alicia. I've got enough on my plate without putting up with a lecture from you as well!"

Alicia bit her tongue. How tempting it was to lash out, but instead she responded with her usual professionalism. ...After all, she reminded herself, she was still there in her capacity as Emily's district nurse, not as a family member.

"Fiona, please come and sit down so we can talk," she said with well-rehearsed patience. "I need to discuss your mother's situation with you."

Fiona half-heartedly complied.

"I hope this won't take long," she said sourly.

"It shouldn't. I'd like to make you a proposition. ...Ah, your kettle's boiling. Can I make the cup of tea for us?"

"Thank you, Alicia. That would be helpful."

While Alicia made drinks for them both and took Emily her usual mug of milky tea, Fiona sat quietly; trying to settle the perpetual restlessness inside her.

When Alicia came back in, she said, "Okay...what's this all about then?"

"I'm aware of what's happening here..." Alicia began.

"And that is..?" asked Fiona curtly, expecting criticism.

"Now, please correct me if I'm wrong, but I am getting the impression that having the responsibility of Emily at home is now too much for both you and Kristine."

Fiona snapped. "What has that girl been saying? ...That I'm not looking after my mother properly, I bet!"

"No, Fiona, nothing like that! This has to do with Emily's level of dependency, not yours or Kristine's capabilities."

"So what exactly are you telling me?"

Alicia glanced through to Emily, whose attention now alternated between her drink and the television screen.

She drew breath to speak, unsure how the proposal she wanted to make would be received; then she said, "I want to suggest something to you. But first I need to, as it were: present my case."

"Okay. I don't know what you're talking about, but go on. I'll listen to whatever you have to say."

Alicia took another breath; which came out more as a sigh. She knew it would be difficult to have Fiona listen without reacting, if what she said did not come out right.

"First of all," she began, thinking carefully. "I want you to know that, speaking both as a professional and from my personal perspective, I think you and Kristine are doing a wonderful job with Emily. Looking after a stroke victim is never easy; especially," she whispered; "someone who also exhibits signs of senility. Between the two of you, Emily's needs are very well covered, and from her level of contentment just at the moment, it is obvious that she is generally quite happy."

Fiona grunted. "You wouldn't say that if you saw her at day-care. She only behaves when one of us is with her."

"Yes," said Alicia supportively. "I heard about that – and about the issue of your sister's sensitivity over helping out. But I also understand where Ruth is coming from, too. Not everyone can cope emotionally when a much-loved elderly relative becomes incapacitated..."

"Some of us have no choice, as you know! ...Anyway, Ruth's well used to her husband's poor health. He had that heart attack, if you remember. She looked after him then."

"Even so, it must have come as quite a shock to find out that while she was away enjoying herself her mother had a stroke. She's probably still dealing with a lot of guilt..."

"...Alicia," Fiona said, cutting in. "I'm sure you didn't bail me up to discuss Ruth's fragile state. If you don't mind, could you please get to the point?"

"Yes, of course. I'm sorry."

Alicia paused momentarily to collect her thoughts; then came straight out with her recommendation.

"Fiona, after some serious consideration, I believe Emily is now ready for the next stage in her ongoing care."

Fiona looked at her austerely. "Are you suggesting one of those geriatric hospitals?"

"Yes."

"Wow!" remarked Fiona; both shocked and saddened. Emily was her mother, after all. Before Kristine showed her round Everglades she had felt that to send a parent to an institution like that must take some real soul searching. Now she was being asked to consider sending Emily, not to a lovely rest-home like Everglades, but to an impersonal hospital of all places. The thought of it made her shudder.

"Well, what are your thoughts?" asked Alicia, mindful of Fiona's time constraints.

"I don't really know," she replied. "For once in my life I'm at a loss for words."

Alicia got up to leave.

"Have a think about it. Discuss it with Kristine and Ruth, and then you can let me know if you want Emily assessed."

She gathered up the instruments of her profession and returned them to her workbag; then turned back to Fiona and said, "Although Emily's current needs are important, so are yours and Kristine's. You are all struggling with this, and I have to admit that just at the moment I'm concerned as much for the wellbeing of Emily's two carers as I am for Emily herself. I'll wait to hear from you."

"Thank you, Alicia," said Fiona; still in a daze.

She watched as her ex-husband's lover left the house; an unexpected feeling of gratitude warming her.

Richard waited while Kristine threw up for the second time in as many hours.

At home for the weekend, he was able to see firsthand how much the nausea was affecting her.

...And much to her dismay, Kristine could hide the truth from him no longer.

"You really should see the doctor about that," he said with apprehension. "It's gone on for ages now. Something more than a tummy bug must be wrong, and I'm worried."

"You've no need to worry," she said, knowing full well what was causing the nausea. "It will pass in time."

"Not if there's something wrong with you; like cancer, for instance!"

Kristine scoffed at the suggestion. "Gee, thanks for the encouragement! Anyway, I know it isn't cancer..."

"...How can you possibly know that without tests? Or is there something you're not telling me?"

Richard was frustrated with her now. He cared enough for Kristine not to ignore her predicament, but she was being far from helpful about it.

Kristine, still looking sickly, had had enough, too.

Keeping her pregnancy a secret did not seem quite so important now. Unable to keep it up, she felt much too ill to make the effort even with Richard.

With tears in her eyes, she said, "I'm sorry, Richard, but you are right. I have been keeping something from you, and I don't have the right to do so any longer. The truth of the matter is: I'm pregnant."

When Richard eventually picked his jaw up off the floor and was able to think clearly again, his first thought was: how could this have happened?

Thinking back, he recalled that using contraception was initiated only when they moved into the flat together, and before that there was just the one time on Ruth's couch...

"Oh dear," he said under his breath, reluctant to let the rising panic surface.

But then another emotion kicked in, and the seed of a realisation began to grow in his mind.

"I guess that means I'm going to be a daddy," he said with an element of shyness.

Kristine looked at him, her fears somewhat dissipating. Surely he would not have phrased his remark that way if he was angry about her news.

"It certainly does," she said, searching his features for confirmation of her theory.

With a shriek of delight Richard threw his arms around her and lifted her up; but then gently lowered her safely to the floor again.

"Sorry," he said. "Perhaps I shouldn't have done that. I didn't hurt you, did I?"

"No," cried Kristine; tears of joy now running down her face. "I'm far too happy – and relieved – to feel any pain at the moment. I thought you would be mad as hell at me for being so careless."

"...You...careless? It takes two to conceive a baby, silly. We were both careless...but who cares about that? We are going to be parents!"

The dilemma facing Kristine now was: should she share her news with anyone else just yet?

There were three aspects of her regular activities that she now had to consider in relation to her pregnancy: her physiotherapy course, her job...and her mother's demands of her. She needed to determine which of them, if any, was likely to be adversely affected by her condition to the extent that those involved should be informed.

Her course, she decided, would not be compromised in any way; likewise, her job should not pose many problems just yet – although it might be prudent to tell Grace that she was pregnant. But as for her mother...

One day soon afterwards, Kristine reluctantly conceded to Richard, "I suppose we shouldn't keep the pregnancy from my family for much longer."

She rubbed her still slender tummy, as if a baby bump was already in evidence.

"Are you apprehensive about your mother's reaction?" he asked intuitively.

"...Mum and Dad both," Kristine replied with a groan. "Dad wasn't too keen on us living together from the start. He reckoned I was too young – and he didn't really trust us, if you know what I mean."

Richard knew very well what she meant; in fact, he had already proved her father's suspicions to be well founded. He felt sick to the stomach that he had overlooked a possibly hostile response from Kristine's family. Would they regard him merely as an opportunist? Her mother never did like him...

"There's only one thing for it," he said quickly, as if to remedy the situation. "We have to get engaged so your father will realise my intentions towards you are genuine."

Kristine looked him in the eye quizzically. Was this his way of proposing?

Then she glanced away; perplexed that he may have suggested it just to save his own skin.

"Is that what you really want – for us to get married?" she asked with uncertainty.

"...One day, yes," he answered in a matter of fact way; taking Kristine by surprise.

"I don't know how to answer you," she said hesitantly. "I guess a part of me was hoping to be swept off my feet by a Prince Charming with a romantic proposal..."

Suddenly Richard dropped to his knee. He took hold of her hand and, looking up into her face, he said, "Kristine, will you marry me?"

Then he leant forward and kissed her tummy.

"Will you...both...marry me?"

Convinced of his sincerity, Kristine laughed and kissed him on the top of his head. She didn't know whether or not she actually loved him, or even if he loved her, but she said anyway, "Yes, Richard, I will...we will both marry you."

Somehow it seemed the right thing to do.

CHAPTER SEVEN

Kristine arranged a get-together with Richard, Emily and both of her parents for the following weekend.

Despite Fiona's request to know the reason for a family meeting, Kristine persuaded her to be patient, and assured her that she would be agreeably surprised by what they wanted to discuss.

Richard had never really met Kristine's parents...and if he was not feeling out of place beforehand, he certainly did the moment he set foot in Emily's house.

"Are you sure we're doing the right thing?" he anxiously asked of Kristine while they waited for Royston to arrive, and for Fiona to finish attending to Emily.

Fiona had wanted Emily quietly occupied and out of the way while they talked, and had attended to every whim her mother was likely to have; including a rose bloom to keep her happy.

When Emily returned to the lounge, she looked with alarm at the strange young man who was sitting beside her granddaughter on the couch. Hunched over her frame, she struggled to walk up to her chair.

She felt self-conscious, making such a concerted effort in front of somebody seated in her personal space who she did not know. As Fiona usually invited her visitors into the adjoining dining room, she wondered why Kristine had failed to do the same on this occasion.

"Hello Nana," said Kristine discreetly, not wanting to break her concentration by introducing Richard.

She did not realise that Emily was already distracted by the young man's presence.

Just then, Richard whispered in Kristine's ear, "Does she always stoop when she walks?"

Kristine glared at him, assuming he was criticising a member of her family. But then she realised his comment came from the physiotherapist in him. Without answering, she touched his hand in appreciation of his concern.

Yet, despite Richard's attempted camouflage, Emily had noticed the secretive whisper.

Feeling uncomfortable that a stranger was scrutinising her efforts, she halted and, wagging the finger of her good hand at him, cried, "No... No... No!"

However, the very act of lifting her good hand from the frame caused her to lose her balance, and Emily started to topple over.

In a flash, Richard jumped up from his seat and caught her before she could fall.

Richard's strong, supportive arms around her gave Emily a curious sense of reassurance. In fact, she marvelled at his strength, and the preparedness of this stranger to come to her assistance.

Showing Emily how to regain her balance, his hand on her back for support, Richard guided her to the chair.

Then, when she was seated, he said to Fiona, "I'm sorry I caused your mother to lose her balance."

Fiona, too, was quite taken with the way Richard had handled the situation. She suddenly saw in him a different Richard from the one who turned her daughter's head only a few short years ago. And from what Kristine told her, it looked like he was in a respectable profession now.

"Thank you, Richard," she said amicably. "I appreciate what you did just now...and so does Emily."

At the mention of her name, Emily beamed up at him. Then she noticed the scar. A horrified look came over her, and she reached out to touch his cheek, but drew her hand away at the last minute.

"It's alright, Mrs Thompson; it doesn't hurt," he said.

From that moment on, Emily and Richard were friends.

Kristine chuckled with satisfaction to see how easily her grandmother and soon-to-be fiancé had become allies. It would make life much easier for all of them, she was sure. Then, while she watched her father park his car and rush up to the house, she pondered her mother's softening attitude towards Richard.

Maybe this little chat will work out alright after all, she thought hopefully.

With Emily settled contentedly in the lounge, the family group gathered around the dining room table.

Richard pulled out Fiona's chair, and gently inched it up behind her when she sat down, further reinforcing Fiona's new, more positive opinion of him; and causing Kristine to smirk with delight.

Later she would tease him about laying on the charm a bit too thick for her usually critical mother.

"Right, Kristine," began Royston as though beginning a ritual. "As we're all here now, would you be kind enough to tell us the reason for this gathering?"

Kristine nervously glanced at Richard who was sitting bolt upright next to her; his hands firmly clasped beneath the table, his eyes cast downwards. She sensed there would be no support from him just yet. It looked like the onus lay on her to start the ball rolling...

"Richard and I have an announcement to make," she said confidently, and then noticed that Richard's averted gaze had developed a disapproving frown.

366

He glanced at her apprehensively. What was she going to tell them – about the engagement or the baby?

In case it was the latter, he decided to cut in.

"If it's alright with you, Sir" he said, addressing Royston directly; "Kristine and I would like to get engaged."

Then, before Royston could react, Kristine added, "Yes, Dad…we're in love."

Richard cast his eyes skyward with embarrassment.

Caught off-guard, Royston looked to Fiona for insight. Yet, Fiona was already forming an opinion of her own.

Without delay she spoke directly to Kristine.

"You're not pregnant, are you?"

Kristine was stunned; this was not supposed to happen. She had planned that her pregnancy would be mentioned gradually, with everyone welcoming the news.

She said in alarm, "What makes you say that!"

"Oh, come on, Kristine," retorted Fiona. "I'm not stupid. That's what this little charade is all about, isn't it? You've got yourself pregnant, and are hoping to soft-soap us into accepting it by supposedly getting engaged. What kind of fools do you think we are?"

Suddenly Kristine saw red.

"I might have known you would act this way. You have never been supportive of my choices."

"Do you call getting pregnant making a choice?"

Fiona sprang to her feet. She was furious now; that her daughter was bringing shame on the family and the pair were attempting to mask the real issue by trumping up a phoney engagement.

It was both humiliating and insulting.

Royston sat quietly while his ex-wife ranted and raved beside him. He had plenty to say on the matter, but chose to reserve his opinion for the brief moment when Fiona stopped to draw breath.

367

When that moment arrived, he calmly said, "Richard, may I have a word with you outside, please?"

To indicate his consent, Richard meekly pushed back his chair and got up; then followed Royston into the garden.

Once outside, Richard could not help noticing the garden; especially the roses. Without realising what he was doing, he remarked on its magnificence.

"You needn't try to avoid the issue, young man," said Royston. "I think you know what I am about to say to you."

"I wasn't trying to avoid it, Sir," Richard responded as politely as he could manage. "I honestly think this is the most amazing display of roses I've ever seen! But you are right: I do know what you have in mind to say. And I'm very sorry it happened this way...but I truly believe Kristine and I are meant to be together. We just seem to click."

"Do you love her?" asked Royston; his fatherly concern easing slightly.

"I think so...whatever true love really is! Certainly I'm devoted to her. I've never had anyone close to me before, and I think Kristine is wonderful. You can be sure I will do right by her."

"Well, good for you, my friend," said Royston, shaking Richard's hand.

Back in the house, things weren't going so well for Kristine.

The whole ugly business had brought on another bout of nausea, and while she retreated to the bathroom, Fiona angrily dealt with a minor request Emily was making.

As Kristine came back downstairs she could hear Fiona grumbling to Emily.

"Do you know what that foolish granddaughter of yours has done?" she said while adjusting Emily's knee rug none too gently. "She's gone and got herself pregnant!"

368

Emily scowled at her, not because of Kristine, but for the slip-shod way in which Fiona had replaced the rug.

Grunting with disgust, Emily tidied it up herself.

From the doorway, Kristine witnessed the action and assumed the disgust was directed at her.

She rushed to Emily and dropped down on her knees beside her chair.

"Please don't be cross with me, Nana. Richard and I love each other. We are going to get married."

Emily looked into her eyes in joyful surprise.

The mention of the word triggered happy memories. She smiled sweetly, and said, "Married..."

"Yes, Nana. We are going to be married. ...Maybe not just yet...but eventually!"

"Don't you think you're over-simplifying the situation?" said Fiona petulantly.

"Just drop it, Mum," said Kristine, shooting her mother a critical glance. "We don't need to subject Nana to all of the details right away."

"Huh! Personally, I think you should get rid of it. You're still only eighteen, for God's sake; and far too young to be carrying a bastard..."

"...Mum! That will do!"

While Emily lapsed into a spell of nostalgia, clutching the girl's hand and occasionally touching it to her lips, Kristine reflected on Fiona's snide comments.

Although Emily was no longer bothered about passing judgement on her indiscretion, the same could not be said for her mother...and yet, surely Fiona of all people would understand her position.

Suddenly a recollection came to mind...did not Fiona conceive out of wedlock? If her memory of past events was correct, her parents only married because Fiona was expecting. Yet, unsure of this, Kristine could not use it as just cause to force Fiona's acceptance in her own case. ...Not in front of Nana, anyway.

When the two men came back in, both apparently in an amicable frame of mind, Kristine breathed a sigh of relief. It looked like that part of the dilemma had been settled. There just remained Fiona.

Would she ever come around and be supportive of her daughter and future son-in-law?

Kristine hoped so.

After Kristine and Richard had said their goodbyes and left, Fiona took Royston to task.

"How can you be so accommodating?" she complained bitterly. "Your teenage daughter has allowed herself to get pregnant, and you don't really care!"

"It's quite simple, Fiona," replied Royston. "They're a young couple in love..."

"...What twaddle! Is that supposed to make it right?"

"If you'll just listen to me for a moment," he continued calmly. "My initial reaction when Kristine told us they were going to flat together was one of horror. I suspected Richard would not be able to keep his hands off her, and it appears I was right there. Yet, the fact that he is dedicated to their relationship has made me change my mind."

"But why? I think it is appalling..."

"...Fiona...before you get up on your high horse again, just cast your mind back a few years, will you?"

"What are you babbling about now?"

"Don't you remember the reason we got married when we did? It certainly wasn't because we were in love!"

"That has nothing to do with Kristine's situation!"

"Yes it has! We married because you were expecting Kristine! We had no choice! Your parents – Emily here and dear Arthur; God rest his soul – forced us to marry. It's what parents did in those days. Have you forgotten that?"

"But Kristine isn't just some reckless teenager trying to spite us, she's the daughter of respectable parents!"

"That doesn't make any difference. In fact, her situation is better than ours was, because they love each other and are marrying by choice. Can't you see that?"

Fiona could indeed see his point, but was not about to admit it. As a mother she had her own scruples; her own wishes where her daughter's future was concerned. She had always been adamant that Kristine would not make the same mistake she once made, and marry someone just because she was expecting his child. And here she was, doing just that.

The thought of it galled her. It would be a cold day in hell before she would give her blessing to this nonsensical relationship.

Alicia's application to have Emily assessed for residential care proceeded slowly.

She knew it would. Bureaucracy rarely expedited these matters, she had found, and this was no exception. All but the most extenuating of circumstances followed a casual and lengthy procedure, requiring much investigation and paperwork. Alicia had already informed Fiona they would need to be patient; for Emily was not considered to be an urgent case.

So when, after a few weeks, Alicia arrived on the back doorstep with a large manila envelope as well as Emily's rose, Fiona showed little interest.

Since Kristine's disappointing news, Fiona had given no thought to her mother's care assessment. Instead, she had settled into an acceptable routine, balancing looking after Emily with her work at the office. The fact that Kristine had agreed to continue with day-care meant that the pressure was off her, and she intended for it to stay that way.

Kristine's pregnancy, she declared privately, should not alter her responsibility to Emily's ongoing care.

"You will only be sitting with her," she had insisted. "It's not as though you have to manhandle her. If you can still work in the rest-home, then as far as I'm concerned you're well enough to chaperone Nana. ...In my pregnancy I had to work right up until I was full term!"

Fiona's control of Emily's regimen was so organized that when Alicia handed her the envelope she took it casually and merely said, "What's in here?"

"...Emily's assessment. It finally came through."

"Oh!" responded Fiona; she had almost forgotten about their decision.

With guarded interest, she took the envelope through to the dining room table, and carefully slit it open. Then she drew out the bulky contents.

"Good grief," she said and pushed the pile of papers over to Alicia. "I think you'd better have a look through, and then tell me what it says."

Alicia picked up the documents. The first sheet was a long covering letter which, she assumed, would require some reading in order to get the gist of it. The following pages were mostly completed forms reporting details of the assessment procedure that had been undertaken. These sheets Alicia flicked through; shaking her head while she did so.

"I don't know why they can't bypass this gobbledegook and get straight to the point," she said pointedly.

After a few minutes she came up with the answer.

"It looks like Emily has been graded to level three."

"What does that mean?"

"As I suspected, if you go ahead with residential care, she will be admitted to a private geriatric hospital."

"How am I expected to afford a private facility?"

"You will be eligible for a government subsidy. We can look into all of that when you've made your decision. Talk it over with the family, and if you want to proceed we can take it from there."

Kristine was finding her hectic workload a struggle now, especially at Everglades.

One afternoon it reached crisis point.

Shortly after she arrived for her duty, an incident caused her anguish from which she could not recover.

The episode involved a new resident, whose affliction caused him to suffer periodic seizures. Fortunately for the resident, he chose the very moment Kristine passed him in the corridor to have a seizure.

Instinctively, she threw her arms around his shoulders to prevent him from careering into the afternoon tea trolley which had been left in the corridor.

Yet, the resident was heavier than she had expected, and much to her horror, both Kristine and the resident fell awkwardly into the trolley; causing crockery and other items to crash noisily to the floor.

The commotion brought staff and visitors running from all directions, fearing a resident had taken a tumble.

On observing Kristine's apparent incompetence in not taking care of a resident properly, some could not help but criticise her for also losing control of the situation and knocking over the trolley. Others present chose to assist the resident, whose seizure had by now passed, to a place of safety; ignoring Kristine's plight in the process.

Kristine's embarrassment was extreme. Not only had she been criticised for attempting to save someone having a fit, but also her fall spoilt the residents' afternoon tea, and she wasted a lot of much needed work time in clearing up the mess and replenishing the trolley.

Yet, embarrassment was not the only thing she suffered that afternoon.

Shortly after the incident, Kristine began to experience pains deep in her abdomen; then later that night, she had Richard awake and concerned because she was spotting.

"I think I might lose the baby," she told him mournfully.

"...Not if I can help it," he argued and, despite the fact that he had not received notification from the Courts that he could drive again, he carefully bundled Kristine into her car and drove with cautious haste to the public hospital.

"You just gave yourself a bit of a fright," a doctor informed her many hours and a couple of tests later. "If I am not mistaken, you've probably been overdoing it – burning the candle at both ends. Your husband will need to make sure you take it easy for the rest of your pregnancy."

The next morning, once Kristine was told that she could go home, the discharging nurse passed the doctor's advice on to an astonished Richard.

"If you and your wife do not want to lose this baby, Kristine must not exert herself or do any lifting. ...And she is to keep off her feet as much as possible."

"But she works in a rest-home," said Richard in alarm. He refrained from remarking that Kristine was not actually his wife yet. "Does this mean she will have to give it up?"

"If she wants to prevent her baby from miscarrying, then she will probably need to review the type of work she does. Kristine seems to be a strong young woman, but it is not worth her taking any chances, especially as this is her first pregnancy."

They arrived home shortly before noon.

With the rest of the day taken off from the clinic in order to look after Kristine, Richard took the opportunity to discuss their precarious new situation with her.

Up until now, Kristine's contribution to the rent at their flat came solely from her part time work at Everglades. It became obvious during their discussion that if she was to give up that job now, then she would no longer be in a position to pay her way at the flat and also finish off the payments on her car.

"What are we going to do?" she cried.

Richard gave her a reassuring cuddle.

"Now, my precious, what is our priority here?" he said. "It's you and the baby – remember? The first thing you must do is promise me you're not going to worry."

"I can't help it! If it wasn't for that stupid loophole that allows them to bring unmanageable patients into a rest-home, this would not have happened...and I would be working for a lot longer than I'm able to."

Richard sighed. He was tired from being up all night, and struggling to think rationally about their difficulties. Although his primary concern was Kristine's wellbeing, he still had the problem of how to make ends meet. They could manage on his income alone for the time being, he reckoned; but after the baby came...

Best not think too far ahead at this stage, he mused as Kristine found comfort in his embrace.

After much-a needed nap, they both felt refreshed.

Fortunately for Kristine, she had no responsibilities for the remainder of the day and was able to rest.

But even so, it troubled her to realise that, although her days of working at the rest-home appeared to be over, she still needed to give them notice of her intention to leave.

As yet, she had not been in touch with Everglades; which meant she would still be expected to work her shift the following afternoon.

With a sense of urgency, she rang to see if Grace was still at the rest-home.

"I'm sorry, Grace left early today," said one of Kristine's nursing colleagues. "She's going out for the evening and doesn't want to be contacted."

"Oh! Who's on call, then? I need to speak to somebody about taking sick leave."

"Just a minute...I'll give you the name of the registered nurse looking after rosters."

"Damn it," thought Kristine after she had jotted down the details. She hated that registered nurse. She was the last person in the world she wanted to speak to.

However, there was no alternative if she wanted to get out of her duty the following day.

The question of giving her notice to resign would have to wait until the morning.

Kristine squirmed when she heard the nurse's squeaky voice on the phone, and expected to be given a hard time about ringing so late about taking sick leave.

Her assumption was correct. In addition to anticipated remarks, the registered nurse also questioned the validity of her request.

"You don't sound particularly sick to me," she said with exaggerated scepticism.

"Well, I am. And I'm on doctor's orders to rest. So could you please replace me for tomorrow?"

Kristine didn't care about her insubordination.

With a sense of empowerment she realised that it really didn't matter what the lazy registered nurse thought of her now. She would never have to see her face or hear her irritating giggle ever again.

"I suppose I've no choice but to replace you then," the nurse responded with annoyance. "You young people have got no stamina...not like when I was training. We had to turn up for a shift even when we felt half dead. Now, if I had my way... Hello... Kristine, are you still there?"

But Kristine had heard enough and ended the call.

Then, as though something in the woman's voice had tainted the phone itself, she slammed it down in disgust.

Later she said to Richard, "It's a weird feeling, knowing I won't be working there again – and a bit scary, too."

"We'll manage," Richard told her reassuringly.

Emily's health board assessment slowly gained momentum in Fiona's mind.

Throughout the days following Alicia's visit, she would often pick up a sheet or two of the papers still spread out on the table, and read a couple of paragraphs: a soulless statistic or the diagnosis of a condition she wasn't aware Emily possessed.

In essence, what she read informed her that she had the right to cast her own mother out into the impersonal snows of residential care.

Could she do it? ...Need she even do it? After all, she and Kristine were coping admirably, now that Emily's outbursts at day-care were under control.

It had done her the world of good, being able to go back to work; like a breath of fresh air in her humdrum daily life. ...And having the freedom to enjoy something of a social life had satisfied a craving for that, too.

If Emily went into care, would all of this be enhanced or severely restricted?

She would still have to visit her mother at whichever hospital accepted her. She could not very well leave her there to rot!

But even so...the agreement she made with Grace, that Kristine be allowed to have Emily at the rest-home for her first hour of work, had been the answer to her prayers. So why should she spoil an arrangement that was already working very well in favour of something untried which might prove to be unsatisfactory?

And as for Emily, how would she cope with uplifted moved from her home and deposited in a strange hospital with people whose conditions were probably far worse than her own?

It must be terribly traumatic, she thought; for someone like Emily to be submerged in the sights, sounds and smells of such an intimidating place.

...It would be worse than remaining at day-care!

The thought of it made Fiona shudder. Even the idea of being associated with a place like a geriatric hospital was more than she wanted to contemplate; as much for herself as for Emily.

...She had always hated hospitals.

Despite Alicia's suggestion that she discuss the assessment with the family, Fiona made the only decision she could justifiably consider.

As far as she was concerned there was no need of any further discussion; for her mind was made up: Emily would stay at home where she belonged. And the sooner she enforced the decision the better.

Early the next morning she reached for the phone to call Alicia and give her the judgement. But as she did so, it rang insistently.

Annoyed that somebody had broken into her train of thought, Fiona picked it up.

"Hello, who's there?" she said curtly.

"Mum, it's me!"

"Oh, look, Kristine; I've got an urgent call to make...can you ring back in a few minutes?"

"No not really. There's something I need to tell you."

Fiona grunted impatiently.

"Alright, tell me quickly, and then I must make this call."

"It's not that simple. I rang to see if I could come over."

"Can't you tell me when you pick Nana up for her day-care session?"

"No. That's what I need to discuss with you."

Fiona didn't like the sound of that.

"What do you mean?" she asked cautiously.

"I won't be able to look after her anymore."

"Why for heaven's sake?" Fiona shrieked.

"Mum...not over the phone. I'm coming round!"

Fiona listened in disbelief as Kristine, after briefly greeting Emily, recapped the events of the last couple of days.

"Sorry to be the bearer of such disturbing news. I would have told you yesterday, but didn't have the chance."

"I don't know what to say," said Fiona; dumbstruck that her plans had been instantaneously overturned.

"I know how you must feel, Mum: your only daughter almost losing your grandchild. But the doctor assured us that as long as I rest up both the baby and I will be alright."

"What?" exclaimed Fiona...she hadn't given the baby so much as a thought. "Don't you realise what you have done to this family by getting pregnant?"

Kristine's jaw dropped. She couldn't believe her ears. What was her mother telling her? Certainly not that she was concerned for the welfare of expectant mother and child! Surely she must have been mistaken.

"Precisely what you mean by that?" she asked.

"Everything was working out well until you got yourself pregnant. But now you've put a spanner in the works."

"And how have I done that? It's not my fault Everglades is so heavy that I hurt myself. ...Anyway, I would have had to leave there sooner or later."

"Yes, when the baby's due. But you could have taken Nana to day-care in the meantime. Now you can't even do that, from what you're telling me!"

"Oh, I see. I'm beginning to get the picture. We're back to how this all affects you again. Never mind my health. It's what you want that counts!"

In a fit of both anger and conscience Kristine rushed out of the house, but then halted her pace. It was vital she keep control not just of her actions but also her emotions, for she still had not been to see Grace to hand in her notice.

The sight of an envelope containing her resignation, still resting on the passenger seat, brought that fact to mind again as she buckled up.

Kristine sighed despondently.

Everglades had been her next port of call, but right now she did not feel like dealing with it.

However, once she had driven off, she steeled herself; deciding it would be better to clear the deck while she was already out and about, as she had more scheduled duties from which she needed to extricate herself.

Grace received the news tersely.

"You're not the only person to give notice today."

"Who else has resigned, then?"

"One of the part-time cleaners – the one who replaced Richard. He was so rude. He said he didn't intend to flog himself to death for peanuts. ...The cheek of it!"

Kristine chuckled under her breath. I must remember to tell Richard about that, she thought to herself.

"At least my resignation is for health reasons," she said; assuming Grace would be more accepting of her dilemma.

380

"Yes... Well... I would hardly call this a health problem, Kristine. Allowing yourself to get pregnant, and then using it as an excuse to leave your job without working off your notice could hardly be termed a health problem! Have you any idea of the difficult position you have put us in?"

"No, I can't say I have thought of it that way. All I know is: the doctor at the hospital said I shouldn't do anything strenuous, and that means just about everything I do here. I can't even take Nana to day-care because of lifting her out of the car and into her wheelchair..."

"...Your grandmother's day-care visits are none of my concern. Fiona will have to make that decision herself."

Grace paused to draw breath, the frustration beginning to get the better of her.

Then she went on, "You said your doctor told you not to do anything strenuous. I take it they gave you a medical certificate to cover the two weeks' notice that you would have been working off. ...Or is giving up work on the spur of the moment your own decision?"

Kristine stalled; at a loss for words.

Indeed, it was just a recommendation by the hospital that she give up work, and the doctor certainly gave her nothing by way of a certificate.

In all honesty, the decision to resign straight away was hers and hers alone.

"I... Um..."

Whatever can I tell her? thought Kristine; searching her mind for inspiration.

Then, as Grace waited for an answer, she mumbled, "The doctor didn't give me a certificate at the time, but I can get one. Would tomorrow be soon enough?"

On the way home Kristine panicked. As yet she had no idea how to get hold of a certificate.

381

The spur-of-the-moment promise made to Grace was purely to cover her bases.

A frantic phone call to the hospital enquiring after the necessary document drew a blank.

After a lengthy wait on hold the receptionist told her there was nothing in her records to state that she must give up her activities, only that she needed to take it easy and let them know if there were problems.

"Does that mean I have to carry on working?" Kristine asked in dismay.

"Not necessarily. You have the option of working or not, but if you feel you need to give up, there's nothing to stop you getting a medical certificate from your doctor. He will already have been advised of your hospital visit."

Kristine drew strength from this, and rang the surgery for an appointment.

"The maximum I can give you on a medical certificate is five days," he told her when she managed to see him.

With further duties scheduled over the next couple of weeks, she quickly totted up to see if five days would be enough, and discovered to her relief that it was.

Thank goodness I only needed to cover the days I was scheduled to work, she thought while she drove back to the rest-home with her precious piece of paper.

As she pulled into the rest-home's staff car park for the last time, she laughed out loud, "That's the advantage of being a casual worker!"

"Gee, what a mission!" she said to Richard later on. "I was beginning to think I was stuck with working out all five of those damnable duties. Now I don't need to go back at all! I hope I never have to see that place again!"

"So that only leaves you with your course at university. Do you think you'll be able to finish it?"

"I don't see why not. With no other commitments to tire me, it shouldn't be a problem. The baby isn't due until after the course finishes, so we can work on our wedding plans In the meantime. What do you say to that?"

"I can't wait," said Richard with enthusiasm.

But then his demeanour altered slightly.

Kristine noticed, and commented.

"What's wrong? Have I overlooked something?"

"No, not at all. I'm thinking about your grandmother. If you and your aunt won't be taking her to day-care, what will Fiona do, now that she is back at work? She's going to be mad as hell about all of this."

"She already is. But I will not live my life just to suit my mother anymore. I've got other things to consider now."

Kristine patted her tummy contentedly.

The future for her and her new family was beginning to look a lot brighter.

Meanwhile, Fiona found herself back at Square One, with all the responsibility of looking after Emily, and nobody to help her out.

In desperation, she made the phone call she was about to make when Kristine wrecked her plans.

But on this occasion, Fiona had very different decision to announce to Alicia.

"Ah, Fiona! I've been expecting to hear from you," said Alicia in her professional voice; somehow she didn't think this would be a social chat. "Have you all come to a decision over Emily's care?" she asked.

In most cases like this, Alicia was used to her clients' families getting back to her after lengthy and sometimes agonising discussions amongst themselves. In all cases, the client was part of the discussion, even if he or she was unable to take part in the decision-making. So when Fiona rang, Alicia assumed that not only had Ruth and Kristine been in on the consultation, but also Emily herself.

Yet, Fiona merely said, "I'm ringing to ask you to pursue the matter of a hospital placement for my mother."

Alicia went quiet.

Two things had come to mind. The first was that it would be a sad day when Emily had to leave her home. But also, a question had arisen she felt sure would not yet have been considered.

"Fiona," she said. "Have you any idea where you would like Emily to go?"

"No. Why do you ask? I assumed that once the decision was made, you would make the arrangements for me. Isn't that what usually happens?"

"...Not really. Families usually prefer to make their own enquiries before coming to any firm decision. But if your family would like me to make a suggestion, I do actually have somewhere in mind that would suit you."

"Please do. I'm open to anything – and the sooner the better. My circumstances have become impossible. I'm working now, and with Kristine pregnant... Did you know she's had to give up work because of it? And not only that... Now she can no longer look after Mum while I'm at work it places me in an situation with my job..."

"...Fiona," said Alicia, interrupting her.

She knew how Fiona could get carried away when she had something on her mind.

"Shall I go ahead and make enquiries at the place I have in mind?"

"Alright, if you say so," Fiona replied pensively. "Where is it, anyway? Not too far away, I hope."

"No, it's not far from your place; in fact, you are already familiar with this one. It's Everglades."

All at once, Fiona halted in her thinking.

"...Everglades? Do you mean...the rest-home where Kristine has been working?"

"Yes. Is that so surprising?"

"But that's just a rest-home! Didn't you tell me Mum was assessed for hospital care...or had you forgotten?"

"No, Fiona... I haven't forgotten!"

Alicia's frustration was beginning to break through her professional veneer now, for she always found it difficult to keep her cool with Fiona.

Yet, experience prevailed and she brushed the irritation aside in the interest of progress.

"The other night Grace came over for dinner. I believe you know her from Everglades..."

"...Yes, yes. I know who you mean. But what has your cosy dinner got to do with this?"

"She told me something about Everglades of which I was unaware, and it might be of interest to you."

"And what is that?"

Fiona was not particularly interested in idle gossip.

"She said the Everglades rest-home is accepting people with a higher dependency level now."

"Since when?"

"Since fairly recently, I think. I only found out about it the other..."

"...So that's why Kristine was making all the fuss," Fiona murmured.

Up until now she had only casually questioned Kristine's criticism that a heavy resident caused her fall, and why she felt the need to resign.

"...What was that about Kristine?" asked Alicia with a mixture of interest and concern.

"It doesn't matter," responded Fiona. "She's decided to give up her job, and will no longer be looking after Mum.

385

It's something to do with her pregnancy. That's why I must get Mum into a hospital as quickly as possible. I can't deal with her on my own anymore."

Now Alicia was confused.

She could not grasp what Fiona was referring to where Kristine and Everglades were concerned. But that was not really any of her business. Her role in this instance was as Emily's primary health worker not her friend; meaning she must heed the wishes of the family; namely, Fiona.

"Would you like me to contact Grace on your behalf, then?" she asked.

"No, I don't think that will be necessary. If, as you say, Everglades now takes in the stage three patients, there's nothing to stop me from seeing her myself. I know Grace quite well now."

"As you wish...and good luck!"

The following day, Fiona asked Kristine to stay with Emily while she ran an errand. Without advising her as to the nature of the errand, she drove straight to Everglades.

Grace received Fiona's visit with surprise. She had never regarded Emily as a permanent resident of the rest-home, nor even considered the possibility that her doting family might one day seek to have her admitted.

"I'm sorry to hear Emily's condition has deteriorated enough to make her eligible for residential care," she said kindly, directing Fiona into the interview room.

"Actually, she's been assessed for hospital," said Fiona, correcting her. "But Alicia informed me that you take more dependent people at Everglades now."

"That's correct..."

"...So does that mean my mother will be able to come here as a resident?"

Fiona's blunt approach caught Grace off guard, and for a moment, practiced etiquette deserted her.

Grace did not know Fiona very well; had met her only a couple of times, in fact. ...Certainly she knew nothing of her personal background.

On the spur of the moment, she had to assume that the woman's insistent manner was born a daughter's need to see her mother receive a level of care she could no longer provide at home.

Grace had come across this many times before, where the loving family wanted only the best for their relative and would stop at nothing to get it.

"Well?" said Fiona, drawing Grace out of her musings. "Can she come here, then?"

"Of course!" said Grace, and then backtracked. "...That is to say, we will give serious consideration to her case. Our clients are selected according to their degree of need, or their position on the rest-home waiting list, whichever is the greater priority."

"And what does that mean where my mother's case is concerned? To me, it is of utmost priority!"

Forcing herself to remain polite, Grace said, "It means that if you will give me a few minutes I'll check our records and get back to you."

Grace left Fiona in the interview room while she went over to the receptionist's office.

Feeling flustered, she said to the receptionist, "Quickly, would you look up our waiting list on the computer. I need to know if there are any urgent referrals. There's a relative here who I want to get off my back as soon as possible."

The receptionist opened up the relevant document and cast her eyes down the list.

"Nothing stands out," she said.

"Excellent. Now, when the referral for Emily Thompson comes through, I would like you to move her name to the top of the list. She's to be given the next available room."

"Emily...Thompson," echoed the receptionist while she made a note of the name. "Isn't that..."

"...Yes: Kristine's grandmother. She'll be coming to live with us – soon, I hope."

"Oh, that'll be lovely! We will all look forward to having Emily with us. She is a delightful lady..."

"...That she is. Now, if you'll excuse me..."

"...Of course."

Back in the interview room, Grace told Fiona, "I have both good news and not so good news."

Fiona looked up at her, not in the mood to be told news she would rather not hear.

"The good news," Grace went on, sensing Fiona's frame of mind; "is that Emily is now at the top of the waiting list for a bed here at Everglades."

"...And the bad news?"

"At the moment we don't have any vacancies."

"Oh, I see."

Fiona's downcast expression confirmed the annoyance she felt at the unwelcome brief.

"...However, that can change at any time," Grace added to try and buoy up Fiona's spirits. Now that she had given her some hope, maybe the wait for a bed would not be so tedious for either Fiona or her mother. "Please tell Emily and the rest of the family that they are welcome to look around the place any time they like. We will, of course, make sure that when the time comes, Emily is given a nice sunny room."

"Thank you," said Fiona, smiling unenthusiastically.

She left the interview room, and strode out to her car.

Disappointed, Fiona rued the fact that the outcome had not been more favourable. ...But, she conceded, it couldn't be helped if there were no vacancies. At least Emily was at the top of the waiting list.

As for bringing her in to look around, there really wasn't any point. For one thing, Emily was already familiar with Everglades, and for another...she knew nothing of Fiona's decision to have her admitted, nor even that there had been an assessment.

If Emily realised what was being planned, her reaction would be hostile to say the least, and that was something Fiona did not want to have to deal with right now.

During the drive home Fiona started to feel more at ease with the situation. Granted, it may be some weeks before a room was vacated; and yet, by the same token one could become available for her tomorrow.

It had been a great help, Fiona reminded herself, that her employer understood Kristine's inability to help out with Emily, for his wife was also expecting a baby and had likewise been told to rest.

"I know how you feel," he had said. "I'm under pressure from home as well. So the least I can do is to offer you all the time you need until the circumstances with the family settle down."

Although Fiona would have preferred to keep working as opposed to spending even one more day minding Emily, she had gratefully accepted the kind offer.

By the time she arrived home, with positive thoughts lifting her spirits, Fiona had reached a decision:

Maybe it would be prudent to inform the family of what was going to happen.

She felt up to the task now.

On Fiona's return from the errand, Kristine quickly noticed that her mother's overall mood was better than when she went out. However, as she brought in no shopping bags, it was obvious she had not been to the store.

Therefore, Kristine could only speculate as to what had brought on the cheerful mood.

"Are you going to tell Nana and me what has made you so chipper all of a sudden?" she asked after her mother had hung up her coat.

Fiona grinned and joined them in the lounge.

"I'll have you know, I've just set in motion the solution to all of our problems," she said boastfully.

Emily smiled innocently up at her daughter, responding to her cheerfulness rather than her remark.

However, Kristine's response to the statement was less naïve than Emily's.

"What's that supposed to mean?" she asked cynically.

Kristine was suspicious: she had encountered this sort of statement from her mother before...there was usually an ulterior motive attached.

She waited nervously for Fiona's answer.

"Don't be like that, Kristine. I know what you're likely thinking. And this time you're wrong. What I've arranged will be good for all of us."

Kristine looked anxiously at Emily who had already lost interest in the conversation.

What was the woman talking about now...and does she include Nana in her scheming?

"Go on," she said; her heart in her mouth.

"You needn't be so wary about it, Kristine. I'm not likely to do anything to hurt either of you, am I? And if I may say so, you should both be grateful for the effort I have put into what has been arranged."

"Just what have you arranged?" Kristine asked uneasily.

Fiona paused for a moment; conscious now that taking matters into her own hands may not be considered by the rest of the family to be her sole prerogative.

With Kristine eyeing her suspiciously, in the corner of her mind she also wondered what Ruth's reaction might be. Oh well, she thought. It's too late now!

"I might as well come right out and tell you..."

"...About time, too!" said Kristine, her eyes still fixed on her mother's.

Fiona ignored her.

Assertively, she announced, "Over the last few weeks, at my request Alicia has been having Nana assessed for long term residential care..."

"...Without discussing it with anybody else?" grumbled Kristine in disbelief.

Fiona instantly sprang to her own defence.

"I'm well within my rights!" she said indignantly. "Nana is my responsibility, and now that the entire workload of looking after her has been dumped on my shoulders again, I am perfectly entitled to do whatever I feel is necessary! So don't get all hoity-toity over it, young lady, because it was you who forced me to consider taking this action. ...And furthermore the idea of residential care for Nana was Alicia's, not mine!"

"Where does Alicia fit into all of this? She may be Dad's girlfriend, but she's not exactly family."

"No, but she is still Nana's district nurse..."

"...Mum, you're worrying me. Would you please tell me what the two of you have trumped up behind our backs?"

"I'm trying to, if you'll just listen! Alicia recognised how difficult everything was becoming for me at home; and for all of us, I should add, because it has had an effect on you and Nana as well."

"Well, I wonder who told her that…"

"…Only after she sounded me out over it. Alicia stayed on here one afternoon, and let you go home early when you were nauseous from your pregnancy. You can't have forgotten that, surely. She stayed because she wanted to talk to me about Nana."

Kristine paused for a moment. When she thought about it, she did have a vague recollection of that happening. She had been too sick at the time to pay much attention.

"Yes. I'm sorry. I do remember now."

"Anyway, as I was trying to tell you; she suggested we have Nana assessed for residential care, and I agreed. Then the results came through. At first I was going to decline, but you told me you could no longer help out with Nana, and I realised there was only one thing I could do now. Kristine, your grandmother is category three, so by rights she should be in a hospital already."

"I had no idea…."

"No. You were so hell bent on backing away from your obligations that you didn't give me or Nana a thought."

"Why didn't you tell me sooner? …And what does Nana think of it all? I presume you've explained it to her."

"No I haven't mentioned it to her yet…."

"…So you chose to leave out the two main players in all this – Nana and me. I suppose Ruth doesn't mind. It will let her off the hook completely, and she won't be plagued by a guilty conscience for not helping out anymore!"

"Alright, that will do; I think you've said enough. The fact of the matter is, I didn't mention it to anyone else, my sister included, because I knew it would get this reaction. And I didn't explain it to Nana because she wouldn't have understood."

Alerted by the raised voices, Emily looked sternly across at Fiona and Kristine.

392

Although the gist of their conversation had gone over her head, of one thing she was acutely aware. They were talking about her...and not just talking, but arguing. Then, when both pairs of eyes latched onto hers, she knew for sure they were plotting something.

Emily wagged her finger at Fiona and slowly said, "No... No... No!"

Then she looked at Kristine as if to enlist her support.

Vivid memories of her early days at the day-care centre came to mind. Fiona had not bothered to find out how she felt about it even then.

Kristine sighed disconsolately.

"I think I should be the one to drop the bombshell on her, if you don't mind," she said to her mother, and then added, "By the way, you haven't said which hospital you and Alicia have decided Nana should go to."

"It isn't a hospital – it's Everglades; and the booking has already been made."

For a moment Kristine felt as though the earth must have opened up and swallowed her.

The mention of Everglades sent a shiver down her spine as she recalled the many difficulties she experienced while working there.

No other member of her family could even guess at the hardships suffered by both caregivers and those residents who could not speak for themselves; all as a result of the apathetic attitude on the part of senior personnel.

While Fiona rambled on about her meeting with Grace, about how impressed she had been when Kristine showed her around the brand new complex, and how much she was looking forward to Emily living in one of the lovely, sunny rooms with their ensuites and warm-air hand-driers, Kristine cringed.

393

In her mind's eye she conjured up the indelible images of caregivers such as herself being too rushed to attend to the residents' individual needs.

Would it be the same for Emily in her absence?

And how would the caregivers cope with her inability to speak properly? Would they take the time to understand what she was attempting to say? Would they string her up on a lifting hoist because, despite Emily's slight stature, they were not allowed to lift disabled residents?

Yet rather than censure the caregivers who would be placed in that position, she sympathised with them; that is, with the ones who, like herself, had always aimed to do their very best for the residents.

As for the others: the ones who were choosy in the way they worked, the caregivers and those in senior positions, who preferred social chit-chat with their colleagues over meaningful time spent with the residents; she hoped none of them would be looking after her grandmother.

"What do you think, then?" Fiona went on. "Isn't it great that Nana can go somewhere she is familiar with and to all accounts enjoys? Grace told me she was very popular with the therapists when you took her there. She was never any trouble for them..."

"...That's because I was still there, stupid!" said Kristine, something vital snapping inside of her.

"Kristine! Don't talk like that, please!"

"Mum, there are a lot of things you don't know about Everglades; things you can't know unless you work there."

"Don't be ridiculous, Kristine. Everglades has developed a good reputation in the short time it has been open, and there is no doubting how beautifully appointed it all is. I'll never forget the hand-driers in their ensuites. That really takes the cake, don't you agree?"

Kristine felt completely defeated. Her mother was on a roll now and could not be stopped.

If she attempted to voice any more of her concerns she would not even be listened to, let alone heeded. It wasn't Fiona who was going to live there; it was Nana — dear, feisty, incapacitated Nana — who had plenty to say for herself, but not the means of saying it. If she didn't get what she needed...

She tailed off in her thoughts with the recollection of that awful time at day-care, when Emily was evicted for being disruptive...not because she was deliberately being rebellious, but because she could no longer express herself properly, and her frustration gave way to agitation.

What would they do if she was a resident at the rest-home and became similarly disruptive? They couldn't very well summon Kristine to deal with her again...and she knew exactly what alternative means they would use...

"...Kristine, I asked your opinion. You do agree with me, don't you?"

"What's the point in my saying anything else, Mum," Kristine sneered back at her. "You don't really care what I think. You only asked because you expect me to go along with all of your plans for Nana!"

With one last, pitiful glance at her anxious grandmother, Kristine fled from the house.

The heightened emotions of pregnancy raced through her as she drove home. Wasn't there anyone in the family she could speak to about it!

Only one person came to mind: her father.

However, before she could discuss the predicament that haunted her, she needed to work out what she should say to him.

Royston, she recalled, was only completely familiar with the Emily he engaged with when he looked after her.

During that time, Emily was still communicative and good-natured. He could understand most of what she said, wanted and needed. He even accepted her foibles where Arthur was concerned.

Yet, once Fiona took over from him, he had little to do with her except socially.

He did not see the frustration that developed between Emily and Fiona. Whenever Kristine saw Royston with her, she was so happy that all she could do was beam at him; giving the impression that nothing was amiss.

How, then, could she convey her grandmother's current emotional state, let alone her fears for Emily's wellbeing as a resident at Everglades?

...And then there was Alicia.

She was very much a part of the family now, so over the months, she and Royston must have talked about Emily.

But Alicia was a professional health worker, so was not at liberty to discuss Emily's medical details outside of that capacity. Therefore, it left Kristine questioning what, if anything, had Alicia already told her father about Emily's irrational outbursts at day-care, about the assessment; or even about Everglades?

Later on, Kristine talked it over with Richard.

"I'm really not sure what to say to Dad," she confessed. "At the moment nobody except for you knows what goes on in Everglades, and Nana needs special care if she is to be happy there. I just don't know what's the best tactic I can use when I approach him."

"Oh, but I do!" said Richard.

He jumped up and fetched his laptop computer; then he placed it in front of Kristine.

"What's this for?" she asked curiously as she steadied it on her lap.

"If your father is the only person you can confide in, then the way to give him all the information is to write it down. ...Send him a letter."

He reached over and clicked open a blank document.

"Okay, start typing," he said. "You can easily make any changes as you go along, and I will be here to help if you have any problems with the computer."

Kristine blew him a kiss in thanks.

Any other time she would have expressed her gratitude with a cuddle, but two things prevented that right now: the expensive new computer balanced precariously on her knee, and the growing bump in her tummy.

She did not want to hurt either by twisting round.

"Here, what do you think of this?" she said later on.

She leant back on the couch so Richard could take the computer off her.

He picked it up; then saved what Kristine had written, and settled back to read it through.

"It all seems to be here," he said afterwards. "One thing became apparent as I read it, though; something I think you should ease back on when you get round to talking about it with your father."

"Oh, what's that?" asked Kristine; puzzled.

"You're a bit too cynical in your comments about your mother and the rest-home. I understand how you feel, but if you're to convince your father that these are facts and not just your feelings, you will need to tone it down a bit. Do you think you can do that?"

Kristine grunted and pulled a face.

"Do I have to? It's taken a lot out of me, just writing all that stuff," she said, pointing at it.

"Okay; we'll go through it again tomorrow shall we?" Richard suggested. "It should all come back fresh in your mind, and you can make your alterations then."

Kristine chuckled contentedly. "However did we get on before we had computers?"

Not only did the finished version contain everything Kristine wanted to say to her father, but also it read so concisely that Richard could not help but comment.

"How could he not take into account everything you are telling him in this?" he stated assertively. "I would be very surprised if he didn't tackle your mother over it!"

Kristine's revelation came as a great surprise to Royston.

As expected, he was initially sceptical; especially as the report suggested, albeit politely, that Fiona was the cause of Emily's aggravation.

"Do you think Emily's situation would have worked out better if I'd stayed with her?" he asked.

"Possibly... Who knows? But it's irrelevant, anyway. You and Alicia could not have lived there together; and even if you had, Nana would still have gone downhill once she suffered the stroke. The thing is Dad: what can we do? I'm so concerned Nana will suffer if she goes to Everglades..."

"...And your mother won't hear a word against the rest-home people. Hmm...that makes it a bit tricky."

Royston paused for thought.

"Okay, love," he said when his thoughts had caught up with his feelings. "Leave it to me; I'll speak to her ...And thanks for confiding in me. It means a lot to know you still value my input where Emily's concerned."

Royston's acceptance of the exposé lifted the weight of care from Kristine's shoulders.

It meant that she could sit back and let her parents sort it out; for she had done everything possible, herself.

398

"Well done, sweetheart," Richard said after she had told him the essence of her father's comments. "You may have just saved your grandmother from a lot of suffering in her golden years."

Yet, Richard was very much mistaken.

The moment Royston voiced his daughter's concerns to Fiona, she rejected them so concisely that he was left with no recourse but to back down.

...For, as it turned out, even before Kristine asked for his help, Grace had rung to inform Fiona that a room was now available for Emily; thus, by the time he left home to go and discuss the matter with her, Fiona had already called in at Everglades and signed the agreement.

With three simple words, Royston was silenced.

"It's too late," Fiona told him without hesitation.

"But that can't be right," Royston stated. "Alicia told me these bookings take ages to go through!"

"Mother's residency at Everglades is signed and sealed; and as far as I'm concerned, there is no going back on it. So you can take your damning report back to Kristine and tell her where she can stick it!"

Despite further distraught protests from Kristine and her father, all of which fell on sanctimoniously deaf ears, Fiona packed up everything she considered Emily would need, and at the last minute sat down with her to explain what was happening.

With the mention of Everglades, Emily's stroke-affected mind thought only of the fun she had there with Kristine, the other ladies in the flower arranging group...and her rose blooms plucked from the rest-home's garden which drew her so much closer to Arthur. The idea of repeating that joyful experience brought a glow to her heart and a smile to her face, and it was this which confirmed to Fiona that the decision to send her to Everglades permanently was the right one.

Emily, she concluded, would be perfectly happy living there, despite Kristine's reservations...and Fiona could not wait to rub her daughter's nose in the fact that she was in the wrong to think otherwise.

"Okay, so you won that round," Kristine conceded when she arrived to help Emily settle into her freshly decorated and sunny room.

Although Fiona had not asked for her assistance, she still reckoned her involvement was needed to make sure Emily did not fret about all that was taking place, and that had once more been forced upon her.

Once they arrived at the rest-home, Kristine wheeled her off to the rose garden, out of the way both physically and emotionally; for she was sure Emily would not be able to grasp what it was all about.

She felt sure Fiona would have believed only what she wanted to believe in Emily's passive reaction to the news.

The difficult times, Kristine suspected, were just around the corner.

There was little Kristine could do now, except pray that the new arrangement would work out alright; that her worries were caused by nothing more than overactive hormones, and most importantly of all, that her grandmother would actually be happy living in Everglades.

CHAPTER EIGHT

During the night, intermittent screams coming from one of the bedrooms greatly alarmed the two caregivers on night duty at Everglades.

"It must be the new lady," said the one to her partner as they hurried down the corridor to investigate. "Nobody else here carries on like that!"

The caregivers burst into the darkened room and found Emily in an agitated state, sitting on the side of her bed.

"Mrs Thompson, what are you doing!" barked one of the caregivers. "...And whatever is all that noise about? You will wake everybody up!"

Emily, still distraught from a nightmare in which Fiona wrenched her from the arms of her husband and dumped her in prison, yelled at the caregivers, "No... No... No!"

Concerned that other residents in the corridor might be disturbed and also create a scene, the caregiver pulled the door to, briefly plunging the room into darkness, before flicking on the light switch.

The sudden brightness caused Emily to cry out.

"Don't yell like that!" chided the caregiver. "Just tell us what you want...please!"

The second caregiver, a little more understanding than the first, quietly said, "I think the light's a bit bright for her." She turned on Emily's bedside lamp and switched off the ceiling light. "Is that better, dear?" she said kindly.

Emily looked beseechingly into the eyes of the stranger. These two uniformed figures were different from the girls who helped her into bed...and where, she wondered, were Fiona and Kristine?

Had they really dumped her in a prison without Arthur? It was all too worrying.

Receiving no response to her question, the kind caregiver, remembering that their new resident was a stroke victim, began to ask questions that required a yes or no answer.

Firstly, she asked if she was in pain, to which Emily lapsed into thought, before shaking her head.

Then the caregiver asked her, "Do you need the toilet?"

Again Emily tried to think, but her mind was in such a whirl she could not work out just what it was she wanted.

The effort to make decisions, after everything that had happened during the day, was just too much, and silently she began to cry.

"Oh, for goodness sake, Mrs Thompson," said the first caregiver. "You were only asked if you want the toilet! What is there to cry about?"

The kind one turned on her colleague. "Don't forget this is her first night here – we need to make allowances! It must all seem very strange to her."

"Well, I hope she gets used to it quickly," her partner responded. "She's going to be here for a long time!"

Then she opened the door, and left.

The kind caregiver sat down on the side of the bed. She touched Emily's hand and, discovering it felt cold, reached for a shawl to place around her shoulders.

Shaking from anxiety and the cold, Emily murmured, "Thank...you;" then clutched the two ends of the shawl with her good hand.

Safely back in bed again, Emily lay gazing up into her young rescuer's face.

402

In the soft light of the bedside lamp everything looked menacing and shadowy to the apprehensive new resident.

Only the caregiver's face was lit well enough for her to see its details, and in that she found comfort.

Though still traumatised after being brought to the rest-home, not only to spend some time with the ladies but also, so it seemed, to stay for a whole night, Emily could see that this girl was a very caring person who was there to help her, and she relaxed a little.

The girl reminded her of Kristine who, only a few short hours ago had sat with her out in the garden.

She remembered that alright; but what she could not remember was the reason she'd been brought here in the first place. Had she done something wrong? Was it some kind of punishment; that she had been made to spend the night in a prison? But if she really was being kept here as some form of punishment, then why was this girl being nice to her when the other was so rude?

She sighed, lost in her own thoughts as the soft voice of her night nurse spoke quietly of...

Emily wasn't sure exactly what she was talking about. It all seemed to wash dreamily over her head.

The caregiver gently pulled the covers up around Emily's shoulders and clicked off her lamp. But instead of closing the door to the corridor, she left it open slightly so that should Emily reawaken she would not be startled by the darkness, and panic again.

The dim corridor night-lights emitted enough brightness for residents who felt the need to stretch their legs, but not enough to disturb those still sleeping who preferred to leave their doors open. She hoped Emily might be able to sleep through the rest of the night. Tomorrow would be a busy day for her: getting used to the rest-home schedule, to having breakfast served off a trolley by yet another set of people, and to having someone she did not know assist her with her shower...

It was a strange new world Emily had just entered. The sympathetic caregiver hoped she would adjust to it easily.

The next morning, as Emily sat in bed enjoying a breakfast of mixed fruit with a drop of cream, followed by toast and marmalade and a cup of tea, she was startled by a knock on her open door.

She looked up to see Kristine standing there.

For a moment, Emily did not know what to do, or even what to think.

She looked down at all the breakfast items on the tray-table in front of her, and then at Kristine in the doorway. Her first thought was that Kristine had come to fetch her home; and yet...she was in the middle of her breakfast. Unnerved, she couldn't work it all out.

However Kristine, seeing Emily sitting up in a rest-home bed in an environment familiar to her well- trained eye, immediately realised what was going through this new resident's mind.

"It's alright, Nana," she said. "Finish off your breakfast. I just popped in to see how you are getting on."

In fact, Kristine had slept very little that night. Traumatised herself by the upheaval her beloved Nana had endured, she felt a mixture of concern and guilt, that she let her mother get away with establishing Emily in a rest-home without seeking consent from the family.

She got up the moment she awoke and, knowing the routine of the residents only too well, timed her arrival at Everglades to catch Emily when she would still be in bed.

Kristine walked over to Emily and squatted down beside her bed.

She looked over the tray, paying special attention to Emily's selection of breakfast items.

Suddenly a voice behind her said, "Is everything alright in there?" Then, when the morning caregiver saw that the visitor with Emily was Kristine, she said, "Oh, hello Kristine. I didn't realise it was you. Do you know this lady?"

"Yes, of course," said Kristine in astonishment.

Had she not brought Emily to the rest-home on many occasions?

"This is my grandmother. She used to come in with me before I started work in the afternoons."

"Emily? Oh...of course! Goodness, she looks so different sitting in bed like this."

Then the caregiver said, "Welcome, Emily. I'm sure you will be very happy living here with us."

Emily glanced at Kristine with a startled look in her eye.

What was that about 'living' here?

Suddenly the penny dropped. Rattling her tray-table, she shouted at the caregiver, "No... No... No!"

As she did so, her cup of tea slopped over her duvet.

Immediately, the caregiver rushed to try and stop the liquid soaking further into her bedding.

Kristine was embarrassed now to think her grandmother was already creating problems for the staff. She knew how busy they were at this time of the morning.

"It's alright," she said to the caregiver. "I'll clear it up."

"Thank you, Kristine...much appreciated."

Then she said to Emily, "Have you finished with your tray, Em...er, Mrs Thompson?"

Emily frowned, as though it was the caregiver's fault that she was stuck in a rest-home and had spilt her drink.

"I think Nana's finished," Kristine replied on her behalf; and added, "Maybe I'll pour her another cup of tea so she doesn't miss out on her fluids, if it's okay with you."

"Yes. That would be alright. The tea trolley is just down the corridor, if you'd like to help yourself... Oh, by the way Emily; I will be in a bit later on to give you a shower."

Kristine turned back to Emily; afraid she might react badly to the way the caregiver casually addressed her.

But Emily was still sulking. As far as she was concerned, she was not going to do anything for anybody if they were going to keep her in prison...

Just then, Kristine remembered who she was dealing with: not so much an anxious new resident, but her own grandmother...and Kristine knew her grandmother like the back of her hand.

She said to Emily, "I'll go and get you another cup of tea, Nana."

Jumping up, she followed the girl out into the corridor.

"I've got a suggestion," she said. "Whenever you want to do something with Nana, take her a rose. Then she will be putty in your hands..."

"...A rose?"

"Yes; from the rose garden out the back. Nana dotes on them. They remind her of her...of my grandfather. He grew roses when he was alive."

"Okay, Kristine. Thanks for the tip," said the caregiver.

Yet, as she rushed the trolley back to the kitchen she muttered to herself, "What time do I have to go outside and pick flowers?"

Kristine remained in Emily's room until the completion of her shower. In actual fact, she stayed with her for the rest of the morning, walking with her to the recreation room, and later on into lunch.

Although it resulted in a long morning for the pregnant Kristine, it was pleasantly different from other occasions when she had been with Emily at the rest-home.

This time, if Emily needed the kind of help Kristine was now no longer able to give, she only had to ring the call bell and sooner or later somebody would come and do all the hard work for her.

This was not something Kristine chose to do, though. She would much rather have attended to Emily by herself. Each time she needed to call in a caregiver, she apologised for doing so; an unnecessary contrition, she was told, for the caregivers were glad to have someone there to help calm their fractious new resident. ...They had been warned by the night staff that Emily Thompson was likely to be a bit troublesome.

Keeping someone like that happy was a godsend.

"I told you Nana would settle in well at Everglades," Fiona gloated when Kristine described her morning at the rest-home. "You doubted me, as always, but I was proved right. An apology would be nice."

Kristine cringed at her mother's cockiness. She was well aware that the reason Emily had settled was because she had her granddaughter fussing over her...

As for her being happy there...that depended on which caregivers were on duty. Kristine knew who was likely to be kind and who could be impatient. Soon enough, Emily would discover for herself which was which. She would no doubt let each of them know exactly how she felt about them, especially those who weren't very patient.

In a way, the thought of it made Kristine chuckle. Emily in full battle cry was a sight to behold...

The trouble was, the caregivers didn't know Emily as well as she did. When disability and frustration prevented

Emily from expressing herself clearly, the helpers over at day-care would interpret her ranting as belligerence. Kristine was sure the people she encountered at the rest-home would respond the same way...

At least, Kristine reflected with satisfaction, she'd had the foresight to tell one of them about the roses.

She hoped the message had been recorded in Emily's notes; and duly passed on.

A few weeks later, Fiona received a call from Grace.

"I'm afraid there is an urgent matter we need to discuss with you," she said in a serious tone.

"Oh! What would that be?"

"Could you come soon? It won't take very long."

Fiona groaned: she was about to leave for work.

"Can't you tell me quickly on the phone," she said with annoyance. "I was on my way out."

"No, not really. ...Although, of course, it has to do with your mother."

"I presumed that. What has she done now?"

"Nothing very terrible. We just need to go over Emily's medications. The doctor would like to discuss them with you before we make any changes."

Changes? What changes? As she set out for Everglades, Fiona puzzled over the unexpected request.

The only medication Emily had ever been prescribed was a painkiller. And she only took those when she needed to: when her stroke arm gave her intermittent problems. ...But the rest-home people already had all those details. What was there to change?

"Please come in and sit down," Grace said, inviting Fiona into the interview room, where the doctor and registered nurse were already pouring over Emily's file.

"Grace, would you please tell me what this is about?" Fiona asked when she saw the severe expressions on their faces. "You've got me worried – has something happened to my mother?"

"No," replied Grace. "I told you that on the phone. The doctor here feels Mrs Thompson requires a little more in the way of medication than she's receiving at present. We need to discuss it with you and get written authorisation before it can be prescribed."

"Then something must have happened, or you wouldn't be doing this. Is she experiencing more pain than before?"

"No...it's nothing like that," said the doctor. "We would like to give Mrs Thompson a little sedative to help her to go to sleep. She is very wakeful during the nights, and has been calling out; which of course not only upsets her own sleeping pattern but also disturbs other residents. We are required to seek permission before administering sleeping aids. Do you understand?"

"Yes...but I don't understand why she can't sleep. She's never had a problem with sleeping before; not while I was looking after her, anyway. What have the staff here been doing, that it has become a problem now?"

Fiona had addressed her enquiry to Grace. However, to those present it sounded more like a criticism, and Grace took immediate exception.

In a civil manner she retorted, "I'll have you know my staff are all experienced and professional in their abilities and ethics. I can assure you that if Mrs Thompson is having trouble sleeping, it is not because of my staff. Now, if you don't mind, Fiona, the doctor is a very busy man so I ask you again: Would you be agreeable for us to give her a mild sedative in the evenings?"

"I suppose so," said Fiona, feeling manipulated.

She started to get up ready to leave.

If that was all they needed to know, it could have been dealt with over the phone; and she was already running late for work.

"Just a minute, please," said Grace quickly, and handed her a form. "May I get you to sign this before you go?"

"Sign what? ...Oh, that's right. I have to authorise it."

"Yes, but this form gives Everglades the authority to alter Mrs Thompson's medications when the need arises. This way, we don't have to keep contacting you about it."

Fiona looked it over, and then glanced at the doctor.

"It's standard procedure," he said reassuringly.

"Alright, if you think it's necessary," said Fiona.

She laid the form on the table and added her signature with the pen provided.

Then she handed both back to Grace, and added as an afterthought, "If mother's sleeping improves, you will ease back on the sedative, won't you?"

"Of course," said Grace.

It troubled Fiona that the medical staff at the rest-home thought it necessary to give Emily a sedative.

Whatever had she been doing to make them take action like that? And why were they so insistent about it?

She decided to seek a second opinion...and her only option for that just at the moment lay with Emily's district nurse. Maybe Alicia could explain why an elderly lady, who had only ever required a mild painkiller in the past, should suddenly be in need of something like a sedative.

"Fiona, you do realise that now Emily is in residential care she is no longer my professional responsibility?" Alicia said in response to the request for advice.

"...So sorry, Alicia. I forgot about that. I should not have bothered you with it."

"...Apology not necessary. I'm still happy to help in any way I can. What did you want to know?"

Fiona explained to her the gist of the conversation with the medical team at Everglades.

"I thought they seemed a bit cagey," she said openly. "They got me to sign a form giving them the right to alter Mum's medication without my say-so. It seemed a bit odd to me."

"...Odd, in what way?"

"I don't really know. It seemed as though they wanted permission to pump her full of pills if it suited them. I know my mother can be a handful, but that doesn't mean she should be drugged out of her brain."

"I doubt if it would come to that!" said Alicia in alarm. "You may have just misunderstood their motives. Perhaps they didn't want to drag you in every time they need to update her meds. Did they say why they wanted to give her a sedative?"

"It seems she hasn't been sleeping very well. Grace told me she's been calling out during the night. ...Apparently it upsets the other residents," Fiona added with scepticism.

Alicia thought for a moment.

"Yes, I suppose it would disturb them. Old people don't sleep as soundly as we young-uns, and can get quite tetchy about being constantly disturbed, so I can understand why Grace and the doctor would want to do that? However, I don't understand why she isn't able to sleep. It was never an issue when she was at home, was it?"

"No...not that I know of."

"Perhaps she hasn't settled as well as we hoped."

Fiona became defensive.

"I disagree. As I predicted, she settled in very well. Just ask Kristine...she'll tell you."

411

That night, Emily begrudgingly allowed her caregiver to help get her ready for bed.

She was young, about Kristine's age Emily guessed, so she accepted the assistance; but nevertheless found her a bit abrupt.

After a while, Emily's calling out increased in frequency and volume; to the extent that every time the caregiver responded to her, she left Emily with the impression that she was wasting her time.

"What do you want now, Mrs T?" she asked during the evening when, on seeing her walk past, Emily called to her in a new unintelligible gibberish that she was devising for the purpose.

Emily had realised that trying to form the words she needed to speak was pointless; even though the speech therapist painstakingly had her practice them.

By the time she had extricated the words from her mind and formed them with her mouth, the chance to ask for something had usually passed, or she forgot just what it was she wanted.

The caregivers, from their perspective, had long since given up persuading Emily to use the call bell. It seemed to them that she could not grasp what she was supposed to do with it, as she kept pulling it out from the wall. After only a few days of continually having to replace it, they stopped handing it to her.

She could not explain to them that she only resorted to yanking it from the wall out of frustration, because when she did manage to press it hard enough to make it ring, it was generally ignored. Thus, Emily's cultivated gibberish came into being.

It was so much easier – and far more productive, she discovered – to just call out in her own distinctive way.

...And Emily found to her immense satisfaction that she could get somebody to come every time she yelled.

There was one drawback, though. Before they asked her what she wanted, they usually told her off for yelling. But Emily didn't mind if it gained her some attention...

As the caregiver stood in the doorway waiting for a reply, Emily grinned at her broadly.

She thought it so clever to get what she wanted just by raucously shouting.

"Do you actually want something, or are you just being naughty again?" the caregiver asked.

Emily took offence.

"Not...naughty!" she stated, and scowled at the cheeky slip of a girl.

...If Kristine ever spoke to her like that, she thought, she would smack her bottom!

"...Well, what do you want then, Emily?" the caregiver cried plaintively. "I've got work to do!"

The distressed look on the girl's face alarmed Emily, and she realised with dismay that there was more than a little bit of mischief behind her calling out this time.

She pointed to her glass of water, which the caregiver had left out of reach.

"...Your glass? Is that what you want?"

Emily nodded enthusiastically. "Yes... Yes!"

She had been given strict instructions not to try and get out of bed by herself. The risk of a fall was too great, and the caregiver knew this.

Remorsefully, the girl apologised.

"I'm sorry, Emily. I forgot to give it to you, didn't I?"

She placed the glass on Emily's bedside table.

"Well done with the talking, by the way," she said, and responded warmly when Emily beamed back at her.

413

"Mrs Thompson's not a bad old stick," the caregiver remarked to her colleague afterwards. "I think her bark is far worse than her bite."

However, she changed her mind about it later on when she attempted to give Emily her new sedative...

The evening medication round was something Everglades' residents were used to. In fact, many of them would even ring their bells if they thought the caregivers were late in bringing them.

Yet, apart from the occasional painkiller, Emily had not needed tablets since she came into the rest-home, and nobody mentioned to her that she had to start now.

Therefore, when her caregiver knocked and walked into her room, switched on the bedside lamp, thus rousing her from the beginnings of a very pleasant reverie, and then told her she had a tablet for her to take; Emily's immediate response was to lash out.

"No...No...No!" she yelled in alarm.

Had Emily still been her old self, fully in control of her faculties, she would have told the girl, nice though she was, just what she could do with the pill and then demand that she not be disturbed again; for her doze that evening had brought her closer to Arthur than ever before.

But as it was, the only expression of annoyance she knew how to make conveyed nothing of her true feelings, and only incited a snub from the caregiver.

"I give up!" she cried, and walked out.

She wrote in Emily's file, 'Refused medication'; then stated to her colleague, "Grace can figure out what to do about it tomorrow!"

Early the next morning, Fiona received another phone call from Grace.

"What's wrong now?" asked Fiona in frustration, having been dragged from the shower to answer the phone.

"We need you to come in and persuade your mother to take her medication at night," she was told emphatically. "Emily really dug her heels in last night and wouldn't allow the caregiver to administer her new tablet. I tried to talk to her this morning, but she yelled at me, and I don't know what she was trying to say. Could you come in today and speak to her, please?"

Fiona could not believe her ears. Had she not handed over responsibility for her mother to Everglades?

She replied, "No, Grace. I'm sorry, but you will have to deal with this situation yourself. I'm not coming in again so soon merely for that; I have a job to go to. You people are the specialists. And from what you assured me yesterday, you are also experts in your field. ...So just do the tasks you are paid to do, and use your own powers of persuasion on her. ...Besides," she added by way of reinforcement, "My mother never listens to me anyway."

Fiona would hear no more of it. What were they paid for, if not to handle their own clients?

She headed back to the warmth of the bathroom again to finish off her ablutions.

Then, as she attended to her makeup in the mirror, she declared to her image, "A place like that should not keep running back to the relatives!"

Kristine found her visits with Emily quite relaxing, now that she wasn't burdened with heavy work anymore.

This placed a different perspective on their relationship, and over the ensuing months the two of them became more like friends than granddaughter and grandmother.

On fine days, Kristine wheeled Emily outside to the rose garden. As if to order, a small gazebo had been erected in the centre of the garden where Emily and Kristine liked to sit; and it became their private haven.

There was never any need of conversation when the two occupied that special place, for Kristine knew where Emily's attention lay. Also sensing the pacifying presence, she was quite happy to sit back and allow Emily and Arthur some solitude for their ephemeral liaison.

Yet, for a reason known only to Emily, once back inside the building, the aura always faded and she would revert to the personality which others there saw in her. ...And that observation was becoming far from complimentary.

Emily's reputation for behaving badly had long-since followed her from the day-care centre to the rest-home. In effect, she was now considered to be a very demanding resident: one whom management was beginning to regret having admitted.

To Kristine, though, she would always be 'Nana.'

Ever delightful when they were together, Kristine saw nothing of the struggle the evening staff had in getting her to take tablets, or her incessant calling out in the night after they failed to do so; for the staff had been told not to bother the family with Emily's unwillingness to cooperate.

Accordingly, Kristine had no idea her grandmother was on sedation; and Fiona chose not to tell her, either.

However, as the ingested medication slowly built up in her system, Kristine noticed a gradual deterioration in Emily's overall bearing.

She suspected something might be wrong when Emily nodded off to sleep during one of her visits.

At first Kristine thought the daily companionship might be tiring her, whereas Emily, though enjoying Kristine's visits, could not keep her eyes open; so effective was the sedative becoming.

Furthermore, no-one at Everglades had mentioned that Emily's sleepiness only occurred during the day.

Even when the caregivers managed to get the sedative into her, having now adopted a trick of crushing the tablet and mixing it with leftover dessert, Emily still did not sleep properly through the night.

It seemed, to the staff that she merely did not like to be alone in the dark, and may have even been forcing herself to stay awake...

The truth behind her insomnia, though, was very different.

The sedative actually prevented Emily from entering the higher state of awareness where she could experience Arthur's presence.

Instead, when she allowed herself to drift off to sleep she would find herself in a frighteningly psychotic state of mind. This brought about a struggle that left her with a feeling of being possessed by something sinister.

By morning, she was so relieved to see daylight that she would immediately fall into a deep and welcome sleep; often failing to rouse again until well after lunch.

Yet, of this Emily had no perception. As far as she was concerned, it was all part of her punishment.

"I think Emily is becoming nocturnal," a caregiver casually remarked to Kristine one morning while they stood over her sleeping form. "She's wide awake through the night and drowsy during the day."

"Yes, I've noticed that. Nana is often sleepy when I'm here these days, and it worries me terribly," said Kristine pensively. "She never used to be like it."

"It's the sedative they've put her on. ...You know she's taking a sedative, don't you?"

"...A sedative? ...Since when?"

417

"Since ages ago now – not long after she came here, in fact. I thought you'd be aware of it."

"No! Nobody has told me anything about that! Does my mother know?"

Kristine was beginning to question certain ethics now.

"Of course she knows! Kristine, you should remember that from when you worked here! Grace and the doctor can't prescribe new medication without permission from the relatives."

Kristine flinched awkwardly.

"Oh dear...how dumb of me to forget that! When it's a relative lying there, you see everything from a different perspective. I have to believe Mum and Grace wouldn't do anything to jeopardise her quality of life."

Regrettably, Kristine decided to give up on her outing to see Emily that day.

Although she would have like to question Emily about the sleepiness, she could not wait indefinitely for her to wake up as this was intended to be a quick call.

She had things to do at home before her university lecture, the last before her final exams, and there was one other reason why she could not stay with Emily: she and Richard had an appointment at the antenatal clinic in town, and she did not want to be late.

Kristine was now at the stage in her pregnancy where antenatal classes were recommended to prepare for the birth of her baby.

"These classes aren't just for the mother-to-be," she had been told. "The baby's father should also be prepared. It's his pregnancy, too!"

The classes began at eleven, and Kristine had arranged to meet Richard outside the clinic.

On seeing him, it was immediately obvious that he was uncomfortable about being there.

"Don't worry," she said in fun. "There'll be lots of other self-conscious Dads at the class too."

"It's not just that," he replied defensively. "My boss thought it weird that I should request time off just to go to antenatal classes."

"...And yet, you still came," said Kristine, touched by his willingness to comply.

"Yes; but it might have to be just the one time."

As Kristine had predicted, several more fathers-to-be also turned up with their partners.

Rather than involve them all in tedious exercises, the teacher made the class interesting.

She taught the mothers how to prepare for and deal with contractions, and demonstrated to the fathers how to massage their partners' backs during labour.

She also advocated relaxation therapy for the men; for, as she put it, "Gentlemen, you may think differently at the moment, but when your wife goes into labour, you will be the one to panic, not her!"

Later, when the day's commitments were behind them, the pair laughed about their experiences at the class.

"I actually quite enjoyed it," Richard admitted. "I might try and go again, after all."

"That would be just great," replied Kristine happily. "It was so good having you there. It made me feel like we're a real couple."

"Well, we are!"

"I know...but we're not officially..."

Kristine hesitated. She had something on her mind, but was not sure whether she should mention it. Usually, the initiative came from the man!

"What?" asked Richard; a smile crossing his face; for he knew what she meant.

"They seemed to think all the participants were married couples. It made me feel a bit out of place, if you know what I mean?"

"I certainly do. We'll just have to do something about it then, won't we?

Richard was beaming now.

"Like what...? Oh! Do you mean...get married?"

"Of course that's what I mean! It's always been part of our long-term plan."

"My goodness!" cried Kristine; blushing at the thought of it. "I suppose we should seriously think about it now. ...For the baby's sake, at least."

"Hey! What about for our sake, too? I've always wanted to marry you, you know!"

"Oh, same here, Richard! I would love to marry you!"

With arms stretched out beyond her bulging abdomen, Kristine hugged him fondly.

"Well, let's do it, then!"

"Just like that?"

"Why not? I don't want anything fancy, do you?"

All of a sudden, Kristine needed to sit down; the reality of their spontaneous decision sinking in.

When they became engaged, she gave no thought to an actual wedding: their engagement was just a step they needed to take at the time.

When a child, she dreamt of one day being a bride, and her mother would have expected her to walk down the aisle wearing a white bridal gown. But now, with all their current priorities, such a wedding was not on the cards. ...Nor was it appropriate in her condition, she chuckled, stroking her tummy.

She would be perfectly happy with a quiet ceremony before a Justice of the Peace somewhere in the city.

"No," she replied sincerely. "I don't want anything fancy, for our wedding, either."

"Alright then...tomorrow I'll make some enquiries about getting married in a registry office, if you like."

"Will you really? I suppose we would need a couple of witnesses. I'd really like Alicia and Dad to be there...don't know about Mum, though. She probably wouldn't want to bother anyway."

Richard laughed.

"She won't have recovered from the shock that we're getting married in a registry office to make it in time!"

A week later, and with the necessary arrangements made, Richard and Kristine were married.

Now heavily pregnant for a slender young girl, Kristine had chosen a white lacy blouse to fit loosely over a long cream skirt that was discreetly let out at the front. She felt an outfit like that was an adequate compromise between the simple attire she would have chosen for herself, and a traditional wedding gown.

Royston and Alicia gladly attended, but Fiona, struggling to cope with both the negative reports she was receiving about Emily and, as expected, the fact that her daughter was getting married in a registry office because she was pregnant, declined her invitation.

Undeterred, the modest bridal party, who had opted for a quiet meal in a restaurant rather than a full-blown wedding reception, treasured the decision.

Kristine, though gleaming with excitement, was also grateful to have been spared the speeches and general wedding protocol her mother would have insisted upon.

When it was all over, the couple went straight back to the flat. Kristine was anxious to lie down. There had been no suggestion of a honeymoon.

That, she had long since decided, would have to wait until after her exams and the birth of the baby.

Richard frivolously suggested, "Perhaps one day Alicia will baby-sit for us while we go away on our honeymoon;" to which Kristine replied with a laugh, "Have you got any idea how funny that sounds? It's supposed to be the other way round: first the honeymoon and then the baby-sitter!"

As far as the staff at Everglades were concerned, Emily's sedation was working wonders now. Yet, even with regular changes to the dosage, her future suitability for rest-home care remained in question.

In fact, mention was made at one of the staff meetings that a psychiatric hospital might be more appropriate for her if the medication did not stabilise her condition.

This was something Grace considered discussing with Fiona, but then decided against it in view of her probable reaction to the suggestion and insistent comments about not wanting to become involved.

"No, we'll wait and see how the more potent sedative works out," she had concluded.

So when favourable reports started to come back from the night staff that Emily was sleeping through the night; that at last their most troublesome resident's behaviour was now manageable, the entire establishment breathed a collective sigh of relief.

The only problem now was, the Emily who was up and about during the day still carried the drug in her system, therefore rendering her more vegetable than human.

In short, as one member of the staff remarked, "Emily has turned into a zombie!"

"A zombie is preferable to a continual nuisance," was the consensus response.

This state of affairs suited the staff very well – it meant they could go about their work without having to rush off and silence Emily's annoying outbursts every five minutes.

Yet, the revised programme did nothing for Emily herself; for a zombie she never had been, nor was she prepared to become one now.

The Emily of old; still alert and responsive behind the mask, silently screamed for release from the eternal prison of her drug-induced sentence.

In a strange way, though, Emily did not really mind this. It prevented her from fretting about the fact that she had been dumped there; for Fiona had maintained no contact with her mother. It also excused her from taking part in some of the home's social activities, especially the irksome and noisy amateur concerts that went on all morning.

The only sessions she actually enjoyed were her flower arranging group and the monthly visits from the nice lady who massaged their hands with oils.

Naturally, she felt differently about Kristine's regular visits, although staying awake was a challenge.

Even after the wedding, Kristine maintained her visits; as much because she felt guilty that Emily was not invited to the ceremony as from her sense of commitment to her grandmother.

Kristine tried to explain away her guilt; yet Emily was always too sleepy to absorb anything but the fact that she was in her room or the gazebo with her granddaughter.

However, there was one aspect of this euphoric state of mind that Emily consciously rued to the point of hysteria.

Deep in her soul she was pining for her lost love; lost to her because no amount of effort helped her to attain that special place in consciousness where Arthur would enter and keep her company, and which had been numbed by the perpetual intake of drugs.

In fact, due to the effect of the sedative, she was devoid now of any emotion except anguish.

Her grief, though not noticeable in her behaviour, had transformed itself into a hurt so profound that only two things eased it: the sight of her granddaughter...and her beloved roses.

In effect, Emily was desperately lonely.

CHAPTER NINE

Such became the pattern of existence for Emily Thompson at Everglades Rest-Home. Her routine hardly changed from week to week.

Every so often Kristine or a rest-home volunteer would come and pick her up for an outing.

On those occasions she would greet them happily, enjoy the outing and express sadness at their departure, but then completely forget all about it.

Even when Kristine excitedly told her she had at long last passed her exams – and on her birthday, too, the significance of the occasion washed right over her.

Had Emily been aware that people were referring to her as a zombie, she would have been inclined to agree!

Yet, all the while, beneath the vacant exterior and painted smiles, lay a soul in turmoil.

Now no longer able to call out, and yet too tormented to remain silent, occasionally a long, low groan was heard coming from her; except it was not so much a sound as a feeling. Anyone who came near to her could not help but share the anguish expressed within the groan.

"It seems like Emily is in pain," a caregiver reported.

"She sounds as if she's in agony," the registered nurse informed the doctor.

"Then we will reassess her pain level," the doctor said, and wrote a prescription for morphine.

"Morphine!" exclaimed Kristine when she heard about it.

Kristine knew from her time working as a caregiver that morphine was a last line of defence in the management of pain; that it affects a person's mind and that in the elderly it can kill.

"Why has my grandmother been put on something like morphine?" she asked Grace in alarm.

"Because she is in a lot of pain," was her reply. "She has been heard groaning, and as she is now uncommunicative, she cannot tell us what is hurting her."

"That's ridiculous. Nana is no more in pain than I am!" Kristine insisted.

"Now how would you know that?"

"...Because I know my grandmother! She's more likely frustrated out of her brain with all the drugs you've been piling into her. She really doesn't need them!"

"The doctor has prescribed them, and he knows what he's doing!"

"But he doesn't know her! Damn it, Grace! Why has it come to this? She's not a vegetable to keep under control; she's a lovely person – who happens to be my Nana!"

"Kristine, please tone down your language," said Grace, mindful of people close by. "You're not at home now...and you won't be doing your unborn child much good, getting all het-up like this..."

Kristine ignored her advice.

"...I know what you're doing! You're trying to kill her off, aren't you? You want to get rid of my grandmother so that you can get in somebody who is less of a problem for you? That is why you pump drugs into them when they become unmanageable. Don't forget, I've worked here, so I know these things."

"Now you're being irrational."

Kristine was almost in tears of despair now.

"I want you to take Emily Thompson off all her meds," she said assertively."...And I want you to do it now!"

"But Kristine, It's not your decision; and your mother has left it up to us."

"We'll soon see about that!"

Kristine rushed off to tackle Fiona. The situation with Emily was intolerable and needed her immediate intervention.

Surely Fiona had a handle on her mother's medication regime! Surely Grace was exaggerating when she said Fiona had left Emily's progress in their hands. Didn't Fiona realise what Management at Everglades were up to?

...And did she not care enough to check that Emily was getting the right kind of medical treatment?

She caught Fiona as she was heading out to her car.

"Mum! Wait a minute! I need to talk to you!" she called out frantically.

Fiona turned in alarm at the unsolicited outburst.

"What on earth is the matter?" she asked in trepidation that her heavily pregnant daughter was not only in a hurry over something, but also seemingly distressed. "You'll go into premature labour if you're not careful!" she said.

"It's about Nana," said Kristine breathlessly. "Have you seen her lately?"

"No. I haven't been there for...let me see..."

"Never mind; you obviously don't go in very often..."

"...No, of course not. Why should I? She's in residential care now. We pay other people to look after her."

Suddenly alarm bells sounded in Kristine.

Slowly she said, "So you don't know about her fragile condition at the moment?"

"What fragile condition? I have not been informed of any changes in her condition, if that's what you mean. And anyway, I have left it up to Grace to adjust her treatment and medication. Why would you ask?"

Oh, my God, thought Kristine in a panic. She's got no idea about any of this!

"Mum, please come back inside. There's something you need to know..."

"...But I'm just going out. You can see that."

"This is urgent. If you care about Nana, then please come inside. ...Now!"

Kristine stood by the front door, the stern expression on her face demanding compliance.

Fiona could see that Kristine meant business, and that she had no recourse but to go along with it.

She said in passing, "Young lady, just because you're married now, it doesn't mean you can take liberties."

Kristine closed the door behind them.

"I'm sorry, Mum, but you are obviously not aware of what is going on at Everglades where Nana is concerned. They're giving her some powerful drugs she doesn't need just to shut her up, and it's killing her spirit. She's more like a vegetable now. You can't talk to her anymore..."

"...Alright, Kristine. If you're that worried about her I'll speak to Grace."

"...Not Grace! She'll just fob you off with some lame excuse. They think they've got all the answers, but they don't know their residents...certainly not Nana. They don't interact with them as real people. I should know; I worked there! The only person Nana has related to is me, and they won't accept my word on anything. They will only deal with you! Mum, you must see Nana for yourself."

"Alright, I'll call in tomorrow before work."

"No...now!" cried Kristine in desperation, a sense of foreboding overwhelming her. "I want you to come in with me right now!"

Fiona lapsed into thought. This was ruining her plans for the rest of the morning. But if the situation was really that bad, then she should at least give Kristine the benefit of the doubt, and go with her.

"I suppose you'd better show me what you mean," she said with reluctance.

Anguish poured freely from Emily's soul now.

Just occasionally it would well up to the surface as a tear, and glisten on an eyelash while her fixed gaze gave away nothing of her feelings.

Her caregiver on the morning shift, a new recruit who was working alone for the first time, said rudely, "What's the matter with you this morning, Emily?" But Emily, too absorbed in her torment, missed the intonation.

Looking directly into the fresh young face, she tried desperately to move her static facial muscles sufficiently to form a smile, but without success.

"If looks could kill!" said the girl sarcastically, mistaking Emily's concentrated effort to smile for a glare. "Come on now, you'll have to get out of that bed at some stage this morning. I've left you till last as it is."

Then Emily, too drowsy to grasp what she was saying, closed her eyes again, causing the tear to drop down onto her cheek.

Just then, Grace tapped on the door and walked in.

She said to the caregiver, "Would you please get Mrs Thompson up now. She has to attend a family meeting in an hour from now."

Then, leaving the girl speechless, she hurried away.

The caregiver turned back to Emily, who had opened her eyes again at the sound of someone else's voice.

"Did you hear that?" she said. "It looks like you've got no choice but to get up after all."

An hour later, Emily's caregiver wheeled her down to the foyer, and applied the chair's brakes.

"I'll leave you here," she said mechanically. "Somebody will come and collect you when they're ready."

Emily, now alert from all the activity, raised her eyes and slowly looked around. She vaguely knew where she was by the sound of the door swishing open and closed as people came through it. With her good hand, she pulled up her collar against the draught created, and tucked the other hand under her knee rug.

A few minutes later, the door swished open again and two more people came in.

This time one of them spoke to her.

Emily perked up at the sound of Kristine's voice.

"Hello, Nana. How are you?"

Kristine kissed Emily on the forehead; then squatted in front of her to make eye contact.

As recognition sunk in, Emily managed a weak smile.

"Look who's here to see you," Kristine said.

She moved away from Emily's line of vision so she could see Fiona.

Yet, rather than step forward to greet her as Kristine did, Fiona held back.

"It's nice to see you again, Mother," she said woodenly.

Emily's smile faded, though not on account of seeing her daughter. The effort involved in smiling was becoming too much for her and she could not keep it up. She looked away, lapsing into drug-induced drowsiness again.

Exasperated, Fiona sighed.

"I don't know why I try to be friendly. She's obviously got no time for me – she can't even say hello!"

This is not going to be very easy, thought Kristine, and wheeled Emily round to the interview room as Grace invited them in.

"Now," said Grace, offering them a seat. "What seems to be the trouble?"

Kristine opened her mouth to make her submission, but Fiona cut in ahead of her.

"My daughter seems to think you professionals aren't looking after Emily properly."

Her eyes wide with indignation, Kristine cried, "Mum!"

"Is that what you think, Kristine?" asked Grace in a tone akin to accusation.

"No, of course not!" she replied, and then realised it was not exactly true.

The purpose of the meeting was to discuss her qualms about Emily's medications, not her overall treatment.

Don't let them browbeat you into admitting something false, Kristine told herself sternly.

"I just think she doesn't need all those drugs; that's all," she said. "You've even got her on morphine now…"

"…And that, as I've already told you Kristine, is because your grandmother is in pain. Would you have us allow her to suffer?"

"What a ridiculous thing to suggest!" said Kristine, irate and still not convinced of their assumption where Emily's pain levels were concerned.

Fiona sat listening to the banter. Then she asked Grace, "What makes you think my mother is in pain?"

"It is documented in her notes; I have them here," said Grace with authority.

She reached across the desk for a red ring binder, which contained Emily's records for the time she had been at the rest-home.

Fiona could see from the volume of pages that a lot had been written about her.

"Look at all these shift reports," said Grace, pointing to the comments made by caregivers on recent duties. "As you can see, Emily has been reported as groaning in pain. Is that not an indication that she is suffering?"

"Suffering, maybe; but not necessarily because she's in pain," Kristine chipped in. "You already had her drugged into a vegetative state. Who wouldn't groan if they felt trapped within their own skull?"

Kristine's voice was becoming raised now.

It was obvious to her, from the fact that Emily had not even batted an eyelid since they came into the interview room, that she was right.

Yet Fiona sprung to Grace's defence.

"Kristine, you can't possibly justify a comment like that. Are you claiming to know Nana's condition better than the doctor and all the qualified staff at Everglades...who, I would remind you, are the ones looking after her?"

"Well, now you come to mention it...yes!"

Fiona and Grace exchanged glances.

"What are your thoughts about it, Fiona?" asked Grace, as though seeking an opinion to contradict what Kristine was saying.

"Personally I don't see that there is a problem," replied Fiona. "It's obvious Mother has deteriorated considerably in recent weeks and that you, as the professionals who have been given the responsibility for her wellbeing, are doing everything you can for her. And by the look of her sitting here, she would appear to be quite comfortable. I therefore have no complaints."

Grace turned to Kristine, whose glare had now fixed in bitter anger.

"What about you, Kristine? Can't you see that you have been mistaken?"

Kristine sullenly remained silent.

There was little point in arguing further. She may not have a leg to stand on with these two, but of one thing she was certain: she was not mistaken. Her grandmother was definitely frustrated rather than in pain.

"Kristine," said Fiona. "Are you going to answer Grace? I want to lay this matter to rest before we leave."

Defeated, Kristine looked forlornly at Emily.

Only the glazed expression on her grandmother's face held the truth.

She said to the others, "What can I possibly say? You've already decided I'm wrong about this. But if either of you took the time to look into Nana's eyes, you would see this whole situation differently."

She leant forward and took hold of Emily's cold hands.

Trying to make eye contact with her again she said, "I'm sorry Nana. We've done you a terrible injustice, bringing here. I hope you will one day be able to forgive us."

Then she got up and left.

That night Kristine could not sleep.

She was profoundly hurt to realise that nobody really cared about Emily except for her.

It distressed her even more to consider the possibility that, with the exception of herself, the people closest to her were ready to give up on someone who had been such an important part of their lives, just because she was old and infirm, and unable to speak for herself.

Did they not remember the happy and vibrant lady who stood so contentedly beside James in marriage not all that many years ago?

All of a sudden, Kristine chuckled as she remembered the look of surprise on Emily's face when she burst into their ceremony, having just escaped Fiona's clutches. Oh how Kristine relished that moment! Was this the same Emily? Deep down inside: definitely! That certainly had not changed! She was still in there; probably screaming...no, groaning now...to try and get out. The whole scenario was dreadful, and despite her efforts there was now nothing she could do about it. If Grandpa knew what they were doing to his beloved Emily he would be horrified...

...Or maybe he already knows...maybe Grandpa, looking down from above, is already well aware of Emily's plight; of the apathy on the part of certain people who should know better, and of her struggle to overcome it.

She raised her eyes to the ceiling, almost expecting to see him there; hoping at least that he could hear her.

"Grandpa," she mouthed. "Grandpa, please help us!"

In the darkness, she sighed and closed her eyes again in the hope that she might be able to drift off; but her mind was still too disturbed.

It looked like she would have another night without proper sleep.

A few minutes later, Kristine quietly got up to go to the toilet; something she needed to do more frequently in her advanced state of pregnancy.

As she stood up from the toilet she heard a click in her abdomen, and then felt a warm rush of fluid descending from her groin.

For a moment she stood still in stunned bewilderment. Then she realised in horror what had happened.

"Richard!" she called at the top of her voice, and sat back down on the toilet as more fluid drained from her. "Richard! Come here! Quickly!"

Within seconds Richard was there.

"Whatever is wrong?" he entreated with some urgency through the locked door.

"My waters just broke! I think I'm going into labour!"

"Good God...already?" he cried in alarm.

"I said so, didn't I? Do something!"

Kristine had panic in her voice now.

"Unlock the door, then!" he said, thinking quickly.

A muffled sound indicated that Kristie had done so, and slowly the door opened to reveal her standing, legs apart, her night dress dripping wet, over a puddle of liquid that looked like water.

"Are you okay, Kris?" he asked, not quite knowing what else to say.

"I don't know; I'm too frightened to move just at the moment," she whimpered.

"You're not giving birth right now, are you?" he asked with cautious anxiety.

"...I don't think so."

"Then let me help you out of there."

Richard reached forward and took hold of her arm. Still supporting herself with one hand on the wall, she carefully stepped away from the puddle on the floor.

"Would you please get me a towel...and I think it might be a good idea if you rang the hospital."

"Okay. Will you be alright for a minute or two?"

"Yes; I'll just have a quick shower and get dressed. Then I suppose we should get going."

Gently, Kristine freshened up and adjusted to the peculiar feeling in her tummy now that, with the loss of the fluid, her baby had moved.

While she did that, Richard warned the obstetrics ward of Kristine's situation and advised them that they would be arriving soon. Then he hastily threw a few items into an overnight bag; something they had been advised to do well in advance of their due date but had not yet done.

When Kristine emerged from the bathroom walking bow legged, Richard couldn't help but laugh.

"You look like you've been in the saddle too long," he said, trying to camouflage his mirth.

"It's not funny," she responded. "My baby has dropped, and there's nothing left of the fluid to cushion either of us. It's quite painful, you know."

"I'm sorry, love. It was a bit insensitive of me. Are you ready to go?"

"Yes, I suppose so."

At the front door, Kristine paused and looked back into their flat. A pang of excitement tinged with apprehension shot through her, and she realised that the next time she passed through the portals of domesticity she would have a baby in her arms...

With her hesitation, Richard also halted.

"Come on now. The car is all loaded up, so let's go," he said, and helped her down the steps.

In her room at Everglades Emily, also unable to sleep, lay back on her bed, staring at the ceiling.

Tonight she felt more alert than usual, and wondered why it was.

Then she remembered: the caregiver had given the night tablets to her whole instead of crushed in dessert. Cleverly, she pretended she had swallowed them, but really she had pushed them into her cheek. Then after the caregiver left, she spat them out.

It was wonderful to be able to think a bit more clearly for a while, even if it meant she couldn't sleep. In the half-light, she looked around her room. It was all reasonably familiar to her now. But she did still miss Arthur's chair which she had at home and Alicia's bunch of roses when she came for her visit.

She longed to have those times again. She even missed Fiona's irritating presence. At least it had been company.

Here she was pushed around like a sack of potatoes, given a cup of tea now and then, and taken to the toilet more often than she really needed to go. But apart from that, nobody paid very much attention to her, now that she couldn't call out anymore.

In a way she didn't mind, though. It gave her back the freedom to allow her thoughts to wander...and whatever was in the medication, it certainly allowed her to detach from her unbearable reality. The only drawback was when Arthur tried to communicate. On those occasions it was an agonising struggle to try and haul herself out from the sluggishness in order to receive him. Often she would find herself groaning under the weight of effort required to do so; unless, as in this instance, she managed to avoid taking the wretched tablets...

More in control of her mental processes than usual, Emily allowed herself to drift away to the one place where she felt at peace: to the state of consciousness where Arthur could find her.

Suddenly the fragrance of roses caught her senses. It was very much like the scent of their favourite whiskey rose...at least, that's what she chose to think.

Abruptly, she opened her eyes, expecting to see Kristine or Alicia, or maybe even one of the caregivers, holding out a posy to her, but it was too dark in the room to make out anything very much...except for one thing. On the far side of the room there was a faint blue haze.

Somehow she felt drawn to it.

Could it be...?

With eyes wide in wonderment, Emily opened herself up to it...and then she saw him.

In an ethereal glow that seemed to light up the whole room, Arthur stood with his arms extended.

Was he beckoning to her?

"Arthur," she said gently as their souls reconnected.

The shimmering form seemed to hover in the corner, but came no closer.

"How wonderful...he wants me to join him," whispered Emily, entranced by the spectacle.

She pushed back her bedcovers, and immediately the room's cool air wrapped itself around her warm skin like tentacles of menace.

Yet Emily didn't notice. She had only one objective now.

Slowly she slid her legs over the side of the bed, and using her good arm, heaved herself into a sitting position.

The incandescence was so inviting, Emily reached for her walker and struggled to her feet. But with her mind in an elevated state of consciousness she failed to check her balance as she began her walk towards him.

Suddenly she tripped over the walking frame; and with a sickening thud fell to the floor.

"Arthur!" she cried when she realised what had happened.

Yet the incandescent glow had disappeared. Emily was alone again, and in darkness.

Her good arm pinned beneath her, she tried to move but could not; for her arm felt like it was broken.

She called out, but nobody came.

Then Emily Thompson, much-loved widow, mother and grandmother, alone and chilled to the bone, lapsed into a state of shock.

A couple of hours later, the night caregivers walked past on their round. From outside Emily's room they could hear a moaning sound.

"I thought the girls said Mrs T. took her pills," said one of them. "It sure doesn't sound like it!"

438

"Do you think we should look in on her, just in case?" asked the other.

"Ooh, no! If we go in there it will set her off, and then we'll have the other residents complaining. The groaning isn't as bad as her yelling. I'd say, let her be."

Kristine gave birth to a healthy boy just before dawn.

Her first time in labour, it had not been an easy birth, and the exhausted girl, pleased it was over, cradled her newborn son with less motivation than she had expected.

Richard looked on; sensing her state of detachment.

"Let me hold him, Kris; you need your rest," he insisted. "You'll have plenty of time with him later on."

He reached out for the precious bundle; then overcome with emotion, sat down beside Kristine's bed where they both enjoyed the spectacle of new life.

"Did you have any thoughts about a name for him?" Richard asked.

"At one time I thought if I had a boy I'd like to name him after Grandpa. I guess we'll get to that soon enough."

"Your grandfather's name was Arthur, wasn't it?"

"Yes. If it's okay with you and Nana, I'd certainly like the baby's second name to be Arthur."

At seven o'clock, the morning caregivers took over from the rest-home's night staff, and received their handover report ready to begin their day's work.

"How has Mrs Thompson been tonight?" they enquired, and were informed that Emily had been quiet except for a late spell of groaning.

"...Nothing out of the ordinary then," the morning staff remarked, and made a note of it.

A short time later, the stifled scream of a young girl was heard throughout Everglades. The caregivers, on entering

Emily's room to sit her up for breakfast and pull back the curtains, found her sprawled out on the floor.

Emily was motionless, her face tinted with cyanosis; her skin cold and clammy to the touch.

The shaken young caregiver, horrified by the shocking sight, stood back against the wall with her hands clasped to her mouth.

"Is she dead?" she asked her partner, who had squatted down beside Emily and was feeling for a pulse.

"It looks like it;" came the ritualistic reply. "I can't feel anything at all."

The two caregivers carefully lifted Emily's limp body back onto the bed, and covered her over as though to keep her warm. Then the senior of the two returned to the office and rang Grace to inform her about the death.

"Okay, I'll come straight in," Grace said, and appeared shortly afterwards.

While the younger caregiver shakily prepared breakfast for the other residents, her partner gave Grace an account of what they found when they entered Emily's room.

"How long do you think she's been dead?" asked Grace.

"...Probably not all that long because parts of her body were still warm when we put her on the bed. ...Maybe an hour or so before we came on duty, I'd say."

Then Grace dismissed the caregiver to continue with her duties. She knew what she needed to do next.

When the phone rang at home, Fiona was still in bed. She heard it ringing, and assumed the call to be from the office asking her to work.

Yet, Fiona had been out the night before and wanted to sleep in. So, convinced it could not possibly be anybody else phoning her at that time of the morning, she let it ring till it clicked over to the answerphone. Then, reminding herself to check it later, she went back to sleep.

Grace had no choice but to just leave the sad message on Fiona's machine, and requested that she get back to her as soon as she possible.

This was a brief Grace had performed either personally, or by message in the event of a relative's absence, with enough frequency that she knew exactly what to say. But she still found it hard to be the bearer of bad news. Grief counselling was something she had not gone into as part of her ongoing training.

The message she left merely stated that regrettably Emily had passed away shortly before daybreak, and that the staff at Everglades wished to offer their condolences to Fiona and all the family.

Grace put down the phone; then, drawing breath ready for the next call she needed to make, she rang to report the death to the on-call doctor.

Fiona had not been back to sleep for long when the phone rang again.

This time, jolted right out of a reverie, her annoyance at being disturbed twice in as many minutes, woke her up completely and she cursed the nuisance.

Abruptly she leapt out of bed and made for the kitchen to answer it.

Assuming the second caller to be the same as the first, she growled as she reached for the phone, "Why can't that office just leave a message?"

Then gruffly she answered it.

"Is that Fiona?" asked a man's voice.

"Yes. Who's this?" she replied. It didn't sound like any of the men she worked with.

"It's Richard. I'm ringing from the hospital to inform you that you have a grandchild."

"The hospital? A grandchild? ...Oh, that Richard! Sorry, I didn't realise who you were for a minute. You say I have a grandchild; does that mean...?"

"...Yes. Kristine went into a premature labour last night, and gave birth this morning."

"Really?" Fiona's surprise robbed her of a response.

"Yes...both mother and son are doing well."

"A son? ...Kristine had a son? ...I always wanted a son."

"Can I tell Kristine that you'll be in to see her later?"

"Of course...and thank you for letting me know."

Fiona hung up the phone and paused to get herself a drink of water. The excitement had made her thirsty.

While she sipped the water she remembered about the first call, and felt guilty that she had jumped to the wrong conclusion as to who might have contacted her.

"Oh well," she said smiling. "It doesn't matter now. I'm a grandma!"

Then she readied herself to go to the hospital.

However, before she left the house, a thought occurred to her: that maybe Royston had not yet heard the good news. He would definitely want to know that he was now a grandfather, she reckoned...and she wanted to be the one to tell him.

So she retraced her steps and picked up the phone to ring him. But a beeping sound in the ear piece halted her. It indicated that a message had indeed been left earlier. Curious now as to who had done so, she clicked it on...

...The message was from Grace.

EPILOGUE

Emily gazed down at the shell she once occupied. Some time had now passed since she vacated it in death.

She watched as her body slowly lost the vibrancy of its aura, and felt an increasing sense of separation from it.

Nevertheless, she suffered no loss in its passing. Death, for Emily, had come not a moment too soon. Over the last few weeks, Emily had progressively grown more tired of it. Her existence had been no life at all for one as naturally lively as her.

The passing had been quite an ordeal.

Having to lie hard on a cold floor, in severe pain from the broken arm beneath her and not able to move, had been a trial beyond endurance.

She had fallen some distance from her bedside locker where the call bell was situated. Her cries of help, muted from the sedative build-up in her system and the fact that she was shivering from shock and cold, prevented her from making herself heard, and so she gave up trying.

With her discomfort slowly worsening, a low and pitiful groan began to emanate from her...until it became almost continual as she longed for unconsciousness to deaden the pain, or for death to release her from the torment.

In her despair, she beseeched Arthur to help her.

He came to her towards the end, when the first vestiges of light peeped through a gap in her curtains.

"Help me!" she murmured as she sensed his presence.

"It won't be long now," he whispered within her soul. "Soon, my precious, we will be together again."

All at once, Emily felt the warmth of his aura. Serenity began to envelope a spirit waiting for its final dismissal.

As the delicate aroma lingered in the air – one that she recognised with profound yearning – she finally allowed the last flimsy tendrils of life to release their hold.

Emily was pleased the Everglades caregivers had had the decency to place her body on the bed again and snuggle it up as though warmly.

She may no longer need it, she reflected as she looked down upon their feverish activity, but it was nice to think that in her final moments she had been treated with the dignity she was previously denied.

Arthur looked down with her.

He understood what Emily had endured in her passing, for he also suffered when cancer claimed his own life.

It was understandable to him that she might want to stay close to her body in order to ensure its safe keeping; for the silver cord connecting her spirit with her body had been sluggish in freeing her emotions.

He knew how that felt, too.

Yet, Arthur also knew he should get Emily away from this tragic scene as soon as he was able; he had waited a long time for his beloved to join him.

He would have waited forever, had that been part of the grand design for her.

And now that fate had intervened and handed her back to him, albeit ahead of her allotted time, the bridegroom was anxious to be reunited with his bride. To receive her now was both a great joy and a blessed relief to him.

"Come with me, Emily," he said, drawing her away. "Your time on earth has ended. Let those left behind tend to your mortal remains. They will ensure you are offered a smooth passage to the afterlife. And then you and I will take a stroll around the garden I've prepared for you. The scent of roses there is just heavenly..."

THE END